THE DRAGON RUSTLER

COWBOYS AND DRAGONS

BOOK 1

ANTHONY A. KERR

Published by Thunder Mountain Books, Co.
ISBN 978-0-9968565-0-8 (paperback)
ISBN 978-0-9968565-1-5 (ebook)

For more information, please visit *www.aakerr.com*, and sign up for updates.

Thank you for reading.

To Jenifer:
Through your love and support,
my dreams are born.

CONTENTS

CONTENTS

MAP OF THUNDERBIRD RANCH

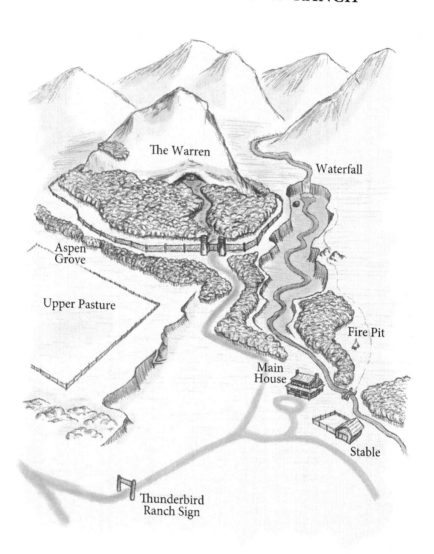

The Warren

Waterfall

Aspen Grove

Upper Pasture

Fire Pit

Main House

Stable

Thunderbird Ranch Sign

CHAPTER 1

MIRANDA

The Lizard-man Always Knocks Thrice

MIRANDA TEETERED ON THE EDGE of a cliff overlooking a cavern so vast, its walls and ceiling disappeared into infinite darkness. Huge creatures with long bodies and bat-like wings swarmed high above. The chamber below seemed alive, pulsing to a steady rhythm, as if the heart of the earth itself throbbed beneath it. But as she looked closer, Miranda realized it was not the floor that was moving, but thousands of robed figures chanting and swaying as one.

She descended a steep stone staircase to the floor below and approached an ornately carved altar. Resting on its smooth surface was a long curved knife and three cracked stone tablets inscribed with characters in a language she could not read. The tablets fit together like the pieces of a jigsaw puzzle, but one fragment was missing. A scaly hand reached out and placed a small stone shard into the gap. Instantly, the tablet began to glow from within, and the cracks in all three disappeared completely.

Miranda's gaze traveled past the altar to a wall of flame

erupting from a rift in the cavern floor. Black smoke swirled and began to take shape. The earth shook, and she realized that the source of the tremor was not an earthquake but deep, menacing laughter coming from something in the flames.

She turned around to face the congregation. They fell silent, their last notes echoing off the chamber's unseen walls. Now Miranda saw that the choir surrounded a man and a woman shackled to stone pillars with thick, rusty chains. She gasped. The man was her father. He moaned as his head lolled from side to side. His ragged clothes were stained with blood.

Miranda shifted her focus to the other column, fearful that she would find her mother there, but saw instead a woman she had never seen before. The stranger appeared to be about her father's age, with fair skin and dark-blond hair like his. She looked up at Miranda with hauntingly familiar deep-blue eyes.

In that instant a wave of nausea washed over Miranda. She felt herself in two places at once. The woman's split lips opened, forming the same whispered words over and over again: "Heal Storm! ... Heal Storm! ... Heal Storm! ..."

Then the scene dissolved into a swirl of colored light as the strange subterranean hell shifted to another scene entirely—a familiar image. Miranda was walking up a brick stairwell leading to a green door, with 412 stamped on a worn bronze plate just above eye level. A gloved hand reached up and traced the numbers with one finger, formed a fist, then knocked three times.

Miranda's eyes shot open, and she squinted at the digital clock resting on her bookshelf; 2:14 a.m. She lay there, straining to hear any movement.

Nothing.

Only a dream? Yet it felt more like a memory—a recent memory—but, somehow, not her own. How could that be possible? When that woman had looked at her—

Knock, knock, knock!

Miranda's heart leaped into her throat. Someone was here! This time she heard the sound of her parents' bedroom door opening and bare feet walking hurriedly into the living room.

She threw off her covers, slipped out of her bottom bunk, and crouched on the cool wooden floor. She looked up to see if the noises had awakened her brother, in the top bunk, but Justin was as dead to the world as he usually was all night long. Good. Miranda crept over to the door of their small room, careful to avoid the boards that creaked even under her slight frame. She placed her ear against the door, and failing to hear anything other than muffled noises, cautiously opened it a tiny crack to peek into the living room beyond.

Blinking away the brightness of the hall light, she saw her parents at the open apartment door. Almost hidden from view in the hallway beyond stood a cloaked figure dressed exactly like the ones in her dream.

"You're not welcome here," her father said, his low voice unusually authoritative.

"Robert and Kaya McAdelind—at last! You have been most challenging to locate," the visitor hissed. "The time is nearing, and you have what we need. Do not deny its presence, we can sense it."

Her father shifted his weight slightly. "It belongs to us and not to your kind. Leave this place now"—a silver knife appeared suddenly in his hand—"or I'll cut you down right here."

The stranger tilted his head to one side. "So be it, McAdelind. I give you one day to turn it over, or your family will share your fate."

"Don't threaten us, Worm," Miranda's dad growled, and

took a step forward.

The visitor moved back quickly and its hood shifted. Miranda sucked in a quick breath as she saw the tiny scales covering the stranger's features, identical to those on the hand that had repaired the broken tablets in her dream just moments before.

The creature's eyes darted to her. The bony ridge where eyebrows should have been rose sharply in shock upon seeing her, exposing vivid yellow irises. Then its eyes narrowed, focusing hard on Miranda, a wicked smile forming on its lipless mouth.

Miranda quickly and silently shut the bedroom door and took a step back, her heart pounding. The creature's presence was cause enough for panic. And her fear had only increased when, just before she closed the door, her father had turned to follow the thing's gaze. Had Dad seen her?

She had to get back into bed quickly. Her parents might come in at any moment, and she didn't want them to know what she'd heard, or worse, what she'd seen.

Miranda turned and bumped into someone standing behind her. She opened her mouth to scream, but a hand shot up and covered her lips, muffling her cry.

"Ssh! It's me, sis," Justin whispered.

Miranda shoved her younger brother hard in the chest, sending him stumbling backward onto her mattress. "What's wrong with you? You scared the crap out of me."

He rubbed the spot where she had pushed him. "I just had a crazy nightmare."

"Hurry, get back to bed," she said, pulling him upright and darting under her covers, where she lay down facing away from the door. "Mom and Dad will be in here any second, and they need to think we're asleep."

Without a word of protest, her brother scampered up the ladder to his bunk. A second later the door opened. Light from the hall spilled into their room, forming a vertical band on the wall at the foot of the bed. The door stayed open. Miranda worried that her brother had given them away.

Miranda heard her mother sigh, "Thank goodness, they're asleep. Robert, I'm worried. Do you think … they know about the children?"

There was a pause before her father answered. "We can't take any chances. It appears we've run out of time."

The door shut and their room was returned to darkness.

Miranda turned over and sat up, listening for the sounds of her parents going back to bed, but instead they returned to the living room. She could hear their muffled voices speaking urgently.

Before she could get out of bed again, Justin swung down and landed without a sound in front of her. "What was all that about? What's going on?"

"No clue," Miranda said, biting her lower lip. She didn't like how worried her parents were, and she definitely didn't like the lizard-man at their door.

"You were spying on them. You must have heard something good."

Miranda crossed her arms over her chest, scowling at her brother in the dark. "I was not spying. I heard knocking at the door and got up to see who was there. I mean, it's the middle of the night! Who comes to your house in the middle of the night?"

"So, what happened?"

"It was weird. There was this guy, or thing, or whatever, and Dad told him to leave. Then he demanded that Dad give him something, or else. … Then the thing looked at me and … smiled."

"What do you mean, a thing?"

"It wasn't human," she whispered.

Justin paused for a moment, then shoved her back against her pillows. "Come on, you're messing with me."

From under her blanket, Miranda kicked him in the leg. "I'm serious. It was wearing a dark robe and it had scales on its face, and no lips." She shuddered again. "It was creep-ola."

Justin paused, seemingly lost in thought. "Was it a brown robe made out of some kind of rough material, and were the scales kind of greenish?"

"How did you know that?"

"Like I said, I was having this crazy nightmare right before I woke up. This may sound completely nuts, but I dreamed I was knocking on the door, and Dad and Mom were there. Dad pulled a knife on me, and then I saw you peeking out the bedroom door. Then everything changed, and I was in a cave with tons of hooded figures, humming and swaying."

The hairs on Miranda's neck stood on end and she began to shake. "Did you see a shadow-monster thingy?"

"Mm-hmm."

"And Dad chained to a large stone pillar?"

"Mm-hmm."

"And a strange woman with blue eyes, like ours, chained to the other one?"

Justin was silent a moment. "No, sis. The other person I saw was ... you."

CHAPTER 2

MIRANDA
The Perfect End to a Horrible Year

MIRANDA JUMPED IN HER SEAT as the last bell of the school year rang. The worst year of her life was over at last. She should have been ecstatic. She was finally headed to high school, and more important, headed away from her annoying little brother. But instead she felt worse than ever. Her mind was swimming with images of lizard men, dark caves, shadowy monsters, and huge flying creatures.

"Hey, anyone home?" Jeanette, Miranda's best friend, waved a hand in front of her face. "Time to celebrate, girl. We're high-schoolers now," she said with a huge grin.

"Ugh. I can't believe we're going to be freshmen—I mean, fresh*women*. Back to the bottom of the food chain," Miranda groaned, shoving a doodle-covered notebook into her backpack. "Yippee."

Jeanette frowned. "Okay, Miss Downer. You've been in a funk all day. Are you going to be like this tonight too? Maybe you should change into black and wear a ton of eyeliner."

Miranda gave her a weak smile and pulled her long black

hair into a ponytail. "I'll be fine, just didn't get much sleep."

Jeanette grabbed her arm and pulled her into the bustling hall. "Come on. Let's blow this place before we get locked in all summer."

The corridors of Hudson Heights Middle School were more frenzied than usual. After a quick stop at Jeanette's locker, they forced their way through mobs of excited students to Miranda's. She quickly popped the lock and began shoving books and loose papers into her already bursting backpack. "Are we still going to the movies tonight?"

Jeanette smiled. "Of course. And guess what? I was talking to Kevin in second period and he and Troy are going to meet—"

"You're dead, McAdelind!"

Miranda spun to see who was yelling her last name, but quickly realized that the threat was directed toward her brother. Justin was frantically running down the hall, colliding with a dozen kids one after another as he attempted to escape from whoever was chasing him and sending their papers and books flying high into the air.

Miranda closed her eyes and took a deep breath. *Not today.* This year had promised to be so good. She was in eighth grade, the ruling class of the school. Her friends were in all her classes. Troy Wilson, the most popular boy in school, seemed to like her. But no. Her idiot brother had done everything in his power to ruin her life. He had kept provoking the in-crowd instead of just keeping a low profile, like every other *smart* sixth-grader. Justin always seemed to be sitting in their seats at lunch or bumping into one of them in the hall. Even though he was almost twelve, he still had the social skills of a five-year-old. Miranda was frankly amazed that anyone still talked to her.

She opened her eyes in time to see none other than Troy, soaked from head to toe, yelling and chasing Justin through the laughing crowd. Miranda pretended that this was nothing out of the ordinary, and kept shoving things into her bag. "What were you saying about Troy? He's going to—"

Jeanette was looking over Miranda's shoulder. "Wasn't that Justin?"

Miranda sighed, "He'll be fine. Anyway. Troy—"

The hall erupted into chants of "Fight! Fight! Fight!" as everyone followed the two boys outdoors.

Jeanette grabbed Miranda's arm and pulled her toward the commotion. "We should see what's going on. Troy looks like he's going to kill your brother."

Miranda groaned. "Fine. Let's see what the dork has gotten himself into this time."

As they pushed through the quickly expanding crowd, Miranda could see Justin, his back to the playground's chain-link fence, his eyes darting rapidly between the now grinning Troy and the tight circle of people surrounding them.

"I told you, twerp, you mess with me and I'll mess you up!" the large boy growled as he wiped dripping hair from his face.

"And I t-told you, to leave m-my friends alone," Justin stammered as he tried to move to his right, but was blocked instantly by a sidestep from the older boy. "I'm not going to let you push us around anymore."

Troy balled his hands into fists. "Well, you're about to see why I *can* push you around."

Jeanette pulled on Miranda's arm. "You need to stop this. Your brother's going to get his face smashed in."

Miranda bit her lower lip. "He's the one who got himself into this mess."

"But he's your little brother."

Just one more embarrassment in the most embarrassing year *ever*. Every time Justin provoked the wrong people, he threatened to knock Miranda farther down the social ladder. She kneaded her hands together, looking around at the faces surrounding her. These were the people she was trying so hard to impress, and yet they were cheering for the boy she liked to kick her brother's butt.

Troy punched one fist into his open palm and advanced on Justin. Miranda could see the fear in her brother's eyes. She took a small step forward.

Justin put his fists up into an awkward defensive position, provoking a burst of laughter from the crowd.

Troy shook his head. "This is going to be so easy."

"Miranda. Do something," Jeanette pleaded.

Miranda took another step forward and yelled, "Stop!"

Troy's fist shot at Justin's face.

But the punch never landed. Troy's arm was held tight, his fist only inches away from impact, by …

"Oh crap," Miranda whispered. Her dad gripped Troy's arm, glaring down at the two boys. Where had he come from?

"Do we have a problem, boys?" he said.

Troy tried to extract himself from their father's viselike grip. Realizing he wasn't going anywhere, he looked down at the ground. "No sir. No problem."

Their dad turned to Justin. "Do you have anything you need to say?"

"Yeah, stop picking on kids smaller than you, you bully." Seeing his father's angry glare, Justin added, "Sorry I dumped a bucket of dirty water on your head."

Their father nodded. "So are we good here?" he asked, looking from one boy to the other. When they both nodded yes, he released Troy's arm.

Troy joined the dispersing crowd and headed for the exit at the end of the hallway. Just before he reached the door, he turned and shouted, "One day, McAdelind, your luck is going to run out, and you're going to get your butt kicked!"

"Maybe, but at least it won't be by you, jerkface!" Justin yelled back. Their dad grabbed him by the arm and whispered something harshly to him.

Miranda saw this as her opportunity to escape, and pushed Jeanette toward the exit. "Let's get out of here before—"

A large hand grabbed her shoulder. She turned to see her father's hard expression, "Oh … Hello, Dad. What are you doing here?"

He looked around, quickly scanning the nearby buildings. "I'm picking you and your brother up today."

Miranda looked at him innocently. "Jeanette and I are going to the movies, then I'm sleeping over at her place. Remember?"

"You'll have to take a rain check on movie night." He said, and guided both Miranda and Justin toward the schoolyard gate. "Say goodbye to Jeanette."

"But I have plans tonight," Miranda protested.

"Your plans have changed," her dad said, increasing their pace toward a waiting taxi.

Miranda turned and Jeanette gave her a weak wave.

"Uh. Dad. Where are we going?" Justin asked.

Their father suddenly tensed and looked to the roof of a nearby building. Miranda followed his gaze and saw someone—or something?—dressed in black move quickly into the shadows. "Not here. We can talk on the way to the airport." He pushed them toward a taxi's open trunk, which Miranda saw was filled with their family's suitcases. "Throw your stuff in."

Miranda stomped her foot down. "Airport? No way. I'm not going anywhere. It's bad enough that dorkhead over here has ruined my life, but I have plans with my friends tonight. Do you want me to go to high school without any friends next year?"

"I'm sure you'll figure out a way to survive," her father

replied flatly, grabbing Miranda's backpack and tossing it into the overstuffed trunk. He slammed the lid shut and guided them to the taxi's open rear door. "We need to hurry, your flight leaves in about an hour."

"What do you mean, 'your' flight?" Miranda glanced in and saw her mother sitting with perfect posture, staring straight ahead, her hands neatly resting on her lap. Then Miranda noticed that her eyes were red and swollen. What the heck was going on? Miranda's stomach began to twist. Something was very wrong.

"Get in kids. We need to hurry," their mom said, her voice breaking slightly.

Miranda stood at the open door. "No way. Not until you tell us what's going on."

Her mother opened her mouth to speak, tears starting to well in her eyes, when suddenly she seemed to catch sight of something in the rearview mirror and turned to look behind the taxi. Miranda followed her gaze and saw several figures in dark robes standing in an alley not twenty feet away. They were motioning toward Miranda, beckoning to her with gloved hands. A chill shot down her spine.

Her mom leaned over. "We need to go. Now!"

Miranda shoved Justin in toward their mom. He glared at her angrily. "Hey!" he said. "It's my turn to sit by the window."

Miranda took one last glance back, but the robed figures were gone. Something told her they were still close by. "Listen, twerp, kids who almost get their butt kicked at school don't get privileges. Now scoot."

"Miranda, please don't be unkind to your brother. I know this is a sudden and unexpected change, but it doesn't warrant such behavior," her mother said, nervously combing her fingers through her long black hair.

"No, but the fact that he ruined eighth grade for me does," Miranda said under her breath, slamming the door shut behind her.

Their father got in the front seat beside the driver. "We're all set."

The scruffy-looking man nodded once and jerked the car into the heavy afternoon traffic, causing a chorus of honks and shouts.

No one said anything for a couple of awkward minutes until Justin broke the silence. "So ... where are we going?"

Their mom's eyes started to well up again. "Your father and I need to go away on a ... business trip for a little while."

"But you just got back from one." Justin's shoulders slumped, then he added hopefully, "Wait. Are we going with you this time?"

No way, Miranda thought. She and her brother were never allowed to go on any of the many trips their parents took each year, disappearing for long weeks to places they referred to only in vague terms, leaving the children in the care of friends or neighbors. But Miranda sensed that their parents were not coming with them.

Her father shifted in his seat, turning to face his family. "No," he said, his face grim, as he looked at their mother for support. "Actually, you two are going on an adventure all your own."

"I don't want to go on some stupid *adventure*. I want to stay here with my friends," Miranda snapped.

Their mother took a deep breath, ignoring Miranda. "What your father means to say is, we are sending you out west to stay on a ranch while we're away."

"Where out west?" Miranda asked.

"And whose ranch?" Justin added.

"Well ... it's actually ... your grandfather's ranch. My father's ranch," their father said. "In southern Colorado."

"Wait—what? Hold on a second." Justin held up both hands in protest. "What grandfather? We have been asking about our family forever, and the only answer you two ever give us is, 'It's complicated.' Now you're shipping us off to stay with a complete stranger across the country?"

"We don't know this person, you might as well drop us off at an orphanage on the way out of town," Miranda huffed.

Their mother frowned, but her voice was soft. "It's not like that."

"It's *exactly* like that! You never talk about our family, and whenever we asked anything, you two always got so upset we stopped asking. How long are you ditching us for?"

Normally, her father would have lost it at a smart remark like that, but now his expression softened, and that made Miranda's stomach tighten into a hard knot. "I wish we knew, but it's an emergency situation, and we could be gone for a while."

Justin scrunched up his face. "Emergency situation? You two are college professors. You're archaeologists! What in the world could qualify as an *emergency* in your lives? Did a mummy suddenly start walking and talking? Did someone discover a new form of ancient writing that needs your immediate personal inspection?" He let out a nervous laugh. "What are we supposed to do on a ranch anyway?"

"We wouldn't be doing this if it wasn't absolutely necessary," her father said. "I can only imagine how difficult this is for both of you, but we need you to trust us."

"Oh, I trust you," Miranda shot back. "I trust that you'll leave us there all summer. I trust that you think whatever academic emergency this is, it's more important than my life. But most of all, I trust that I will be on my own, struggling to keep my little brother out of trouble while you two are having fun somewhere in the world."

"I can actually take care of myself, by the way," Justin said half under his breath.

"Please Mom, I'm begging you. I will be absolutely

miserable, bored out of my mind, and you know it. Why can't I just stay with Jeanette's family, and Justin could go over to one of his weird little friend's houses?"

"Nice, sis, love you too," Justin said. He turned to their mother. "As much as I don't want to give her the satisfaction, I have to agree with Miranda. Just let us stay here. Don't make us go somewhere we don't know."

"This is harder on us than you can possibly imagine," her mother said, a sob escaping. She closed her eyes and took a deep breath. Their mother was never emotional. She was the rock of the family. The situation must be bad, very bad. "I need you both to do what we ask without a fight. This *is* an emergency. We need you to be with someone who can keep you safe." Their mother paused and swallowed hard. "And that person is ... your grandfather."

"We don't really have a choice here," their dad said.

"Of course you have a choice. You always have a choice. You and Mom just always choose to leave us." She crossed her arms and glared at her father. "But whatever. It's just a perfectly horrible ending to a totally horrible year. So why not spend it on some stupid ranch in the middle of nowhere?" She was fighting back tears now and turned to face the window so no one would see her cry.

"I know it doesn't seem like it now, but this is the best course of action open to us." Her father sighed and turned back around in his seat to face forward. "Besides, you might be surprised. It won't be nearly as boring as you think."

CHAPTER 3

JUSTIN
Tall, Dark, and Cowboy

*A*S JUSTIN RODE THE ESCALATOR up toward the arrivals area and baggage claim at Denver International Airport, he marveled at how quickly his life had been turned upside down. If he had been even remotely excited to go on this "adventure," as Dad had called it, he would have been thrilled by his very first flight, his first real trip *anywhere*, by the prospect of seeing a new part of the country and meeting his long-lost grandfather.

But Justin didn't care about some stupid ranch, and he felt worried about meeting a man his parents had always kept a secret. They must have had a very good reason for keeping their distance. Why would a man hide from his own parents? Justin's mind was filled with scenarios explaining his dad's behavior, none of them good.

Justin glanced over at Miranda. He longed to talk to her, to snap her out of her teenager-ness just long enough to reassure him that everything was going to be okay. *Good luck with that.* His sister had stopped being nice to him ages ago, blaming him for all the issues he was having at school. But the popular kids were complete jerks who fed off the misery of everyone they excluded from their little clique. He had spent most of his life being bullied, and this year he had decided to fight back. The only problem was, instead of his big sister standing up for him the way she used to, she was now one of his tormentors, and part of Justin hated her for that. So he said nothing.

At the top of the escalator Justin scanned the crowd waiting for arriving friends and family. Jostled by the eager passengers, he suddenly felt small and insignificant as people hurried by all around him. He wasn't even sure who he was looking for.

When the surging wave of people had finally dissipated, Justin noticed a tall man dressed from head to toe in black, crowned with a matching black cowboy hat, holding up a sign with MCADELIND written on it in red marker. He was about the same age as their parents, with dark brown eyes and close-cropped light-brown hair. He looked like he'd just walked off a western-movie set. Dad had said not to expect their grandfather himself at the airport, but he hadn't said just who to expect in his place.

The man walked quickly over to them, his polished black heels clacking on the floor. Shifting the sign to his left hand, he tipped his hat with his right. "Are you two the McAdelind kids?" he asked flatly.

Justin stepped forward. "Yes, sir. I'm Justin. And this is my sister, Miranda."

Justin noticed the man's face harden at the sound of her name, then he relaxed, inclined his head toward her and said, "Beautiful name you have there, Miss Miranda."

Miranda hesitated, then said "Thank you" with a slight nod. "May I ask, who are you? You don't look old enough to be our grandfather."

He smiled slightly. "Nope. Can't say that I am. My name is William O'Faron. I work for the old man. He sent me to fetch you two, with his apologies. It's nothing personal. Your granddad has an urgent matter to attend to, and it's taking up every second he can spare. Don't worry, you'll meet him soon enough. Either of you need a snack or to use the facilities?" When they both shook their heads no, he turned and headed toward baggage claim.

After grabbing their suitcases, they headed outside to the parking garage. A short walk later they were standing at the rear gate of a large red pickup truck. Mr. O'Faron tossed their bags roughly into the truckbed next to a wooden crate, then went to the passenger-side door and opened it for them.

Miranda shoved her brother and yelled, "I call shotgun!"

"Hey!" Justin protested. "You had the window in the taxi and on the plane. It's my turn to ride in front."

Mr. O'Faron pulled a lever at the side of the passenger seat, causing it to tilt and slide forward. "Actually, you need to hop in the back. I'm sure you're old enough to sit in front, but I'm not taking any chances."

Justin stood openmouthed. "Are you serious?"

"Very," Mr. O'Faron said, pointing to the backseat. "Get in."

Justin grudgingly climbed in, grumbling under his breath. He watched his sister reach over to push the seat back upright so she could get in front, but Mr. O'Faron was standing in her way. "You're in the back too."

Justin couldn't help smiling. Miranda reluctantly pulled herself into the back of the cab and sat down with a loud "*Humph!*" She glared at her brother, daring him to say something, but Justin just grinned at her. "Shut up," she said and turned to look out the window.

Mr. O'Faron shut the door and walked around to the other side of the truck. Before sitting down, he took off his immaculate black cowboy hat and placed it with care on the passenger seat. Well, that explains *that*, Justin thought.

* * *

"Are we close to the ranch?" Justin asked after they had been driving for a little while. It kind of looked like they were in the country.

Mr. O'Faron shook his head. "Nope. Your granddad's ranch is in southern Colorado. It will take a bit over four hours to get there."

"Four hours? You're joking right?" Justin said.

"Afraid not, son. You're in the West now. Things here are further apart."

As they traveled along the highway, Justin could see towering buildings sitting at the foot of mountains. He was struck by how big Denver was. He had imagined the West as a landscape of ghost towns, saloons, unpaved roads, cattle, and dust. Not cities with skyscrapers.

As they approached the city's downtown, Mr. O'Faron exited the freeway. They were soon in an industrial area, surrounded by a bunch of warehouses nestled among railroad tracks. Mr. O'Faron brought the truck to a stop in the parking lot of an old rust-colored building with no windows, one door, and a dozen loading docks. He turned around to look at Justin and his sister. "I have to drop off a package … for your granddad. Stay put until I come back. This should only take a minute." He grabbed his hat and stepped out of the truck. Once outside, he put the hat on, positioning it just right with a glance in the side mirror, and walked around to the truck bed.

Justin watched him remove the large wooden crate, straining slightly as he lifted it with care. He then quickly walked toward the warehouse's lone door and kicked it several times. It opened immediately, but just wide enough for him to enter. Before the door slammed shut behind him, Justin caught him stealing a look back in their direction.

Justin turned to Miranda. "So? Are we ever going to talk about last night?"

"No," Miranda said, not meeting his eyes.

"Come on, sis. I'm freaked out about what happened at home and I'm worried about Mom and Dad. Please talk to me."

Miranda let out a humorless laugh. "What do you want me to say? Mom and Dad can obviously take care of themselves."

"Maybe. But what about us? We both have the same nightmare about Dad beaten up and chained to a pillar, then a lizard-man comes for a social call in the middle of the night, and the next day we are sent off to Colorado 'for our own safety'? That's kind of messed up."

"You know what, Justin? You're right. It's completely messed up, but what can we do about it? Nothing. We just need to survive staying in this lame place for a little while, then we can go home."

"What's wrong with you? Aren't you even a little—"

Bang!

Their heads jerked forward in unison to see the door to the warehouse flung open. Mr. O'Faron stormed out of the building, his face flushed, waving something in his hand emphatically at whoever was inside. "This'd better not be a trick!" he yelled. "If it is, I'm coming back here and …"

His head snapped toward the truck, as if he had remembered that Justin and Miranda were still there. Instantly, his whole demeanor changed, his furrowed brow and deep scowl replaced with the stoic expression he had worn earlier. He turned away from the door, kicking it shut with his heel, and walked over to the truck. He carefully set his hat back in its place of honor and settled into the driver's seat.

"Everything ... okay?" Justin asked.

Mr. O'Faron turned partway around in his seat. "Nothing you need to worry about." Although his face remained emotionless, his dark eyes were burning. He started the truck, and as they drove past the docks toward the exit, one of the garage doors started to rise slowly.

Justin peered into the dark interior of the warehouse. Although he could see nothing there, an image of dozens of reptilian men, crouched in the dark recesses of the building, licking their lipless mouths in anticipation as they waited for the truck to come within their scaly reach, flashed into his mind, as vivid as his dream of the night before. The more he concentrated, the clearer the picture grew. He thought he could hear something, soft at first, nothing more than a quiet hissing noise, then building in intensity and volume until he could make out words, repeated over and over in an eerie chant: "Bring us the children!"

Justin shot his sister a glance. Her eyes were wide with terror.

Mr. O'Faron shook his head, as if trying to clear his mind, and the truck slowed to a crawl. He began to turn the truck toward the opening warehouse door.

Justin heard the eerie voices, louder and faster: "Bring us the children!"

"Mr. O'Faron! Where are you going?" Miranda whispered, almost too soft to hear.

But O'Faron didn't respond. He just kept looking ahead, inching the truck forward.

The chanting continued to grow in intensity, until it felt like it was coming from all around them: "Bring us the children!"

Justin closed his eyes and put his hands over his ears in a

vain attempt to stop the noise. In his mind's eye he could see the creatures swaying back and forth as they chanted. In the center stood a taller figure draped in a black cloak covered in glowing golden symbols. His snakelike eyes seemed to be looking right at Justin as his mouth parted into an eager grin.

Justin's eyes shot open and he shouted, "Mr. O'Faron! Stop the truck! You can't go that way!"

Mr. O'Faron mumbled something and the truck came to a stop just as something in the front seat began to vibrate. He rubbed his temples. "*Ugh*. My head." He reached into his pants pocket and pulled out a cell phone. He looked at the number before punching the talk button. "Uh … Howdy, Mac … Yes, I have them. … We're on our way now. … Okay, see you then." As he spoke, he spun the wheel hard to the right, stomped on the gas, and veered away from the warehouse, sending both Justin and Miranda crashing back against their seats and lurching against each other. The truck's tires squealed as it turned back onto the highway.

Justin looked out the rear window at the warehouse disappearing into the distance. Standing on the dock and watching them leave were the robed figures he had seen in his mind. He felt his whole body shaking but couldn't stop. What the heck was going on? He looked over at his sister, and she met his gaze, her eyes still wide. Justin mouthed, *What was that about?*

She shook her head quickly. "Not here," she whispered.

Justin kept looking over his shoulder, each time expecting to see hundreds of creepy creatures sprinting down the highway in pursuit. Whoever had come to their house had followed them here, but why? What could they possibly want with two middle school kids—or anyone else in their family? And what was Mr. O'Faron doing with them? Was their grandfather somehow involved with these creatures too? Justin shuddered. Only one thing was clear: their parents must be terribly wrong. He and Miranda definitely weren't any safer here than back home.

CHAPTER 4

JUSTIN
M.V.R.H.

J USTIN'S HEAD BOUNCED HARD off the window of
the truck, waking him with a start. "Ouch," he said,
trying to rub the pain away. He quickly glanced around
for his sister. She sat, brooding as she had ever since they
had left New York, staring out the window, frowning. He
doubted that she had slept at all. "How long was I asleep?"

"Three hours," Miranda answered, without looking at him.

Judging by the kink in his neck, that sounded about right.
"Where are we now?"

"We're just outside La Garita," Mr. O'Faron answered—like
that was supposed to mean something to them.

Justin leaned in closer to his sister and whispered,
"Anything … *weird* happen while I was asleep?"

She shook her head, but shot the back of Mr. O'Faron a
hard look before returning to staring out the window.

"Did you try to call Mom and Dad?"

"Several times. It's just going straight to voicemail. They
must still be on their flight to—wherever it is they're going."

Justin's stomach growled. "I'm starving. Are we almost

there?"

"Yep," Mr. O'Faron said, pointing out the front window.

By the light of the rising full moon, Justin made out two massive wooden pillars flanking either side of the road and connected overhead by a big flat board with the words THUNDERBIRD RANCH carved into it.

"Our grandfather must like vintage cars," Justin mused.

His sister made a *tsk* sound, her way of letting him know he had said something dumb. "Don't be a dork. I seriously doubt the ranch is named after a car."

Mr. O'Faron nodded. "Your sister's right. A thunderbird is a massive storm-generating winged creature in Native American folklore."

Justin could just make out a meandering stream and a dozen or so buildings. "Which one of those is the ranch?"

Mr. O'Faron laughed. "All of it. Thunderbird Ranch covers the entire valley and a fair bit into the mountains beyond." He pointed to the structures in the distance. "There are several houses, a couple of barns, stables, and garages."

"*Several* houses?" Justin asked. Coming from a two-bedroom apartment in Manhattan, it was hard to fathom the need for more than *one* house.

"Sure. Your granddad's, a handful for the full-time staff, and the bunkhouse for the seasonal help."

"Awesome. Are we staying in the bunkhouse?"

Mr. O'Faron shook his head. "You and your sister will be staying with your granddad. His home has been pretty empty for a while now." He glanced back over his shoulder at them, his expression serious. "I think you two might be exactly what this place needs."

Justin elbowed his sister to get her attention and mouthed, "*What the heck does that mean?*" But she just shrugged and looked back out the window.

The road split, and they took the path to the right, followed immediately by a quick left, pulling up in front of the largest of the ranch's houses. It was three stories tall, with a massive wraparound front porch.

As soon as Mr. O'Faron turned the engine off, the screen door swung open and a small Asian lady bounded out onto the porch. She smiled broadly at them, jumping up and down, waving excitedly. Each time she leaped into the air, her white apron and crimson dress flared out like a parachute, exposing a pair of bright gold shoes.

Mr. O'Faron opened the side door and slid the seat forward. "I'll grab your bags and take them to your rooms. You two should probably go introduce yourselves before she explodes."

As soon as they set foot on the porch, the crazy jumping woman scooped them both into a tight hug. Her arms were like iron bands squeezing the air out of them. A second before Justin thought he actually might pass out, she pushed them away and began to giggle with glee. Her laugh sounded almost musical, like a bell choir at Christmas. She shook her head, eyes closed. "I can't believe you two actually exist." She had a very slight, unplaceable accent. "I mean, I know you exist. You're right here. And look at you!" She waved her hand up and down, as if magically revealing them for the first time. "You both got your mother's raven hair and copper skin, but those blue eyes are most unmistakably McAdelind. You look so much like your parents."

"You know our parents?" Justin asked.

"Of course. Don't be silly." She giggled again, touching a string of large gleaming pearls around her neck reflexively. "But just look at you …" She broke off, paused, and regarded them very seriously. "You must be Justin, and you're Miranda. Welcome!" She clapped her hands together. "Okay. It's late. To the dining room. We need to get you two a decent meal, then off to bed."

"Doesn't our grandfather want to meet us first?" Miranda asked. Justin could tell from her tone that she wasn't sure she really wanted to meet the man.

"Oh, he's very busy tonight, my dears. You'll meet him soon enough," the woman replied.

"Excuse me, ma'am," Justin asked timidly, "but who are *you*?"

She slapped her hands on her knees. "Of course you don't know me, we just met," she said, giggling. "My name is Mrs. Lóng."

"Nice to meet you Mrs. ... *errr* ... Long," Justin stammered.

She shook her head vigorously, her black-and-silver ponytail slapping both sides of her face. "Not 'Long,' *Lo-ong*," she said, with a rising intonation. "It's a Chinese name."

"Sorry," Justin said. He doubted he'd ever be able to pronounce the odd vowel just right. "What exactly do you do on the ranch?"

Mrs. Lóng opened the screen door and motioned them inside. "I am the housekeeper, cook, gardener, handywoman, watcher of kids and grandkids, and whatever-else-they-need-done-on-the-ranch person," she said, winking at Justin as if they were sharing some private joke. "I am the M.V.R.H. This place would absolutely shut down if not for me."

"What does M.V.R.H. stand for?" Justin asked as he looked around the massive entry hall. It had polished hardwood floors and spotless white walls reflecting the light coming through several of the open archways that led to rooms along both sides. He had never been to a home so ... empty ... before. There was nothing to see except a wide wooden staircase on the left—no furniture, no family pictures, no paintings, nothing. Everything was completely bare, as if it were for sale.

"Ah. Of course you don't know. Why, it stands for Most

Valuable Ranch Hand." She wrapped her arms around her stomach and giggled in her strange musical way, then turned on her heel and leaped into an arched opening to her right.

Justin looked at his sister, who was making a circular motion with her index finger around her ear, the universal sign for *crazy*. He smiled and nodded in agreement. But crazy or not, Mrs. Lóng seemed to be the person they would be stuck with until their parents sent for them, or came to get them. Justin shrugged and followed his sister into the room. "Whoa. This is as big as our whole apartment."

"Hardly," his sister said, trying hard not to seem impressed.

The room was as empty as the hall, with the exceptions of a brilliant flower arrangement in the middle of the huge table and an enormous fieldstone fireplace.

"Okay. Grab a seat, I'll be back in a second," Mrs. Lóng said as she disappeared through a swinging door at the rear of the room.

There were twelve seats at the mammoth table, but only two at the far end had place settings. Miranda walked over to one of the seats, so Justin took the other. He pulled back the heavy chair, and cringed as it made a loud grating noise as wood scraped against wood.

Mrs. Lóng emerged, using her behind to open the door. Her arms were laden with plates of all sizes, piled high with enough food for an army. Justin watched in awe as she expertly set all the dishes down. The smell was incredible, like a steakhouse restaurant. He surveyed everything as if he were a king gazing upon a feast in his honor. There were steaks, mashed potatoes, sweet corn, beans, rolls, and some kind of yellowish pudding for dessert.

"Oh my gosh. I am so-o-o-o-o starving," he said, his stomach growling in agreement.

Mrs. Lóng let out a small laugh, "Well? Don't wait for a written invitation. Eat up."

Justin tore into the food with gusto, piling as much as he could on his plate and shoveling mounds of food into his mouth. The steak was juicy perfection, the potatoes smooth and creamy, the corn sweet and salty, and the roll, soft and buttery. He stopped to take a deep breath and massage his stomach, trying to clear more room for food, when he noticed two sets of eyes on him. "What?"

"Just checking to make sure you weren't going to explode," quipped Mrs. Lóng. Then she turned to Miranda, "What are you waiting for, dear? Do you not like the food?"

"I don't eat red meat. The potatoes and veggies will be fine," Miranda said, and poked at the corn with her fork.

Mrs. Lóng raised an eyebrow, "No red meat?" Then she shook a finger at Miranda. "Of course you don't eat red meat. Why make anything easy for me? You know, where I am from, you eat what is given to you and you are thankful. None of this custom-order nonsense kids think is their right, these days."

"Oh really," Justin interrupted, trying to say anything before his sister said something rude in response. "Where exactly are you from, Mrs. Lóng?"

She looked at him and smiled. "Jiangxi province, in Southern China. Now don't interrupt me when I am on my soapbox, dear," she said, before turning back to his sister. "Now what am I supposed to do with you?"

"You don't have to do anything, the vegetables are fine," Miranda replied blankly.

"Nonsense. I live to serve the needs of picky eaters. You stay put, I'll be right back," she said and bounded into the kitchen.

"That is one crazy old lady," Miranda said, shaking her head.

Justin put his finger to his lips. "Ssssh. Not so loud. She seems fine to me. You're being rude," he said and shoved another piece of steak into his mouth.

"Whatever. Let's just get through this so I can go to bed."

Justin was starting to say something when the door swung open again and Mrs. Lóng burst into the dining room holding a large platter with a whole rotisserie chicken resting on it.

Justin almost choked on a spoonful of potatoes, "How in the world …"

"Here you go, dear," she said, pulling out a long curved knife and carving a piece of chicken breast, sliding it onto Miranda's plate.

Did the cook always keep a whole roasted chicken on hand just in case? Justin could tell his sister was freaked out by this too, but instead of saying anything, she grabbed her fork and took a tentative bite. Instantly, her hard expression melted. She quickly devoured the rest of the chicken.

"Glad you like it. Here you go, dear," Mrs. Lóng said, as she carved two more pieces and scooped some mashed potatoes and corn onto Miranda's plate.

Mrs. Lóng plopped down with a sigh, sinking into the chair at the head of the table. She was smiling and giggling, almost manic with glee.

Justin began to smile too. "What?"

"Oh nothing, just happy you two like the food."

"Oh we totally do. It's fantastic," he said, and shoved another spoonful of potatoes in his mouth. Then he paused, another forkful of steak poised at his mouth, and looked at her. "Do you want to have some too?"

Her face became suddenly very serious as she looked off in the distance, staring at nothing.

Justin put down his fork and spoon. "Earth to Mrs. … Lóng," he said, trying hard to pronounce her name right. "Hello?"

Mrs. Lóng turned slowly to stare at Justin with unfocused

eyes.

His heart began to race. This was the same vacant expression Mr. O'Faron had worn when they were at the warehouse earlier. Were the lizard people here too? "Mrs. Lóng, why aren't you eating with us?"

Her eyes snapped back into focus and she raised her right hand. Between her index finger and thumb was a small brown bottle. "Because I poisoned your food, dear."

CHAPTER 5

MIRANDA
Please Pass the Antidote

IRANDA JUMPED BACK FROM THE TABLE, knocking her silverware to the floor. Justin was wiping his tongue with his napkin, spitting out anything he could onto his plate. Mrs. Lóng started choking with laughter. She grabbed her sides as if her lungs were going to burst. Tears were streaming down her face.

Miranda leaped forward and grabbed the butter knife off the floor, holding it menacingly at the crazed cook. "Where's the antidote?" she yelled. But this action caused the woman's laughter to double in intensity.

When Mrs. Lóng had finally regained enough composure to speak, she turned the small vial around so that Miranda could read the label: PURE VANILLA EXTRACT.

Miranda threw the knife down on the table. She felt her face turn red with anger and her heart pounding.

Her brother, finally realizing that they had been the targets of a practical joke, looked down at the plate of already-been-chewed food, and moaned, "Oh, man. Look at that. And I was still hungry too."

Mrs. Lóng wiped the tears from her eyes and looked at Miranda. "You were so uptight, I thought I would lighten the mood for you."

"Well, it wasn't funny," Miranda huffed and sat back down, arms crossed over her chest. "Not funny at all."

"Oh come on, that was funny. One of my best jokes yet." Mrs. Lóng sighed, still smiling, "I get it, you don't want to be here, that is pretty obvious, but trust me ... ." She leaned forward, a very serious look in her eyes, and whispered, "This is a magical place." Then she smiled again, sat back, and crossed her arms behind her head. "I've always found jokes a great way to dissipate stress and fear." She turned to Justin. "And don't worry, dear, there is plenty of food left. What would you like to eat?"

But Miranda wasn't willing to let the incident go so easily. "That was just plain mean, and you know it. I'm not sure what you were expecting our reaction to be, but I'm not amused. And frankly, I don't want to enjoy myself. I want to go home." She stood up and turned to leave the room. When she got to the archway, she looked back at her brother and said, "Are you coming?" and, not waiting for an answer, headed up the stairs.

Miranda paused halfway up the first flight and waited for her brother. She heard him say something to Mrs. Lóng, before she saw him round the corner at full speed, glide like a hockey player across the polished wooden floor, and bound up several stairs at a time until he caught up with her.

When they reached the top of the stairs, Miranda could see the upstairs hall was a twin of the one below, except that it was lined with large wooden doors instead of open archways. Miranda noticed several of the doors to the left were ajar, so she approached the first one and peered inside.

The room was definitely intended for a boy. The walls were painted bright orange and accented by dark-blue furniture.

Covering almost every inch of wall space were faded Denver Broncos posters. Opposite the door, nestled between the room's two windows, was a large overflowing bookshelf. Resting on a bed with an orange-blue-and-white checkered quilt was Justin's suitcase.

Miranda turned to look at her brother, who just stood there with a goofy, concerned look on his face. She guessed he was attempting to look sympathetic or something, and probably trying hard to think of anything to say that wouldn't make her angrier. Miranda fought the desire to snap at him, and motioned with her thumb back toward the room. "This one is yours," she said, and moved to the next open door.

She heard Justin let out a long sigh, but she didn't turn around, sure that if she did, they would start fighting, or worse, she would start to cry.

The next room turned out to be a large bathroom, so she continued to the third door. On the bed, she saw her suitcase lying on a checkered blue-and-white quilt. Unlike her brother's room, this one had nothing decorating its sky-blue walls. Not one picture, poster, or bookshelf. Nothing. The dark wooden bed frame matched the low dresser with a mirror and the nightstand, but other than those basic furnishings, the room had no personality at all.

Miranda walked over to her suitcase and began piling its contents onto the floor, looking for her toothbrush. When she found it, she headed to the bathroom, but stopped when she noticed a square space on the bedroom wall that was slightly darker than the surrounding area. She walked over to it and moved her hand across the line from dark to light to see if the area had been patched, but it was smooth. She walked around the room, looking closely at each section of the wall, and quickly discovered several other areas where the discoloration was apparent. Leaning against the foot of the bed, she took in as much of the room at once as she could, looking for a pattern to the shapes.

"That's weird," she said to herself.

"What's weird?" said Justin, suddenly beside her.

She jumped. "Knock much?"

He shrugged. "We've shared a room our entire lives. Knocking didn't really occur to me." He looked around the room, "So what's weird?"

Miranda waved her hand around the space. "The walls are blank except for these areas where the paint is slightly darker."

Justin inspected the wall. "Yeah, looks like there were pictures or something hanging up and someone took them down. You know how back in the apartment the floor was faded in spots where the sun always hit. This looks like the opposite of that."

Miranda nodded, still looking at the empty walls. "So someone took all the posters down from this room but kept all those old football ones in yours? Seems kind of strange."

"I'm pretty sure I'm in Dad's old room. You know how much he loves football. Whose room do you suppose this was?" Justin asked.

Miranda answered with a shrug, then yawned so wide, her jaw hurt. The day's events had finally caught up with her, and she was fading fast. She looked over at her brother as he echoed her yawn.

"We should get some sleep." She could see him about to protest and cut him off with a raised hand. "We can talk tomorrow. I'm too tired to think about anything right now."

Looking defeated, Justin turned and exited the room, calling back, "Goodnight."

Miranda grabbed her toiletries, went to the bathroom, and got ready for bed. When she returned to her room, she shut the door, walked over to the bed, and began to slide the empty suitcase under it but stopped suddenly when she heard paper tearing. Getting down on her hands and knees, she looked for the cause of the sound. Hanging down from the bottom of the box springs was a piece of paper. Miranda moved her suitcase aside and wedged herself as far under the bed as she could until she could reach the piece of paper and pull it out.

Miranda plopped heavily down on the bed and turned over the yellowed, torn note several times before opening it.

My dearest Em,
   No one has ever given me a gift like you gave me today. I will cherish it for the rest of my life, as I will cherish you. I wish I had more to give you, to show you how much I care. One day I will. I'll have my name back, I know I will, because you believe in me, and that belief makes me a stronger, better man. I will give you the world someday, but until then, take this note as promise.
   Yours always,

The bottom part of the note, where the signature should have been, was missing. Only the left half of the name's first letter was still intact, possibly a *B*, *E*, *F*, or *R*.

Miranda read the note twice more before carefully folding it back up, placing it in her suitcase, and shoving them both under the bed. Miranda let out a sigh, wondering if someone, someday, would write her a note like this one. Thanks to her brother, her social life, she assumed, had pretty much come to an early end. So, probably not.

Miranda lay there for a moment wondering about the note. Was this Em's room? If so, where was all her stuff? And who was she anyhow?

CHAPTER 6

MIRANDA
Fireside Chats

MIRANDA AWOKE SUDDENLY. The night was quiet. Nothing like Manhattan. There, unless you live high up in a tall building, all night long you hear a continuous symphony of urban sounds: traffic, people out late, sirens, alley cats. You get used to it. But on this ranch, in the middle of nowhere, Miranda could hardly hear anything: a few insects, that was all. Could it have been the lack of familiar sounds that had woken her up?

Miranda was lying there, trying to go back to sleep, when she heard something else. She sat up in bed, tilting her head, listening intently to a slight rumbling noise, barely audible, but coming closer. Someone talking in the distance—no, two distinct voices. And they were definitely coming nearer.

The front door slammed shut with enough force to shake the floor in Miranda's room. The voices were clearer now. Two men were speaking, though she still couldn't make out the words. One of them seemed agitated; his voice was slightly louder and had an edge to it.

Miranda hopped silently out of bed and crept over to the

door, trying to see if she could make out any of the words. She couldn't. If she were going to do some proper spying, she would need her brother as backup. She tiptoed out of her room and down the hall to Justin's.

A small moan escaped Justin's lips as she walked over to his bed. What was he dreaming about? She shook him lightly. Nothing. She shook him harder. He rolled over. "Justin," she whispered. Another moan escaped his lips. She leaned in close to his ear and whispered as loud as she dared, "Lizard men."

Justin shot up, his eyes wide with terror, flailing his arms wildly in all directions.

"*Sssh!*" Miranda said as she tried to pin his arms down to his sides.

Justin's eyes shot wildly around the dark room. "What the heck?"

"I need your help."

"And you thought scaring the crap out of me was the best way to get it?"

Miranda pulled back and crossed her arms. "It worked, didn't it?" She motioned toward the door. "There are a couple of men talking downstairs and I want to find out if one of them is our grandfather."

"I was having a bad dream. I was in a cave or something, chasing someone down a bunch of passageways, but lost them in a round room with shiny things on the walls."

Miranda was curious to hear more but didn't want to miss the conversation below, so she just shrugged. "Dreams are weird. Let's go see if Grandpa's home."

Justin jumped out of bed and followed Miranda to the door. When she had confirmed that the men were still downstairs, she slowly pulled open the door and glided silently out into the corridor. Light was flickering faintly on the walls from the hallway below.

With Justin as her shadow, she moved silently down the old staircase, keeping as close to the wall as possible. On the landing halfway down, they crouched low as Miranda peeked into the hall below. The coast was clear. The voices were coming from the room opposite the dining room, but they were so low, it was difficult to tell what they were saying.

Miranda looked back at her brother, and made a motion indicating she was going down to the main hall to get a better look. Justin shook his head vigorously. Miranda waved him off and started down the stairs, hugging the wall as she descended. She glanced back toward Justin when she was halfway down. Her chicken brother was frozen on the landing. Miranda beckoned to him to follow. He shook his head again. She pointed at him hard and then moved her hand across her neck in a slicing motion. He sighed and began creeping slowly down the stairs.

Miranda turned and continued the rest of the way down the stairs to the main hall. She inched forward silently until she reached the arched entryway to the room where the men were talking.

Miranda leaned forward to peer in. The room was large, with a fieldstone fireplace identical to the one in the dining room. Facing the fire were two leather-upholstered chairs with backs so high, their occupants were entirely hidden from view.

"Did they let their parents know they made it okay?" said an unfamiliar voice, deep and gravelly.

"Miranda tried several times in the truck, but I'm not sure if they tried again later." Mr. O'Faron.

"*Humph!*" snorted the other man. "Who knows what harebrained scheme that idiot son of mine is up to?"

Miranda looked at her brother and mouthed, "*Grandpa.*"

Justin's face was flushed—Miranda assumed because of the remark about their dad being an "idiot." Justin mock-slammed his fist into his open palm and then pointed in the direction of their grandfather. Miranda raised her finger to her lips and turned back around.

"Everything went okay picking them up?" their grandfather asked.

"Yep. Airport to here without a hitch."

The old man grunted in acknowledgement.

Miranda looked at Justin, who raised an eyebrow. Why didn't Mr. O'Faron let their grandfather know he had delivered the package?

"So ... what are they like?" their grandfather asked.

"Well, the boy takes after his father as far as I can tell."

"Great. That's just what this place needs." It was becoming painfully obvious why their dad had stopped talking to this man. "And the girl?"

There was a long pause before Mr. O'Faron responded. "Hard to tell," he said, then paused as if choosing the right words. "But there is something about her, the way she carries herself, that reminds me of ... Em—"

"William," their grandfather said curtly, cutting him off, a warning in his voice.

Dead silence followed. No grunt. No *humph*. Even the fire refrained from popping or crackling.

Miranda's mind was racing. Who is this Em person? she wondered. I'm sleeping in her room—a room that has, by the looks of it, been purposefully cleansed of any evidence of her existence. A room with a secret note from a boyfriend. Someone obviously known to the people in this house. And I remind Mr. O'Faron of her?

Justin tapped Miranda on the shoulder and mouthed, "*Em?*"

Miranda just shook her head and turned back to continue spying on the men.

"I've spent the last twenty-odd hours looking for the

wyrmling, or how someone could have gotten into the sanctuary. Nothing. Are you positive you didn't see any signs that someone had forced their way in?" their grandfather asked.

"No. But forget *in* for a moment. How in the heck did they get it *out*? Something that size, under our noses, is very troubling. It looks like we either have a thief who knows what he's doing or someone who is intimately familiar with our security system. I can't believe this is happening again."

Their grandfather grunted. "This time is different. Last time it was a couple of bars and the family stone. This is even more serious. Cisco thinks it's an inside job."

"I suppose that's possible, but who would steal from us? Everyone on the ranch has worked here for years. Why would they make their move now? No. It's got to be one of the other families—or possibly even the Tribe. But there have definitely been some strange things going on. On my way out of town today, I stopped at the Trading Post. Old Miller was telling everyone how he saw something flying low, just above the trees last night." Mr. O'Faron let out a dry laugh. "Of course all the speculation was about government drones and UFOs. And just before I came down here, I saw Red in the trophy room sniffing around. He seemed very agitated."

Their grandfather let out another *"Humph,"* then said, "I think it's unlikely to be one of the Nineteen or the Tribe." His voice dropped to a low growl. "But it has to be someone with intimate knowledge of our world. It would be a mistake to ignore any possibilities, especially when the stakes are so high." There was the sound of a chair scooting against the floor and another grunt as their grandfather strained to stand up. "I'll see you to the door."

Panic surged in Miranda, and she moved quickly toward her brother, practically shoving him up the stairs to the first landing. At the top of the staircase, she pulled him into a shadow, where they crouched and waited.

Miranda could see the silhouettes of both men exiting the room. Mr. O'Faron walked out first, his tall, lean frame crowned by his precious hat. He was followed closely by a large man, almost as tall as he was, but much broader in the shoulders. Miranda thought about moving out of the shadows to get a better look but knew that would expose their hiding spot.

Then as if reading her mind, their grandfather turned suddenly and faced the stairs. Miranda froze, the rush of blood in her ears making it hard to hear anything. Were they busted? Did he see them? Maybe the shadow wasn't as concealing as she had thought.

"Do you think they know?" he said, then turned back to Mr. O'Faron.

"No. They would have said something."

Their grandfather grunted. "I suppose it's better that way, considering the situation. We'll have Billy keep them busy so they won't have time to wander around." The men turned and walked away from the stairs, toward the door.

Miranda needed to get herself and Justin back to their rooms, and quickly. Miranda grabbed her brother by the arm and forcefully guided him up the stairs. At the top of the hall she paused in front of his room. "We'll talk tomorrow," she whispered.

"But what was that about? And who's Em?"

The front door shut, and a bolt slid into place, locking the house for the night. Then a set of booted feet started an uneven walk toward the stairs.

"No time now. Tomorrow," Miranda whispered and shoved her brother toward the door to his room.

Miranda silently ran down the hall to her own room, shut the door, and leaped into bed. It wasn't until she heard a door farther down the hall close that she allowed herself to let out the breath she had been holding. Their grandfather didn't suspect they were awake after all.

Her mind began to swim with questions. What weren't they supposed to know about this place? What other families was he talking about? Why would someone break into a ranch, anyway? Were they stealing cattle or something? And who the heck was this Em person?

Miranda decided she wasn't going to let anything prevent her finding the answers to these questions. After all, if she had to waste her whole summer in this stupid place, she was going to figure out what was really going on around here.

CHAPTER 7

JUSTIN
Billy, the Kid

J USTIN AWOKE HUNGRIER than he had ever been in his entire life. Smells from the kitchen had intruded into his dreams, causing him to awaken to the grumble of his stomach. He rolled over and looked at the clock. Six-thirty in the morning—the earliest he had gotten up on his own without an alarm clock ... ever. Well ... excluding Christmas, of course.

Justin walked over to his suitcase to grab some clothes. He had not bothered to unpack the night before, half wishing that his parents would show up and take him and Miranda home. He sighed and rifled through his clothing, selecting an orange T-shirt, red socks, and a pair of faded jeans.

As he slipped on his pants, he felt something in the pocket. He pulled out an object wrapped in paper about the size of a granola bar. Turning it over, he saw his mom's handwriting: *Don't open. Keep safe.* He frowned. That's weird, he thought. What in the world could this be? He was strongly tempted to disobey her written instructions, but hesitated. His birthday was coming up, but surely they would be back in Manhattan by then, wouldn't they? Not wanting to think about the possibility of being stranded on the ranch for months, he decided to keep an eye out for a safe place to stash the package. He put the wrapped object back in his pocket, zipped up his suitcase, and pulled it over to the closet.

He walked down the hall and knocked lightly a couple of times on Miranda's door. When no response came, he knocked a little louder.

There was a strange croaking noise, then a cough, then, "Come in."

Justin pushed the door open. Miranda had propped herself up on one elbow and was glaring at him. "Do you know what time it is?" she asked, still sounding a little rough.

Justin sauntered into the room. "I reckon it's time to rise and shine, and have some grub, little lady." He flicked his hands up from his sides like pistols and pointed them at his sister.

"You're such a dork," she said, flatly, "You know that, right?" Then as if remembering something, she grabbed her cell phone from the nightstand. She frowned. "I wonder where Mom and Dad are? No texts or calls, and every time I try them, it goes straight to voicemail."

"I'm sure they're just in the middle of a flight, or the time zone isn't right, or something. We'll hear from them today." Justin wished he felt as confident as he sounded. "Come on. I'm starving."

Justin left Miranda alone long enough for her to wash up and get dressed, then together they went downstairs to the dining room. Two steaming plates were already positioned at the places where they had sat the night before. Justin made a beeline for his chair.

"Before you sit down, you might want to check for a whoopee cushion, plastic spiders, or trick chair leg," Miranda said, inspecting her own seat.

Justin had hoped she'd gotten over Mrs. Lóng's joke of the night before, but he could tell from the look on her face that she was going to hold onto this one for a while. He did think the joke had been pretty funny, even though its timing was bad. But regardless of what they might think of the crazy old lady's welcoming tactics, her cooking more than made up for her eccentricities.

Justin dropped into his seat and proceeded to devour the feast in front of him: scrambled eggs, fresh biscuits, breakfast potatoes with diced tomatoes and something green and spicy, and a couple of thick slabs of bacon. He paused only to slurp water and orange juice alternately. When he had finished his first assault, Justin stopped and looked up to see how much damage his sister had done to her plate. It was only then that he noticed Mrs. Lóng sitting at the head of the table.

"What the heck! Where did you come from?" he said, almost falling off his chair.

Miranda looked up and spat out some food in surprise. She eyed Mrs. Lóng suspiciously. "How did you get there? I didn't even see you walk in!"

Mrs. Lóng laughed in her strangely musical way. "Oh, children. So distracted by eating the absolutely delicious food I made for you." She flourished her hands in a theatrical gesture. "You are quite welcome. It's a curse to be such an incredible chef that people forget their manners."

Justin finished chewing a mouthful and said, "Thank you, Mrs. Lóng." He surveyed the room. "Are the other people joining us soon?"

The old woman just giggled. "Silly boy, they have been up for hours. We let you sleep in this morning, assuming you would be too exhausted from your travels yesterday." She stood up suddenly and with a twirl that sent her red dress and white apron flaring out around her, bounded into the kitchen.

Miranda leaned forward across the table. "I'm telling you, she wasn't here one moment, then she was the next." Pointing her fork at him for emphasis, she added, "She's a sneaky old lady. We need to keep an eye on her. I bet you she's the one that's swiping things. You heard them last night, whoever it is moves in and out unseen."

"Oh come on, she's harmless. Strange. But harmless."

Miranda frowned. "Well, it's your funeral. When she sneaks up behind you and slits your throat with a kitchen knife, you'll be wishing you listened to me. Frankly, she gives me the heebie-jeebies, and I don't trust her one bit."

Justin thought his sister was being a little dramatic but kept his mouth shut.

Mrs. Lóng came through the door to the kitchen holding a couple of sheets of paper. She placed one down in front of Justin and one in front of Miranda. "This is your list of chores while you are here at the ranch. Everyone is expected to earn their keep. That includes short- and long-term guests." She gestured toward them with both hands.

Justin quickly scanned down the list of items. "There are, like, twenty things on here."

"Sixteen to be exact, and yours and your sister's lists are slightly different. I took the liberty to add the day of the week on which each chore is to be done, a brief description of the task, and where you go on the ranch to do it."

Miranda raised her hand. "Shouldn't the people who usually do these chores continue to do them? I mean, we will probably just screw things up and they will have more work redoing them."

"She has a good point," Justin interjected. His sister was a master at getting out of work, so he went along with her.

Mrs. Lóng looked from Justin to his sister, then back again, her eyes hardening. She sat down silently and folded her hands in her lap. "Let me make this perfectly clear, because I will only say this once." Her eyes began to smolder. In fact, Justin thought they actually started to glow slightly. "I am in charge of you two while you are at this establishment. I expect the chores to be done correctly, and on time. If you do a job poorly in an attempt to get out of doing your assigned work, I will make you do it over and over again until you do it right. And since you seem to want to back each other up, even on ill-thought-through tactics, it should be no problem for you also to back each other up to ensure the chores are done correctly." She paused and looked at Justin, then Miranda. "Do I make myself clear?"

Justin sank down in his seat. "Yes, Mrs. Lóng."

The old lady looked over at Miranda, who was sitting there with her arms folded tight across her chest. They stared at each other for what seemed like hours. Then Mrs. Lóng said, "I can stare at you all day, young lady, but we have work to do. Did I make myself clear, or do I need to repeat myself?"

"Crystal," Miranda said through clenched teeth.

Mrs. Lóng clapped her hands together and smiled broadly. "Well then. Now that we have that business behind us, let's move on to reviewing the lists and my expectations, shall we?"

* * *

Fifteen minutes later they were standing outside one of the ranch's many corrals, waiting for someone named Billy to arrive. Justin remembered his name from the night before but couldn't remember the context. Realizing that the moment might be their best chance to talk, he said, "It's no wonder Dad left this place and never looked back. There's not a lot of love going on around here."

Miranda did not reply, but just continued to lean on the

fence, her chin resting on a post, staring into the empty corral beyond. In fact, she hadn't made a sound since the end of their discussion with Mrs. Lóng.

"Maybe this Billy guy will be okay," Justin said.

Miranda let out a long sigh. "I doubt it."

"Do you want to talk about the past couple of nights? You know, try to make some sense of everything?" Justin asked.

"Not really."

He decided to try a different approach. "I know being lectured sucks, trust me, I became an expert this past year. But it's not like we did anything wrong. She's just letting us know who's in charge."

"Uh-huh," Miranda replied, still gazing at the ground.

"So what's all"—Justin motioned with his hands toward his sister—"this about?"

Miranda turned her head, lifting it off the fence slightly to meet his eyes. "This is about being trapped. This is about being at the mercy of crazy cooks, grumpy old men, and strange ranch hands who are in love with their hat." She turned back and leaned her chin down on the fence once more. "That's what this is about."

"I understand, but it's not like this is the first time Mom and Dad took off and left us with other people."

"At least we were in Manhattan. We could go where we wanted and wouldn't have to do their housework for them." She looked over her shoulder down the driveway back to the main house. "You were asleep most of the way here, so you don't know how remote this place really is. Nothing, and I mean *no-thing*, within thirty miles of here except farms and a small general store." She looked back over the empty corral. "You know what was within thirty miles from our house in Manhattan?"

"New Jersey and Connecticut?"

"No. *Everything.*" She closed her eyes and sighed. "We are

prisoners here."

A high-pitched engine revved to life behind one of the large barns. Justin and Miranda turned toward the sound. A blue all-terrain vehicle careened around the corner, both wheels on one side high off the ground. The ATV leveled off and shot toward them, sending a thick plume of dust shooting into the sky in its wake. A matching trailer laden with a pile of miscellaneous items anchored the ATV to the earth and kept it from flipping over. The driver was hunched low over the handlebars, his features obscured by a black-and-purple baseball cap pulled down over wraparound sunglasses. Gunning the engine, the stranger headed directly toward Justin and Miranda. Justin sprang back and slammed into the fence as Miranda spun around. They both pressed themselves flat against the rough boards, trapped. At the last moment, the driver grinned and veered away, throwing a spray of dust and gravel over both of them.

The stranger remained seated, his gloved hands revving the engine to keep it from stalling. "Hop on. We have a lot of work to do," he said, not even turning to look at them.

Justin pushed away from the fence and put himself between the driver and his sister. "What's the big idea? You could've hurt someone!"

The driver let go of the handlebars and stood up. He was at least a foot taller than Justin, broad in the shoulders and muscular for his age, which seemed to be around sixteen. "Relax, small fry. I was just fooling around," he said and patted Justin on the head.

"That wasn't very cool. You could have hurt us," Miranda said, but at the same time, Justin noticed a twitching at the corner of her mouth as she fought back a smile.

The boy leaned back in his seat and crossed his arms over his chest. "Not a chance. I've been driving this thing since I could walk."

"I doubt it," Miranda said, smiling now. "You must be Billy then."

"Yep. Billy O'Faron."

"O'Faron, huh? As in Mr. O'Faron's son?" Justin asked.

Billy looked away. "Not by choice."

"I'm Justin. This is my sister, Miranda."

"I know who you are, McAdelind," Billy replied flatly. "We have a busy day, so let's get moving." He pointed to the seat behind him. "Hop on."

"There's not enough room for the both of us," Justin said.

Billy looked over his shoulder. "Your sister can sit there. You're in the trailer."

Miranda looked over at Justin and shrugged, then climbed on behind Billy.

"Typical," Justin muttered under his breath.

Billy revved the engine loudly several times, yelling over the noise, "Hold on to something back there, squirt!" and the ATV shot forward.

Justin clung to the side of the wagon, his feet hitting the ground with each jarring bounce. He thought he could feel bruises blooming on his backside.

Justin had been wrong. This Billy guy was definitely *not* okay.

CHAPTER 8

MIRANDA

The Warren

JUSTIN HAD BEEN RIGHT FOR ONCE, Miranda thought. This Billy guy really *was* okay. It had not crossed her mind she might meet someone cool in Nowhereville, Colorado. Billy was also kind of cute, which didn't hurt either.

A large dip in the path threatened to throw her from the ATV's seat, and she instinctively wrapped her arms around Billy's waist. He smelled of earth and sun, and she couldn't resist leaning in a little closer, but quickly pulled away, afraid he might notice, and returned to holding onto his shoulders instead.

Stealing a glance back at her brother, checking to make sure that he had not been thrown out of the trailer, Miranda saw he was clinging to its sides with white knuckles, each dip in the uneven path tossing him mercilessly into the air.

"Can you slow down a bit?" she yelled over the whine of the engine.

"We're almost there!" Billy called back over his shoulder.

Miranda frowned, but didn't press further.

They shot up a hill, over a rutted service road and into a narrow valley, crossing into a section of the ranch previously obscured by the massive walls of the surrounding cliffs. Billy slowed the ATV and zigzagged up the hard-packed dirt track, avoiding bushes and boulders.

Could Billy be the boy who had written the note to Em? Miranda wondered. Granted, she didn't know for sure if the signature started with a *B*, but he was the first nonancient person she had seen since they arrived. Still, the note seemed to be much older than the boy she was clinging to.

They continued to climb through the small canyon until they crested a hill and entered a vast pasture. Billy opened the throttle and shot forward, causing her brother to yelp in surprise. Ahead of them there stretched a seemingly endless wood-and-wire fence. Billy pulled up within a couple feet of the massive barrier and cut the engine. He motioned for Miranda to climb down first, then vaulted off in the opposite direction.

"Show off," Justin muttered under his breath but still loud enough for Miranda to hear.

She turned around to tell him to shut up, but when she saw how beaten up and disheveled he looked, she decided to keep her comments to herself.

"Okay," Billy said loudly, drawing their attention back to him, "in two days, we will move the cattle from the lower elevations up to this pasture, where they will graze until the end of summer. However, before we can, we need to check the entire length of the fence to ensure there are no gaps or damaged areas." He gestured toward the section of fencing to his left. "I've already been around the entire fence that way." He turned to his right. "But we have about another ten miles of fence to inspect before we can move the herd in."

"So ... we just walk around until we find a hole in the fence and fix it?" Justin asked.

"Normally yes, but since we are short on time, we will slowly drive along the fence instead. If either of you notice a gap, hole, or section that looks somewhat weak, point it out. Any questions?"

Justin raised one hand, rubbing his backside with the other. "Yeah. Can I walk?"

* * *

By midday they had covered about six miles of fence and only found two places that needed repairs. Justin opted to walk the entire way. It wasn't hard for him to keep up since Billy drove slowly. Occasionally he would gun it and race ahead, waving back at Justin as a joke—which Miranda could tell her brother didn't find very funny.

They continued along the fence until it turned at a right angle and disappeared behind a rocky outcropping. Billy cut the engine and gestured up the hill away from the fence toward a wooded area where white trees with brilliant green leaves shimmered when the wind blew. "Let's have lunch up there," he said, grabbing a small cooler from the wagon.

"Those are birch trees, right?" Miranda asked.

"No, aspens," Billy said, and continued up the hill.

Miranda felt her face flush. She hated being wrong, especially in front of a boy. She shook her head and followed Billy up to the trees, where he was standing, looking back in the direction of the fence, not saying a word. She turned to see what he was looking at, and her breath caught with awe. From this new vantage point, a vast valley surrounded by majestic mountains stretched out before her.

"Beautiful, huh?" Billy said, then plopped down on the grassy slope, opened the cooler, pulled out a sandwich and a can of soda, and handed them to her.

Miranda nodded and tore into the sandwich with zeal,

surprised at how hungry she was. She had eaten her sandwich and finished about half of her can of soda when Justin came plodding up the hill, sweating and breathing hard.

"Break time," Justin said and dropped to the ground. He pulled a sandwich from the cooler, not bothering to see what it was before devouring it in three bites. He chugged a soda, belched loudly, and lay down on the soft grass. Knitting his hands behind his head, he closed his eyes and said, "Wake me when it's time to go."

Billy stood and grabbed the cooler, "Time to go."

Justin opened one eye. "Seriously?"

Billy looked annoyed. "Yes, seriously. We have a lot left to do before sunset."

Justin propped himself up on his elbows. "I just got here."

"You're the one who wanted to walk."

Miranda raised both hands, like a referee. "Billy, would it be okay if Justin rested for fifteen minutes? This has been a big change from New York, and the altitude is hard on both of us."

Billy frowned but nodded. "Fair point," he said, then looked over his shoulder at the stretch of fence they had yet to inspect. "I'll drive ahead and give the fence a once over, and you and your brother can chill out here. I'll be back in about thirty minutes."

Miranda gave him a coy smile. "Thanks." Billy just turned and jogged down the hill to the ATV. Miranda felt so lame. What was she thinking?

"Thanks, sis."

"You owe me," she said, watching Billy disappear into the distance. "He seems cool." She looked at her brother to make sure he got the point. The least Justin could do was to not embarrass her in front of a cute boy, even if Billy was older and obviously not interested. But Justin's eyes were shut and he was snoring slightly. "Of course, you're already asleep," she said.

The shade of the aspens shielded them from the heat of the noonday sun, making it quite comfortable. Miranda lay down onto the ground, taking the opportunity to relax until Billy returned. The clouds were migrating across the sky at a lazy pace. A breeze rustled the leaves overhead, and Miranda felt her eyes closing slowly on their own. She continued to listen to the wind move through the branches above until its gentle melody lulled her to sleep.

Miranda became aware that her breathing was slowing, matching someone else's. Beneath her was a stone floor, and the air was dank and cool. She was remembering someone too, a girl a little older than herself, with fair skin and dark-blond hair. Something about her was so familiar. Miranda looked into her deep-blue eyes, strangely hard and serious for someone so young, and she realized she had seen her before. But where? Miranda looked at her again and she was overwhelmed with such a profound feeling of failure and loss, it took her breath away, and she began to sob.

Miranda opened her eyes, realizing that she had fallen asleep and had a dream. She was still lying under the protection of the aspens, and Justin was standing above her.

"Are you okay?" His brows were knitted together in concern.

Miranda sat up and instinctively wiped her eyes with her palms. She drew them away, staring at the beads of moisture. She really had been crying, that part wasn't only a dream.

"Who are you?"

She looked up at her brother. "What do you mean?" she said. He was looking into the woods behind them. "Justin, why did you ask me who I am?"

He looked down at her. His eyes showed more whites than normal. "That wasn't me. I didn't say anything. The voice came from the woods." He paused, shaking his head as if to clear it. "I mean, I think it must have come from the woods.

It felt like it was in my head."

Miranda jumped to her feet facing the grove of trees behind them. "Who's there? Come on, we're not playing around. Is that you, Mrs. Lóng? If it is, that's not funny!"

"*Who are you?*" This time the voice was faint. Justin was right, it sounded as if it was coming from the trees, but it *felt* like it was definitely in her head as well.

Justin took a step back, away from the woods. "I don't like this. It's like those lizard things."

Miranda shook her head and grabbed his hand, pulling him toward the grove. "No, this is different. Come on. Let's see what's in there."

Hand in hand, they picked their way through the thick cluster of bone-white trees, heading toward the place where the voice seemed to originate. After a couple of minutes, they emerged onto a strip of grass below a twelve-foot-high chain-link fence topped with loops of razor wire. About twenty feet beyond the first fence was a second one, its twin, creating an imposing barrier.

"What the … ?" Justin said, staring at the obstruction. "This looks like a prison."

Miranda walked toward a sign posted at eye level about ten feet away. In bold black capital letters it read:

DO NOT ENTER

TRESPASSERS WILL BE SHOT ON SIGHT

NO QUESTIONS ASKED

Justin let out a low whistle, "Whoever posted that means business."

"No joke. What do you think is back there?"

"Nothing that is of interest to you two," said a voice behind them. They jumped and whirled around. Billy stood there with his arms crossed. "Come on, you guys, let's get out of here before we get shot by accident."

"What is this place?" Miranda demanded.

"Is this part of Thunderbird Ranch?" asked Justin.

"And why would they shoot anyone?" Miranda added.

Billy held up his hands to stop the barrage of questions. "Let's go back to the pasture and I'll tell you all about it. Okay?"

They nodded and had started to follow Billy when they heard a galloping sound approaching them quickly from behind. Miranda turned to see a man on horseback emerge from the woods on the other side of the fences. He was wearing a light-colored cowboy hat and a faded red-and-black plaid shirt. He held the reins in one hand and a rifle in the other. "Oye!" he shouted and leveled the gun at them.

"Don't shoot!" Justin yelped and raised his arms straight into the air.

Miranda wanted to walk over and slap him on the back of the head, but she didn't want to make any sudden moves herself. "Justin," she stage-whispered, "put your hands down. You look like an idiot."

He shot her a glare and slowly lowered his hands.

The man on the horse moved closer to the inner fence. His thin mustache bent down into a frown and he lifted the muzzle away from them. "Billy, you know this area is off-limits to outsiders," he scolded. He spoke with a slight Latin American accent.

Billy's eyes narrowed. "The McAdelind boy just wandered off looking for a place to relieve himself," he said, indicating Justin. "His sister and I just came up to get him and continue mending the upper-pasture fence."

The man nodded but said nothing. His eyes never left the three of them as his anxious horse did a complete three-sixty.

Billy turned to Miranda and her brother and spread his

arms wide, collecting them and guiding them away.

Before they disappeared into the forest, the man on the horse called out, "It was nice to meet you, Miranda and Justin! I'm sure I'll be seeing you two around the ranch."

Miranda turned and the man on the horse tipped his hat to her. She gave a weak smile and followed Billy down the hill toward the pasture.

No one said a word until they arrived back at the ATV. Then Billy turned on them. "What were you doing wandering off like that?" he demanded. Shaking his head, he continued. "Listen carefully: there are things up here in the mountains that will make a meal out of you without a second thought. You two need to be smarter about wandering off without someone who knows this land."

"We heard a voice and went to see who it was," Miranda said.

"We heard talking," Justin added, shooting her a look that said, *Too much information.* "It was probably that guy on the horse."

Billy frowned. "That was Mr. DeSoto, head of security. You'll want to keep your distance from him."

"Head of security?" Miranda asked. "What kind of ranch needs a head of security?"

Billy paused for a moment, then looked up the hill. He took a step closer and whispered, "A ranch that has one of the largest gold mines in Colorado."

"No way," Justin said.

"It's true. You guys stumbled onto one of the most closely guarded secrets of the valley."

Miranda studied his face. Billy was holding something back, but she wasn't sure what. "Does the mine have a name?" she asked, trying to trip him up with details.

"We call it the Warren," he said, not missing a beat.

"Why the Warren?" Miranda pressed.

"You've obviously never been in a mine before." Billy said with a chuckle, causing Miranda's face to flush. "Listen, I've already said too much. We need to get back to work. When I scouted ahead, I found three areas to repair. Good news, we can finish this today. Bad news, we're going to have to hustle to get it done before dinner."

As they drove away along the fence, Miranda glanced back at the grove of white trees. Billy was hiding something. If he wouldn't tell them what, they were just going to have to find out on their own.

CHAPTER 9

JUSTIN
The Discovery of Fire

WHEN HE WALKED INTO the dining room that evening Justin was bone-tired. Miranda wouldn't be joining him tonight. She hadn't said much after hearing that weird voice in the woods and almost getting shot. As a matter of fact, she had seemed pretty distracted all afternoon, and when they got back to the house she told him she wasn't hungry and quickly disappeared upstairs.

How she could work all day and not eat dinner was beyond Justin. He was starving.

"Hello, dear. How was your day?" responded the now familiar voice of the quirky cook.

Justin jumped in surprise and turned to face Mrs. Lóng. "You really have to stop sneaking up on me. You're going to give me a heart attack," he said, grabbing his chest. "It was okay. The work sucked, I walked for a hundred miles, and I probably got way too much sun."

Mrs. Lóng scooped an enormous serving of lasagna on his plate. "What did you think of Billy?"

"He's a jerk." Justin said, shoveling a forkful of food into his mouth. "This is delicious by the way. Thank you."

Mrs. Lóng laughed. "Now let's not beat around the bush! Billy is ... complicated ... for sure. I've been watching him since he was a baby. He was the sweetest, most hardworking and respectful boy you could imagine." She shook her head sadly. "All that changed about a year ago."

Justin swallowed a large mouthful of lasagna. "What happened?"

Mrs. Lóng sighed. "I suppose what happens to most young men his age, they begin to see the world as it is, and not as they wish it to be."

Justin nodded, then shook his head. "I have no idea what that means."

Mrs. Lóng laughed. "Maybe not now, but some day you will."

After dinner, Justin helped Mrs. Lóng clear the table. While he was washing the dishes, she took some dinner up to Miranda's room. After only a couple of minutes, Mrs. Lóng came bounding back into the kitchen and announced she had a surprise for him. Justin pressed her for details, but no matter how nicely or how many times he asked, Mrs. Lóng would only smile in response.

When he had finished cleaning, she shooed him out of the kitchen through a back door and disappeared into the pantry. She emerged a second later carrying a closed picnic basket. "This way," she said, heading off toward a part of the ranch Justin hadn't seen yet.

They passed a large vegetable garden, then crossed a wooden bridge that led to a dirt path. The winding path continued to snake up a hill for about a mile. Eventually they came to a stop at a large meadow that overlooked the valley below. Justin could see the path continued into thick woods farther ahead, but his eyes were drawn to a number of objects near the center of the grassy oasis. Arranged around a large stone-lined fire pit were several enormous split-log benches. "Cool!" he exclaimed and ran over to the ring of blackened stones. Gray ash swirled in the center of the circle as wind whipped over the hilltop. Off to one side of the pit sat a stack of split wood.

"Have you ever started a campfire before?" Mrs. Lóng asked. Justin shook his head. She walked over to the pile, carefully picking out small pieces of wood, and scooped up a handful of twigs and dried grass. She knelt down next to the stone ring, depositing the contents next to her. She reached into her apron pocket and pulled out a box of wooden matches, motioning for Justin to come and join her.

Justin knelt down beside the stones. Mrs. Lóng handed him the matchbox and placed the dried grass in a pile in the center of the ring. She made a teepee of sticks over the grass, leaving an opening facing him.

"See how I did that?" she asked. Justin nodded. Next, she took the little cone of sticks apart, handing the sticks to Justin one by one. "Now you do it."

Justin carefully arranged the sticks in a similar pattern.

Mrs. Lóng smiled. "Good. Now light a match and hold it to the dry grass. When the grass starts to burn, lightly blow on it until the twigs catch fire."

On the third match, Justin ignited the dry grass and blew a slow, steady stream of breath until the glowing embers flared enough to ignite the kindling.

Mrs. Lóng walked back over to the pile and grabbed some larger pieces of wood and continued to build the little teepee. "Very good, Justin," she said with a strange gleam in her eyes. "You learn quickly. Fire seems to come naturally to you."

"Thanks for showing me how. I always wanted to learn, but camping doesn't really seem to be our family's thing."

Mrs. Lóng let out a loud laugh. "You don't know your

parents very well, do you?"

Even though he knew she couldn't really mean it, the comment hurt him a little. But looking around at his grandfather's ranch, he realized that it was true: there certainly were some things about his father, at least, that he really didn't know. "Do you think I'll be able to make campfires often?" he asked, trying to change the subject back to something less confusing.

Mrs. Lóng thought about this for a moment, pursed her lips, and then emphatically nodded her head. "I see no reason why not." She shot a hand out toward him with her index finger raised. "But you must practice caution and always respect fire." She gestured toward the hills and the trees around them. "Up here, fires could mean disaster for the ranch and the land. It is too dry to make any mistakes."

"Rule number one: you need to keep the fire small. Rule number two: always ensure that the fire is completely out before leaving it. And rule number three: if something happens and the fire spreads beyond the stones, come to the house and get help immediately. Understand?"

Justin nodded, "Yes, ma'am."

Mrs. Lóng smiled at Justin warmly, opened the picnic basket, and produced graham crackers, marshmallows, and chocolate bars. "Now. What do you say we have some dessert?"

CHAPTER 10

MIRANDA
The Valley

MIRANDA COULDN'T HELP BUT SMILE as she walked to the stables. Every Sunday they were allowed some time off from their endless round of chores, and earlier that morning, Billy had said he was going to show her "someplace special." After an exhausting three days on the ranch, Miranda was looking forward to a change of pace. She was secretly hoping that Billy would take her to Alamosa—a real, if small, city in the San Luis Valley, and not far away—to escape the confines of the ranch. Maybe to see a movie, or eat at a restaurant. Anything was better than one more second in the middle of nowhere.

But when she got to the stables, Billy was standing there holding the reins of two horses. She forced a smile, trying to hide her disappointment. "Oh, so, the 'someplace special' is around here."

He nodded "Is that okay?"

"No, it's great. I've been looking forward to doing

something besides chores." She cast a sideways glance at the horses. "But, is it possible to walk there? I'm not really great at riding, and I don't want to embarrass myself." Actually she was downright hopeless. Miranda held the honor of being the only kid she knew to get thrown off a pony-ride pony at a fair.

Billy shrugged. "Sure. No worries." He led the horses back to their stables, returning a few minutes later.

Soon they were walking at a leisurely pace over the river and up the hill behind the house and past the fire pit that Justin had mentioned before. He asked her if she wanted to have S'mores with him later, but when it came down to hanging out with her little brother or a cute older boy, cute older boy would win every time.

Billy led Miranda down the meandering dirt path deeper into the mountains. Eventually the path veered left, and Billy led them up a sloping hillside through a thick pine grove and up to a rocky ledge.

The view was amazing. Miranda could see everything: the valley with the farmhouses, the winding river, the stables, the fire pit, and the twisting trail to the pasture. But what really caught her attention was the seemingly endless prison-like fence enclosing the Warren, disappearing from view here and there around low hills only to reappear farther off. Tracing the outline of the fence with her eyes, Miranda recognized the aspen grove where she and Justin had heard the strange voice. She also noticed two guard towers framing a wide gate, which she had not been able to see from the aspen grove itself.

"Pretty impressive view from up here," Billy said. Then, noticing that her gaze was fixed on the gate, he added, "Don't even think about it. I told you, that place is off-limits."

Miranda watched a couple of men on horseback patrolling the perimeter, inside the fence. Movement in the tower caught her eye and she realized there was a guard up there too. "I didn't realize gold mines needed so much protection."

"It's a very large mine, and they don't want to take any chances," Billy said. "Come on, let's keep moving." He guided Miranda away from the ledge, and they continued on the path between two large boulders.

Before the fence disappeared out of sight behind them, Miranda turned and quickly studied the road leading to the gate. She felt confident that she could get there on her own.

Miranda caught up to Billy and followed him down a steep gravel-strewn slope, almost falling several times as she half ran, half slid down to the box canyon below. In the distance, Miranda heard the muffled roar of falling water.

When they got to the river at the bottom of the canyon, Billy expertly hopped from rock to rock over a shallow spot in the water, crossing with practiced ease. He pointed at the rocks Miranda should step on, and said, "Be careful on that third one, it's a little loose."

Miranda took a deep breath and began leaping from one slippery stone to the next. On the very rock Billy had indicated, her footing faltered and she fell forward into the icy-cold water. She was able to catch herself so that only her hands and feet got soaked, but it was enough not to only chill her to the bone but also embarrass her deeply.

Billy ran forward and helped her the rest of the way across. "You all right?"

"A little wet and really cold," she replied through chattering teeth. "Oh, and—*ouch*—I think I hurt my pride."

Billy smiled. "I've fallen in this river more times than I can count. Don't sweat it." He took a blanket out of his backpack and wrapped it around Miranda. "We're almost there."

They continued through the canyon, with the sound of roaring water growing ever louder. As they came around a tight corner, Miranda's eyes fell on one of the most amazing waterfalls she had ever seen. It must have been thirty feet tall and about half as wide. A rainbow arced through billowing clouds of mist above the mighty cascade plummeting down a steep stone wall.

"Wow!" Miranda exclaimed over the rush of water. "That's one of the most beautiful things I've ever seen."

"It is, isn't it? This is where my Dad would take Mom and me for picnics when I was little," Billy said, with a distant look in his eyes. "Before they split, that is." He gestured toward a rock with a flat top perched close to the waterfall, but not so close that it was wet. "We would eat over there, and talk about all sorts of things."

"What things?" Miranda asked.

He shrugged. "What it was like for the first people to find this spot. How cool it would be to have a house on the hill up there and see this all the time." He paused. "What it would be like to have enough money to own this land."

Miranda looked at the falls. She felt somehow ashamed. This wasn't her ranch, it belonged to her grandfather—that mysterious man she had spied on a couple of nights before, but still had yet to meet. He was out of the ranch house before she and Justin were even awake, and came home long after they had fallen exhausted into bed. She never even caught a glimpse of him during the day. It was almost like he was avoiding meeting his own grandchildren, and every time they asked about him, Mrs. Lóng made some excuse about how busy he was dealing with urgent matters. Until now, Miranda hadn't given it much thought, but her father's family was probably rich—especially if they really did own that gold mine. But her own family wasn't rich. Her parents were college professors. They had enough to live comfortably but no more. "How long have your parents been divorced?" she asked.

"They were never married, but they broke up about ten

years ago." Billy gazed into the waterfall. "Things were bad well before that. Sometimes I wonder if they ever really loved each other at all."

"Why do you say that?"

"Oh, just the more you find out about your family, the more things seem messed up." He looked down at the ground at his feet. "You know, when they stop being your parents and start being humans. When you find out stuff you wish you hadn't known about them. It's hard when your view of everything changes like that."

For a second, their eyes met. Billy seemed to want to say more but hesitated.

"Billy!"

Miranda's eyes shot to the source of the voice. Standing on the top of the canyon rim and glaring down at them stood Mr. O'Faron, his immaculate black hat pulled low on his brow, obscuring his eyes in shadow. "Playtime is over. I need you to take Miranda back to the main house. Then meet me at the stables."

Billy glared up at his father. "Yes, sir." He turned to Miranda. "I'm sorry. I was hoping to show you ..."

"It's okay," Miranda said. "Thank you for showing me *this*."

Billy looked back at his father. "We'd better go." He set off in silence, walking ahead of Miranda.

Just before they passed back through the two large boulders, Miranda stole a glance over her shoulder at Mr. O'Faron. He was standing stoically, arms crossed over his chest, watching them. A gleam of sunlight flashing on metal caught her eye: loops of razor wire atop a chain-link fence, glittering in the light of the setting sun.

Everywhere she went, it seemed, the Warren challenged her to find a way past that fence.

CHAPTER 11

MIRANDA

Diversions

MIRANDA FOUND HERSELF RUNNING *down a long corridor, frantically searching for someone. A thief! A cool breeze hit her face as she ran, yet it seemed impossible to force air into her lungs, and she felt she was going to either throw up or pass out. There was the sound of someone running in the distance, and she felt an overwhelming sense of despair as she heard herself say, "Leave my child alone." Yet somehow the voice was at the same time someone else's too.*

Miranda was running as fast as she could now. The smooth walls of the corridor became a blur as she raced past. She was drawing closer to her quarry; she could smell him. She turned a corner, followed the scent into a round room with two stairways, but he was not there. She hesitated for a moment, then out of the corner of her eye she saw a figure heading down a descending set of stairs. She launched herself after him. He smelled different now, but she felt sure she was on the right trail.

Miranda emerged at the bottom of the stairs into a dimly lit room. Boxes, crates, and barrels of every size were neatly stacked along the walls. With a strength she did not know she had, Miranda tossed the objects around as if they were made of Styrofoam.

But there was no one there. "No!" Miranda heard herself wail.

Panic took over and she felt her strength fail. A sob escaped her throat. "Don't take my baby!"

Ring, ring, ring! The bell was both muffled in the distance and also right near her. Hearing it as if she was in two places at once. Ring, ring, ring! Miranda cocked her head to one side, staring past the smashed barrels and boxes at a stone wall weeping with moisture.

Ring, ring, ring!

Miranda kicked off her covers and ran to the window. The trees on the brow of the hill behind the house were silhouetted by a flickering orange glow that lit up the sky and was reflected off the low clouds above. She heard distant voices shouting "Fire!" and saw people scrambling to cross the bridge over the river.

Miranda turned to look at the clock: 11:45 p.m. She had only been asleep for a couple of hours. Billy had escorted her back to the ranch, where they had arrived just after dinner, and then he had headed off to meet his father. They had seen Justin at the fire pit on the way back, but he was so engrossed with his fire, he hadn't even noticed them walking past. Mrs. Lóng was nowhere to be found, so Miranda had improvised dinner from some leftovers she found in the refrigerator and gone to her bedroom to read.

Miranda turned to the pile of dirty clothes she had dropped before crawling into bed, intending to put them back on, only to find that her shirt was missing. That's weird, she thought. But she didn't want to waste time looking for it. With all the ranch personnel distracted by the fire, she finally had a chance to snoop around the Warren, so she pulled another top from the dresser drawer and put it on. It was now or never.

But what if there were still a guard or two at the gates? She would need someone to cause a distraction while she found a way to slip inside. Billy was out. He knew more than he was letting on. There was only one person she could trust, or at least only one person she could convince to help her. She took a deep breath and ran down the hall to Justin's room.

She knocked once, then ran inside. Justin was still asleep, one arm hanging awkwardly over the side of the bed. She shook him hard.

Justin groaned and looked at her through half-open eyes. "What's ... going on?"

"I swear you could sleep through the end of the world." She threw back his covers. "You need to get up now. There's a fire on the hill."

Justin bolted out of bed and ran over to the window. "Oh no!" he whispered. He sprinted to the closet and quickly put on his clothes. As he hopped on one foot to pull on a sneaker, he moaned, "That's where the fire pit is."

"Did you forget to put the fire out?" Miranda asked.

"Of course I put it out." He paused while he pulled on his other sneaker. "I'm positive I did."

"That's good enough for me." Miranda grabbed his arm and pulled him toward the door. "Come on, now's our chance to see what's really going on in the Warren while everyone's distracted."

"But we should help them," Justin protested as they sprinted down the stairs, taking them three at a time.

Miranda shook her head. "There's, like, twenty people out there who know what they're doing. The last thing they need is two kids in their way."

"But—"

Miranda stopped and grabbed her brother by the shoulders. "Justin. Please. I know something strange is going on. I think it has to do with the weird voices and lizard guys, and I don't buy for one minute that all that security is for a gold mine. I want ... scratch that ... I *need* to know what's happening here." She punched him lightly on the shoulder. "So, are you with me?" He nodded. She smiled and pulled him out the door. "Let's go," she whispered, guiding him in the direction of the woods by the river. When they reached the trees, she pulled him down into a crouch.

"I don't feel right about this. What if they catch us?"

She glanced up at the glowing hillside. "They'll be busy with the fire for hours. This is our only chance—"

A twig snapped nearby and they froze.

Mrs. Lóng was running through the woods toward the stream, skillfully ducking and jumping through the thicket. Her normal red dress and white apron had been replaced with a red shirt and white pants. It wasn't until the last gleam of firelight reflecting off her pearl necklace had vanished in the distance that they dared to breathe.

"Where in the heck do you suppose she's going?" Justin asked.

"It doesn't matter, she's weird. Okay. Stay low, and try not to make any noise." She looked around one more time to make sure the coast was clear, then took off through the trees as fast as she could.

They had only been running for a little while when there was a flash of lightning followed almost instantly by a deafening clap of thunder, so loud it stopped them both in their tracks. Another flash—another *boom!* Miranda's ears were ringing. They both hit the ground hard.

Miranda looked back in the direction of the thunderclaps.

The storm seemed to be centered directly over the hill where the fire was blazing. Thick, dark clouds gathered above and rain started to fall in a torrential downpour. They were drenched to the skin in seconds.

"Come on!" Miranda shouted over the storm. "We need to keep moving!" She helped Justin to his feet, and they both kept running. After tripping over countless downed trees and shrubs, running for what seemed like miles, they finally slowed to a stop. Completely winded and shaking from the exertion, Miranda leaned against a tree to catch her breath. She looked back at her brother, who was bracing himself against his knees, rainwater dripping from his hair. They were now at the edge of the forest. Ahead of them stood the double fence that enclosed the Warren.

Miranda took a couple of steps forward and looked to her left. No more than fifty feet away was the gate flanked by guard towers that she had seen from the hill above. She waited there a moment, checking for any sign of guards. The towers looked empty; the dead-man zone between the two fences and the open area beyond appeared likewise void of any sign of life.

Justin came up beside her. "What … now?" he said between labored breaths.

"It looks clear … I say we run … for the gate … and see if it's open."

He nodded, and they sprinted onward.

Justin let out a low whistle. "Who are they … trying to … keep out of here?"

"Or … are they trying to keep something … in?" Miranda wondered aloud, walking tentatively up to the gate. It was closed.

She took a deep breath and pushed against it. The gate swung wide open.

Justin laughed. "Well, that was easy."

"Yeah, a little too easy. The gate should have been locked." Miranda whispered. Had the guards been in such a hurry to get to the fire they forgot to lock the gate? If that was the case, no wonder stuff was missing.

"So. Where to now, sis?" Justin asked.

Miranda looked quickly around. Besides the fence, the gate, and the road, there was nothing to see but thick woods crawling up a steady incline. "Let's keep to the road, we'll move faster," she said and started to jog along the worn path.

After a quarter of an hour, they heard the rapid clomping of a horse's hooves accompanied by frantic voices.

Miranda dove into the woods, pulling her brother along with her. They crouched low, waiting for the rider to pass. The horse slowed to a stop not far from where they were hiding. Static crackled from a walkie-talkie. "Cisco, do you copy? We need all hands at the fire immediately," the voice on the radio shouted. Miranda recognized it as their grandfather's.

"Copy that. I just finished securing the Warren. I'm on my way now!" shouted the rider and kicked his horse back into a gallop toward the gate.

Miranda watched the horse and rider until they disappeared out of sight. "Come on," she said, once again pulling her brother along behind her. They continued up the path, with lightning intermittently illuminating the way.

The trail seemed to lead to a dead end as they found themselves facing a steep rock wall. "There must have been a turn we missed. Let's go—" Miranda began. Then a flash of lightning illuminated the mouth of what appeared to be an enormous cavern only a few yards away.

"Whoa," Miranda said. Slowly she walked into the cave with Justin following, gripping her arm hard. It was pitch-black inside. Miranda was cursing herself for not bringing a flashlight when another lightning strike showed just enough of the space for Miranda to see it was not very deep at all, and ended in a huge steel barn-style door at the back.

"This way," she said, stretching one hand out in front of her and dragging Justin along through the dark with the other. Miranda's fingers finally made contact with the large door, and she ran her hand over the cold metal searching for a handle. Her fingers closed around a steel bar, and with a hard tug, the door slid open just wide enough for them to squeeze through.

Dim light spilled through the small opening, exposing a wide stone-walled passage. Miranda tiptoed over to the left wall with Justin following close behind. Hidden sources of dim light in the ceiling pierced the gloom here and there. She kept one shoulder against the cold stone as they moved slowly forward through the passage, all her senses alert. Her fingers grazed small cracks and crevices in the walls; she felt the gradual slope downward of the floor; she heard water dripping in other passageways she could not see; she smelled the chalky scent of stone mingled with some strange musky odor; and, more than anything else, she felt the presence of something else, something alive—something *animal*.

They came to an intersection. Instinctively, Miranda took the passage to the right. The musky smell was stronger now. She released Justin's arm and picked up her pace, starting to jog down a long corridor, with a couple of huge steel doors on both sides.

"Sis ..." Justin whispered.

Miranda kept moving. She could sense that whatever she was seeking, it lay just ahead, and nothing was going to stop her now.

"Miranda," Justin whined. "I've got a bad feeling about this."

Miranda ignored him and broke into a run. Speeding along the corridor, she came to a crossing where, again out of pure instinct, she turned left, sensing that her destination was within reach.

They passed another intersecting corridor, and a change in the air alerted Miranda to the presence of an immense chamber just ahead of them, and she skidded to a stop. Justin slammed into her back. "What the … ?" he gasped.

Shadowy things were moving fast past the entrance to the chamber. Miranda took a step forward, but Justin held her back. His viselike grip on her shoulder began to shake and he made a strange choking noise, barely above a whisper. Miranda looked back over her shoulder to see what was wrong. Justin was staring wide-eyed at something in the corridor behind them.

Miranda could just barely make out the shape of a huge reptilian head. Its eyes glowed slightly, reflecting what little light was available in the dim passageway.

"*Ummm … Hello,*" it said in a deep, smoky voice.

Miranda realized with a start that the creature had not uttered the words out loud. She had heard them in her head. Just like the voice in the aspen grove.

The beast quickly looked back over one shoulder, as if trying to see if they were actually looking at something more interesting behind it. Satisfied, it seemed, that it was indeed the object of their scrutiny, the creature turned back to face them and took a step closer, out of shadow and into a patch of light.

Two parallel rows of sharp spikes began at each eyebrow and extended backward, growing longer as they reached the back of the beast's dark-red scaly head. Huge bat-like wings flexed and extended gently on either side of its massive torso as it stalked toward them on four clawed feet.

The creature cocked its head to one side, studying them, then said, "*Can I help you?*"

CHAPTER 12

JUSTIN

Here Be Dragons

JUSTIN WAS STARTLED BY a high-pitched scream. His ears rang from the sound reverberating off the walls of the stone tunnel. He wished desperately for it to stop, and looked around for the source of the shrieking. Then, to his surprise, he realized that the sound was emanating from his own open mouth.

He slammed his mouth shut and tried to speak, but his voice didn't seem to work. He tried to move, but his muscles would not respond to his desperate command to run. He was scared of a lot of things, but he had never experienced such terror before. Then again, he had never been prey before either.

The red dragon was lying on the ground, its huge front paws pressed hard around where its ears might be, its eyes closed tight with a pained expression on its face. It opened one eye tentatively and fixed it on Justin. *"What is wrong with you, kid?"* The dragon shook its head and struck it with one paw several times, as if trying to clear water out of its ears. *"It's bad enough you screeched like that in such a small space, but really, yelling in my head too—you can't block that sort of thing."* Then it paused and cocked its head again. *"Wait a minute. How are you doing that?"*

Justin felt himself being tugged backward. He forced himself to turn away from the dragon to see who was pulling him. Miranda gripped his arm, her eyes wide with fear, her mouth twisted grimly. She was moving her lips, but no words came out. Justin tried to read her lips, at first with no success, but finally he made out one word: *Run!*

This was enough to start his legs going, pumping them as fast as he could. He held onto his sister fiercely as they ran down the passageway. Justin heard the heavy footfalls of the dragon pursuing them, its claws scraping on the stone floor. *"Wait! You don't want to go in there."*

They burst out of the passageway into a chamber so massive, Justin felt overwhelmed by sudden vertigo as he struggled to get his bearings. More dragons, three black ones this time, soared above in the shadowy heights, their massive beating wings sounding like a symphony of bass drums. One swooped down, sending Justin and Miranda plunging to the cave floor.

"Strangers!" a new voice said, this one higher-pitched than that of the first dragon they had encountered, making it sound almost female.

"Perhaps the thieves have returned?" said another.

"Let's catch them and find out," added a third.

"I prefer to eat first, ask questions later," replied the first.

"Run!" shouted Miranda, finally finding her voice. She took off at a full sprint, hugging the wall of the cavern.

Justin followed as fast as his legs could carry him. Somehow Justin sensed rather than saw another dragon swoop low behind him, its front claws outstretched. At the last second, Justin dropped to the floor, tasting blood as his chin banged on stone. Looking up, he saw the four sets of gleaming outstretched claws and an armored belly of an enormous black dragon swoop past only inches above his prone body.

"You are losing your touch, Shadow," chided one of the dragons circling above. *"Now watch a true champion catch its prey."*

Justin was on his feet again. He could sense that this new dragon who claimed to be a champion was going to try to cut them off, could see the intent forming in its mind. Ahead, he saw light spilling through a broad opening in the cavern wall.

"Head to the right!" he shouted to Miranda, diving through the aperture just as a huge black dragon landed not ten feet ahead of them. Justin misjudged his leap, and his shoulder struck the edge of the opening in the rock wall. He spun out of control and fell sprawling on the ground again, but sprang to his feet and fled into the passageway ahead.

"You guys are good. I'll give you that," growled the black dragon as he pursued them into the stone passage.

Miranda was ahead of Justin now, and he struggled to catch up to her. He could feel the enormous beast closing in on them from behind as its hot breath hit his neck.

Miranda cut to the right, heading into an intersecting passage, with Justin right behind.

The black dragon was moving too fast to follow; its momentum sent it skidding past the entrance to the corridor. Justin watched over his shoulder as it slid out of control and into a roll, letting out a deafening roar of frustration.

The passage they were now running through was lined with steel doors similar to the ones they had passed earlier. Miranda stopped at one and tugged hard on the handle. When it didn't budge, she ran to the opposite wall and tried another. This one was locked too. Justin could sense that the black dragon behind them had regained its footing but had not regained sight of them. The third door Miranda tried slid open, and she disappeared inside. Justin followed her into the darkness, and silently slid the door shut behind them.

Justin and his sister leaned their backs against the cold steel door, trying hard to catch their breath. Without the sparse light from the corridor, they were blind in the utter blackness of whatever space they were now in.

They waited there until they felt the dragon move past them down the corridor. Justin could sense its frustration and disappointment as it continued down the long passage until he could sense its presence no more.

"What now ... Miss ... I-Need-to-See-What's-in-the-Warren?" Justin asked through gasping breaths.

"We wait for ... a couple of seconds. Then we ... run for it," Miranda replied, equally winded. After a minute or two, when she had a chance to relax a little, she added, "You did see what I saw, right? There are actually dragons here."

"Yep. I saw them," Justin replied. Then, thinking about the voices in his head, he added, "And I, *heard*, them too. Right in the middle of my head."

"Yeah, me too."

They heard something moving across the room, a bulky mass shifting and air being forcefully exhaled from enormous lungs. They froze.

"*Who dares enter my lair?*" said a strong, female voice—a voice Justin recognized.

The dragon moved closer. The sound of scales scraping on stone was now only a few feet away. Justin felt the heat from her body, smelled her distinctive musky odor. Her breath stirred the hairs on his arms.

Miranda slid the door back open. Now that their eyes were adjusted to the darkness, the dim light from the corridor was enough to reveal the large chamber hewn from the living rock. Were they in a prison for dragons, Justin thought—or a stable? The dragon recoiled from the feeble light. She was grayish-blue and smaller than both the red dragon they had first encountered and the terrifying black dragon that had chased them, but still larger than a Clydesdale. She blinked several times, adjusting to the light, and her huge reptilian eyes met Miranda's.

"*You!*" the dragon exclaimed. "*Who are you?*"

With those words, Justin was able to place the voice as the one they had heard in the grove. But Miranda was already out the door and pulling Justin behind her.

They continued running through the corridor. Now the doors on either side were sliding open on their own. Huge dragon heads peeked out through the doorways. Most were bluish grey, but one was mottled green and another dull yellowish brown.

The dragons yelled after them, "*Thieves!*" "*Intruders!*" "*Stop them!*" and lunged at Justin and Miranda as they passed, snapping their knifelike teeth, trying to catch them in their great jaws.

Justin and Miranda turned down a wide corridor to their left, which Justin recognized as the first tunnel they had entered after gaining access to the secret complex. He couldn't help but let out a small, hopeful laugh. He kicked it into high gear, sprinting as fast as he could, closing the distance to the exit.

Justin made it to the massive steel door, still slightly open just as they had left it, and squeezed through the gap with Miranda following close behind. They tumbled into a tangled heap on the other side. Justin stood up quickly and strained to close the portal. He stole a glance back into the cave as he did, where he saw several dragons racing in their direction. Justin threw all his weight into the effort, sweating and grunting as he slammed the door shut with a resounding clang.

"Come on!" he yelled, grabbing his sister and pulling her to her feet.

They ran out into the open air beyond the cavern's entrance. The ground was still slick from the rain, but the downpour had stopped. Justin greedily gulped in the fresh, cool air. He looked back over his shoulder to confirm that the dragons had not somehow followed them, but there was no sign of pursuit. Justin bent over, resting his hands on his knees, trying to steady himself.

Then he started to laugh. To his surprise, Miranda joined him. Soon they were doubled over in laughter. Justin wasn't exactly sure what they found so funny. Rarely did he and Miranda find the same thing amusing, but he soon realized they weren't laughing at anything in particular, but sharing instead a deep, primal laugh, a laugh that is only brought on by the sheer, unadulterated, joy at finding oneself alive.

The world went white. Bright lights assaulted him from all angles. Justin's eyes stung and he saw spots through his tightly closed lids. He heard sounds of men yelling and clicks of guns being cocked. He reached out for Miranda but couldn't find her. He spun in a circle, his eyes shut, trying to find a direction where the lights weren't blinding him.

"Kill the high beams!" shouted a man in a husky, angry voice.

Then the world went suddenly dark. Justin stood, trying to make out the details of the dozen or so objects around him, but still only saw flashing spots where the lights had been seconds before. When he could finally see again, he realized that he and Miranda were surrounded by people, and three of them were quickly approaching. The man in the center was their very angry grandfather, the one to his right was Mr. O'Faron, and to his left, Mr. DeSoto.

All three looked like they had plunged down a filthy chimney. Dirt and soot covered every inch of their bodies, their clothes were ripped and even burned in places, and they were soaked from head to toe.

Their grandfather walked to within a foot of them, glaring down with his hard, deep-blue eyes. His large gray mustache twitched, as if he were going to say something, then reconsidered. Finally he thrust out his arm, pointing back down the long path toward the ranch. "House! Now!"

CHAPTER 13

JUSTIN
Truth and Consequences

THEIR GRANDFATHER PACED back and forth in front of the study's cold, empty hearth. His heavily muscled arms were crossed over his barrel chest. Every once in a while he would let out a grunt or a sigh, apparently trying to work out what to say to his two grandchildren. Standing in silence on either side of him were Mr. O'Faron, Billy, Mr. DeSoto, Mrs. Lóng, and a young woman Miranda and Justin had not met yet. She was maybe in her mid-twenties, with long reddish-brown hair.

Justin glanced over at an old wooden clock on the wall: two in the morning. The adrenalin from their race through "dragon mountain" had worn off about an hour before, and now he was fighting to keep his eyes open.

Justin continued to watch their grandfather closely. This was really the first time he had seen him up close and in the light. Justin was hoping to glean any information about the man who was, for better or worse, in control of their immediate future. He was a large man, almost as tall as their father, but a good bit broader. His tan skin was weathered, resembling aged leather, which had the effect of making his white hair look even whiter. But what really caught Justin's attention were three wide, equally spaced scars that started on his left brow and cut deep furrows all the way down past the collar of his soiled shirt.

What circumstances had led to those scars? Up until tonight, Justin would have thought an accident with one of the farm machines was the cause. But after seeing the dragons, he suspected something more ominous had occurred.

Their grandfather stopped pacing and faced them. He shifted his eyes from Justin to his sister and back again. "What am I going to do with you two?" he said, then resumed his pacing. This time he kept his piercing blue eyes locked on them, like a predator viewing its prey.

"I think you should tell us what's really going on here," Justin said.

Anger flashed across their grandfather's face and he ran over to Justin, placing a hand on each armrest of the chair, their faces inches apart, with noses almost touching. "Did I give you permission to speak?"

"N-no, sir," Justin stammered.

His grandfather pulled back, glaring at him for a long moment. "We just had an acre of woods go up in flames. Care to explain to me why you set that fire, boy?" he said, his eyes still locked on Justin.

But Justin said nothing.

Their grandfather's face started to redden. "Nothing to say for yourself."

"You didn't give him permission to speak," Miranda spat.

Their grandfather snapped his fingers and pointed at her in warning, then turned back to Justin. "Speak up, boy."

"I didn't set anything *on* fire. I had a camp fire going and I—"

"You were up there earlier tonight with a fire, correct?" he replied, arms spread in a question.

"Yes, but—"

He held up his hand silencing him, and turned to Billy. "You told me when you walked past there at dusk, he was already gone. Did you see any smoke?"

Billy looked at Justin, his face hard as a stone. "No, sir. But he must have left it smoldering. I didn't see anyone else up there tonight besides Justin."

Miranda jumped to her feet. "Now wait one minute. You don't know it was still smoldering. For all we know, lightning from the storm caused the fire." Then she glared at Billy. "Besides, what were you doing up there anyhow? When we walked back to the ranch Justin was still at the fire pit."

"I realized I … dropped something … on our walk … and went back to get it." Billy stammered.

Their grandfather stepped between Billy and Miranda, grabbing back their attention. "The storm didn't happen until the blaze was well established. But that is beside the point—"

"The fire was out when I left," Justin insisted.

His grandfather's expression remained hard. "You were the only person lighting fires up there, Justin. It was centered on the pit you used tonight. A fact is a fact. There was a forest fire that could have cost people their lives. You need to accept responsibility for your actions."

Justin sat tight-lipped, refusing to meet his grandfather's gaze. He could feel a burning in his throat, and he was trying hard to fight back tears of frustration.

His grandfather shook his head sternly. "I'm sorry Justin, but—"

"I will accept responsibility for the fire," Mrs. Lóng said, stepping forward. She met Justin's eyes, smiling softly at him before turning to face his grandfather.

Everyone's attention was on the old cook. Their grandfather gave her a perplexed look. "What do you mean, *you* accept responsibility?"

"I was the one who showed Justin how to start the fire in the first place, and I was the one who told him he could use the fire pit when his chores were done. I should have supervised him until I knew he was ready for that level of responsibility." She paused and looked around, daring anyone to challenge her. "I am the one ultimately responsible."

The room was dead silent. Justin looked from face to face, and stopped when he came to Billy's hard expression.

"Ying, I appreciate your intent here, but the boy needs to understand that there are consequences for his actions."

"I think he understands that just fine," Mrs. Lóng said, her voice soothing, and walked over to stand next to Justin. "I suggest both of us share in this equally."

Their grandfather studied the old cook for a moment before letting out a sigh. "As you wish." He turned to Justin. "You and Mrs. Lóng are banned from starting any fires on this property. In addition, you will spend every evening after your chores are completed, cleaning up the downed trees and other debris." His face became hard again. "Is that clear?"

Justin looked up at Mrs. Lóng, who nodded to him encouragingly. "Yes, sir, perfectly clear," he said.

Their grandfather held his gaze for a moment, then turned to address the other people in the room. "Okay, people, we had an incredible stroke of good luck. That rainstorm saved the ranch," he said, looking from face to face, "You all did exceptional work tonight. I'll see you all tomorrow morning. Dismissed."

Everyone started silently filing out of the room.

Mrs. Lóng squeezed Justin's shoulder, and he looked up at her. "Thank you, Mrs. Lóng," Justin said. She was still dressed in the same red shirt and white pants she had been wearing earlier. But unlike everyone else in the room, there wasn't a sign of ash, mud, or water on her anywhere. Had she actually changed into an identical outfit? "By the way, I saw you running through the woods tonight. Where were you going?"

"I was heading toward the river, dear. You need a lot of water to make a thunderstorm." She winked at him, then took a step back and started walking toward the arched doorway that led to the front hall.

Justin started to follow her but stopped when he heard a shrill whistle.

Standing in the middle of the room was Miranda, her arms crossed, an angry look on her face. "You're joking, right?" She looked around at everyone, her eyes coming to rest on their grandfather. "Nobody is going anywhere until someone explains what the heck is going on in the Warren."

"I'm sure by now a smart girl like you has already figured out it's a gold mine," their grandfather responded, deadpan.

Miranda rolled her eyes. "Right, and the gold just happens to be protected by a bunch of dragons?"

Justin could see this had the effect his sister intended, as everyone in the room looked suddenly at their grandfather to see his reaction. But he kept his eyes focused on Miranda, not moving a muscle, with no change in expression, no eyebrow raised, no twitching of his mustache, nothing.

"That's a fine imagination you have there, missy." He looked behind him at the rest of the ranch hands and staff, his gaze finally narrowing in on Billy. "Did someone tell you that fanciful story?"

"No, Justin and I saw them with our own eyes."

"Saw what? Dragons? I think maybe you saw some funny shapes in the smoke from the forest fire tonight. That's what I think."

"There wasn't much smoke inside the mountain."

Their grandfather noticeably stiffened. His eyes locked on her. "What do you mean, *inside* the mountain?"

Justin stepped forward. "Miranda and I went in through that big steel door at the cave, and—"

Their grandfather swung around to face Mr. DeSoto. "Cisco, I clearly remember you telling me everything was secure."

Mr. DeSoto nodded. "I made sure the main portal and the gate were sealed before I joined you to fight the fire. The gate was unlocked when I got to it, and I read Johnson the riot act for leaving it like that. I can assure you the perimeter gate was secure when I left the Warren though. The kids must have slipped in during the time it was unlocked." He looked at Justin and Miranda, pulled a walkie-talkie from his belt, and left the room. A moment later he walked back in and nodded. "The main portal is still locked down tight, but I have the men doing a sweep and inventory now, just in case."

"The door was unlocked when we got there," Justin said.

Their grandfather's anger seemed to lose some of its edge. "Did you see anyone else?" He knelt down on one knee in front of them, his joints cracking with the effort. "This is important. Was anyone else in the mountain tonight?"

Miranda shook her head. "No, we didn't see anyone." Justin could tell from the look on his grandfather's face he was hoping for something more. "But, we did *hear* something," she added.

"What exactly did you hear?" Mr. DeSoto asked expectantly.

"We heard a lot of crashing, like someone smashing wood," Miranda said, then quickly turned toward Justin and gave him her best *I'll explain later* look.

But they hadn't heard anything, especially not something being smashed. What was she talking about? Justin wondered. Movement caught his attention and he glanced back over at Billy, who was pale and staring intently at Miranda. He looked completely disheveled, but not like the others. There wasn't a speck of ash on him, but his shirt and pants were torn in several spots, and his boots were covered in thick grayish mud.

"Cisco, see what you can find out," their grandfather said.

The head of security stepped out into the hall again. When he returned a minute later, he had a grim look on his face. "Several of the crates in the eastern storage room were smashed to bits. It looks like one of the wilds may have gotten in there. I told Johnson and Garcia to skip the other areas and do an inventory of the hatcheries." He paused before delivering the next bit of news. "It's not good, Mac. In addition to the missing wyrmling from the first break-in, we now have five eggs unaccounted for: three domestic blacks, a domestic blue, and a wild blue."

Justin watched his grandfather closely. His eyes narrowed as he frowned at Mr. O'Faron, whose face was so red, it looked like his head was going to explode.

Their grandfather stood with a grunt and some effort, then walked back over to the hearth. With a yell of frustration, he slammed his fist into the wooden mantelpiece, making everyone in the room jump. When he turned back around, Justin saw that his face was twisted with anger. "I want to know who is doing this, how they're getting through our security, and I want to know now!" he yelled, causing the occupants of the room to jump again. "There is too much at stake. Someone is making me look like a fool," he concluded, striking the mantel again for emphasis.

The radio in Mr. DeSoto's hand crackled. "Cisco? You there? Over."

"Yes. Over," Mr. DeSoto replied.

"We just did a comprehensive sweep of all critical areas.

Your office door was forced open."

"What— How— Is anything missing?" Mr. DeSoto sputtered.

"It doesn't appear so. Your door was forced and some cabinets were open. Over."

Justin noticed a confused look on Mr. DeSoto's face. His eyes darted rapidly back and forth, as if he was trying to work through a complex math problem in his mind. Then his face hardened, and he glanced from Mr. O'Faron to Billy. "Mac. If it's okay, I'm going to see if anything's missing."

Their grandfather shook his head. "In a moment. If something's gone, it's too late now. I need you here until we find out what the kids know."

"But—" Mr. DeSoto began to protest, then fell silent as their grandfather shot him a look.

"Sit down, kids," their grandfather said, his voice calmer now, even though his face was still red and wore a grim expression. He motioned for them to take the seats they both occupied moments before.

He pulled over an ottoman, letting out a grunt as he collapsed down onto it. His bushy gray eyebrows hung over heavy lids. Clasping his hands together as if preparing to say a prayer, he brought his fingertips up to his lips. "Now, tell me what you saw," he said through his clasped hands, "and don't leave out any details."

As Justin considered where to start, he looked around for Mrs. Lóng for some encouragement, but she wasn't there. Where in the world would she have gone at a time like this? But before he had a chance to speak, Miranda took control. She explained how they had entered through the unlocked gate and door into the Warren, how they ran into the red dragon, and how the black one had pursued them through the corridor. When she got to the part where they were in the room with the smaller blue dragon, Justin noticed his grandfather look at Miranda, his eyebrows knitting together, as if he were working out something important.

Neither Justin nor his sister mentioned anything about hearing the dragons speak. Something deep in his gut told him to keep his mouth shut about that little fact. Plus, since Miranda hadn't said anything, he figured she must have a very good reason not to.

Miranda turned and looked at their grandfather. "Now it's your turn," she said, locking eyes with him. "Oh—and don't leave out any details."

CHAPTER 14

MIRANDA
Taking The Oath

MIRANDA WAS ALMOST POSITIVE that she saw a smile flash across her grandfather's face, but it happened so quickly, she began to doubt her own eyes. Here she was, staring at this man she barely knew, her father's father—but a stranger. He was broad and strong, like a warrior from an ancient tale, with the scars on his face as testaments to past battles. There was also a power there, a presence very few people had, and as she looked at his imposing figure, the righteous indignation she had felt began to disappear.

Their grandfather stood up tall. "Frankly, I'm both surprised and disappointed that your parents haven't told you anything about our family."

"Honestly, we are too," Miranda said, turning to look at her brother. She could tell by the way Justin was gazing off into the distance that he felt the same way. He was thinking about Mom and Dad, who were so far away now—in so many ways. Miranda was angry with her parents for all that they had concealed from their own children. But the thing that most upset her when she let herself think about it was that they kept leaving her behind.

"We didn't even know we *had* a grandfather until a couple of days ago, let alone that he lived with a bunch of dragons," Justin added. "As a matter of fact, we don't even know what to call you."

Their grandfather gave a single nod in acknowledgment. "I have to get used to this too, you know. Why don't you just call me Grandpa. That's what your dad called my father when he was little, but if that doesn't work for you, 'sir' is also perfectly acceptable."

Miranda and Justin exchanged a look. "If it's okay with you, sir, I mean, Grandpa," Justin said, "I think we'll both go with 'Grandpa.'"

Miranda nodded in assent. She noticed the slightest smile at the corner of her grandfather's mouth before he looked around the room once, took a deep breath, and plunged in. "What I am about to tell you is not to be repeated outside of this ranch, or more specifically, to anyone who is not a part of our world."

Miranda and Justin nodded in unison.

"Unfortunately, I'll need more than a nod. You two must take a solemn oath to keep this secret." He leaned forward, his face inches away from Justin's. "Do you, Justin McAdelind, solemnly swear to protect the secrets of the dragons, of this ranch, and of our family? Do you swear to protect this with your very life if necessary? Do you swear to protect dragons from the desires and exploits of anyone who might bring harm upon them? If so, then say, *I do.*"

Justin gulped. "I do."

Their grandfather nodded, then turned to Miranda. "Do you, Miranda McAdelind—" His voice broke for a moment, and his eyes looked glossy. "... Solemnly swear to protect the secrets of the dragons, of this ranch, and of our family? Do you swear to protect this with your very life ..." He trailed off, then cleared his throat. "If necessary? Do you swear to protect dragons from the desires and exploits of anyone who might bring harm upon them? If so, then say, *I do*."

"I do," Miranda whispered.

Their grandfather nodded to her. "Well, you've seen the dragons already," he said, shaking his head in disbelief. "How you two greenhorns managed to get in and out of there without getting yourselves killed is beyond me. Dragons are very territorial and are apex predators. If they don't know you, they will attack without hesitation. Not many creatures, or even trained humans for that matter, can evade them when they're zeroed in on their prey. The security measures you *evaded* we put in place as much to protect people from stumbling into their domain as it is to protect the dragons themselves."

"Protect the dragons?" Justin asked. "From what I've seen, they don't need much protection."

The corner of their grandfather's mouth twitched slightly. "They may seem indestructible at first glance, but they do have their weaknesses. Since ancient times, dragons have been hunted and slaughtered for one reason or another. Mostly they were killed out of fear and superstition, or to protect herd animals, but occasionally they were killed for arcane reasons."

Miranda raised an eyebrow, "'Arcane reasons'?"

He nodded. "Dragons are ... *special* creatures, and in the hands of the right people, knowledge of them can be used to heal any wound, destroy hated enemies, or even prolong one's life."

"That's pretty cool. It's like the Holy Grail and the Ark of the Covenant all rolled into one," Justin said.

Their grandfather ignored the comment and continued.

"It is our family's responsibility to protect the dragons from the greed and ambitions of humanity." He looked back at the others still gathered around the room. "All of us have sworn an oath to protect them and knowledge of their existence, at any cost."

"Are these the only dragons in the world?" Miranda asked, pointing in the direction of the Warren.

"No, child. Not even close. We are only one of the nineteen families that raise and care for dragons around the world."

Nineteen, Miranda thought. When had she heard that before?

Grandpa gestured behind him with a thumb. "Everyone in this room is descended from one of those families. Mr. DeSoto is from a South American family. Miss Ddraig is from a family in Wales, and Mr. O'Faron is ..." He paused for a moment, frowning at the man in black. "Well, Mr. O'Faron's family has worked side by side with the McAdelinds for generations.

Miranda looked instinctively to Billy. He was glaring at her grandfather, his eyes narrowed into angry slits. Then, sensing her gaze, he snapped around to meet her eyes. His expression quickly melted to one of blank indifference. He bowed his head slightly to her, then turned and exited the room. Grandpa barely glanced in the boy's direction as he left.

"We raise dragons? You mean, like, *breed* them?" Justin's comment brought Miranda's attention back to the conversation.

Their grandfather nodded.

"Why?" Miranda asked, but when her grandfather's eyebrows rose questioningly in response, she added, "I mean, if we're trying to keep them a secret, why breed them?"

"To keep the lines going. To preserve the species."

"Like a dragon zoo?" Justin asked.

"Not so much like a zoo as a reserve. But you're essentially correct."

The woman they hadn't met yet, Miss Ddraig, stepped forward and cleared her throat. "Aye, on the ranch we have a small number of wild dragons. There's even some in the surroundin' mountains. We keep 'em both under control an' out of sight." She had a strong accent that sounded a bit similar to English or Scottish, but was definitely unique, with *r*'s rolling off her tongue almost musically.

"Miss Ddraig is our dragon trainer," their grandfather said. The name was strange, beginning with a thick *th*- sound Miranda had never heard before. She looked at the young woman skeptically. She looked barely old enough to drive, let alone train dragons.

"Whoa, wait a minute. Those are *trained* dragons?" Justin said, pointing in the direction of the Warren.

The young woman laughed, her reddish-brown eyes sparkling. "Aye, some of 'em are. We train the domestics. Wilds are far too dangerous to train."

"What exactly do you mean by 'domestic'?" Miranda asked.

"Millennia ago," their grandfather replied, "our ancestors succeeded in domesticating dragons, more or less the way humans bred wolves into dogs. But dragons in some ways are more like cats than dogs—meaning that they only allowed themselves to be domesticated opportunistically, like the wild desert cats in ancient Egypt. Our ancestors needed a way to contain and manage the wild dragon populations. Eventually, they were able to create a line of dragons that were loyal to humans, using them much as other ranchers use horses." He paused again. "There were, however, certain changes that occurred during the domestication process, ultimately separating the species into two quite different species. They *can* interbreed, although they prefer not to, and we keep their breeding programs strictly separate, because of genetic issues."

Miranda crinkled up her face. The dragons she and Justin had encountered had looked and behaved pretty much like those in the legends, stories, and movies she had seen. "Like what kind of changes?"

"Well, for the most part, domestics tend to be smaller, but certain breeds are stronger or faster than the wild dragons," their grandfather said. "The domestics' body coloring is muted, even dull, while wilds have vibrant hues and markings. But probably what sets them apart most is their lack of breath weapons, the hallmark of their species."

"Breath weapons? You mean like breathing fire?" Justin asked. His question drew concerned looks in his direction.

Grandpa nodded. "Yes, like breathing fire—or poison, or lightning, and many other weapons. Something in the domestication process deprived dragons' of this ability."

"Can they talk?" Miranda asked, looking at her brother out of the corner of her eye.

Their grandfather considered this for a moment and shook his head. "According to old stories, mere legends maybe, they once could learn the languages of humans—something happened a long time ago and dragons lost their ability to speak. But they can communicate fairly well through their body language. When you've been around them as long as I have, it begins to feel like speech." He let out a wide yawn. "Okay, I think that is enough for tonight. We are all exhausted."

"But—" Miranda and Justin said in unison.

Grandpa raised a hand, silencing their protest. "Tomorrow Miss Ddraig will begin instructing you both in dragon care and dragon lore. You will report to the Warren after lunch." He looked behind Miranda and her brother. "Mrs. Lóng."

"Yes," she said, causing Miranda and Justin both to jump slightly. She must have snuck back in while their grandfather was talking.

"Please adjust the chores for the kids accordingly." He looked at Justin. "And don't forget, you will be spending every evening cleaning up the fire damage."

"We will do as promised," Mrs. Lóng interjected.

Their grandfather stood up with a groan as several of his joints cracked like popcorn. He turned to address everyone else. "All right. Hit the bunks. I'll see you all in about …"— he looked down at his watch and frowned—"three hours."

CHAPTER 15

MIRANDA
The Rock and the Sweaty T-Shirt

MIRANDA COULD SENSE that something was different about her room even before she walked in. She quickly looked around, but nothing seemed out of place. Everything was, mostly, in the right spot, just not in the exact location where she knew she had left it. She took a quick inventory of all her belongings. The shirt she thought she had misplaced earlier was definitely missing. That didn't make any sense. Who would take her dirty shirt?

She ran back down the hall to her brother's room.

Justin was squatting by his open closet door, examining his suitcase.

"Are you okay?" she asked, walking over to him.

He turned and faced her. "Did someone go through your stuff too?"

She nodded, and looked around her brother's uncharacteristically messy room. His clothes were scattered haphazardly all across the floor. The bookshelf was emptied onto the floor, and in the closet, boxes were tipped over. "Not this bad though. What the heck do you think they were looking for?"

Justin stood up and reached into his pocket. "I think they were looking for this," he said, holding up a white package.

Miranda walked over to his outstretched hand and took the package from him. She recognized their mother's looping script immediately. "'Don't open. Keep safe,'" she read aloud. Miranda looked at Justin with a questioning expression.

He shrugged. "It was in my pants pocket. I've been carrying it around with me since we arrived. Do you have any idea what it is?"

"Nope. Let's open it and find out."

Justin made a grab for it, but Miranda was too quick and put it behind her back. "Come on, sis, Mom specifically wrote on there *not* to open it." He held out his hand, "Plus she gave it to me to keep safe."

"They also said we would be safe here, and as soon as we landed, lizard people were trying to lure us into a warehouse, and we've been chased by dragons. What Mom and Dad want is irrelevant now. We are on our own, and someone was snooping through our stuff looking for something. Probably this." She held up the wrapped package so they both could see it clearly. "Who even knows if this is what they were after? We're in the dark until we find out what it is."

Justin pursed his lips. "Okay, but I'm opening it."

She tossed it back to him and smiled. "Be my guest."

Justin pulled the thick paper away from a grayish-brown object inside. He let the wrappings drop to the floor and held the object in his hand. It was a stone. "It's a rock. Why would they give me a rock to keep safe?" He turned it over. "And look, it's all marked up with scratches. You don't think they're losing it, do you?"

"Let me see that for a second." Miranda grabbed the stone and held it close to her eyes to get a better look. "It looks kind of familiar … ." She studied the marks her brother had noticed. The scratches were too neatly spaced to be accidental. She realized they were in fact a series of lines and triangles. "Justin, I think this is writing. This looks like, what's it called, uniform?"

Justin let out a small laugh. "You don't listen much at home, do you? *Cuneiform*. It's the world's oldest writing system."

"I pretty much tune all of you out when you talk about that archaeological stuff." She rubbed her finger over the indentations, and the symbols started to glow. The stone became hot in her hand; a feeling of déjà vu overwhelmed her. A wave of nausea overtook her as darkness closed in from all directions, with an intense feeling of emptiness. Miranda tried to look around, but no light pierced the endless void. In the distance, there was a rumble, like a low growl. It built in intensity until it shook her to the core.

"*Soon, young one. Soon you will be with me, and I will be free,*" hissed a voice, oozing malice.

Then Miranda heard something else, a sound small at first, but gaining in strength, pushing back the void. It was another voice. "… Miranda … Miranda …." The familiar sound filled her with hope and strength and pulled her back into the light. The evil seemed to retreat, as the familiar presence commanded her attention.

Her eyes began to flutter and the world she knew came back into view.

"… Miranda. Can you hear me?" Justin was leaning over her.

She sat up slowly with his help. "What the heck just happened?"

"You turned over the stone, then your whole body began to shake like crazy. A second later your eyes rolled back into your head and you passed out."

"I heard a voice."

Justin nodded. "I heard it too. Who do you think it was?"

"I don't know. I didn't recognize it. It wasn't like the dragons. It seemed far away, not in my head."

Justin shivered, "It was creepy."

She opened her clenched fist, suddenly realizing that the stone was gone. "Where did it go?" she said, frantically looking around.

"Relax. It's back in a safe place," he said, patting his pants pocket. "I think it's probably best if I keep it right here from now on. You said it looked familiar. Do you remember where you saw it?"

She nodded. "Yeah. It looks like a piece from one of those tablets in the dream we had back in Manhattan. The broken ones on the altar."

Justin slapped his forehead with the palm of his hand. "Oh, man. You're right. Wait—why do our parents have a piece of a broken old tablet that you and I dreamed about? And why the heck would Mom give it to *me* for safekeeping?"

Miranda shrugged. "Not sure. But, I'll bet you a hundred bucks, this is what the lizard-man wanted from Mom and Dad that night." She paused to consider for a moment. "Maybe she was worried about it being stolen if they took it with them.

"And she figured it was safest *here*? So far Mom and Dad are zero for two."

Miranda nodded, then remembering why she had come into his room in the first place, said, "So, is there anything missing?"

Justin shook his head. "Nope. How about your stuff?"

"The shirt I wore earlier today is gone. But I noticed it was missing before we left for the Warren."

Justin crinkled up his nose. "Seriously? Someone

actually swiped your stinky clothes? Why? That's just plain disturbing."

"Who knows? But I think you're right about the stone, whoever was in here was looking for it. You don't think those lizard-men were in here, do you?" Miranda asked, as a shiver ran down her spine at the thought of those creepy creatures going through her things.

"No, but I think it might be someone working closely with them."

Miranda nodded. "Well, if it's someone on the ranch, it has to be Mrs. Lóng. She disappeared from the study for a while tonight."

Justin's face contorted, and he looked at Miranda as if she were suddenly speaking a different language. "Mrs. Lóng? What's the matter with you? Of course it's not Mrs. Lóng. Why in the world would she go through our stuff in the middle of the night when she has access to it all day? No. It has to be Mr. O'Faron. We saw him drop something off for the lizard-guys at that warehouse. Maybe that stolen 'wyrmling' thing Mr. DeSoto mentioned—whatever that is. He must have snuck in here when everyone was distracted to swipe it."

"That can't be right," Miranda said finally, shaking her head. "Mr. O'Faron was fighting the fire all night. You saw him— he was covered in soot and mud. Not to mention, he was with us from the time we left the dragons, until just now."

"I suppose it could have been Billy. He left early tonight too."

Miranda's scowled at him. "Billy just turned sixteen. Mrs. Lóng told me the other day. What could a teenage boy possibly want an old stone for? And why would he take my dirty shirt? That's just stupid." And creepy, Miranda thought, if Justin was right.

Justin shrugged, "It could be someone else entirely. It

sounds like stuff keeps getting stolen from the ranch. Maybe it's all related."

"Agreed. We need to find out more information about the stuff being stolen, and keep our eyes open. Someone on this ranch is a thief, and we're going to catch them red-handed."

CHAPTER 16

JUSTIN
Mr. DeSoto

J USTIN WAS AMAZED at how much shorter the trip
to the Warren was in the light of day. Before he knew it,
he and his sister were standing in front of the towering
main gate of the enclosure.

Mr. DeSoto was waiting for them. He dismounted from
his horse and limped over to the gate. He quickly typed a
series of numbers into a keypad, and with a grunt pushed
the door open just enough for them to enter through.

After Mr. DeSoto had led his horse through and shut the
gate, he took off his hat and bowed to them. "I can't say I'm
pleased you two made it so easily around our security," he
said, giving them both a stern look. Then he smiled, his
brilliant white teeth sparkling in the noonday sun. "But I'm
glad you both finally know the truth about this place."

Justin looked at the older man's leg. "Did you hurt yourself
last night in the fire?"

"No, why … Oh, you mean, why am I limping?" He pulled
up his pants leg above his knee, showing them a prosthetic
leg. "No, this happened to me a long time ago."

"If you don't mind my asking, how did it happen?" Miranda asked.

"Well, let's just say, no matter how tame some of these beasts might seem, they are still wild animals." He let his pants leg back down and winked at them. "But hey, injuries like this come with the territory."

Justin immediately thought about the deep, jagged scars on his grandfather's face and gulped.

Mr. DeSoto threw his head back and laughed. "Sorry, *mi hijo*. I didn't mean to scare you. You'll be fine, I'm sure. But it's important to know that these are beasts just like any other wild animal, even the ones we call domestics. If they get spooked or hungry or backed into a corner, all bets are off. Don't ever let them think they have the upper hand, and make sure you put them in their place every so often."

When they started walking up the path, Justin asked, "Grandpa said your family is from South America. Are the dragons there similar to the ones here?"

Mr. DeSoto laughed. "Not even close. They look like feathered snakes with wings. But just as deadly. They are masters of blending into their environment, so much so that people used to think they were magic and could disappear."

"Cool. Do you have one here?" Justin asked excitedly.

The security chief looked away and said tonelessly, "No. My brother back home would never allow it."

Justin scrunched up his face. "Your brother? You're an adult. What can your brother do to stop you?"

Mr. DeSoto shook his head. "Not all siblings get along as well as you and your sister, *mi hijo*," he said and shrugged. "Plus, he is the dragon lord of the family. He can do what he wishes. That is why I … left."

"Did you two get into a fight?" Justin asked. If Mr. DeSoto thought that Justin and Miranda got along, then his relationship with his brother must be really bad.

A dark look flashed over the older man's face. "Something like that."

They walked the rest of the way in silence until they reached the cave. Justin was shocked to find that even in the bright light of day he could barely tell anything was there. Near the dark entrance, Mr. DeSoto placed his hand flat against a black panel Justin had not noticed the night before. A green light moved up and down once, followed by a loud click and the sound of metal sliding against metal. Mr. DeSoto walked over to the handle and pulled the door aside far enough for all of them to pass through. Once they were inside, he slid the door shut, and it automatically locked behind them. "I'm not sure what happened here last night, but this door is secured with handprint identification and a magnetic locking system."

Justin shrugged. "It was unlocked when we got here. The front gate was open too."

"Maybe the storm knocked out the power?" Miranda suggested.

Mr. DeSoto frowned, his thin mustache drooping down into an almost perfect arch. "That seems unlikely. Our backup generators have backup generators. Were the lights on?" Miranda nodded. He motioned for them to come closer and said in a low voice, "No one thinks the two of you could have broken into this place, but this is very serious business. If we don't find out who *is* breaking in and put a stop to the thefts … Well, the consequences to your family could be severe. Until the night before you two arrived, there had been zero incidents for ten years under my watch. Now we've had two break-ins and some pretty serious stuff stolen." He lowered his voice even more. "I trust you two. Keep your eyes peeled and your ears open and let me know if you see anything suspicious. Trust no one. I think that among the three of us we can catch whoever is stealing from your family." He looked down the wide hallway. "Here comes Miss Ddraig. Let's keep this between us for now, okay?" They both nodded. His demeanor changed, and his face looked stern. "Now I'd better not catch you two sneaking in here again, or it will be the last thing you do. *¿Entiende?*"

"Cisco, enough with the scare tactics already. I'll be takin' our young criminals off your hands." Justin turned around to see the approaching form of Miss Ddraig, the dragon trainer, making her way up the wide passage. She flashed them a warm smile. "Come along, kiddies," she said in her singsong accent as she corralled them down the long corridor.

Justin looked over his shoulder at Mr. DeSoto. The older man winked at him. Something about this didn't feel right.

"Pay no attention to Cisco, he's all jaw, that one," the young dragon trainer said once they were too far away from the head of security for him to hear.

"What are we doing today, Miss Ddraig?" Miranda asked, struggling with the unfamiliar last name.

"You can call me Miss D, by the way. I know my last name is a bit hard for you Americans to pronounce. Oh, we'll do a little of this, a little of that. Mostly gettin' you two familiar with this rough-as-ten place, so you blokes actually have a fightin' chance of livin' through the summer."

"Rough as ten?" his sister asked.

Miss D laughed. "Sorry. Hard to break old habits. 'Rough as ten,' slang for a dangerous place, mostly used to describe shady pubs back home, but equally fittin' here."

"What brought you to Thunderbird Ranch?" Justin asked.

"Well, a boat an' train mostly," she responded with a smile. "Seriously though, the families have a sort of … exchange program … through which you live an' work on dragon ranches outside your home country in order to gain experience with different breeds an' various care techniques."

"Why *this* ranch? There must be ones in more exotic locations?" Miranda asked.

Miss D nodded. "Oh sure, an' I've been to a lot of 'em, I have, but this one is special."

"Special how?" Justin asked.

"Well, for one, the Ddraigs an' the McAdelinds have been close families for centuries. Their bloodlines have crossed many a time, if you catch my meaning," she said with a wink. "For another, when I was a little girl, your father came an' lived with us for a time. I thought he was one of the coolest blokes around, I did. So I always wanted to come an' see where he grew up."

Miranda stopped dead in her tracks. "Wait a minute. You thought *our* dad was *cool*?"

Miss D laughed. "Aye, I did. He was older, tidy, smart, had a great accent, an' was one of the best dragon trainers in the world."

"You're talking about *our* dad?" Justin said, pointing back and forth between himself and his sister.

"Aye, *your* dad." Miss D pushed them both back into motion along the corridor. "Come along now. There's somethin' I want to show you two before we begin workin' with the dragons today."

CHAPTER 17

JUSTIN
The Trophy Room

*A*S THEY WALKED DOWN the seemingly endless tunnel, Justin marveled at how different the caverns and tunnels of the Warren looked with the lights on. The walls and floors were so highly polished that they reflected the bright overhead light, making it feel almost like daylight in the subterranean complex. There was still the musky animal smell, that made Justin think of the times he had been to the zoo in summer, the smell of big, wild things that were never meant to be contained in a small space. He also had the same weird feeling he had had the night before, when he sensed the dragon's intention to trap him and Miranda. He sensed dragons circling in a massive chamber to his left, and even more dozing in smaller chambers along several passageways to either side. Justin wasn't sure how he knew these things; he just did.

They soon passed the corridor that they had run down the night before. Justin glanced nervously around, expecting to see a large black dragon charging toward them, but thankfully the passage was empty and quiet.

After several minutes of steady walking, they came to a circular chamber with four arched doorways arranged in a cross formation. Between each pair of archways was a life-size statue carved out of the very rock itself. There were also two wide stone stairwells, one going up and the other going down. Filling the walls between these structures were shelves lined with tall shiny objects.

Justin leaned back and stared up into the endless black void where a ceiling should have been. "Holy cow. I totally had a dream about this place," he said, remembering the image of chasing someone into this very room. "What exactly is it?"

"This is the trophy room," Miss D said, and following his eyes upward added, "an' no, we have no idea where that goes. The stairs end about twenty feet up. Whatever it was goin' to be, they never got round to finishin' it."

"Trophies for what exactly, best of show at the Dragon Kennel Club?" Miranda said as she inspected one of the unnervingly lifelike statues of a grizzled old man with muttonchops joined by a thick mustache. He looked like someone straight out of the old west, but instead of a six-shooter strapped to his belt, he was armed with a long sword.

"Nothin' so civilized, I can assure you," Miss D said and winked at her. "It's a kind of tournament, or in the spirit of bein' in the West, a rodeo. Each year, the Council of Twenty meets an' as part of that gatherin', the families compete in different events. It helps ensure any hostilities that arise are restricted to the games."

"Sounds like it would just make them hate each other more," Justin said, inspecting a shelf next to one of the statues. He had an overwhelming feeling that someone was watching him, and he glanced out of the corner of his eyes at the stone figure. It was of a creepy dragon lady with a slight smile on her lips. Not the kind of smile that lit up a person's eyes, not a welcoming smile, but the smile of a predator certain it is about to catch its prey. She held a scepter in one hand and a stone tablet in the other. The detail was amazing; she looked as if she might jump off the wall and grab him at any moment. A chill ran down Justin's spine, and he suddenly became very interested in what his sister was looking at on the other side of the room. As he walked hurriedly past the statue, her snakelike eyes seemed to follow him everywhere.

"Look here. This one says 'Wyrmling Roundup Champion 1986, R. McAdelind,'" Miranda said, pointing to a golden statuette of a man wrestling a small dragon.

"Are those Dad's?" Justin asked.

"Aye. That's Robin's section of the trophy room."

Justin cringed at the name *Robin*. He could only remember one time when his mother had called his father by that name, and it just didn't sound right. As far as he was concerned, his father was Dr. Robert McAdelind. He didn't like thinking about his dad as a boy named Robin. That was just too weird.

"What's a 'wyrmling' anyhow?" Justin asked, remembering his grandfather mentioning that one had been stolen from the ranch.

"It's a baby dragon. Dragon's have five developmental stages in their life cycle: egg, wyrmling, juvenile, adult, an' ancient."

Justin continued to read the plaques on the trophies: 1987, 1988, 1990, 1991—then nothing. "What happened after 1991?" he asked Miss Ddraig.

She shrugged. "I imagine that is when your father went off to university."

"Whose trophies were here?" Miranda asked, as she inspected a set of empty shelves next to their dad's.

The dragon trainer joined Justin and Miranda. "Not sure. Those have been empty since I arrived. Probably space reserved for you two," she said, and nudged Miranda with her elbow, knocking her slightly off balance, before turning and walking across the room to another section of trophies.

"I don't think so," Miranda whispered, indicating a spot on the empty shelf.

Justin looked to where she pointed. There was a thick layer of dust covering the entire shelf, broken occasionally by an almost perfectly round spot of thinner dust. "There were trophies here, but it looks like not for a while," he whispered.

"But whose?" Miranda wondered aloud.

"It looks kind of like the walls in your room. I bet it's the same person," Justin said.

Miranda nodded. "My thoughts exactly."

"Over here, I want to show you somethin'," Miss D shouted from across the room, the words echoing up into the endless space overhead.

She pointed to a bunch of shiny trophies on one of the lower shelves. "These are the awards we won at the most recent family tournament. This section over here is mine," she said proudly, pointing at a pair of dragon statuettes, one silver and one bronze, that read:

RING RACING—G. DDRAIG (MCADELIND)

"Why does it say 'McAdelind'?" Justin asked.

"When you're on a family exchange, you're formally part of that family. Did you notice that a year was missin' from your Dad's wall? That's the year he represented the Ddraig family in the tournament."

"These look pretty new. How long ago was the tournament?" Justin asked.

"Last summer. Actually the next one is coming up in about a month."

"Whose are these?" Miranda pointed at a couple of gold trophies marked only with MCADELIND.

The dragon trainer paused for a moment, then said softly, "Those are Billy's."

Miranda crinkled her face. "Billy's? Why isn't his name on them?"

The dragon trainer blushed. "Well … you see … it's complicated, you know. Political stuff with the Council, really." Then she started to walk hurriedly toward the archway on the right. "Now come along, kiddies. It's dragon time."

Justin and Miranda jogged down a short corridor to where Miss D stopped at the edge of an unfathomably large cavern. Massive stone pillars were spaced along the walls about two hundred feet apart, supporting colossal arches meeting at a center point on the ceiling far above. Each of the pillars was lined with hundreds of lights, making the subterranean space feel as if they were standing under the bright sunlight outside.

"This place is massive," Miranda said as she craned her head back trying to take it all in. "It looks even bigger with the lights on."

"Oh. This is where we were last night," Justin said, recalling the place where the black dragon had attacked them.

"Welcome to the Grand Corral," Miss D said, and spread her arms wide. "One of the greatest structures in the world, an' another reason why this ranch is quite unique." She turned back to face them. "Believe it or not, this is one of two corrals in this complex: one for the domestic dragons an' the other for the wild ones. If we were allowed to let people know this existed, it would surely be one of the wonders of the world."

Justin looked around the cavern. It was hard to see all the way to the far side, or even to perceive how far the ceiling was above them. He couldn't imagine that the mountain was much larger than this cave, but it had to be. "How in the world did they build this?"

"Well, like the other families, the McAdelinds used dracs

to build these secret structures. They are the only creatures capable of doin' anythin' quite like this."

Justin shot a questioning look at the dragon trainer. "What exactly is a ... drac?"

She regarded him skeptically for a moment, then said, "Aye! That's right. I keep forgettin' you two don't know anythin' about this stuff." She blushed slightly. "Not that it's a bad thing, mind. I'm just sayin', everyone else who comes to work on a dragon ranch is already familiar with the trade." She gestured toward the carved benches along one wall of the cavern, indicating that they should take a seat. "Their real name is *umu dabrutu*, quite a mouthful, eh? So we call 'em dracs, or draconians, and they're ... well I guess you might describe them as ... dragon-men, or lizard-men."

Justin and Miranda turned and looked at each other. So, it was a draconian that had visited their apartment in New York in the middle of the night. And draconians, dozens of them, that they had seen in the warehouse where Mr. O'Faron had stopped on their way to the ranch.

Miss D shrugged. "Honestly, I don't know much more about 'em myself. They've been around forever, servin' the families, helpin' to care for the wild dragons, but they really never talk to anyone. I always thought they were kind of daft myself."

"I haven't seen any draconians around here," Miranda said, looking around the massive structure.

"Aye. Neither have I. Not sure why though. They're usually lurkin' around the dragons' lairs." Miss Ddraig held up a finger. "You know, if you want to find out more about 'em, you could ask Mr. O'Faron. From what I hear, he's quite the expert on dracs."

Miranda shot Justin a glance. There had to be a good reason why there were no draconians working on the ranch, so why had Mr. O'Faron dropped off a package to them?

"Yeah, I bet he's an expert all right," Justin said under his breath.

The dragon trainer put two fingers to her lips and blew three, short, shrill whistles that echoed off the cavern walls.

Justin sensed the dragon approaching before he actually saw it. Enormous bat-like wings beat rhythmically as the large beast lowered itself from some hidden perch. For something the size of a large horse, it landed with astonishing grace. Justin stared up at the dragon and gaped in wonder.

CHAPTER 18

JUSTIN
Dragonspeak

J USTIN HAD SPENT SO MUCH TIME the previous
night trying to get away from the dragons, he had not
really had any time to look at one closely. In daylight,
the beast was awesome and terrifying at the same time. The
dragon was smaller and more slender than the ones they
had run into already, with thin cordlike muscles visible
beneath a sleek reddish-brown scale-covered hide. It turned
its streamlined head and regarded them with seeming
indifference. When it met Justin's gaze, he felt terror build
inside him. He wanted to run, but those wolflike eyes with
their round pupils and brilliant red irises held him in place.

"This is Flare," Miss Ddraig said, as she walked over and
lovingly stroked the dragon's foreleg. "She's a Welsh Red, an'
consequently, *my* Welsh Red. I brought her here with me."

"*Strictly speaking, this is my human, but she can believe
what she wants,*" the dragon said, holding her head up high.

Justin looked at his sister, and she smiled at him, nodding
slightly to acknowledge that she too had heard the dragon
speak.

"Are all red dragons Welsh?" Miranda asked.

"Oh, no," replied Miss D. "The wild reds aren't Welsh at all."

"So Flare is a domestic dragon?" Justin asked.

The dragon's head snapped around to glare at him, an indignant look on her face. *"Domestic dragon? Humph! That's a daft label coming from a domesticated ape."*

"Aye. That's how we refer to 'em, but they are in fact almost a different species from the wild ones, mind," Miss D said, completely oblivious to Flare's thoughts on the matter.

"You said Flare is a 'she.' How can you tell a female dragon from a male one?" Justin asked.

Flare let out a snort, *"Please! How completely daft are you? You're a right sledge, you are."*

"Without inspectin' their nether parts, you mean?" Miss D said with a wink.

Justin and Miranda both grimaced.

"Size, coloration, an' horn length mostly." Miss Ddraig continued. "Males tend to be larger an' broader, with slightly more vividly colored hides, an' will typically have longer horns. You get to the point where you know just by lookin' at 'em. We think dragons can tell by other means too, like pheromones."

"So, what do dragons eat exactly? I can't imagine you can pick up a bag of Dragon Chow at the store," Justin said with a nervous chuckle, hoping beyond hope that the answer was not: humans.

"Varies by breed. Some prefer fish, some sheep, but to keep pryin' eyes off the Warren, this is strictly a beef operation."

"Beef? You mean like steaks?" Miranda asked. Justin noticed his sister turning a light shade of green.

"Aye, no. I mean cattle. A meal of a whole steer can hold a dragon a week or more. However, the more active they are, the more they need to eat."

"Do they eat them ... alive?" Miranda seemed to force

herself to ask the question.

"You mean, do they prefer live prey, the way snakes do?" Miss D replied. "Indeed they do. But a dragon doesn't play with its prey, it kills instantly, by—"

Miranda really looked as if she might barf, Justin thought.

"Maybe that's enough details for now," Miss D said. She motioned for them to stand up.

"Now, come over here slowly an' introduce yourselves to Flare properly. Dragons have a powerful sense of smell, an' she will respond better to you in the future if she associates your scent with mine."

Justin and Miranda rose in unison and slowly walked over to the large beast. As they approached, Flare narrowed her eyes and regarded them both with suspicion.

"Hold out your hands, palms up," Miss Ddraig instructed. "This shows that you have no ill intentions toward her."

They held their arms out as instructed and Flare leaned down, smelling Miranda's hand first.

"Hi, Flare. I'm Miranda McAdelind."

The dragon let out a snort. *"Smell one human, you've smelled 'em all."*

Justin laughed, and the dragon regarded him suspiciously for a moment before leaning over to smell his hand.

"Hi. I'm a domesticated ape," he said with a smile.

Flare reared back away from him, a stunned look in her eyes. *"You can hear me, human?"* she said, her telepathic voice breaking slightly.

"Yes," Miranda said.

The dragon swung her head to stare at his sister.

Miss Ddraig looked at Miranda. "Yes, what?"

"Yes ... my brother is a domesticated ape," Miranda said, and she and Justin both laughed.

"Kids, this isn't a game. Justin, please introduce yourself properly."

Justin grinned at his sister, then cleared his throat and said, "I am Justin McAdelind."

"If you can really understand me boy, say 'Dragons are magnificent creatures.'"

"Dragons are *vain* creatures," Justin said, trying hard not to laugh.

Flare let out a low growl and lunged at him. Justin tried to retreat but fell hard onto his back. The dragon put one great clawed paw on his chest, holding him in place, her big muzzle inches away from his face. She drew her lips back into a snarl, exposing long, sharp fangs. *"Watch your mouth, human. I don't care whose spawn you are. I'll rip you to shreds if you disrespect me like that again, I will."*

Miss Ddraig ran over to Justin's side, holding up both hands with her palms facing outward toward the enraged dragon. "Flare! He didn't mean any disrespect. He's completely daft, a downright sledge he is, and he will apologize immediately," she said. Then out of the corner of her mouth she whispered, "Apologize. Now."

"I'm s-sorry, Flare. Honest. I was j-just joking," Justin stammered, fighting hard against the weight of the dragon's paw to draw in enough air to form the words.

Flare leaned in even closer, so her snout was touching his nose. *"I'm not sure I believe that you're sincere,"* she growled.

"Back down, Flare!" yelled a deep, smoky voice.

The dragon and Justin turned their heads in unison toward the sound. Stalking down the arena, his head held low to the ground, his tail swishing from side to side, was the red dragon they had seen the night before. In the bright lights of the corral, the approaching dragon looked truly magnificent. He was almost twice as large as Flare, his reddish-gray scales shimmering as his massive muscles flexed with each step, his eyes never leaving Flare's.

"The boy offended me, he did," she said with a growl.

The big dragon turned and regarded Justin. "*Were you screaming again?*"

"*He was insolent, he mocked me!*" Flare said, not showing any signs of backing down.

The red dragon continued toward her. "*Well, you are a vain little wyrmling. I'm sure you deserved it.*"

She growled at him, "*How dare you? I am a champion. You will show me some respect.*"

"*No. You are a visitor here, and you will behave accordingly. The boy is under my protection. If you want to indulge your ego, come here and try to do so with me.*" The male dragon reared up, extending his wings out in an impressive show of his truly massive size.

Justin could feel Flare's body shake. She carefully removed her paw and slowly backed away.

The other dragon turned his gaze away from Flare and addressed Justin. "*Now, apologize to our guest.*"

Justin scrambled to his feet. "Flare, I'm sorry. I was just joking around and didn't mean to offend you," he said, trying his best to sound as sincere as possible.

"*See that it doesn't happen again, boy,*" she ordered curtly, refusing to make eye contact with him.

"*Flare,*" the other dragon growled warningly.

She looked at Justin and her face softened. "*What I meant was, apology accepted,*" she said, and extended a forepaw to him.

Justin took a step forward and placed his hand on her proffered paw.

"Uh, what in bloody 'ell just happened here?" Miss Ddraig said, her eyes going from the dragon to the boy.

"*Don't let her know you can hear us,*" warned the other dragon. "*At least not yet.*"

Justin looked at him and nodded, then turned to Miss D. "I guess we came to an … understanding."

The trainer looked up at her dragon and gently rubbed her neck. "Why don't you go back to your lair for a while? I'll visit you soon."

Flare nodded her head once, then turned and walked through one of the large arched entrances.

Miss Ddraig turned on Justin as soon as the dragon was out of sight. "Why did you do such a daft thing like that for? You're not all there, are you! You could have gotten yourself killed. Never, an' I mean *never*, insult a dragon. That was one of the most idiotic things you could have done." She was pacing back and forth, throwing her arms in every direction as she spoke. "I have a mind to ban you from being around the dragons for your own safety."

"Wasn't even close to the most idiotic thing I've ever seen," the red dragon said, as he sat down on the stone floor.

Miss D stared at Justin for several minutes, shaking her head, as if she were having a conversation with some unheard voice. Then she sighed and said, "Well, you're alive an' Flare seemed to be fine with you in the end. I imagine you're a right bag of nerves too." She snorted, laughing. "I guess that's as good a lesson on what not to do with dragons as I could have come up with." She turned to the big dragon sitting nearby. "Red, can you watch over 'em for a few minutes, please? I'm goin' to go fetch a couple of things."

The dragon nodded his massive head once in acknowledgment, then lowered the rest of his large body to the ground and closed his eyes.

Miss Ddraig pointed at Justin and Miranda. "You two behave. I'll be right back." She jogged out the same arch through which Flare had exited.

Justin looked at the large dragon lying nearby. "So your name's Red, and you're a *red* dragon?"

The beast opened one eye and sighed. *"What's your point, kid?"*

"Whose creative mind came up with that name?"

"Your dad's creative mind," he said and sat back up. *"You'd have thought you'd learn something about respect after being schooled by a petite little juvenile dragonette."*

Miranda laughed. "He's always getting his butt kicked."

Justin shot his sister a dirty look. "Zip it, you."

"Why did you tell us not to say we could hear you?" his sister asked, changing the subject, but was still grinning widely.

"There's something going on around here, and I think if anyone suspected there are humans who can actually dragonspeak, it would put you two in even greater danger."

"Wait—you mean there are no other people who can hear you?" Justin asked.

"No. There are stories of course. A long time ago, all riders could hear their dragons, but something changed, something lost to time. Sometimes, I could have sworn your pop knew what I was thinking." Red looked off into the distance. *"But I was young, and he left, so I never got around to asking him."* Red looked down at the ground and shook his head. *"Is he coming here soon—?"* He stopped in midsentence and sprang to his feet, his head low, his back arched like a cat's, his tail held high, as if readying himself for a fight.

Then Justin sensed it too. He swung around to face the corridor to the trophy room. An intense desire to destroy, to harm, to kill, was moving quickly toward them.

Something enormous raced through the opening, spread its great wings, and took instantly to the air. It wasn't until Justin saw the creature with his own eyes that he truly understood the differences between a wild and a domestic dragon. It had all seemed so academic to him when his grandfather was trying to explain it. Now, as he watched a true wild dragon make a tight circle in the air above him, it seemed to make frightening sense. This creature was a truly dangerous animal. Its body was covered in thick, glistening deep-blue scales, and its back bristled with sharp, pointed spikes. It was leaner than the other dragons Justin had seen so far, and its neck and tail were longer, making it look more reptilian than the domestics.

"*I knew I smelled the thief in here! Where is my child, wretch?*" it shouted at them.

Red put himself in front of Justin and Miranda. "*Calm down, Azuria! There is no thief here.*"

"*Do not shield your masters, mongrel.*"

"*Return to your lair, or I will drag you there by your neck,*" Red retorted angrily.

"*If I have to get past a filthy subbreed to exact revenge, so be it,*" she said.

Red growled and leaped into the air at the blue dragon. Azuria anticipated this move and easily dodged to the side. Red went flying past her. Justin realized with horror that this had been her plan all along, that the taunting was intended to get Red to make the first move. She now had a clear path to her real target as her eyes locked on Miranda.

The wild dragon took in a deep breath. Her scales began to shimmer and seemed to flex independently, rubbing against one another as small arcs of electricity danced across them.

"*Hit the ground!*" Red shouted as, with mighty beats of his wings, he dove between them and the blue dragon.

As Justin dropped to the floor, his whole body began to tingle, and every one of his hairs stood on end. There was a deafening cracking noise, as if the whole mountain had just split open. He brought his hand up to shield his eyes as a blinding flash of light collided with Red.

The dragon cried out in pain and crashed into the stone floor, the edge of his shoulder billowing smoke. "*Azuria! Stop!*" Red yelled desperately.

"Miranda! This way!" Justin called, pointing at the exit

behind them. But she waved him off and ran in the opposite direction. Justin hesitated for a moment. What the heck was she doing? That way led back to the room the dragon had come from in the first place. Miranda was going to get herself killed. But she was on her own now. He turned and ran as fast as he could to the closest exit.

When he reached the archway, Justin turned to make sure his sister had made it to safety. To his dismay, the blue dragon had shifted in the air and was blocking Miranda's escape. Now she was cornered between the creature and one of the massive stone pillars.

Red was crawling toward the blue, trying to pull himself back up to reach Miranda in time.

The beast turned to look at Red for the briefest moment. Her crystal-blue eyes with their catlike pupils regarded his approach with utter indifference. Justin could tell in an instant that she knew the injured dragon was no real threat to her.

Miranda used the blue's momentary distraction to her advantage and made a run for the far exit.

Azuria snapped her head back around. *"Not this time, thief!"* she cried as blue-white electricity crackled over her glittering body. She opened her mouth wide and unleashed a blinding flash of lightning from her gaping maw.

Justin watched in stunned horror as the bolt struck his sister square in the back, sending her flying through the air and into the stone wall of the Grand Corral.

CHAPTER 19

MIRANDA

Azuria

MIRANDA FELT HERSELF ENVELOPED in utter darkness. There were sounds all around her. People were shouting, but none of the words made sense, as if someone were constantly changing radio stations nearby. She forced herself to concentrate on just one of the sounds, but it was impossible to focus. There was pain too; her arms felt as if they were being pulled free from their sockets. She tried to speak, but the words came out all wrong. Something bad happened. Everything was all mixed up, she felt … scrambled. Then she became aware of a scraping noise. It continued steadily, and she concentrated on that one sound. The longer she focused on it, the more all the other things became clearer.

She slowly opened her eyes. There was a carved stone ceiling far above her, and she seemed to be floating on her back. Sounds of fighting grabbed her attention, and what she saw didn't make sense. Dragons were fighting each other. People were running around, shouting and throwing ropes into the fray. And she wasn't floating; it was her own boots that were making the scraping sound she heard as she was dragged roughly across the floor.

She looked up to see her brother pulling her along by her arms as hard as he could. She tried her voice again. "What ... what happened?"

Justin's face was red and streaked with sweat. "We're ... almost ... to the ... tunnel. I'll ... tell you ... then ... ."

They passed under an archway, and her brother propped her against the cold, smooth wall. "Are you okay?" he asked, crouching down next to her.

Miranda massaged her hands, trying to return some of the blood to her numb fingers. When she readjusted her position against the wall, the small of her back came in contact with the hard surface, sending pain shooting through her entire body and making her scream.

Her brother shifted to get a better look at her back. "Yikes," he said, his face going pale. "That's one nasty burn. How do you feel otherwise?"

Miranda took a quick inventory of the rest of her body. The wound on her back—easily visible, since half the back of her shirt had been incinerated—was by far the worst injury she had sustained, but also her head felt as if she had just been smacked by a log, and her rear was sore from being dragged across the floor of the Grand Corral. "I'm pretty tired of being knocked unconscious and slightly humiliated from having my baby brother revive me, but other than that I'm alive. What happened?"

The ground shook, drawing their attention back to the struggle taking place in the middle of the corral. Red had Azuria pinned to the ground with an immobilizing hold from behind, while Flare gripped the blue dragon's mouth closed from the front. Miss D was crouched low, trying to get in close enough to put the glimmering silver rope she held coiled in her hands to use. Mr. O'Faron was busy dodging Azuria's lethal tail in order to secure her hind legs. Circling the dragons and shouting out commands, looking every bit the part of dragon rancher, was their grandfather.

"Get off of me, you treacherous lapdogs!" Azuria was screaming at the two red dragons as they worked in tandem with their human companions to secure the enraged beast.

Red leaned in close to the blue's head and whispered, *"I would show a little more respect to your executioner. Because if that girl dies, I will rip out your throat myself."*

Miranda stood on shaky legs and took a step toward the arena. "I'm okay!" she shouted.

Every eye turned to her as she slowly walked forward. Justin ran up beside her and offered his arm to steady her.

"That's impossible. I hit you with a bolt. You should be dead." Azuria whispered.

When they were less than twenty feet away, their grandfather raised his hand, telling Miranda to come no closer.

With a deafening roar, Azuria threw Flare and Red from her and sprang at Miranda.

Justin knocked Miranda sideways, sending them both clear of the dragon's snapping jaws.

Azuria let out a cry of frustration as her momentum made her overshoot her target. She turned quickly, coiled her long body, and leaped at them again.

Miranda didn't have time to dodge; she instinctively turned her head and held out her hand in a feeble attempt to ward off the attack. There was a ground-shaking collision, and she flinched instinctively. But Azuria had not touched her. Miranda looked back and gasped to see a huge black dragon standing on the back of her assailant and pinning her to the floor.

Within seconds, Flare, Red, and the other humans were

back on top of the incapacitated Azuria, quickly securing her legs, arms, and mouth with the strange silver rope.

It wasn't until the black dragon dropped down on all fours that Miranda saw Billy riding on its back. He looked down, inclined his head toward Miranda, and with a terse command sent the massive black beast into the air. Miranda watched in awe as the dragon made a wide circle above them, banked into a roll, and landed silently a short distance away.

"*Showoff,*" said Justin and Red in unison.

Billy slid smoothly from the black's back, patted it on the shoulder, and said softly, "Good work, Nightshade." Then he walked quickly over to Miranda. "Are you okay?"

"Thanks for saving me," she said, blushing slightly.

"*Nice. I took a bolt of lightning for her, and it doesn't even warrant a thank-you,*" Red said.

"Apparently neither does dragging her fifty feet out of harm's way, or knocking her out of a mad dragon's path," Justin replied.

"What is he talking about?" Billy asked, looking at her brother over Miranda's shoulders.

"Nothing," she said, not turning to face Justin or Red.

Billy came up next to Miranda. "That burn looks pretty bad. Maybe you should sit down for a while."

Miranda stood up straighter. "It's fine. Come on, I want to see what's happening," she said and headed toward the fallen blue dragon.

"All secure?" her grandfather yelled as he continued to circle Azuria, keenly inspecting the coils of silver rope binding the beast. When Mr. O'Faron and Miss Ddraig nodded, he looked over at Red and Flare, who were still holding onto the unconscious wild blue. "Okay, you two can get off now," Grandpa said.

Red groaned as he stood up and Miranda gasped when she saw his wound. The scales on his shoulder were burned black and oozing dark-red blood. She walked over to him, and placed a hand on the foreleg below his injured shoulder. "Oh, Red, I'm sorry. I didn't know it was that bad. Are you going to be okay?"

The Welsh Red pulled himself up proudly. *"'Tis but a flesh wound, my lady."* Then wincing in pain, he added, *"Actually it feels like I was shot by a bolt of lightning, but never fear, I'll be all right in a couple of days."*

"Dragon saliva is better at healin' cuts an' scrapes than anythin' we'd be able to come up with. It's an antiseptic an' a coagulant, an' it stimulates rapid healin' of the dragon's cells." Miss D chimed in, unaware of Red's comment.

Justin frowned. "I'm not sure I follow what that all means."

"It means we have magic spit, kid," Red grunted. *"I lick my wounds, bye-bye booboos."*

"You," Grandpa shouted back at Billy's dragon. "Drag this no-good lizard back to her lair."

Nightshade nodded and grabbed the blue by her tail, pulling her backward through the tunnel she had emerged from earlier.

"Miss Ddraig, a word please," her grandfather said flatly to the dragon trainer. Then he turned to Mr. O'Faron. "William, please take Miss Ddraig's mount and make sure the wild makes it back to her lair."

The ranch hand nodded and followed the black dragon through the archway with Flare close behind.

After they were gone from sight, their grandpa turned to Miranda and Justin. "You two all right?"

"For the most part," Miranda said, wincing as she touched the small of her back.

Their grandfather placed a hard, weathered hand on her shoulder and gently turned her around. "Let me have a look." He touched her back lightly. She let out a yelp. "Sorry," he said. "What exactly happened? Miss Ddraig said she heard a lightning attack."

Justin stepped forward. "Miranda started to run and the dragon shot her in the back with lightning."

"Right." Grandpa chuckled drily. "She'd be crispier 'n burned bacon if one of those bolts had hit her." He pointed to the burned wound on Red's shoulder. "A dragon can take an artillery shell to the chest and have nothing more than a nasty bruise to show for it. If your sister had been hit …" His voice trailed off, and he cleared his throat. "She wouldn't be standing here. More likely one of the Welsh Red's scales, or a piece of stone, heated from the lightning, hit her in the back."

"Red's wound is from the first shot," Justin said. "I'm telling you, the second one hit Miranda square in the back. Then Red wrestled the blue to the ground."

Their grandfather regarded him seriously for a moment. "Sorry. What you think you saw is impossible," he said, then turned to Miss D. "What in God's name were you thinking leaving the kids alone in here? Where was your head?" His face flushed with anger.

Miss D lowered her gaze. "I went to get a saddle to show 'em—"

"I don't want excuses, Gwen. They're the only family I have. Got that?"

She nodded and stammered, "Aye, sir."

He turned to Red, reached up, grabbed him by the chin, and roughly pulled his head down so they were eye to eye, man to dragon. "And I expect more from you." He pointed to the dragon's wound. "You were lucky this time, but if you hadn't been, they'd be dead." He motioned to Miranda and Justin for emphasis. "You need to be better than this. They are my family. You need to protect them at any cost. That is your duty. Understand?"

"Hey, Gramps!" Justin said, marching toward him, his hands balled into fists. "First off, he *did* protect us 'at any cost.' See this hole in his body?" Justin pointed at the oozing wound. "That isn't from sitting on his butt doing nothing. Second ... off ... he tried to save us, so you should be thanking him, not yelling at him."

Miranda was shocked to see her brother stand up to an adult. Sure, Justin had a tendency to get in over his head with older kids, but he never talked to people in positions of authority like this.

Grandpa just glared down at Justin. "The operative word here is *try*," he said, not budging. "In this world, the world you and your sister are now a part of, *trying* doesn't earn you ribbons, *trying* gets you killed. This Welsh Red knows his first responsibility is to get you to safety before engaging in battle. He failed to do that."

"You weren't there. That wasn't possible."

"*Justin, it's okay,*" Red interrupted.

Justin looked over his shoulder at the dragon. "I'm not going to let you take the blame. What you did was brave."

"*Lord McAdelind is correct,*" Red said. "*I lost my temper and acted foolishly. Bravery is irrelevant if it costs the lives of the ones we are sworn to protect. I should have been smart, not brave.*" He hung his head low.

"Bravery could have gotten your sister killed. The dragon knows this," Grandpa said, his voice rising.

Justin took a step forward and stabbed a finger in the air at the older man's chest. "His name is Red, by the way, and at least he was here for us. Where were you when we needed you? Where were you when Miranda needed *your* protection?"

Their grandfather flinched, taking a half step backward, then narrowed his eyes and pointed to the exit. "Get out of my sight," he whispered.

The room was so silent you could have heard a spider crawling on the vaulted ceiling. Miranda watched her brother lock eyes with their grandfather for the briefest moment, then turn on his heels, and stomp off through the nearest exit.

Mr. O'Faron reentered the Grand Corral. "She's locked in her lair—" He broke off. "What's going on? Is everything all right?"

Miranda's grandfather did not look up but continued staring at the spot where Justin had been moments before. "How did the wild blue get in here, and where is DeSoto? I've been trying to reach him for the past fifteen minutes."

Mr. O'Faron looked over his shoulder. "He's coming. I ran into him in the trophy room, he said he was doing an inventory."

As if on cue, the head of security limped into the Grand Corral. "The door to the wild's area was unlocked and wide open. I just radioed Johnson, and he's doing an immediate sweep of the area."

"Why were you doing an inventory and why in Sam Hill weren't you responding to my calls?"

Miranda noticed that Mr. DeSoto's eyes narrow for just a second before he dropped his head apologetically. "I was checking out a hunch. There are more eggs missing from the nursery."

"What ... How ..." her grandfather stammered, spittle flying with every word. "We need this solved. Now, Cisco! Take one of the dragons with you and see if you can pick up a scent. I want you to bring me whoever is stealing from us so I can deal with them myself. You understand me?"

Mr. DeSoto inclined his head. "I will redouble my efforts." He looked over at Red. "But I don't need a dragon's help, sir."

Miranda thought her grandfather's head was going to explode. "You will use whatever means are at your disposal, Mr. DeSoto. Or you will be on the first plane back home. Understand?"

"*Claro*, my lord," he said stiffly. He bowed deeply before limping back toward the trophy room.

Billy cleared his throat. "Sir, if it's okay, I'm going to take Miranda to Mrs. Lóng to see if she has anything for that burn."

The older man just gave him a wave of his hand without turning around to look at them.

"Come on," Billy whispered.

As they exited the Grand Corral, Miranda looked back. Red was lying down and carefully licking his wound. Her grandfather was still standing beside the injured dragon, staring at the floor, lost in thought.

CHAPTER 20

MIRANDA
Storm

MIRANDA AWOKE THE NEXT AFTERNOON feeling very sore but otherwise fine. Billy had walked her back to the main house, where Mrs. Lóng seemed to almost faint at the sight of Miranda's wound, but pulled herself together long enough to produce a bowl of thick green smelly goo and a steaming hot mug of something fragrant. The paste felt slimy and cool on Miranda's back, and caused a tingling sensation to spread throughout her body. The warm drink was sweet, pleasant and somehow familiar. She started to think back through all the happy times in her life—finishing first in the district track meet, her first kiss with Taylor Mason, sitting on her dad's lap as he read aloud to her, her mom's protective hug. The last thing she could remember was stumbling up the stairs to her room, leaning heavily on Mrs. Lóng, who tucked her under the covers. Miranda blushed with embarrassment to think of how pathetic she must have looked to Billy.

Knock, knock, knock.

"Come in!" she shouted.

Billy's head poked through the partially opened door.

Miranda let out a high-pitched scream, and pulled her covers up around her neck.

Billy quickly disappeared back out the door but spoke through the crack. "Sorry. I just wanted to see how you were feeling."

"You just startled me, is all. I thought you were Justin," she said. "I'm feeling a lot better though, thanks for asking. Ready and rearing to get back to work in the stables."

"That's good," Billy said, still on the other side of the door. "Actually, that's the other reason I was coming to see you. Your granddad feels it would be best for you to learn about dragons as quickly as possible. He asked me to show you the ropes. If you're up to it, that is."

"What about Justin?"

There was a pause before Billy replied. "Your little brother is working full time on cleaning up the burned area."

"That's not really fair. Justin wasn't responsible for what happened the other night." Miranda frowned. She couldn't believe she was actually defending her dorky brother, but keeping him away from the dragons was wrong.

"It was more the way he talked back to your granddad. The old man isn't used to being challenged. On this ranch, his word is law."

"It still doesn't make it right," Miranda said. Then when she got no response, she added, "Okay. I'll be down in a couple of minutes."

After Billy had closed the door, Miranda peeled herself gingerly off her mattress, washed up, pulled on some clothes, and went to the bathroom. She had to at least make herself semipresentable.

Billy was waiting for her on the front porch. He looked as ruggedly handsome as always, leaning against one of the pillars, and grinning at her in his lopsided way. "Your chariot awaits," he said, indicating the ATV at the bottom of the steps.

Miranda returned Billy's smile and walked with him down the stairs. He helped her onto the vehicle, climbed on in front of her, and revved the engine to life. Soon they were rocketing up the dirt road to the Warren. They made their way through the main gate and up the winding wooden path to the cavern entrance. They dismounted the ATV and walked through the large steel door and down into the massive stone cavern.

"I was wondering if you'd be up for another trip to the waterfall? I want to show you something." Billy said.

"You mean like, now?"

"No, no. After lessons. Plus, we should go around dusk, it will be harder for anyone to spot us then. My Dad would be furious if I took you back there."

Miranda's eyebrows furrowed. "Why would he be mad? That doesn't make sense. It's one of your favorite places."

"My father is only interested in what makes *him* happy these days," Billy spat, making Miranda jump a little. "Sorry. My Dad and I don't have the best relationship."

"I don't want to make things worse between you two. Can't you just tell me about—whatever it is?"

Billy shook his head, "No. There's something you need to know, and it'd be better if I showed you."

Miranda nodded. "Do you want to meet at the house or the stables?"

"Too many eyes. I don't know if you noticed yet, but it's impossible to be alone on this ranch. Mr. DeSoto, Mrs. Lóng, my Dad, your granddad, they always seem to be everywhere, all the time."

Miranda nodded. He was right, the adults always seemed to pop up in the strangest places, almost as if she and her brother were constantly being watched. "We'll just meet in the valley then?"

"I think that's best. I'll leave you a 'survival pack' in the flower bed to the right of the front steps to the main house."

They walked for a while in silence, until Miranda recognized one of the passages she and her brother had run through a few nights before. The corridor was lined with big steel doors, some open, some closed. "Are these where the dragons sleep?" she asked, looking at one of the open portals.

"Yeah. We call them lairs." He walked over to the nearest doorway and motioned for Miranda to join him. He knocked on the open door a couple of times, then said, "Thunder. May we enter?"

Miranda heard a shifting of weight, as something massive moved inside, scraping scales against stone. "*I guess*," said a deep voice, tinged with sadness. This was followed by two soft snorts.

"The dragons communicate with us using a few simple sounds and body language. Two snorts means yes, one snort means no. After a while you begin to recognize other cues that help when you're riding." Billy led Miranda through the open door.

Thunder's lair was dimly lit, but Miranda could still see everything inside just fine. It was larger than she had imagined, with a high ceiling and a pool of clear water in one corner. The floor at the far end the room seemed to be covered with what looked like massive mounds of sand and rock.

Sitting off to one side was a very large grayish-blue dragon, looking annoyed. "*Please don't let my desire for privacy interfere with your inane curiosity*," he said and made a huffing noise.

Miranda looked at him apologetically. "We're sorry to

disturb you. I was just curious about what your lair was like."

Billy regarded her for a moment. "Good read. You're a natural. This is Thunder. He's my dad's dragon." Then he turned to Thunder. "Thunder, this is Miranda McAdelind."

She noticed the dragon tense slightly and sit up straighter. He tilted his head and regarded her closely. *"Lord McAdelind's granddaughter?"* he said, no longer moody.

Careful to mind Red's advice, Miranda pretended that she couldn't understand dragon speech in front of Billy. "Are all the lairs the same?"

Billy shook his head. "Not quite. They vary slightly by breed. This is a domestic blue dragon's lair. They are also called Scottish Blues, Thunderbirds, or Storm dragons, and they are naturally coastal creatures, so this lair is more humid than most others, and it has a large pool. Welsh Reds prefer rocky, warmer lairs, and Romanian Blacks favor dark ones with lots of vegetation. We try to make them all as comfortable as possible."

Miranda looked back at Thunder, who was in turn still regarding her with interest. "How are you doing, Thunder?" she asked politely.

The dragon bowed his head slightly toward her. *"Better, now that I am in the presence of a Lady McAdelind. It has been far too long."*

All at once, a stream of images flashed through Miranda's mind, fleeting pictures of the young girl, about her age, she had seen before in dreams, of an older woman who looked familiar, and of a sleek, beautiful bluish-gray dragon, soaring effortlessly through the clouds.

Miranda staggered back, slightly dizzy. She shook her head a couple of times, trying to clear her mind. She looked up at the massive blue with a questioning expression. *"Who were those women?"* she thought, willing the dragon to hear her. Thunder took a step away from her. Had he heard her thoughts? Miranda didn't want him to retreat and took a step toward him.

"*Um*—what's going on?" Billy said, and Miranda became aware that he was watching her intently.

Miranda cleared her throat. "Glad to have met you, Thunder. Thank you for allowing me into your home." She turned and walked as quickly as she could out the door. Once outside, she leaned against the cold stone wall and took a deep breath.

"Are you okay?" Billy asked.

Miranda gave him a weak smile. "Just a little worn out from yesterday. Give me a second to catch my breath."

"You sure everything's all right? You looked like you were going to attack Thunder, and he seemed genuinely scared. It's not unusual to feel some animosity toward the dragons, especially after being attacked by one. I mean, look at Mr. DeSoto. He got his leg bitten off by one, and now he won't even get near them."

"I noticed he seemed a little weirded out about taking a dragon with him yesterday. If dragons freak you out, why work on a ranch full of them?"

Billy shrugged and looked away. "Sometimes it's the only choice you have."

Miranda let out a small laugh. "Everyone has a choice. Are you saying he doesn't?"

Billy's deep brown eyes bored into her. "You'd be surprised." He smiled. "Anyhow, enough of that. Let's keep moving," he said and guided her down the passageway.

The very next lair they passed Miranda recognized from two nights before as the one she and Justin had ducked into to hide. She paused there for a moment, looking at the closed door.

"Nothing in there worth being concerned about," Billy said with a snort.

"What does that mean? Who's in there?"

"Nothing really. Barely a dragon. An old blue."

Billy tried to lead her away, but Miranda refused to budge. "Who is in there, Billy?"

"Just a crazy old beast that rarely comes out of her lair."

Miranda walked over to the door and put her hand on the cold steel. "What happened to her?"

Billy shrugged. "Not sure exactly. I asked Dad once, but he just said to leave her alone. Come on. Let's get to the corral."

Miranda hesitated for a moment. She felt drawn to this place, but she didn't know why. She gave the door one last glance, then hurried after Billy. When she caught up to him she asked, "What's her name?"

"You mean the blue's name? It's Storm."

Miranda sucked in a quick breath. The dream she had had in New York before they came here swept over her. She was back in the massive cavern, with the woman, beaten and chained to the stone pillar, telling her over and over again, *Heal Storm!*

CHAPTER 21

JUSTIN

What Is Behind Door Number … ?

J USTIN GRABBED YET ANOTHER burned piece of
wood and carried it over to the ever-growing pile. The
intense high-altitude sun made sweat pour down his
face, which was already covered in soot and grime. With
a grunt, he threw the log onto the stack, arched his back,
and with filthy hands, tried in vain to loosen his knotted
muscles. He took a deep breath, longing for some fresh air,
but everything just smelled like smoke.

He looked around at the small circle of burned wood and
brush he had spent all morning stacking. "This sucks!" he
yelled loud enough to ensure that the sound echoed back
from the other side of the valley, then he plopped down on
the now barren earth and added quietly, "This totally sucks.
Not to mention, it's completely unfair."

No more than ten minutes before, a fast moving ATV had
shot down the road toward the Warren. He could see two
people riding it. The driver was most likely Billy, since the
person riding behind him, her long black hair flapping like
an ebony flag, was obviously Miranda.

Justin was furious. Not only was that slimeball, who basically blamed him for the fire, heading to the Warren to be with the dragons, but his sister was with the guy. Justin had checked in on Miranda every hour the night before, terrified that she was going to die, and instead of coming to let him know she was fine, she goes off with that jerk. Justin clenched and unclenched his fist as his mind stewed over the injustice of it all.

A gentle hand rested on his shoulder, diverting his attention. Mrs. Lóng was standing beside him. "Justin, are you okay?"

"Yes," he snapped. His eyes began to water and smoke filled his lungs. He coughed several times. Tiny flames danced on the pile of logs he had just stacked.

Mrs. Lóng's gentle touch became viselike as she turned him to face her. "It's all right, Justin, sometimes there are still embers that remain in the charred wood, it will burn itself out soon. You just need to relax."

She guided him away from the fire, and he took in deep breaths. The flames disappeared and the smoke died down.

"See, I told you," she said with a reassuring smile. "The fire wasn't your fault. I know that, your sister knows that, and in his heart, your grandfather knows it too. You remind him too much of your father, and a past he tries hard to forget. But you and your sister are threatening to tear down the lie he has shielded himself with, and that scares him."

"What are you talking about?" Justin asked.

"Let me finish please," Mrs. Lóng said softly. "It was wrong of him to be so hard on you, but the reality is, he was. There is no need to play the victim. Be more like your father. Take control of your own destiny. He was one of the few people who ever stood up to your grandfather, and he was the better for it."

"*Right*. And it drove him away from his own family. Good

point."

Mrs. Lóng smacked Justin lightly on the side of the head. "You are more like him than you know." She let out a long sigh. "So, are you ready to get back to cleaning up the woods?"

Justin looked down the valley and to the gate of the Warren. He shook his head. "No, ma'am. I think I am going to go learn how to ride dragons instead."

* * *

Justin was winded from the run, but there was no way breathing hard and a stitch in his side were going to stop him from being with the dragons today. He was probably already in a ton of trouble for just being here, but no member of the security team seemed to have gotten a memo on not letting him in. Plus, he wasn't going to let his grandpa yelling at him get in the way of keeping an eye on his sister and learning more about the dragons.

When he finally made it into the Grand Corral, Justin couldn't see Miranda anywhere—or anyone else. No Miss Ddraig, no dragons, no one. Justin started to get a little freaked out. The place was far too spooky to be wandering around alone. Where was everyone? He was thinking about leaving, but decided instead to take a seat and wait for someone to show up. For the inside of a mountain, the place was very noisy. There were a lot of strange noises seemingly all around him—a distant scraping sound, a small rock falling from the ceiling, water dripping somewhere to his left. After about thirty seconds of trying hard not to panic, he decided to visit the trophy room to distract himself.

If I keep myself busy looking around, I won't have to worry about being scared to death, Justin thought. I can take a closer look at some of those cool trophies while I wait. Instinctively, he crept along as silently as he could.

When Justin was only a few paces from the trophy room, the sound of something echoing off the walls of the corral sent him flat against the corridor wall for a moment. He looked back to make sure there was nothing sinister following him. When he didn't see anything, he turned to continue on his way, but a movement caught his eye and froze him in place.

In the trophy room, the form of Mr. O'Faron, black hat and all, strode purposefully across the archway at the end of the corridor where Justin was hiding. Hmmm. I wonder what you're up to now, Mr. O'Faron? Justin thought. Not wanting to lose sight of the man, Justin crept forward and peered around the corner of the archway.

As if sensing something, Mr. O'Faron glanced over his shoulder, but Justin swung his head out of view before he was spotted. He took a deep breath, counted to three, and slowly looked around the corner again. The man was nowhere in sight.

Justin figured, based on the direction in which Mr. O'Faron was heading, that he must have gone down the back passageway. Now what in the world could you be doing back there? Justin wondered. Crouching down and half running silently on his tiptoes, he made his way around the trophy room to the edge of the entrance to the corridor where Mr. O'Faron had disappeared a moment earlier.

Once again, Justin slowly peered around the corner. The passage beyond was almost pitch-black, but he could just make out the silhouette of a man walking rapidly away from him. There was the faint *click* as he turned on a flashlight. Justin could now see Mr. O'Faron standing in front of a door. He fumbled with something in his hands, keys probably, then looked back down the corridor. Justin ducked out of sight again, but when he looked into the corridor again, it was empty.

He must have gone through the door already, Justin thought. What is back there anyhow? If I try to follow him and he comes back through the door, I'll be caught, and I'm in enough trouble already.

"What do you think you're doing?"

Justin spun around to find Mr. DeSoto glaring at him.

Where in the world had he come from? No one had been there a second before. "You scared the crap out of me," Justin said.

"Well, I imagine if you weren't sneaking around, you wouldn't have anything to be scared of. Now answer my question. What are you doing here?"

"I came to learn how to ride dragons, and while I was waiting, I thought I saw someone walk down this corridor."

Mr. DeSoto frowned. "Not a chance. That whole section is off-limits. No one goes in there. Even if they did, they would need the key to get through the door, and the only person who has that is your grandfather. Trust me, he keeps that locked up tight."

"Interesting." Justin looked back over his shoulder to the door through which Mr. O'Faron had apparently disappeared. Obviously it was not as secure as everyone thought. "So, what's back there anyhow?"

"Nothing. It's been closed off for years. I think it's just a bunch of empty lairs. If we suddenly ran into space issues, I'm sure that section would be opened up." Mr. DeSoto stroked his thin mustache for a moment, as if considering what to say next. "So, *mi hijo*. Besides seeing shadowy figures walk down corridors to nowhere, have you noticed anyone or anything else suspicious?"

Justin was tempted to tell him about seeing Mr. O'Faron walk through the door, but something in his gut told him to keep his mouth shut, at least for now. "You mean besides being on a ranch full of dragons?"

Mr. DeSoto glanced over his shoulder as if making sure they were still alone. "Nothing? You know, I just saw Billy walking with your sister, not more than ten minutes ago, and I overheard them talking about meeting later. It reminded me, he's been acting kind of, well, strange lately. I would hate for Miranda to get involved in anything he is up to."

"Don't get me wrong, if being a tool was a crime, he'd be a lifer. But I haven't seen him do anything suspicious." Justin paused. "Is there gray mud in the hatcheries?"

Mr. DeSoto thought for a moment. "No, the hatcheries are clean and sterile, why?"

"Not sure. Billy just had some gray mud on his boots the night of the fire, and I don't remember seeing anything like that around."

Mr. DeSoto stroked his chin, lost in thought. "No. Me neither." Then he leaned down and whispered, a gleam in his eyes, "I think you might be onto something here, *mi hijo*. Keep a close eye on Billy O'Faron. Okay? Fill me in on any details you notice—no matter how insignificant they might seem."

Justin nodded, suddenly feeling uncomfortable. "I should probably see if Miss D is there now," he said, and hurried back to the Grand Corral. Partway along the corridor, he glanced back to look at the trophy room. Mr. DeSoto was nowhere to be seen.

CHAPTER 22

JUSTIN
Sage

J USTIN WAITED AT ONE OF THE STONE benches in the Grand Corral as Miss Ddraig led three dragons single file into the arena. The first was her red dragon, Flare, the next was a small blue, and the third was an ancient green. All three sported saddles, with long straps that crisscrossed their bellies and chests and wrapped around each front leg. It looked as if leather octopuses were attacking them.

"Justin. I'm glad to see you here, boyo. Mrs. Lóng radioed ahead to say you were on the mitch an' headin' this way. I'm glad your granddad didn't scare you away yesterday."

Justin frowned at the dragon trainer. "You know I have no idea what you're saying half the time, right?"

"Just pointin' out that dodgin' chores to be here is the right call." She shrugged, "So, are you ready to learn about the fine art of dragon ridin'?" She motioned to him with a flick of her head to come closer.

Justin got up and slowly approached the dragons. He held out his hands, palms up, the way she had instructed him the day before. He went to the familiar red dragon first. "Good to see you again, Flare."

"*Wish I could say the same thing about you, ape,*" she said with a snort.

Justin gave her a scowl and walked over to the small grayish-blue. Its scales shimmered under the artificial light. It looked … new, as if it had just come off some mythical-creature assembly line. Its head was held high and its chest was puffed out, making it look slightly larger than it actually was.

"This is Steel," Miss D said. "He's a juvenile Scottish Blue. Only two years old, but in dragon years, a teenager."

Justin stretched out his hand. "Nice to meet you, Steel."

The young dragon bent his head down and sniffed long at Justin's hand. "*I hope he picks me to ride. I'm ready.*"

Justin smiled at the blue's enthusiasm, then crossed to the broken-down-looking green dragon. Miss D followed him over, and put her hand on its wrinkled, drooping head. Next to young Steel, it looked beat up, dull, and just plain tired. "This is Sage. He's the … senior … dragon of the ranch."

This introduction drew silent laughter from the two younger dragons that only they and Justin could hear. Sage turned slightly to glare at the juveniles. "*You'd show some respect if you knew what was good for ya. Keep it up, and I show you both what this old dragon can still do.*"

Justin frowned at the other dragons. "Do I get to choose which one to ride?"

"Aye. Before you bond with a dragon of your own, or if you find yourself in need of ridin' an unfamiliar dragon, you should always follow your gut."

"Then I would like to ride Sage," Justin said and moved in closer to the old green, stroking the side of his scarred and sagging face.

Laughter to his right caught his attention, and he turned to see Miranda and Billy walking into the arena, followed close behind by Billy's black dragon, Nightshade. Justin turned quickly away, pretending not to notice they had entered.

"Over here, kiddies!" Miss Ddraig said, waving a hand frantically. As if they might somehow miss the three dragons lined up in a neat row, Justin thought.

Justin was trying hard to look everywhere except at his sister. Even when she was standing next to him, he found himself suddenly very interested in a sore on Sage's foreleg.

"I thought you were busy cleaning the woods?" Miranda said, placing her hand on his shoulder.

"And I thought you were still in bed," he replied, shaking her off. "So nice of you to let me know you're okay."

"All right, *Dad*. Since when do I report to you?"

"You should at least let *me* know you're alive."

"Someone is sensitive today." Miranda scowled at him.

"Just leave me alone," Justin said and turned away from her.

"Fine. Be that way," Miranda snapped and stomped back to where Billy was standing.

"Maybe this is too soon after last night's *events*. We should continue tomorrow, when things cool down a bit," Miss Ddraig said.

Justin shook his head and walked over to Sage. "No way. I'm fine. Let's ride."

Miss D stared at him for a moment, looking concerned. Justin felt sure that she was going to say no and that he would be forced to go back to cleanup duty. But to his surprise, she smiled and said, "Here, catch." Then threw him a wide leather belt, like the ones furniture movers wear to support their lower backs, but with mysterious clips on the sides. "Put this on."

"What's this for?"

"You'll see, just put it on like a normal belt." He secured the thick leather around his waist. Miss D gave an adjustment strap a firm tug to make sure it was on good and tight, then guided him over to the side of the ancient dragon. "Now ask Sage to lie down so you can get onto the saddle."

Justin rubbed the old dragon's neck. "Sage, can you lie down for a second?"

The dragon looked back at him, let out a sigh, then with a series of grunts, moans, and creaking joints, settled to the ground. The younger dragons giggled.

"Be especially gentle with the old geezer. You might accidentally snap his spine," Steel said, chortling silently again.

Sage growled and swung his head toward the young dragon, bumping Justin off balance in the process. *"One more comment, and I'm coming over there, and we'll see whose spine snaps."*

"Justin. Be careful," Miss Ddraig said, misreading the old dragon's intentions.

"Sorry, youngster," Sage said, swinging his head back around to the front.

"Now, place your foot in the stirrup an' push yourself up, throwin' your other leg over the saddle."

It took Justin two tries before he was able to pull himself up, but to his dismay he somehow ended up facing the wrong direction, toward the dragon's rear.

Flare snorted and said, *"Oh, this is goin' to be better than I thought."*

Justin ignored the comment, but couldn't help blushing at his mistake. Once he was oriented right way round, Justin's stomach felt suddenly queasy. He was on the back of a dragon. What in the world was he doing? He didn't know anything about riding dragons, or any other creature for that matter. This was nuts. He was going to die.

"You okay?" Miss D asked. "You look like you're goin' to heave."

Justin had to force himself to look down at her. "I'm fine," he said weakly.

Sage swung his head around. *"If you're going to be sick, I want you off my back."*

Justin looked over at his sister and Billy. They were both watching from one of the stone benches. Miranda looked concerned, but Billy wore his usual annoying smirk. Justin sat up straight and looked straight ahead. "I'm fine," he said, meaning it this time.

"See that hard thing stickin' up at the front of the saddle? That's called the horn. Most of the time you'll be holdin' onto that. But when the dragon is takin' off, or landin', or makin' some more complex maneuvers, you'll want to grab onto the two handles at either side of the horn. Those are called gullet grips. For what we're doin' today, you won't be needin' those." She stepped further away from the dragon. "Finally, reach back an' grab those two straps hangin' off the cantle, the back of the part you're sittin' on."

Justin twisted around slightly in the saddle to see two short leather straps with steel loops at their ends attached to the back of the seat. He grabbed hold of both of them and looked back at Miss D. "These two?"

"Aye. Now attach the loops to the clips on your belt." She pointed, indicating the clips on either sides of the belt Justin was wearing that had puzzled him when he put it on. Justin snapped them into place with a *click*. "Now mind, I know they don't look like much, but those little straps will save your life. When your dragon pitches an' rolls or dives an' climbs, they'll keep you from flyin' off to your death. Any questions?"

At the mention of death, Justin had that sick feeling again. Instinctively, he triple-checked all the straps to make sure they were secure. "Don't I need something to, uh, steer the dragon?"

"Humph! Just like a human to want to treat us like some

common beast of burden," Flare said with a snort.

"You mean a bridle. No, not with dragons. We help guide them with voice commands an' also by shifting our weight in the saddle. Lean forward an' they dive, lean back an' they climb, lean left an' right an' they turn. Easy-peasy."

"Right. Sounds easy," Justin said sarcastically. "So, I just lean back to take off?"

Miss D laughed. "You'll bloody well do no such thing! No flyin' today. We are just going to walk around a bit, so you get a feel for the saddle an' guidin' the dragon. I'll be ridin' Flare beside you the whole time."

"Plus there is no way that relic could make it off the ground even if he was carried," Steel said.

"It was a mistake for the boy to even pick a has-been like that one," Flare added.

Justin could feel Sage's muscles tense. He could sense the anger and humiliation radiating from Sage. Nervous about what the dragon might do, Justin leaned forward in his saddle and gently patted his thick, wrinkled neck. "It's okay, Sage, don't let them get to you. They're just being jerks."

"No, they are being disrespectful children who need to be taught a lesson in humility," Sage growled.

Miss D turned around at the sound of the angry dragon. "Justin. What's going on?"

"I ... don't know," Justin said. He leaned down and whispered to Sage, "They're just being dumb kids. Whatever you're thinking, please don't do it. Please, Sage."

Steel lay down on the ground and sighed. *"The human is right, of course. In fact, he is probably saving your life. I'm sure if you started to fly, the sheer stress would cause you to break apart."*

"You want to see what I can do, child?" Sage retorted.

Justin saw Billy and Miranda out of the corner of his eye stand up and walk quickly toward him.

Steel stood up, puffed out his chest, and said, *"Bring it on, old one."*

Justin sensed Sage's intention only a fraction of a second before the dragon moved. "No, Sage!" he yelped, as the great green beast reared back on his hind legs and spread his wings wide. Justin grabbed the horn of the saddle, desperately trying to hold on. He heard Miss Ddraig and Billy yelling something, but he felt too overwhelmed by the anger emanating from Sage to make out any of the words.

"I'll show you exactly what this 'old one' can still do!" the ancient dragon yelled. The words blasted through Justin's and Miranda's brains, but came out as a mighty roar to Billy and Miss D. Sage dropped back on all fours, causing Justin's head to smack into the scales of the dragon's neck. He saw stars and could not focus his eyes for a moment, but he could tell that the dragon was pivoting. He looked up and saw that they were now facing down the full length of the Grand Corral.

"Please, Sage. Don't do this," Justin whispered.

"Sorry, son, but a dragon's got to do what a dragon's got to do." And the beast launched himself forward.

CHAPTER 23

JUSTIN
Glory Days

THIS MUST BE WHAT IT IS LIKE to ride a rhino, Justin thought. His legs were spread so wide over Sage's broad back that it was nearly impossible for Justin to push himself up in the stirrups to prevent being jarred with each step the dragon took. Huge batlike wings extended out on either side of him. Justin could see that the thin membranes were torn in several spots. From past fights? he wondered.

Sage started to beat his wings rapidly, but there was no movement upward. He tried several small leaps to get airborne, only to come back down hard again. Justin could feel the dragon's angry determination yielding to frustrated rage. Suddenly the beast turned to the right, heading directly for the closest wall.

"Sage! What are you doing?"

"*I need some height,*" the dragon responded.

They were rapidly closing in on the wall. "I *really* don't think this is a good idea," Justin whimpered.

The dragon sprung into the air, slamming hard into the

wall about fifteen feet off the ground. His claws locked into the rough stone and he rapidly clambered up the surface, with Justin clinging desperately to the horn of the saddle to keep from keeling over backward. When Sage was about a hundred feet above the cavern floor he stopped, his whole body tensed, readying himself to push off.

"Please, please, please, don't do this," Justin pleaded, but all hope disappeared with the sickening sensation of free fall as the dragon launched himself from the wall.

Justin grabbed onto the gullet grips so tightly, he thought his fingers were going to break. After several seconds of the dragon frantically beating his great wings in the air, he tucked them tightly against his body and dove to the ground below. The floor was coming up fast to meet them. In seconds, they would smash into it. Suddenly, instinct kicked in and Justin did the only things that seemed right: he leaned back and pulled with all his might on the gullet grips.

Sage's wings spread instantly, turning the dive into a fast glide, mere feet above the floor. *"Great timing, son,"* the dragon said, beating his wings rapidly, sending them farther and farther up into the air. *"My vision isn't what it used to be. I thought we had a couple more feet."*

Justin felt faint. Of course, of the three dragons, he had picked the one that was not only crazy but also blind. "Let's just land and get this over with. I think you've proven your point."

"The kid is right. You are too old to be doing this. You've had a good run. You don't need to prove anything to anyone anymore," Sage chided himself.

Justin winced as he sensed how defeated Sage felt. In the same moment, he felt, rather than saw, the dragon's memories of his glorious youth, what it had been like for Sage to be proud and invincible, to soar effortlessly over the vast land below. But even more, Justin felt the dragon's loss—

of loved ones, of hope, of dignity. Justin tried to speak, but his voice caught in his throat. Finally he said, "You know what? I've changed my mind. Let's show those idiots down there what an old-timer can do."

Sage looked back, winked, and beat his wings hard. He was now so low to the ground that he kicked off from the floor with both feet, launching them up into the still air of the Grand Corral. When they were nearing the roof, Justin pulled back hard on the saddle and Sage responded instantly with a tight back flip. Once they were level again, the dragon leaned left, then right, zigzagging back and forth, banking slightly with each turn. Justin was too amazed to feel frightened.

As they neared the far wall, Justin guided the dragon into a lazy turn until they were facing the cluster of humans and dragons at the other end of the corral. "You want to show these youngsters a thing or two?" Justin shouted over the rushing air.

"*You got it. Hold on tight, we're about to go old-school on their shiny little behinds.*" The dragon beat his wings hard to gain altitude.

Justin gripped the horn of the saddle and stood up slightly in his stirrups. "Let's do it!" he yelled, but as the dragon fell into a dive, his yell quickly turned into a scream.

Sage was flying crazily, twisting and turning in the air, turning loops into flips and flips into dives. Justin had no idea which direction was up. But it wasn't until they were heading upside down into the ground that he realized, neither did Sage.

Pulling back on the horn and leaning hard to the right, Justin tried to turn the dragon before he became nothing more than a smear of human on the stone floor. As before, Sage responded instantly, but this time *instantly* was a little too late. The dragon collided with the ground before he had completely righted himself, his forelegs buckling under his own weight and speed. His chin smashed into the ground with a sickening thud.

Justin gasped, but the safety belt held him tightly in place, keeping him from flying over the dragon's head. He gripped the saddle's horn as Sage's still body skidded to a halt not a hundred feet away from where they had started.

Miss D, Miranda, and Billy were in motion even before the dragon had stopped moving. Justin could see the panic on Miss D's and his sister's faces, and a look of astonishment on Billy's.

Justin tried to unclip the life-saving saddle straps from the belt, but his trembling fingers could not handle the task. So he unbuckled the belt, leaving it attached to the saddle, and slid to the ground. He walked slowly to the dragon's motionless head and touched his sagging cheek gently. "Sage. Sage, can you hear me? Are you okay?" but there was no response. Justin closed his eyes and rested his forehead against the dragon's. *"I'm sorry, Sage. I shouldn't have pushed you like that,"* he thought, willing the dragon to hear his apology.

"I knew there was something special about you, son."

Justin jerked back. Sage regarded him with one half-open eye. *"You can hear me ... like this?"*

"Loud and clear. And just to put the record straight, our ... incident ... is this old prideful fool's fault, not yours."

"Justin, are you okay?" Miranda said, running up beside him.

Justin nodded, never taking his gaze away from the old green dragon. "I'm fine."

Sage tried to get up, but winched in pain and lay back down. *"I think I broke something."*

The dragon trainer came running up and grabbed Justin, spinning him around to face her. "Have you gone completely mental?" she squeaked, her voice a full octave higher than normal.

"Miss D, I think Sage may have broken something on the landing. Can you please take a look at him?" Justin replied softly.

Miss D immediately undertook a full inspection of the old dragon. "His left foreleg is broken. We'll need to get him to the examination room an' set the bone. Not an easy task, mind. Billy, can you an' Nightshade help me move Sage?"

"I'll come with you," Miranda said, staring at her brother for a moment before walking away.

Justin didn't care what his sister was thinking. His attention was focused on the old dragon as he slowly limped out of the room on three legs. Nightshade steadied him on his injured side while the three humans guided him on the right.

"I told you he'd break apart," Steel said.

Justin's hands clenched into fists and he started to shake.

"Really. Did you see how hard it was for him to take off in the first place?" Flare added, laughing. *"I was stunned to see him in the air."*

"Okay, that's enough!" Justin said. He turned and marched straight toward the two young dragons. Flare narrowed her eyes and stood her ground, but Steel wasn't sure what to make of this small human advancing toward him and backed away. Justin pressed in on him, and when he was standing nose to nose with the juvenile blue he reached up and grabbed him by the lower jaw, the same way he had seen his grandpa do with Red the day before. He pulled the dragon's head down hard so they were eye to eye. "You'd better hope that when you grow up you're *half* the dragon Sage is."

"Watch yourself, human," Flare growled. *"We don't answer to you, an' I already talked to you once about addressin' us with respect."*

Justin let go of Steel's snout and walked over to Flare. He met her gaze levelly. "I will talk to you with respect when you've earned it, *lizard*. Let me repeat what Red told you yesterday. You are a guest here, and *you* will show the humans and the dragons who live here respect." Justin took another step toward her. "Do I make myself clear?"

Flare lowered her head and let out a low growl. But now her predator eyes, which had scared him motionless before, held no power over him. Boy and dragon remained locked like this for a moment, the dragon's powerful back muscles flexing involuntarily as if she were deciding what move to make next.

"I said, *Do I make myself clear?*"

To Justin's surprise, both dragons winced, and their eyes widened. They both began to back away from him slowly. "*Yes,*" they said in unison.

"Good. Now the two of you get out of my sight." Justin pointed to one of the exits. He watched the beasts as they slunk out of the Grand Corral, their armored bellies almost scraping the ground. Steel looked every bit as ashamed as Justin thought he should, but Flare held her head high.

After they had left, Justin sighed. Sensing something behind him, he turned around. Towering above him, not ten feet away, was Red. "How long have you been lurking there?"

"*Long enough. You've got some guts, kid, I'll give you that,*" he said and laughed.

Justin frowned. "So, *you* were the reason they backed down."

"*Come now. Don't sell yourself short. That was all you. You probably weren't aware of this, but your words have a certain ... power ... behind them. Even I felt a bit ... intimidated. Plus, I was just here to make sure no one did anything stupid.*" The massive dragon lowered his body to the ground. "*What you did for Sage was very honorable."*

"If by honorable, you mean dumb, then yes, I totally agree with you." Justin felt tears beginning to well in his eyes. "He got hurt and it was my fault for pushing him."

Red reached out a massive forepaw, extended a single claw and placed it gently under Justin's chin, then raised the boy's head. *"Now you listen to me. That was Sage's decision, not yours. He's been around for a long time, and unfortunately no one has asked him to do anything as long as I can remember. I was shocked to see him out here in fact. But I was proud of you for choosing him and not one of those other idiots. You've got heart."*

Justin nodded. "But somehow I always seem to screw things up."

"I didn't say you had brains." Red laughed. *"Well, that might change over time—or maybe not. Either way, never stop, it's what makes you better than other humans. As a matter of fact, I have a proposition for you."*

"What kind of proposition?"

"If you're up to it, I would like to be your dragon. You know, show you the ropes and teach you the finer points of riding. After all, I was trained by the best: your Dad. And since he's not here to teach you, I'm the next best thing."

Justin felt a twinge at the mention of his dad. He missed his parents so much. Even though they traveled a lot, he knew they were always looking out for him. But now, he felt alone, vulnerable and scared. He looked up at the big dragon and his heart soared. Red was kind of family. His dad had raised the dragon, which must make the beast like Justin's older brother or something. Justin wrapped his arms as far as he could around the dragon's neck and said, "I can't think of a better idea."

Red cleared his throat with a dragonish growl. *"Okay, okay, enough of the hugging already. We're a couple of take-no-*

prisoners cowboy dudes." The dragon pulled away. *"So, are you ready to get started?"*

Justin stuck his thumbs into his front belt loops, and spat on the ground at his feet. "Shoot, partner. I was born ready."

Red shook his head. *"Okay, that's just plain embarrassing. Now grab a saddle and hop on before I change my mind."*

CHAPTER 24

MIRANDA

Rendezvous

MIRANDA LOOKED THROUGH the window at the sun low in the sky to the west. It would be another hour before dusk, but she had no intention of waiting until then. Her plan was to go to the place where she and Billy had agreed to meet before the sun was behind the mountains and just wait until Billy arrived. That way she wouldn't accidentally run into a mountain lion or fall off a cliff.

She was heading down the stairs when she ran into Justin coming up. "Watch out," she said and gave him a little shove to the side.

"Hey! What the heck." He looked up at her suspiciously. "Where are you going?"

"None of your business," she said and skipped down the remaining stairs.

Justin turned and bounded down after her. "It's going to be dark soon. You shouldn't be out there alone … Wait a minute. Please tell me you aren't meeting Billy somewhere."

Miranda spun around, jabbing a finger into his chest. "What if I am?"

"Well, if you are, I don't think it's a good idea," he said, shrinking a little. "For one, you were struck by *lightning* less than a day ago. For two, Billy totally blamed me for the fire and got me into trouble. I don't trust him one bit."

"Do you think after lecturing me earlier, I'll listen to *anything* you have to say?"

"Well, if you weren't such a self-centered jerk that you forget to let your brother know you're *alive*, then maybe I wouldn't have to lecture you!"

Miranda narrowed her eyes. There was a tiny part of her that suspected Justin might have a point, but she would never give him the satisfaction of hearing her admit that. "Just leave me alone. I can take care of myself. I don't need my *little* brother watching out for me." She turned and stomped out the front door.

Miranda was so angry, she almost forgot to grab the pack Billy had left for her. It was right where he had said it would be. She swung it over her shoulder and almost fell to the ground. It was heavier than she anticipated. What was in there? Bricks? Maybe there was something she could leave behind? But not here. If Justin came out looking for her, he would follow her for sure.

After running across the bridge and up the hill, Miranda found herself totally exposed on the scorched land by the fire pit. She looked back down at the house and saw her brother come out and look around for her. Miranda dropped to the ground and crawled over to one of the massive piles of debris. She pulled herself into a crouch and peaked around the edge to see if he had spotted her. Justin was standing in the center of the lawn alternately looking up the hill and toward the Warren. Then he suddenly took off up the road toward the hidden dragon sanctuary.

Miranda let out a small laugh, "See ya." She stood and ran as fast as she could down the path to the waterfall.

The sky was turning steadily darker and the air was beginning to cool. A shiver ran up her spine as the sweat from running started to cool against her skin. Miranda quickly took off the backpack and pulled on the jacket she was carrying. She thought about taking a second to look in the pack but felt she couldn't afford to be spotted by her brother or not making it to the waterfall before it got too dark. Instead she hurried off down the path at a brisk jog.

Miranda reached the point where the path turned sharply down a hill toward the valley below. She quickly navigated down the slope covered with loose gravel toward the river. In the distance, she could hear the rush of the waterfall, but it was now too dark in the box canyon to see it clearly.

When she reached the edge of the river, Miranda crouched down and strained to see where the rocks were. "This is stupid. I'm going to end up dead, or worse, in the river again," Miranda said out loud. She was starting to feel very alone and maybe a little scared too. "Okay, Billy O'Faron, let's see what you put in here for me." She unzipped the pack and looked inside. In the dim light she could barely make out the contents. There was a box of some sort, something that was soft like fabric but crunched when she touched it, a flashlight, and something that looked like a small fire extinguisher.

The sound of gravel shifting nearby made her heart jump. Miranda quickly pulled the flashlight out, aimed it where she had heard the noise, and pushed the button. A beam of intense light shot out, illuminating the bushes and rocks in front of her. She quickly moved the beam around, looking for any sign of an animal. But after an intensive scan of the area, nothing seemed out of place.

Miranda shone the light back into the pack to see what

exactly was in there. The fire extinguisher thingy was actually a can of bear mace. That might come in handy. Miranda took it out and placed it on the ground next to her. The crunchy material was some sort of reflective silvery fabric, and the box was a metal container labeled SURVIVAL KIT.

Having the flashlight and the mace did make Miranda feel better, but she was starting to get seriously freaked out. She shone the light around one more time: still nothing. She closed the backpack, threw it over her shoulder and, holding the mace in one hand and the flashlight in the other, carefully made her way from one wobbly stone to the next. With the aid of the flashlight, and her prior knowledge of which stones not to step on, she was soon across the stream and sitting on the table-like rock near the waterfall.

"Billy, where are you?" she said quietly to herself.

Miranda was answered by the sound of a rock coming loose and falling down the steep wall of the canyon, echoing as it bounced off a dozen rocks. She shone the flashlight to the spot where it landed. "Billy? Is that you?" Another rock echoed off the wall behind her, and she spun the light there. "Okay. This isn't funny." But there was no response. The hairs on the back of her neck stood on end, and goosebumps formed on her arms. Something nearby was watching her, and it was everything she could do not to run screaming from the valley.

She slid slowly off the big rock and crouched beside it. She gripped the canister of mace and the flashlight until her knuckles were white.

Miranda heard the sound of something above her like a sail catching a gust of wind and shone the light toward the top of the canyon ridge. Two glowing eyes reflected the flashlight back at her for a second before whatever it was averted its face from the beam. An enormous two-legged reptilian creature sat perched on the edge of the canyon, its gaping mouth dripping saliva from rows of gleaming teeth while it flexed its two massive batlike wings as if ready to dive at any moment. It shifted its weight from one clawed foot to the other, sending another rock bouncing down the canyon wall.

A sound behind Miranda made her spin around. What she saw in the flashlight's beam made her heart catch in her throat. On a large boulder, not twenty feet away, and cutting off any chance for escape, was another one of these horrifying beasts.

Miranda raised the flashlight to scan the ledges and high rocks above her. The beam reflected off the eyes of a third, then a fourth, and finally a fifth monster, all fanning out their wings and shifting from side to side, like vultures readying to swoop down on fresh carrion.

Miranda shone the light again at the closest of the creatures, the one perched on the boulder behind her, almost dropping the flashlight with her trembling hands. When the beam hit its face, it recoiled slightly and smashed its long spiked tail down several times on the ground. It was definitely the largest of the five. Then it arched its menacing tail high above its head, and Miranda let out a small gasp. The tail was tipped with a long curved spike thrusting out from a bulbous segment, like a giant scorpion's tail.

She was in trouble. Big trouble. Cornered here in a box canyon, with no way out. Why hadn't she been able to sense these creatures? They looked kind of like dragons, but she knew in her heart they weren't. Maybe she could communicate with them anyway. "Are you one of the dragons from the Warren?" she asked, her voice trembling slightly. The creature turned its head slightly but didn't respond. "Because my grandfather runs this place, and he would be pretty upset if anything ever happened to me."

The giant beast shifted but made no indication of having understood her.

Miranda tried to drive her thoughts into the animal's mind, as she had with Thunder. *"This is my grandfather's place. Go away, or you'll be sorry."* But it only tilted its head slightly to the side again before jumping down off the rock. The ground shook when it landed. Miranda shone the light around at the other creatures to make sure they weren't about to swoop down upon her. Each remained in place, wings spread, ready to strike. "Billy, where are you?" she whispered and crouched low behind the table-like rock.

The lead creature licked its lips with a long forked tongue and slowly advanced on Miranda, wobbling slightly as it walked on its two muscular legs, its wings spread wide for balance.

Miranda looked desperately around for a place to run, or hide. She knew it was only a matter of seconds before the creature was upon her, and she doubted that using the entire can of mace would do anything. Her light revealed an open area below the table rock. It appeared that the flat rock, thick and heavy though it was, was balanced on two separate stones, making a small cavelike opening. Not wasting a second, Miranda dove for the small hole and shimmied inside.

The earth shook as the strange creature advanced quickly toward her. It let out a blood-curdling screech. The beast lowered its head to the ground and peered with one gleaming eye inside the hole. Miranda pulled herself up into a tight ball at the far end of the tiny cave. The beast flicked out its forked tongue, licking her booted feet and legs. Her whole body began to quiver, and she pulled farther away from the creature. It let out another screech, then jumped on top of the rock. Loose sandy dirt showered down around her, making its way into Miranda's eyes and lungs.

She couldn't breathe, she couldn't see, but she could sense the enormous weight of the giant reptile perched on the stone above her head about to crush her. She was going to die.

CHAPTER 25

MIRANDA

Wyvern Attack

"THINK, MIRANDA," MIRANDA whispered aloud. "Think." She had to do something fast or the table rock would be her tomb in a matter of seconds. But what? What could she possibly do against a creature like this? Remembering Red and how he had fought the wild blue dragon, Azuria, Miranda realized the only thing that could save her now was a dragon.

She squeezed her eyes tight, and directed her thoughts toward the Warren. *"Help me! I'm being attacked by some kind of scorpion-tailed creatures! Anybody, please! Help!"*

Instantly, Miranda felt another mind connect to hers. *"Where are you?"* The voice seemed to be somehow far away and in her mind at the same time. She wasn't alone after all.

"In the valley with the waterfall."

"Show me exactly where." Miranda was able to place the voice: it was the mysterious dragon, Storm.

Miranda pictured the valley, the creatures, and the stone she was hiding under.

Storm responded immediately. *"Your assailants are called wyverns. Their sting is deadly."*

"That's just great. *And while I'm at it, I'll try to keep away from their rows of knife-like teeth, and their razor-sharp claws,"* Miranda thought back sarcastically.

"That would be wise. Do whatever it takes to stay alive. I'm coming." Then the connection was gone, and she was alone again.

Miranda heard a scraping noise behind her, and turned to see the wyvern using its chin to scrape away the dirt by her head, digging inexorably down. Something poked her feet: she looked to see what it was. The animal had swept its tail around to the opening of her hiding place, and its scorpion-like stinger was probing around, tapping at her boots. Miranda instinctively pulled away from the barb— closer to where the creature was trying to dig her out.

Something long and wet and slimy wrapped around Miranda's neck, choking a scream in her throat. She tried desperately to pry the vile thing off, but the wyvern was too strong, it was pulling her swiftly toward the freshly dug hole. The stench of rancid meat on its breath made her gag, as she realized that the appendage gripping her by the throat was the monster's tongue.

In her struggle, Miranda's foot kicked the can of bear mace. It was a long shot, but she had nothing left. She dragged the canister with her foot toward her right hand. Tiny flashes of light danced across her vision; she was about to lose consciousness. She felt darkness closing in around her.

"Don't give up!" Storm said, nearer this time.

Miranda's hand closed around the canister of mace. She pulled the safety pin free with her teeth and pointed the canister in the direction of the wyvern's mouth and squeezed the handle.

Miranda pressed her eyes shut tightly as the jet of mace

burst from the can. The tongue released immediately. Miranda gasped for breath, each gulp of air forcing the darkness away. The beast let out a gurgling screech and withdrew its spiked tail. Miranda knew that her hiding place had become a death trap and the next attack would be her end.

Miranda squirmed out from beneath the table rock and peeked over the top to see the creature thrashing its head back and forth, clawing at its tongue, its jaws gaping wide, as labored gasps and rasping cries issued from its seared throat. Miranda scanned the cliff wall, where she could barely make out the shapes of the other wyverns. She could only hope that their attention was focused on their injured companion. Her exit from the valley was no longer blocked. It was now or never.

Miranda pushed off the table rock and ran down the long valley at a full sprint. She heard a screech and dove behind a low rock just as one of the wyverns glided past her. She started to get up, but the rock exploded as the monster slammed its spiked tail down, missing her by inches.

The earth began to shake. One of the wyverns was right behind her on foot, closing quickly. She could feel its foul breath on the back of her neck, and knew it was only seconds from snapping her in two. She cut quickly to the right, running toward the valley wall. The wyvern overshot her and skidded to a stop, sending up a spray of gravel into the air. It couldn't maneuver on two legs as well as a human. Miranda could try to use this to her advantage, but probably not for long. Running was useless. Maybe she could spray it with a dose of mace and buy a few seconds more for her rescuer. She raised the canister in both hands, ready to spray the beast in the mouth or eyes as it charged.

The wyvern clawed at the ground and lowered its head. Miranda braced herself for the charge.

There was a roar from above and the beating of massive wings. Both Miranda and her attacker looked up at the same time to see a slender blue dragon plunging toward them, landing without a sound between them. The dragon spread its wings wide and crouched low to the ground, its tail swishing back and forth, readying to attack. The light from Miranda's flashlight danced off its blue-gray scales, highlighting a latticework of deep scars on Storm's wings and back.

"*Get on, I might be able to outrace them in the air,*" the dragon ordered. Miranda tried to take a step forward, but her feet were locked in place. "*Now, youngling!*"

"I can't," Miranda whispered back.

Two of the wyverns had landed beside the first, cutting off any chance for escape.

"*Your hesitation has doomed us both,*" Storm said with a growl. She whipped her head around to face the approaching creatures. Her lips pulled back in a snarl, revealing rows of dagger-sharp teeth. "*So, it is a fight then?*"

Without a moment's hesitation, the blue sprang at the leading wyvern. She moved so quickly, it didn't even have time to react. Her mouth closed around its throat, but her body continued past it. In one fluid motion, still gripping its long neck, she tossed her head backward, using her own momentum to send it over her head. The beast crashed into the opposite canyon wall with a thud, blood pulsing from the gaping hole in its neck.

Even before the wyvern had slid to the ground in a lifeless heap, Storm was in motion again. Her tail swept the legs out from under the attacker to her right, sending it flipping onto its back. Its talons snatched uselessly at the air in a vain attempt to right itself. The dragon pinned the creature to the ground with her back legs and used her front claws and teeth to rip and tear at its chest and neck. Miranda watched in shock as the dragon fought viciously for their survival. She wanted to help, but what could she do with nothing but an almost-empty can of mace and a flashlight?

Just then, Miranda saw another wyvern position itself behind the blue dragon and raise its scorpion tail high for a killing strike. "Behind you!" Miranda yelled at the top of her lungs, sending the image of what she was seeing to Storm at the same time.

As the wyvern's tail struck down toward the dragon's back, Storm rolled to one side, and the spiked barb plunged into the chest of the creature lying on the ground. It let out a gurgling wail and started to convulse uncontrollably.

The other two creatures descended on opposite sides of the dragon, snapping at her ferociously and smashing their tails down as Storm barely evaded strike after strike. Miranda knew it was only a matter of time before one of the barbs caught the dragon. She had to do something. Quickly working her way around the canyon wall, she came up behind one of the wyverns, took aim, and threw the canister of bear mace as hard as she could at its head. "Hey, ugly! Over here! I thought I was the one you were after!" As the massive beast turned its head toward her, she flashed a beam of light into its eyes, temporarily blinding it.

This was all the opportunity Storm needed. She rolled toward the distracted creature, knocking it over like a bowling pin, ending in a crouch. *"You should have run,"* she scolded.

"You're welcome," Miranda replied tartly.

With a great heave, the wyvern that had its barbed tail lodged deeply in its dead companion's chest extracted the stinger and began to advance on Miranda and Storm as the two remaining monsters joined it in a loose triangular formation. Storm kept shifting her position, ensuring that she always stood directly between Miranda and the advancing terrors.

"This human is under my protection. You will not harm her," the dragon growled.

Miranda's head started to spin. While the battle before her played out, in her mind's eye she saw a nearly identical scene enacted. Overcome, she fell to her knees. The slender, scarred blue dragon before her seemed to melt into a younger version of herself. She was shaking, staring wildly at three approaching creatures before her. Miranda could sense her fear and hopelessness, her desire to flee nearly overpowering a primal desire to protect.

The scorpion-tailed creature in the center let out a screech that snapped Miranda back to the present. The image of the younger dragon was gone, replaced by the real dragon in front of her, protecting her from the advancing nightmares.

"Never again," the blue said, tensing her muscles and readying to pounce on her enemy.

Miranda knew that Storm's first attack had caught the creatures completely off guard. This time they would be anticipating her. Miranda closed her eyes and reached out with her mind to the dragon; she wanted to warn her to not to try the same attack again. But when Miranda touched the blue's mind again, the fear she was feeling melted away and was replaced by a primal desire to fight, to protect, to kill. She began to tingle with energy as pure, raw electricity began to build throughout her body, moving rapidly toward a single spot, gathering deep in her chest. If she didn't find a way to release it soon, it would consume her. Yet there was a wall, dark and thick, that would not allow the energy to be released. Miranda pushed with her mind, but nothing happened. She pushed harder. The wall move slightly, but the intensity of the energy was becoming too much to bear; her whole body felt as if it were on fire. She heard a scream and realized it was coming from her own mouth. Her eyes flew open, and the pain dissipated immediately.

But the dragon in front of her wasn't so lucky. She was writhing in pain as small arcs of electricity crawled across her shimmering back. The three wyverns were starting to retreat, their eyes wide with fear.

Miranda heard the deep, steady beat of great wings behind them: another dragon. Within seconds, Red's massive form came diving over the canyon wall directly at her assailants. In a panic, they fell over each other trying to turn and take flight.

"*Not so fast, you filthy wannabes!*" Red yelled, landing by the nearest one. He grabbed its tail with his mouth and swung it hard to the ground. With a twist of his head, he ripped the end of its tail from the creature's flailing body.

Someone slid from Red's back and ran toward Miranda. She was expecting to see Billy or her grandfather, but to her surprise it was Justin, with a huge grin on his face.

"Did you see that? We were all like ... *whoosh* ... and *pow!*" he said, throwing punches in the air.

A gurgling wail made Miranda and Justin turn to watch Red rip the throat out of his fallen prey. "All righty then. That's totally disgusting," Justin said, turning away from the gory scene. His eyes went wide and he pointed at Storm. "What's wrong with her?"

Miranda turned to see the blue writhing on the ground, her eyes wild with fear, her mouth open but no sound coming out. Bolts of electricity arced around her body as the scales on her back vibrated rapidly. Her chest and abdomen were swelling to the point of bursting. Miranda ran toward her. The dragon shook her head, trying to warn Miranda away, to no avail. When she reached the dragon, the net of electricity extended and wrapped around her outstretched arm. Miranda turned one dancing bolt around in her hand. It felt hot and sent a tingling sensation throughout her body.

To her amazement it didn't hurt—and more important, it didn't kill her.

Miranda pressed forward until her hand was touching the dragon's body. She closed her eyes, reaching out to Storm with her mind. Storm's pain was almost overwhelming, and Miranda wanted to cry out, but she forced her way deeper through the building energy, trying to reach its origin. The closer she got to it, the harder it became to move ahead. Finally she saw it, a crackling ball of electricity. She visualized her hands reaching out and grabbing the sphere, willing it to dissipate.

When Miranda opened her eyes, the blue dragon was staring at her. The pain was gone from her face and there was no sign of the electricity. "*What ... did you do to me?*"

"I don't know. I wanted to help, and I felt the energy and tried to release it."

"*You touched a part of a domestic's mind that isn't supposed to be there. We can't use breath weapons and you turned on something that is impossible. I could not release the energy. It almost killed me.*"

Rapid movement of someone coming down the valley past the waterfall caught their attention. Billy was running as fast as he could toward them. Where had he been all this time? Miranda wanted to scream at him for not being there for her, but before she could, her brother ran to intercept him.

CHAPTER 26

JUSTIN
Not By Chance

"**H**EY, CREEP! YOU ALMOST got my sister killed," Justin spat, his fists clenched as he charged at Billy. "What are you talking about?" the older boy said, looking around and noticing the dead creatures littering the canyon for the first time. "Wait. What happened here?"

"Oh, like you don't know." Justin jabbed his finger at Billy's chest.

Billy's face flushed. "I don't know what happened, but if you keep poking me, I'll break that finger off."

Justin was too angry to even notice the threat. "Seems pretty convenient that you ask my sister to meet you here just when a bunch of …"

"*Wyverns,*" Red chimed in silently.

"… *Wyverns* decide to have a party in the canyon. And even more convenient that you just happened to show up *after* all the fighting was over."

"If I were you, I'd watch the accusations, twerp. I was on my way here, and I had a run in with Mr. DeSoto."

Justin took a step forward, so that he was only inches from

Billy. "You know what I think? I think you're a liar."

Billy's hands shot out at Justin, shoving him hard in the chest and causing him to stumble backward. As Justin fought to regain his balance, one foot caught on a rock. He crashed to the ground, the wind knocked right out of him.

As he lay there gasping for breath, Billy's face came into view above him. "Don't, for one second, presume to know anything about me, rich boy," he hissed, and stepped down on Justin's chest.

Justin fought to get Billy's weight off of him so he could breathe, but the bigger boy wouldn't budge. Justin began to panic, but just when he thought he was going to pass out, Billy was gone.

Justin rolled over onto his hands and knees, moaning. He slumped heavily, looking down at the muddy boot print on his chest.

"Get off of me, you dumb lizard!" Billy said.

Red had his massive front paws, claws extended, on Billy's chest, pinning him to the ground.

Justin groaned as he stood up.

The big dragon turned to Justin. *"Oh good, you're up. I'll hold this loser down so you can come over here and knock the wind out of him,"* Red said in his smoky voice.

Miranda poked her head around from the far side of the dragon, and said, "Don't crush him just yet. I need to ask him a couple of questions first." She paused to lean down until her face was only inches from Billy's. "Like where the heck were you when I was getting attacked by a pack of *wyverns?*" she screamed.

The sound of galloping horses caught Justin's attention. He turned to see his grandfather, Mr. O'Faron, and Mr. DeSoto rapidly descending the steep hill. The three experienced cowboys had little difficulty guiding their horses down the treacherous incline.

"What in Sam Hill is going on here?" Grandpa yelled as he dismounted and approached Red. "Let him up—now."

The red dragon snorted and turned to Justin. *"Your call, kid."*

The last thing Justin wanted was to see Billy set free, but he could see that his grandpa was getting ready to let loose on Red, and Justin's anger at Billy gave way to concern for his friend. "It's okay, Red. Let him up."

The large dragon nodded and slowly stepped back off the boy.

Billy scrambled to his feet, dusting himself off. Justin half expected Billy to lunge at him, or yell, or make up some story about how Justin had ordered Red to kill him or something. But he just walked away, glaring at Mr. DeSoto the entire time.

Their grandfather hurried over to Miranda. "How did—" His voice cracked and he had to pause to clear his throat. "What are you doing here?" He broke off again. "And what were you thinking, bringing the dragons out of the Warren? Maybe I made a mistake by allowing you full access to the drag—" He broke off as he noticed the beam from Mr. O'Faron's flashlight come to rest on one of the dead wyverns. He flicked on his own light and began rapidly scanning the area. Seemingly entranced, he walked over to one of the corpses and crouched down beside it. After a minute of dead silence, he turned to Red. "Is it you who took them down?"

"Red took care of the one over there," Justin said, pointing to where Mr. O'Faron was examining the wyvern with its throat ripped out. "She"—he pointed to the blue dragon crouched low in the shadows by the canyon wall—"must have killed the other two before we arrived."

Grandpa strode over to the blue. They stood together for a long moment, man and dragon, gazing unblinkingly into each other's eyes. Grandpa shook his head slightly and turn away from the blue without a word as the dragon looked away. Justin sensed her intense shame, which perplexed him. What had the dragon done to feel ashamed of? Before Justin could ask her, the slender beast launched herself into the dark sky and was gone.

Miranda joined Justin as their grandfather approached them. He turned to Mr. O'Faron, Mr. DeSoto, and Billy. "I've got the kids. You three go on back to the house and let the others know what happened. I'll have Red dispose of the wyverns' bodies."

The two older men hesitated for a moment. Mr. O'Faron was visibly shaken, and Mr. DeSoto licked his lips and looked around the canyon, his eyes narrowing. Grandpa gave the men a dismissive wave, and they led the horses back up the steep slope out of sight.

Billy held back and drew close to Justin. "Call me a liar again, McAdelind," he whispered harshly, "and I'll do more than knock you on your butt."

Justin flinched, but said nothing. He followed Billy with his eyes until the older boy was out of sight.

"What happened here?" Grandpa asked.

"There were five of those creepy wyvern dragon-thingies, and they tried to kill me, but two of them got away," Miranda explained. "If it hadn't been for Storm, I'd be dead."

"Seriously? What does a guy need to do to get some credit around here?" Red moaned, flopping down on the ground theatrically. *"Humph."*

Grandpa nodded, his face stony again, and his eyes returned to the spot where the blue dragon had been crouching moments before. Justin watched as the older man's rugged fingers traced the deep scars zigzagging down his face. He looked around the dark valley, then slumped, looking defeated. "I don't like this place much. Too many bad memories. I'd appreciate it if you two didn't come back here ever again."

He walked over to one of the fallen wyverns, lost in thought. Then, without any warning, he bellowed at the dead creature, a wordless anguished cry, and kicked it hard in the head. When the echoes of his shout faded, he walked around the wyvern, shining the beam of light on its head, neck, and back. "Did someone ask you to come here tonight?" Justin knew the question was aimed at his sister, and kept his mouth shut.

She hesitated before answering, "Yes."

"Who?"

"Billy," she said, looking down.

He seemed to consider this for a long moment, then nodded. "Okay." He walked over to the next wyvern and scanned it as he had the first. When he didn't find anything of interest, he asked, "How did Storm get here?"

Miranda looked at Justin, who shook his head and mouthed, *Not yet.*

"When the wyverns attacked, I screamed for help, and she came."

Their grandpa stood up and looked back over his shoulder at the roaring waterfall. "There's no way she would have been able to hear you. She must have followed you and been here in the canyon already."

Then he walked over to the biggest of the three dead wyverns, the one lying in a heap by the valley wall. He knelt to examine something closely, then beckoned to Justin and Miranda to come close. "See this?"

Justin and his sister looked closely at the back of the wyvern. Sharp spikes the length of baseball bats bristled down its bony spine—everywhere except in the space between its wings.

"Did the spikes there get knocked off when Storm threw

the wyvern against the canyon wall?" Miranda asked.

Grandpa shook his head. "Take a closer look."

Justin drew nearer and noticed that the missing spikes appeared to have been cut and filed down level with the animal's back. "Someone made it like this."

Grandpa nodded. "Which means this isn't a wild wyvern, it's a mount." He stood up and shone his flashlight around the ridge, his face grim. "It also means, this attack was no coincidence."

CHAPTER 27

JUSTIN
Of Course I Know Kung Fu

*A*FTER BREAKFAST ON THE MORNING following the wyvern attack, Justin had just been heading out to start his morning chores when he caught sight of the old cook standing in the shallow part of the river. She was up to her knees in the rushing water, shifting back and forth, her arms wheeling in a weird kind of dance.

"Mrs. Lóng, may I ask you a question?" Justin asked.

"Sure, dear."

"What are you doing?"

"My morning exercises. What does it look like I'm doing?" She made a motion like trying to push with both hands against an imaginary wall.

"It looks like you're trying to stop the river from flowing," Justin said with a smirk.

Mrs. Lóng stopped, sighed, and turned to look right at him with her piercing dark eyes. "Why, dear, that is exactly what I am trying to do."

Justin's first reaction was to smile, but when Mrs. Lóng kept looking at him instead of returning to her routine, he thought she might be serious. "For real?"

She continued to stare at him silently, then shook her head. "Of course not, child. Is there no such thing as sarcasm in New York City?"

Justin laughed. "In abundance. You're just a pro."

"Years and years of practice." She closed her eyes and began pushing the imaginary wall again.

"I guess I was wondering if you were doing some form of karate or something."

She stopped again and lowered her head, shaking it slightly. "No, my poor confused child, I am not doing karate. This is called t'ai chi. It is Chinese. Karate is Japanese."

Justin shrugged. "Looks kind of the same to me."

She held up a hand. "Okay. Please stop talking. Is there something you need before I am forced to drown you?"

Justin hesitated for a moment. He felt stupid asking a small old lady for help, but he didn't really know who else to turn to. "I want to learn how to protect myself."

Mrs. Lóng put her hands on her hips. "And you assumed, since I am Chinese, that what, I know kung fu or something?"

"But ... you were just ... I thought—"

She laughed in her musical way. "Oh, child, relax. I am teasing you. Of course I know kung fu. As a matter of fact, I know many forms, including the t'ai chi that I was just doing." She then crossed her arms and scowled at him. "Why do you want to know how to defend yourself? Did something happen?"

Justin's face flushed and he looked down. "I just think it's time I learn how to take care of myself."

Mrs. Lóng was splashing toward him now. When she stood only a foot away, she reached out a hand and gently raised Justin's chin until their eyes met. "What happened?"

"Billy shoved me last night and knocked me down, and now I can't even think about him without being afraid. It was humiliating." Justin felt tears welling. "I'm tired of being so weak. I hate being small. I hate being afraid all the time. I thought coming out here, I would finally get away from being picked on, the way I am at school, but it's even worse."

Mrs. Lóng placed both hands on his shoulders. "It's okay to be afraid. Fear keeps us from harm. Fear keeps us alive. But do not give into your fear, do not let it rule your actions. If you do, soon it will start to corrupt who you are, and you will become a slave to your fears." She pulled him into a hug. "Embrace your fear. Control it. Master it. And soon it will be your ally."

A sob escaped Justin's throat. "I just want to teach him a lesson. I want him to know he can't push me around."

Mrs. Lóng pulled out of the hug, but still held him. "I want to be very clear, child. I will teach you martial arts, but only so long as you agree to use your skills for self-defense." Her face softened. "What Billy did was wrong. He of all people should know not to hit a child, after the way his mother used to—" She broke off. "But I am not in the revenge business. If you want tips on that, talk to Mr. DeSoto. Do I make myself clear?"

Justin nodded. "Yes, ma'am. Self-defense only." Then he smiled at her. "But if he attacks me first, I can beat him down, right?"

Mrs. Lóng smiled wickedly. "Of course, dear."

* * *

Over the next week, Justin's schedule was jammed with activity. Chores in the morning, dragon-riding in the afternoon, cleaning up the burned acre in the evening, and martial arts lessons before bed. By the end of the day he was so exhausted, sleep came quickly. Unfortunately, so did the next morning.

Everything was going really well. Justin and Red were working on some advanced aerial maneuvers and stunt routines. The woods were almost cleared, thanks in no small part to the never tired and shockingly strong Mrs. Lóng. Justin would often stand and stare in awe as the petite Chinese lady cleared more wood that an entire lumber crew could, without even breaking a sweat. The self-defense training was exhausting, painful, sometimes humiliating—and almost always totally fun.

At first Justin was a little worried, as the first two lessons focused on nothing but the right way to stand, breathe, and make a fist. But he had watched enough movies to know this was all part of the deal. However, the cook surprised him on day three by showing him some holds and throws. Mrs. Lóng said they were going to spend their time focusing on basic self-defense and not on any single form of martial arts. She mixed wing chun, t'ai chi, and some modified kung fu into forms "focused on situations someone like Justin might find himself in," as she put it. Situations like facing a bigger, stronger opponent or, simply, Billy.

It was during one of these sessions that Justin found himself lying on his back, looking up at the painted sky of twilight, as Mrs. Lóng's face swam into view above him. "You all right, dear?"

Justin strained to sit up. There was a new sore spot in the middle of his back from where it had just made forceful contact with the earth. "That was awesome. I definitely need to know how to do that flip."

"It is really simple, like most of what you have learned, the key is using your opponent's force against them. Are you ready to try it against me?"

Justin laughed, "I think I need to see it a couple more times before I'll understand how you did it."

She nodded. "Very well. Face me again and try to punch

me in the nose."

After the first day of pulling his punches and trying not to actually hit the old lady, he realized there was nothing he could do to land a punch, even if he gave it everything he had. Justin bent his knees, adjusted his weight slightly until he felt balanced, balled his fist tight in the correct form and punched as hard and fast as he could. His fist shot past Mrs. Lóng's face as he felt her iron hands wrap around his wrist. The next thing he knew, he was once again staring up at the sky, but this time the sky was gone, having been replaced by thick clouds.

"What in Sam Hill is going on here?" said a deep, gravelly voice.

Justin scrabbled to his feet to face his grandfather. "Nothing, sir. We were just, um …"

"Exercising," the old cook said.

Grandpa shook his head. "Whatever." He addressed Justin. "If you're done getting your butt whipped by an old lady—"

"Hey!" Mrs. Lóng said, her hands on her hips.

Grandpa chuckled. "Relax, Ying. No harm intended. I'm far older than you are."

"Hardly," she said under her breath.

"Anyhow, if you are done here, I need your assistance," Grandpa said.

Justin eyed him suspiciously. Had someone else burned down something that needed cleaning up? "Seriously?"

Grandpa crossed his arms over his broad chest. "Yes, seriously. We have a situation on our hands, and Mr. DeSoto said you're turning into quite the dragon rider. I need your help."

Mr. DeSoto? Was the security chief watching him all the time too? That was just plain creepy. "You're serious?"

"Why do you keep asking me that, boy? Of course I'm serious," he said. "Now come on, I'll explain once we're inside."

Justin and Mrs. Lóng followed Grandpa into the study. The old man walked over to the mantelpiece, where he pushed something hidden and tiny on its top surface. Suddenly the painting over the fireplace slid up into the ceiling, revealing a large flat-screen television behind it.

Justin's jaw dropped. "Seriously?"

His grandfather's eyes narrowed. "Are you having a stroke, son?" He turned the TV and some kind of digital recorder on.

The old man has TiVo *too*? Justin thought. "You've had a TV all this time, and I've been reading my dad's stupid old books?"

"Of course we have a TV. How else do you think we watch the Broncos? Anyhow, the TV isn't what I wanted to show you. It's something Mr. DeSoto brought to my attention."

His grandfather turned up the sound. A news anchor was speaking somberly in front of an image of a mound of fur lying on a grassy field. "… Another bison was found mutilated today by rangers at the Rocky Mountain Arsenal National Wildlife Refuge, just north of downtown Denver. This is the third case this week of an animal in the preserve found cut open with all its internal organs removed. Investigators are at a loss as to who, or what, might be responsible for this. Very little blood was found on, in, or near the carcasses. Refuge officials are asking anyone who may have seen anything or have any information regarding who might be behind these attacks to please call Crime Stoppers at—" Justin's grandfather clicked the TV off.

"Okay, that's just gross. But what does that have to do with us? Aren't cattle mutilations the realm of the Men in Black or chupacabras or something?"

"All those legends come from some place. Animal mutilations, like this one, can only mean one thing. We have a wyrmling on the loose."

"You mean a *baby* dragon did that?" Justin asked, wide-eyed. "What is a baby dragon doing in Denver anyhow? I thought all the dragons were around here."

His grandfather nodded. "That's exactly what we're going to find out." He started toward the door. "But first we have to catch the little worm before this makes national news. Now stop asking questions, we need to mount up and ride."

Justin stopped dead in his tracks. "Whoa, whoa, whoa. What do you mean 'mount up and ride'? Are you saying we're flying dragons to Denver?"

"That's exactly what I am saying."

Justin rubbed his hands together vigorously as a smile quickly spread across his face. "Then what are we waiting for? Let's ride!"

CHAPTER 28

JUSTIN
Wyrmling Roundup

IN LESS THAN THIRTY MINUTES, Justin was riding Red above the low clouds that had moved in from the west, concealing their flight path from the ground all the way up to where some AWOL baby dragon was sucking the organs and blood out of a bison herd near Denver.

"We actually knew about this yesterday, but had to wait for the cloud cover to come in so we could move in undetected," Grandpa said, his voice sounding metallic over the wireless battery-powered headset Justin was wearing. They were flying in a close V formation, all sporting the same electronic gear. Justin and Red were on the far left, next to Miss D and Flare. His grandfather flew point on his massive gold dragon, Argo, and to the right was Mr. O'Faron on Thunder. On the far right was Billy on his black dragon, Nightshade.

"Justin, you'll be our spotter. The dragons will get us close, but once the wyrmling starts movin', we will need eyes on it," Miss D said.

Justin would have been having the time of his life, if it weren't for Billy being there too. To Justin's surprise, his nemesis didn't even acknowledge his presence. In fact Billy seemed distracted, scanning the night sky constantly.

"Grandpa, why isn't Mr. DeSoto with us?" Justin said. DeSoto always seemed to be nearby. Where was he now?

"He needs to keep an eye on the ranch and see if he can catch the varmint who's stealing from us," Grandpa replied.

Miss D motioned for Justin to switch channels on his headset so they could have a private conversation. When he gave her the thumbs up, she said, "Plus he's absolutely terrified of dragons, he is. Since he got his leg chomped off, an' all. He keeps a healthy distance from the lot of 'em."

Justin scrunched up his face. "Then why work on a dragon ranch? That seems like the last thing he would want to do."

Miss D thought about that for a moment. "Aye. Seems that way, doesn't it? I suppose you'll have to ask him that one. It may be all he knows, so he stays on at the ranch. Your father is a rarity among the families. He well may be the only bloke I've ever heard of who just walked away from this life. We'd best switch back to the main channel now. Don't want to be missin' anythin'."

Justin nodded and flew in silence for a while. Riding a dragon through the night sky, its powerful wings carrying him effortlessly onward, Justin had a hard time understanding why his father would have given this all up. "Just out of curiosity, how do we catch the baby dragon once we find it?" Justin asked no one in particular.

"Luckily for us," Miss D said, "we have several Wyrmling Roundup champions in our midst." She pointed with her chin toward the two O'Farons. Justin remembered the golden dragon trophies in the massive round room at the heart of the underground complex. Billy's name wasn't on them, but he had won them as a contestant at the last Dragon Rodeo for the McAdelind family.

"Has Grandpa won any trophies?" Justin asked, forgetting

he was talking on an open channel.

"*Humph!*" the old man said. "I won my fair share, but what's more important is, I have decades of *real* experience."

"*He was one of the best,*" Red said in his silent, smoky way. "*He stopped taking risks after—*"

"We're getting close. Keep alert, and stay in formation," Grandpa said, bringing everyone's focus to the task ahead.

Just in front of them, Justin could see the orange glow of a large city below the clouds. Realizing they were already over Denver, Justin turned to Miss D. "If I had known dragon-flying was this fast I would have asked Red to take me someplace a little more happening than La Garita."

"Aye, but if it were only that simple, boyo," the dragon trainer said with a wink. "If it were, I'd be in Cardiff every weekend gettin' together with me butties from university."

"Focus!" his grandfather said harshly. "We're here." Justin looked down and noticed a large dark area in the clouds. "Argo, got anything?"

"*Not yet,*" the old gold dragon said silently to himself, overheard only by Justin, while also shaking his massive head so that his human rider could understand.

"Okay. We will proceed down through the clouds and fan out. If you spot this little worm, call it out. Once we have a visual, William and I will engage." He looked around at all the riders. "Everyone got that?"

Justin stole a glance over at Billy, who was scanning the sky behind and above them. What was he looking for?

Justin's attention snapped back to reality as Red tucked his wings and entered a steep dive. They were knocked around by turbulence as they continued to free-fall through the seemingly endless damp clouds. Justin looked around for the others, but the cloud cover was too thick and he couldn't see more than a couple of feet in any direction. On a hunch, he tried closing his eyes and reaching out with his mind, and suddenly he could sense the dragons around him. Flare was to his left, but flying more slowly through the clouds and getting knocked around quite a bit more than Justin and Red were. Argo was farther away to the right and moving just as fast as Red. Justin could barely sense Thunder gliding effortlessly through the clouds. But when he tried to locate Nightshade, the dragon was nowhere to be found.

Justin opened his eyes just as they emerged below the cloud cover, and his heart almost stopped as he saw the ground rushing up to meet them. He tried to pull back on the horn of his saddle, but the big red dragon continued his downward plunge.

"*Red!*" Justin thought, as emphatically as he could.

"*Relax, kid. I know what I'm doing. Trust me. And would you please stop yelling in my brain!*"

Justin grabbed the two gullet grips and clenched his teeth, preparing for the inevitable impact. But Red's wings sprang out wide and caught the air like two giant parachutes, slowing their descent enough to pull into a fast glide, just high enough over the bushes and tall grass of the wildlife refuge to skim above them without grazing them.

Red turned his head slightly so he could look back at Justin. "*Told you. I've still got it. No skid marks. No one can track us, I don't care who tries.*"

"*Except for the trail of vomit I just left behind us …*" Justin relaxed his grip a little and sat up taller in the saddle. "*A little warning next time would be awesome.*"

"*I didn't want to interrupt your scanning for dragons.*"

"*Wait. You could feel that?*"

"*Not exactly feel, but I can sometimes see what you're thinking. You broadcast your thoughts sometimes. Which leads me back to the brain yelling. Cut it out. I can hear you just fine when you, uh, think at me.*" The big dragon beat his wings rapidly several times to gain altitude again as they sped low over the dark grassy plain, dodging the occasional tree.

"So, what are we looking for exactly? Can you see the wyrmling, or smell it, or something?"

"No. Part of our natural defenses when we are young is to be almost scentless, and really hard to spot when still. Your grandfather was exaggerating the ease of catching a wyrmling in the wild. It can take hours, even if you have twice as many riders as we have today." Red was silent for a moment, then added, *"We do have a secret weapon, however."*

"We do?" Justin asked, not remembering any mention of special dragon-detection gear.

"We sure do, kid. You."

"Me? How am I possibly a secret weapon? Are you going to stake me to the ground as bait?"

"Hmmm. That actually might work, but I was thinking more along the lines of your dragonspeaking ability. You're like a dragon-detecting radar. Remember how you told me you could feel Nightshade's intention to jump in front of you and Miranda? I imagine you could use that same kind of ability here. Dragons can't do what you can. When we speak to one another, it's like humans talking. We can talk, yell, and whisper mentally, but only up to a certain distance, half a dozen dragon-lengths if we're not distracted. You have a whole different thing going on. You can actually read our minds, and from what I can tell your mind-reading range is a lot greater than our dragonspeaking range."

Justin thought back to the night he and Miranda had snuck into the Warren, and then about the feeling he had just had in the clouds as he reached out to locate the dragons near him, even though he couldn't actually see them. *"I'll try."* He closed his eyes and visualized his field of vision spreading out all around him like ripples on a pond, pushing the edge farther and farther away and into the blackness beyond. Soon, he could feel Flare far behind him, slowly searching every inch of the land below her as she flew. Her desperate desire to look good by being the first to find the wyrmling was bordering on obsessive.

"*Flare's kind of a freak, isn't she?*" Justin said, his eyes still closed as he searched with his mind.

"*You have no idea,*" the big red dragon said with a sigh. "*This one time, a couple of months ago—*"

"*Sssh,*" Justin whispered, trying to concentrate. He had felt something. Something like fear, just at the very edge of his mental reach. "*Head slightly to the right,*" he said, and Red instantly made an adjustment to their course. The feeling of terror increased with each beat of Red's massive wings. With the other dragons, Justin usually sensed words or images, but now he sensed only an intense feeling of terror.

"*I don't see anything.*"

"*We're getting close. It's right ahead of us in that grove of trees. I can't read its thoughts, but it's very afraid.*"

"*Probably thinks we are going to eat it,*" Red said with a snort. "*Not uncommon for wilds to eat a rival's young.*"

"*Okay, that's pretty gross.*"

The dragon laughed. "*I suppose so. A lot of species do it. It's a way to ensure that a particular line continues. Survival of the fittest and all that Darwin jazz.*"

"*I should probably signal Grandpa—*" Justin felt something big moving quickly toward them from above and behind. He looked up, but the sky was so black now, he couldn't see anything. He quickly scanned all around and below but saw nothing. "*Okay, that's just weird. I don't see any—*" An intense desire to kill washed over him from something behind. "Red, move!" Justin yelled, and Red responded immediately, beating his wings hard to pick up speed and altitude.

"*What the—!*" The impact hit Red's underside so suddenly

that the air was forced from his lungs in a small explosion. The dragon's head lolled listlessly as he pinwheeled out of control toward the ground.

CHAPTER 29

JUSTIN
Get Along, Little Dragon

JUSTIN'S WHOLE BODY HURT from the jarring force of the attack. However, being strapped to the back of a huge, heavy dragon about to do a back flop onto the plain below made any kind of pain he felt disappear behind a veil of panic. "Red! Wake up!"

"... *Just five more minutes ...*"

"*Wake up now, you big lizard, before I'm a smear on the ground!*" Justin yelled into the dragon's mind.

They were close to the ground now, and Justin did the only thing he could think of, he closed his eyes and waited for the life to be crushed from him. Then he felt the dragon roll as he slammed hard into the saddle. Justin opened one eye, and looked around. They were on the plain, safe for the moment.

Red shook his head, trying to clear the fog away. "*What the heck hit me?*"

Justin scanned the sky. "*I have no idea. Whatever it was blends in perfectly with the night. It's not the wyrmling, is it?*"

"*Kid, if a baby dragon hit me with that much force, I don't want to meet it."* He shook his head. *"No, this was definitely something bigger. Do you see anything?"*

After making another fruitless scan with his eyes, Justin decided to try with his mind again. He reached out, and detected two creatures near the trees, one projecting nothing but raw fear, the other, an intense desire to kill.

"Up ahead. The baby and something bigger … hunting it … or …" Justin tilted his head to the side. There was definitely another creature out there besides the wyrmling—a dragon, he thought—but Justin couldn't quite read it. He could tell it was hunting something, but he wasn't sure that the baby dragon was the creature's intended prey. Was it hunting Red—and Justin too? A chill ran down his spine.

As if reading his thoughts, Red said, *"Time to call in reinforcements."* Then the dragon tensed every muscle in his body and sprang into the air, rapidly flying in the direction Justin had indicated.

Justin tried the headset. Static. He must be out of range. He closed his eyes and cried out "Argo!"—and, silently, *"Argo!"*—at the same time. As he looked into the moonless, starless night above, he still saw nothing but the shadowy shape of a grove of trees rapidly approaching. He decided to continue to use the one sense that seemed to be working the best. Closing his eyes and opening his mind, Justin felt the larger—it was a dragon, right?—ever more desperate to catch its prey. The baby dragon was on the move, running rapidly through the tall grass. So the wyrmling was the hunter's prey after all. *"We don't have a lot of time, Red, whatever hit us is closing in on the baby dragon."*

Ahead of them, there was a screech, and Justin sensed the dragon's anticipation of victory, of ripping into its prey. *"That sounded familiar. Like one of those wyverns from the canyon."*

Red surged forward. *"Indeed."*

They were close. Justin strained and could barely make out a shadow moving off into the sky. He tried to sense its intentions, but they were so close to the wyrmling now, all he could pick up is its terror. *"Red, we can't wait for the others. We need to try to catch the wyrmling before that thing comes back. What do I need to do?"*

"I'll show you," Red said. He showed Justin a rapid series of his own memories of a boy, maybe sixteen or seventeen, jumping off the dragon's back and onto a fleeing wyrmling. The boy grabbed the small horns protruding from the baby dragon's head and simultaneously pulled them hard to one side, all the while digging his boots into the ground to skid to a stop before binding the creature's flailing feet together with a silver rope.

"You're kidding, right?" Bile rose into Justin's throat. The back of his neck and cheeks felt hot.

"We should probably wait," Red conceded. *"Maybe we can place ourselves between them until your grandfather gets here."*

There was another screech, this one closer than the last. *"I'm not sure we can wait. I'll stop the wyrmling, you cover me."*

"Your call." They could hear the wyrmling's racing footsteps now. Red zigzagged back and forth, keeping as close to the wyrmling as possible as it ran swiftly through the tall grass. *"You ready, kid?"*

"I suppose so," Justin said with as much confidence as he could muster. He tried to stand up in his stirrups but was jerked back into place.

"Safety straps," Red said with a chuckle.

Justin unclipped the straps from his belt and immediately felt like he was going to die. *"This is a bad idea."*

"Well, of course it is, but why let that stop you now?"

Justin stood up clenching the saddle tight with his knees, trying to get a sense of how to anticipate Red's twists and turns. Below him, he could see the wyrmling clearly now.

It was larger than he had imagined it would be, about the size of a tiger, but moving at cheetah speed. Its wings were tucked back tight against its sleek body.

Justin tensed and readied to jump.

"Don't forget the rope."

Justin looked over at the silver coil strapped next to one of the saddlebags. *"What do I do with that?"*

"Well, you use it to tie the little worm up before he cuts you open like one of those bison."

Justin swallowed the vomit trying to force its way into his mouth. He unstrapped the silver rope. *"What's this made out of?"* Justin asked, gripping the unnaturally light coil of rope in his shaking hand.

Red shrugged, almost knocking Justin off his back with the motion. *"Not sure exactly. It's really strong though, and dragons can't break through it."*

Everything Red had just showed him vanished from his mind as the reality of his situation hit home. Justin was about to land on the back of an untrained baby dragon, which was much stronger and weighed a lot more than an eleven-year-old boy and could bring down a full-grown bison for dinner. Justin was going to die.

"Okay, get ready. One ... two ... Jump!"

Justin threw himself from the saddle and slammed onto the back of the wyrmling. He wrapped his arms around its long, slender neck. It let out a cry and stumbled, losing its balance, but kept running. All Justin could do was hold on for dear life. *"Now what? Red!"*

Red was keeping pace above them. *"Stop playing horsey and bring it down."*

"I got that. How?"

"Grab its horns and pull it to the side like I showed you."

Justin tried to wriggle his arms up to grab onto the small horns protruding from the back of the wyrmling's skull, but before he could wrap his fingers around them, the dragon bucked and almost threw him to the ground. Justin redoubled his grasp around the creature's neck. *"This is insane. I'm going to die and it's not even in a cool way. Death by baby dragon is completely lame!"*

"Well, at least it's death by dragon. That's pretty cool, right?"

"Not helping."

"Try for the horns again."

Justin started to reach up, and again the wyrmling bucked. This wasn't going to work. He closed his eyes and reached out to the little dragon with his mind. He could feel how terrified it was, how all it wanted to do was escape. Whatever was out there, he wasn't going to let it hurt the wyrmling. He hadn't been able to stop the bullies who had harassed him at school, but he and Red could stop whatever was trying to harm this little guy.

Justin was so lost in thought, he failed to notice that they had stopped moving. He opened his eyes. The wyrmling was looking back over its shoulder at him, wide-eyed. Justin could no longer sense fear in the small dragon, only sadness.

Justin slid off its back and knelt on the ground so they were eye to eye. "I'm not going to hurt you. I know you're scared. We're here to take you home," he said, realizing he wasn't certain whether baby dragons could understand human speech the way the adults could. Regardless, the wyrmling let out a soft snort and sat down in front of him.

Red landed a short distance away and slowly stalked closer. *"Not exactly how I've seen it done in the past, but whatever you did worked."*

"It's just scared."

"She's just scared." The large dragon corrected him.

Justin reached out and gently stroked the side of the wyrmling's snout. The small beast leaned into his touch, rubbing her cheek against his hand. Justin gave the dragon a quick once over, looking for injuries. *"That's weird."*

"What's weird?"

"She's not injured. Not a scratch."

Red sniffed the air. *"I smell fresh blood. Maybe whatever hit me is still out there."*

A symphony of beating wings signaled the arrival of the rest of their party. Justin kept sending protective feelings toward the baby dragon to keep it calm. There were footsteps behind him. Justin turned to see his grandfather standing nearby. Justin heard a click, then the beam of a flashlight hit the ground near the wyrmling, startling her. Justin reached out again to stroke her cheek.

"Back away, son, slowly."

"It's all right, she's just scared. But I have her calm now."

Grandpa moved closer to Justin's side, studying the dragon. After a moment he said quietly, "I'm not sure what in that little mind of yours thought going after the wyrmling by yourself was a good idea, or how you're even sitting here like this with her. But I'm going to let that slide. We've got a bigger problem."

"Do you mean the other creature?"

"What other creature?" He shook his head. "Never mind, you can explain later. No, look at her, what do you see?"

Justin studied the dragon closely. Her hide was a mottled blue-gray, and she had a short neck, nubby little horns, and round pupils. "She's a domestic," he said. "How in the world did she get here?"

Grandpa leaned in closer. "Not just any domestic," he whispered. "One of *ours*. This was the first thing stolen from the ranch the day before you and your sister arrived." He paused for a moment, looking around at the rest of the party standing just outside of earshot. "The real question isn't *how* she got here, but *who* brought her here, and more important, *why?*"

Justin looked over at Billy, still on Nightshade's back, barely illuminated by the reflected light from his grandfather's flashlight. The dragon was so dark, Justin could barely make out his outline in the moonless night. Then he noticed something. There was dirt on the dragon's belly, as if it had slid into home base somewhere along the way. Justin narrowed his eyes and said under his breath. "Oh. I think I know who. But I have no idea why."

CHAPTER 30

MIRANDA
The Key

MIRANDA BOUNCED A TENNIS BALL off the stone wall outside Storm's lair for about the millionth time, catching it with no effort from her position seated on the cold floor. Every once in a while, she would try something really complicated, like bouncing it off the floor, then the ceiling, then the far wall, then back to her. But she didn't really feel like getting up and chasing it down the corridor on her rare miss, so she kept most of the throws pretty basic today.

Miranda had been trying to talk to Storm for days now. At first she had tried asking politely; when that approach met with utter silence, she tried entering Storm's lair. That had been a disaster, starting with a swipe of a tail and ending with Miranda on all fours trying to get her breath back. Yelling and insults hadn't worked either. Neither had begging. Storm just wouldn't talk to Miranda. The dragon was stubborn in the extreme. Unfortunately for Storm, so was Miranda. "Eventually you're going to have to talk to me. I am even more pigheaded then you are. You just don't realize it yet!" Miranda yelled back over her shoulder at the stall door.

The blue dragon had saved her life in the canyon. When Miranda had needed someone most, Storm had been there for her. She wanted to thank her rescuer, but more than that, she felt a strong connection to the dragon, and knew that Storm felt the same way. They were tied together, connected somehow, and Miranda wanted to know why. But the stubborn dragon wouldn't even acknowledge her presence.

Miranda closed her eyes and rested her head against the cold wall. It had been a long couple of days. She had had to work with Billy in the sables, and the massive amount of energy she had to expend to stay angry at him was exhausting. The cuter the boy, the bigger the jerk. What was wrong with them? It had to be something to do with testosterone. Her dad wasn't like that though; maybe something happened to boys when they finally become men. There is no way her mom would have put up with Billy's behavior.

The thought of her parents made Miranda suddenly very sad. She was terrified that something had happened to them. They had never gone this long without calling—not even when they were on one of their remote digs somewhere in the Middle East. What made it worse was that she and Justin had no way of contacting them, no idea where they were, no idea when they would come and get their children. Miranda remembered the image of her father tied to the pillar. Is that where he was now? Chained to a rock somewhere underground, broken and bleeding? Had the vision been a premonition and not just a crazy dream? What could she do to help him? Nothing. She was so weak.

"You are far from weak."

Miranda jumped. Storm's proud head was barely visible in the dark shadows of the lair.

"You don't know me that well," Miranda said, wiping her eyes with the back of her sleeve.

Storm inclined her head slightly and said, *"Perhaps."* She took a step forward into the corridor, her sleek blue-gray scales shining under the fluorescent lights. The dragon's huge round eyes, similar in color to Miranda's own deep blue, watched her intently. *"But the girl I fought for the other night had enough courage for the both of us."*

Miranda looked down at the ground. "So it took me bawling my eyes out to finally bring you out of hiding?"

The dragon pushed the door all the way open with her snout. *"Please come in. You are right, it is time we talk."*

Miranda followed Storm into her spacious cavelike home. The only light came from the corridor beyond, casting deep shadows in all the corners. However, there was enough light to clearly see the lattice of scars all across Storm's scaly back. The dragon seemed to have sensed her gaze and quickly turned, hiding her back in the shadows, then sat on her haunches like a huge cat, with her tail curled around her front paws.

"Did you get hurt the other night?" Miranda said, sinking down opposite the dragon against the wall, beside the door.

"I think you know those scars are not from the other night. But you are correct, in a way. I was in pain from the other night and did not want to be disturbed." Storm tilted her head and regarded Miranda for a long moment. *"Some wounds are deeper than others."*

"So, why talk to me tonight? I've been trying to get through to you for a week."

"Because I saw your heart open up and you ... you remind me of someone who was very special to me."

"I wanted to thank you for saving me from the wyverns the other night."

"I know."

"So why didn't you just let me?"

"*Because I don't deserve thanks.*" Storm turned to the door. "*Someone comes.*"

At first Miranda couldn't hear anything, but gradually she perceived the sound of booted feet clomping down the long corridor and muffled voices deep in conversation. She started to rise, but Storm gestured with a raised front paw for her to stay seated.

Moments later, Miranda heard her grandpa barking out orders near the open door. "William, I want you and Billy to take the wyrmling to the nursery. Justin, Gwen, please come with me." This was followed by the sound of footsteps walking away down a distant corridor.

Miranda leaned away from the wall. "Is—"

"*Silence,*" the dragon whispered harshly. "*The O'Farons remain outside my lair.*"

"I need to know we are on the same side here." Mr. O'Faron said, sounding exasperated.

"What side would that be? The one where you get everything you want and I get kicked to the curb?" Billy replied.

"This isn't about you."

Billy laughed humorlessly. "It would be nice if something, *anything,* ever was."

"You have no idea what you're talking about."

"No, I know exactly what I'm talking about. Putting family first. *Our* family. Isn't that what you've taught me? And here you are, sacrificing everything to get what *you* want. Now get your hands off of me!"

"You're just too young and stubborn to understand. I'm warning you, Billy—"

"And I'm warning you, Dad. Don't touch me again, and don't get in my way. I can take care of myself. I've gotten quite good at that," Billy hissed.

The sound of Billy hurrying away down the corridor was

followed by a series of curses from Mr. O'Faron before he too departed.

"*They are gone*," Storm said, curling up on the floor with her front paws curled neatly underneath her.

Miranda realized she had been holding her breath and let the air escape slowly through her teeth. "What was that about?" she whispered.

Storm snorted. "*I feel sorry for Billy. He has had a hard life, he deserves better than that.*"

"Do you know what they were talking about?" Miranda said, standing and walking over to Storm.

Storm closed her eyes, lifted her nose, and sniffed delicately. "*They have left the area. Go now while the coast is clear.*"

Miranda crossed her arms over her chest. "You're joking, right?"

The dragon's eyes opened slightly. "*I never joke. Go. Now.*"

"Fine." Miranda turned and stomped out the door, which Storm closed quietly but decisively behind Miranda with her tail. She turned. "But I'll be back every day, so you'd better get used to having company." She started to leave but stole one last glance at Storm's lair, then took a deep breath and exhaled slowly. This was going to take time. She just had to be patient. They were finally talking—which was progress.

* * *

Miranda cut through the trophy room on her way to find her brother. The light was dimmer in the large circular space than in the other rooms and corridors. She walked instinctively over to the section of shelves inexplicably void of trophies. Miss D had said there had never been anything there, but faint perfect circles of less dust indicated otherwise. There had been trophies there, Miranda was sure of it, just not for some time. But why were they missing?

Miranda walked over to the next set of shelves. The dust was thick here too, but there were rows of trophies all labeled MCADELIND. She looked across the rotunda to the shelf that held Billy's gleaming new trophies. Surely, these couldn't be Billy's too. They were way too old.

There was the sound of a door shutting in the distance, down the dark back corridor. Miranda slipped quickly up the spiral stairway that went nowhere. She quickly climbed until she was hidden in shadow but still had a view of the trophy room.

A man in a black cowboy hat with his back to her walked out of the dark corridor that led to the locked-off area of the subterranean complex. He paused for a moment in the middle of the room, looked down each of the adjacent passages, then walked quickly over to the empty shelves. He pulled something small out of his pocket, stood on his tiptoes, and placed it at the back of the highest shelf, well out of sight. Then he turned and headed toward the corridor that led out of the Warren. Before he left, he turned and looked behind him.

Miranda instinctively ducked down deeper into the shadows. The man didn't look up. He sighed, took a handkerchief from his back pocket, and removed his hat: Mr. O'Faron. He wiped the sweat from his forehead, then walked quickly out of the room.

Miranda waited several minutes before walking back down the spiral staircase. She glanced down the corridors: no one. She walked over to the empty shelves and climbed up them like a ladder until she could reach the topmost one. Lying in the far back corner was an old-looking key.

"Uh … What are you doing?"

Miranda almost fell from fright. Justin was staring up at her, one eyebrow raised.

"You scared the crap out of me. I didn't even hear you."

Justin put his hands together in prayer position and bowed low. "I'm a ninja, remember?"

"Right. Is anyone else behind you?"

Justin looked over his shoulder. "That's a negative."

"Good," she said, grabbed the key and dropped to the ground.

"What are you doing there? Storing nuts for the winter?"

"Wow. I almost forgot how funny you are. I was getting this." She tossed him the key.

He turned it over, examining it closely. "What does it unlock?"

Miranda smiled. "That is what we're going to find out. Come on."

Justin shook his head. "Do you have any idea how late it is? It's almost two in the morning. Besides, I can't." He handed the key back to her. "Grandpa is waiting for me. He's walking me back to the house. I told him I wanted to look at Dad's trophies first."

Miranda crinkled her face. "Meeting Grandpa? What did you do this time? Is your punishment dusting this place? Because if it is, it might take longer than cleaning up the woods."

"Nice. I'm not in trouble. Actually ... I kind of kicked butt tonight," he said, smiling broadly.

"Are you sure you don't mean, you got your butt kicked?"

"Who's the comedian now? I do have some skills, you know." He pounded his chest with a fist. "I singlehandedly captured an escaped dragon."

"Whatever."

"As hard as it may be to believe, I jumped off Red's back in midflight and landed on the back of a wyrmling, brought it down ... sort of ... and captured it." He blew on his fingertips, then rubbed them on his chest. "I know. I'm awesome." He looked around at the shelves. "Anyhow, I wanted to look at Dad's trophies. Wyrmling Roundup was his event at the dragon rodeos. Miss D said he was awesome."

"Really?"

"I know, hard to picture Dr. Robert McAdelind doing anything crazy or … you know … physical, but apparently it's what Thunderbird Ranch is known for. Grandpa was really good at it, and Billy won the event this past year, and apparently Mr. O'Faron was really good at it too.

Miranda looked back at the old trophies with no name on them. "So these must be Mr. O'Faron's."

Justin turned to look, "Probably."

Miranda held up the key. "So is this."

"You mean that key is Mr. O'Faron's?"

"I hid and watched him come from back that way and stow it up there."

Justin looked down the dark back corridor. "I saw him disappear down there about a week ago too, but Mr. DeSoto was here, and I couldn't follow him. He said Grandpa has the only key though."

"Obviously not." She smiled. "I bet that's where he's keeping the stolen stuff from the ranch. No one would ever think to even look back there. Sure you don't want to keep Gramps waiting a little longer?"

Justin looked over his shoulder toward the exit. "I can't. We'll also need some flashlights. I went back there once. It's pitch-black." He frowned. "Plus, I don't think Mr. O'Faron is the thief. He's kind of weird and quiet. But he seems completely dedicated to Grandpa."

Miranda shook her head. "He delivered a package to the dracs, he's been sneaking in and out of a place that is supposed to be locked, and he and Billy got in a huge fight tonight, something about being faithful to the family. He's definitely up to something." She sighed. "But okay." She carefully climbed up the shelves again and placed the key back exactly where she had found it. "We'll go back there tomorrow and see what we can find. Deal?"

Justin glanced nervously down the dark corridor. "Deal."

CHAPTER 31

MIRANDA

History Lesson

THE NEXT MORNING, MIRANDA was back on stable duty with Billy. He was brooding, in an even darker mood than he had been in ever since the wyvern attack.

"So, where were you last night?" he asked, finally breaking the silence.

"Oh, so we're talking again?" Miranda said, not looking at him.

"Only if you want to." He held up his hands in mock surrender.

"I was reading," she said, lying. Miranda wasn't quite ready to give up the silent-treatment punishment she had imposed on Billy, but she knew that if she wanted to find out what had happened between him and his father the night before, she was going to have to give in a little. "What about you?"

"We flew up to Denver to capture an escaped wyrmling," he said, shrugging as if this were an everyday thing.

"How do you think it got there?"

He paused, looking down at the ground. "Your guess is as good as mine."

What is he hiding? Miranda wondered. "Was it the stolen one?"

Billy shrugged again. "Seems that way."

Justin had already told her that the baby was most certainly the missing Thunderbird Ranch dragon when they had walked back to the house with their grandfather the night before. "Where else could it have come from?"

Billy frowned. "I don't know. If you're so curious, why don't you ask our so-called head of security?"

"He just seems weird to me, that's why."

Billy stared at her for a moment, then went back to mucking out the stalls. Miranda was very thankful that the dragons didn't need cleaning up after. They had their own special self-flushing "toilets"—for lack of a better term—in the Warren. After dealing with horse poop on a daily basis as part of her round of chores, she couldn't even imagine the mountains of waste that full-grown dragons must produce.

She sighed. The subtle approach wasn't getting anywhere with Billy. Time to switch tactics. Maybe something more direct. "So, how are things with your dad?"

Billy stopped. "My dad? How are things with my dad?" His face flushed. "He's a selfish, self-centered idiot, who is willing to squander away what little we have for a—" He stopped and looked at the ground.

"A *what*? What happened?"

Billy shook his head. "It's a long story, and I really don't want to talk about it."

"Okay, but if you ever do—"

"I don't." He strode from the stable in a huff.

"What did your father do to you, Billy O'Faron?" Miranda muttered to herself.

* * *

After lunch, Miranda caught up with her brother in the Warren. Justin was just finishing takeoff-and-landing practice with Red when she walked into the Grand Corral.

Miss D waved her over to where she was standing next to a very sulky Flare. "Hi-ya, Miranda. Haven't seen you around in a bit," Miss D said. "Finally ready to give dragon ridin' a go, are you? Come an' have a watch until you're up."

Miranda shook her head. "I'm content just seeing my brother excel at something for once. I would hate to embarrass him."

Flare snorted. *"Brazen words for someone who has yet to prove herself capable of anythin'."*

Miranda scowled at the young dragon. "I was joking."

"Aye, I got that, Miranda," Miss D replied, her eyes fixed on Justin and Red. "I'm not completely daft, an' as unlikely as it might seem, we actually have this thing called sarcasm in Wales too. Excellent landin'! Now, let's try the jump start once more."

Miranda had no idea how you "jump-started" a dragon, but the idea sounded interesting. Granted that the blue ones definitely had that electric thing going on, but Red's breed, well at least their *wild* dragon counterparts, breathed fire. Miranda watched attentively as the big dragon crouched low to the ground, then suddenly leaped straight into the air, beating his wings rapidly to gain altitude. The entire time Justin was in perfect sync with its movements. "Oh, I get it. Hah. He jumped to start flying, instead of running."

Flare shook her head. *"It's remarkable you can even stand there an' talk at the same time without passin' out."*

Miranda glared at her.

"What else did you think it meant?" Miss D asked, her attention still focused on Justin and Red.

"You know, like a car— Never mind."

"Okay, Justin! That was tidy. Now let's try a high-speed—" Miss D was cut off by the sound of klaxons blaring throughout the underground complex. Flare sprang into action, putting herself between the corridor to the main doors and her mistress. Red and Justin landed lightly near Miranda.

"What's that noise?" Justin yelled.

Miss Ddraig shook her head. "No idea!"

Mr. DeSoto came running into the Grand Corral, an automatic rifle in his hands. His limping gait was more pronounced when he ran, Miranda noticed. "Did anyone come in here?" he said, his eyes darting around the massive chamber.

"No! Cisco, what's going on?" Miss D asked.

"We had another break-in," Mr. DeSoto said. "I have a team guarding the main entrance, so this time we're going to catch the dirty thief. I'll need the three of you to come with me. Once you're cleared, we're going to do a sweep of the entire place. We got him this time." He stroked his thin mustache.

Miranda looked toward the corridor that led to the trophy room. "Is someone guarding the back entrance?"

Mr. DeSoto gave a wicked smile. "That's the beauty of this place. There is no back entrance. Now if you please, you three come with me. You two"—he pointed to the dragons with an expression of disgust—"get back to your lairs."

Flare growled. *"I will not be ordered around by a damaged ape."*

Mr. DeSoto took an unsteady step back and raised his gun at the dragon.

Miss D yelled and placed herself in front of Flare. "Lower your gun. Now!"

Red nudged the younger dragon toward the door. *"Let's not make this any worse than it already is."*

But Flare refused to budge. *"How dare he order me around like a common dog!"*

Red snorted. *"Your ego is totally out of control. We will comply because obedience is important to the humans we serve. Now come, wyrmling, before you make matters worse."* He stalked off ahead of the others.

Miss D shot DeSoto a murderous look and placed a reassuring hand on the dragon's neck. "It's okay, girl. Just ignore the sledge with the gun. They'll catch the thief an' it'll all be over soon enough."

Flare held her head up high and followed Red down the corridor.

The siren continued to wail deafeningly as the four humans walked to the main entrance. Standing at the door were three men Miranda recognized as members of the ranch's security detail. Each was holding an automatic rifle at the ready.

"What exactly did they take this time?" Miranda asked, as Mr. DeSoto tried to pat down the dragon trainer, like a police officer at a drug bust.

"Another egg, and some gold."

Miss D batted his hands away. "That's quite enough, thank you very much."

He scowled at her. "You could have stowed the egg when the sirens went off, but the gold might still be on your person."

"Come off it, Cisco," Miss D said. She turned to Miranda and Justin. "Kiddies, turn out your pockets an' pull up your pant legs so Inspector Clouseau here can see that you're not hidin' a thirty-pound bar of gold in your clothes." She glared at Mr. DeSoto. "Or are you satisfied that the McAdelinds aren't stealin' their own money?"

The security chief's face darkened and he narrowed his eyes. "Funny you should mention *McAdelinds* and *stealing* in the same sentence." Then, apparently remembering there were people other than the dragon trainer present, he smiled broadly and said, "I'm not worried about the kids, Gwen. But you ..." He let his voice trail off and turned to the men at the door. "Let them through, they're clean."

"Come on, let's get out of here an' let the thugs to their work," Miss D said, pushing her way through the armed men.

When the three were outside in the open air, she shot a dirty look back in the direction of the security team. "Did you see that daft idiot pull a gun on Flare? I have a mind to tell Lord McAdelind about this straight away."

"What did he mean by 'Funny you should mention McAdelinds and stealing in the same sentence'? Did we take something?" Justin asked, as they walked down the path to the Warren's main gate.

"Let's just say the dragon families have complex relationships an' leave it at that." Miss D stopped as if considering something and looked back at the main entrance to the underground complex. "You know, I never really thought much on it, but all this land belonged to Cisco's family generations ago."

"You mean like the McAdelinds bought it from the DeSotos?" Miranda asked.

"Well, no, not really. Old family drama an' the like. You've heard of the conquistadors?"

Both Miranda and Justin nodded.

"Well, some of those blokes were not only interested in God, gold, and glory. A few were from one of the dragon families sent over to the New World to see if dragons were indigenous here. As it turned out, not only were there dragons in North and South America, but there was also a Native American nation who had worked to keep 'em under control."

"Wait. You mean Native Americans were riding dragons

before Columbus came to America? That's insane," Justin said with a laugh.

Whatever Native American nation that was, Miranda had a sneaking suspicion their mom was one of them.

"More insane than the fact there are dragons at all?" Miss D said, raising an eyebrow.

"Point taken," Justin conceded. "Go on."

"Anyhow, Cisco's family was responsible for all the dragons west of the Mississippi an' in Central an' South America."

"What about east of the Mississippi?"

"That's where your family comes in, boyo. By right, the Drake family had claims on what became the United States, but instead decided to grant temporary guardianship to the DeSoto family. There wasn't a huge risk for the Drakes to lose power or control of the New World, because there weren't any dragons left on the east coast. That was early in the eighteenth century. Now, fast-forward a hundred years. The young United States bought a huge piece of territory from France—"

"The Louisiana Purchase," Miranda interjected.

"An' they say you Yanks don't know your history." The young trainer winked and continued. "For some unknown reason, High Lord Drake turned over his claim on the U.S. to a small dragon family from Scotland named McAdelind."

"Why?" Justin asked, struggling to keep up with Miss D's long strides.

"Aye, mun. Did you not catch the part about 'some unknown reason' a second ago? No one knows, an' if they do, no one ever tells. Which is not really a rare thing among the dragon families—secrets are the nature of the business. Anyhow, your many-great-grandfather herded the wild dragons in the plains to the mountains of what is now Colorado. I imagine the DeSoto family was none too happy about losin' control of all the Americas, but probably even less so about losin' all the gold here in Colorado."

"Did they fight each other?" Justin asked, eager for a story about battle.

Miss D smiled. "Aye, they did, but that is not how these things are settled among the families. The United States was expandin' rapidly, manifest destiny, mind, an' the McAdelinds were aligned with the side that was winnin' the push westward. By the mid-eighteen-hundreds the DeSoto family's territory was now south of the Rio Grande, an' all this territory became your family's responsibility." She paused and stretched her back, tilting her arms from side to side above her head. "But does Cisco's family feel like they've been robbed—?" She let the question hang for a moment. "Maybe. Maybe not. I've not heard a word about it, an' Cisco has worked for your grandfather for over a decade."

"So, even given that motive, you don't think he could be the person stealing everything?" Justin asked.

Miss D laughed. "Aye, no. Cisco is many things, but a thief? He can't bloody well steal the land out from under your family, can he? An' I don't see what he could hope to gain from liftin' some dragon eggs an' gold. If he tried to set up his own ranch, the Council would shut him down straight away." She looked up at the setting sun. "Enough spoutin' then. Time to eat. We'll continue our studies before bedtime."

CHAPTER 32

JUSTIN
The Secret Room

J USTIN AND MISS D RETURNED to the Grand Corral
to continue his training after Mr. DeSoto had come by
the ranch house after dinner to report that there was
no sign of the thief anywhere. When Grandpa had started
bellowing that his head of security was an incompetent
nincompoop and threatened to fire him, Miss D and her
pupil took that as their cue to make a discreet exit.

However, their evening training session appeared to be
doomed from the start, and they decided to call it quits
after Justin almost decapitated himself. Miss D had been
guiding him through the rings course, trying to get him
comfortable with another one of the Dragon Family Rodeo
competition events, when the accident happened. Ring
racing—the dragon equivalent of show jumping for horses—
involves flying through a series of giant hoops hanging from
the ceiling by thick wires at different heights and facing in
different directions. To complete the course, the dragon
and rider must fly through the rings in the correct order,
without touching any part of them, in the shortest time

possible. Points are deducted for missing a ring or touching it, and extra points are awarded for doing as many tricks as possible between the hoops. This is of course where everything went wrong.

Practice was going very well until Justin got confused on the order of the rings and guided Red into a corkscrew heading toward the wrong ring. Red, who *did* know the correct order, but was trained to respond to the commands of his rider, tried to pull out of the aerial maneuver early and correct their course. Unfortunately this meant that he headed directly into one of the wires. If the dragon hadn't been so experienced and pulled up just enough to catch the wire full force on the chest himself, they would have been carting Justin off in two boxes. Despite shaking so badly he could hardly stand, Justin wanted to get right back on and try the event again.

Red, however, insisted on calling it a night. *"I know how much you love crashing dragons into things, kid, but I'm calling it quits before one of us, most likely me, ends up dead."*

Justin was just about to argue when he saw Miranda standing near the entrance to the corridor that led to the trophy room, beckoning for him to follow her before she disappeared through the archway. Justin understood: now was their chance to see what Mr. O'Faron was doing in the locked, off-limits section of the underground complex.

Red had already left the Grand Corral, off to wherever he spent his free time. Once when Justin had asked to see his lair, Red just changed the subject. Later when Justin asked Miss D where the dragon's lair was, she said it didn't really matter, because Red was never there.

Making certain that Miss D was still preoccupied with taking off Flare's tack, Justin slipped into the corridor and began sprinting on tiptoe to the trophy room. But when he got there, it was completely empty. Walking to the center of the circular chamber, he peered down each of the four corridors connected to it. The passageway directly opposite the one leading to the Grand Corral led to the wild dragons' exercise arena—another massive underground cavern. To Justin's left was the way to the exit, and to his right, the dark back corridor that led to a locked door. Justin couldn't help but glance over at the statue representing the figure he thought of as the Dragon Lady. She was as creepy as ever, with her knowing smile and eyes that seemed to follow him everywhere.

"What are you smiling about?" Justin said out loud. "Do you know something—"

"Boo!"

Justin spun to see his sister standing behind him. She held a lit flashlight just below her chin, making her face look even scarier than usual. "What's wrong with you? You gave me a heart attack." He grabbed his chest and staggered backward.

Her lips turned up slightly into a devilish grin. "Who's the ninja now?"

Even though he kind of felt like punching her for scaring him, it was good to see her smile. There hadn't been a lot to be happy about lately. "Where did you appear from?"

"I was just up those stairs in the shadows. A surprisingly good hiding place, if I do say so myself." She tossed Justin one of the two flashlights she was holding, flipped on her own and shone it down the dark passageway. "Come on, let's see what good old Mr. O'Faron is hiding back there."

Justin switched on his light as well, glanced once more at the unnervingly grinning statue, and quickly followed Miranda down the cobweb-festooned corridor, following a clear trail of recent boot prints in the gray dust.

When they reached the rusty iron door at the end of the corridor, Miranda reached in her pocket and pulled out the key she had watched Mr. O'Faron hide. "I got this from the shelf while I was waiting for you," she said, then paused. "You ready?" she asked, more to herself than to Justin. She took a deep breath, put the key in and turned. *Click.* She exhaled and pushed against the enormous door. It swung open easily and without a sound, opening into a small chamber with several passageways leading from it.

The air in this section of the underground complex was different—cooler, slightly stale-smelling, and more humid. The light from the flashlights dissipated quickly down the long corridors, making them all seem infinite. There were no signs of the renovations that had been made over the years in the other section of the Warren, no recessed fluorescent lights lining the ceilings, no fancy security systems, only the occasional empty light socket dangling from lines of tacked-up electrical wire and lair doors left ajar on rusty hinges.

"Now where?" Miranda asked.

"This way," Justin said, indicating the trail of boot prints that led into one of the passageways with a flick of his flashlight.

"Nice one," she said, and took the lead.

They walked for a little while. The path turned left, then right again. Justin was beginning to think he might have missed something when the trail stopped in front of a well-maintained, closed lair door, which looked almost new compared with the others. "What do you think's behind there?" he asked, taking a step back. "You don't think he's keeping a dragon back here, do you?"

Miranda shook her head. "I'm willing to bet it's the missing eggs and gold." She reached for the door handle. "But there's only one way to find out," she said, yanking hard on the door and sliding it back with little effort.

Justin peeked around the edge of the door and quickly scanned the interior with his light, ready to turn and run. But nothing came flying out at him. The room was so deep and dark, he couldn't see anything inside at all. Miranda joined him as he took a step closer to the edge of the doorway to investigate further. At the very back of the space, his light reflected off several objects. "Do you think that's the missing gold?"

"Looks like it might be," Miranda agreed. They stepped gingerly inside. Their flashlights revealed boxes stacked against the back wall, a table with dozens of golden Dragon Rodeo trophies in neat rows, freshly polished and gleaming, and pictures and maps pinned to the wall. They were both drawn to a large world map with pushpins carefully connected by strings in several colors. Each pin secured a collection of newspaper clippings, pictures, and handwritten notes, some of them yellowed and curled up with age.

"What do you suppose this is?" Miranda asked.

"You see this all the time on crime shows," Justin said, "It's a way to keep track of timelines and connections between events and people." He reached up and pulled off a note that looked new, pinned near Manhattan. Scratched out on the top was *Robin?* and added below, *Robin, Kaya, and kids!* The last word was underlined several times.

"Okay," Miranda said, looking over Justin's shoulder. "That's a little creepy. Do you think he was looking for Dad"—she gulped—"or *us*? Maybe he was the one who let the drac know where we lived?"

Justin looked back up at the wall again. "I don't think so." He pointed to a tiny note pinned to southern Mexico: "See there." Then to someplace in Europe: "And there." Then a place in England: "And there. They all have the same thing written on them: 'Em.' Actually, it's written all over the place. What the heck is an 'Em'?" Justin scrunched his face. "Wait a second. These are all places Mom and Dad have been recently."

"I found a note under my bed to an 'Em.' They have to be

the same person." She glanced back down at the trophies. "And these are all for an 'M. McAdelind,' from around the same time as Dad's." She snapped her fingers, "Em is *M*."

Justin stared at her, his eyebrow arched. "Uh ... of course *m* is *m*—and *o* is *o* and *p* is *p*. What's your point?"

She shook her head. "No, I mean Em, *E-M*," she said, spelling the name and pointing at the map. "'Em' and 'M. McAdelind' must be the same person. 'Em' must be a nickname."

Justin looked back at the board again. "Who do you think she is?"

A voice behind them said, "Her name is Miranda McAdelind."

Justin felt as if his heart had jumped right out of his chest. He spun around to see Mr. O'Faron standing in the doorway, a sad look on his face. "She's your aunt, and the love of my life."

CHAPTER 33

MIRANDA
Lord Drake

MIRANDA GRABBED ONE OF THE trophies on the table, brandishing it like a golden club. "Stay back!"

Mr. O'Faron raised both hands. "I'm not going to harm you … honest." He looked at the map, his eyes glistening. "Actually, I'm glad you found this place."

Miranda lowered the trophy slightly. "What do you mean, *glad* we found this place? What is all this stuff?"

Mr. O'Faron took a step toward them; Miranda and Justin stepped back. She didn't like being cornered and started to move in a wide arc toward the door. Her brother followed her lead and soon they had switched places with Mr. O'Faron. He reached up to one of the pins and pulled off a picture, placed it on the edge of the table. Then, taking several steps back, he said, "Look at this picture."

Miranda kept her improvised weapon pointed at Mr. O'Faron as she lunged forward and snatched up the photo. She looked at it quickly, not wanting to lower her guard, and handed it to her brother. "A picture of a girl and two guys.

So what?"

"Recognize anyone in the photo?" Mr. O'Faron asked.

Justin nodded. "That's Dad on the right." He held his flashlight closer to the picture, then shone it at Mr. O'Faron. "The guy on the left is you. Well, a way younger version of you."

Mr. O'Faron chuckled. "We were all younger then. And that girl in the middle is your Aunt Em." He turned to Miranda. "You're not only named after her, you even act like her. When I first met you, I was completely taken off-guard."

Justin let out a small nervous laugh. "Wait. We have an Aunt Em? Like Dorothy in *The Wonderful Wizard of Oz*? I suppose we are pretty close to Kansas."

Miranda decided to take a closer look, specifically at the young woman in the middle. She looked familiar, as if Miranda had seen her somewhere before. But where?

"Just before you two arrived," Mr. O'Faron said, "I tried to find Robin, to let him know what I'd found out about Em, but before I ever got the chance, you two showed up at our door." His thoughts seemed to drift someplace else for a moment. "Funny how the world works. We hadn't heard from him in years, not since he and Kaya ran off. We had no idea you two even existed."

Miranda gripped the trophy tighter. "Why the sudden urgency to get in touch with our father?"

Mr. O'Faron stepped over to the map. "I wanted to let him know I had found new evidence that Em was alive."

"Alive?" Justin said. "Wait a minute, I'm missing something. Can we go back to the part where we learn what the heck is going on?"

Mr. O'Faron looked at his watch and sighed. "It's a long story, and it's getting late. We don't have time right now—"

Miranda took a step forward. "Actually, you have all the time in the world. Unless of course you want Grandpa to know about your little stash."

The older man locked eyes with Miranda for a moment, then shook his head and smiled. "You're so much like her, it's scary. Okay, fine, but I'm giving you two the *Reader's Digest* version."

Miranda nodded. "I can live with that ... for now."

"What's a *Reader's Digest*?" Justin asked, but Miranda silenced him with a wave of her hand.

Mr. O'Faron took a deep breath. "A little over twenty years ago, your aunt was attacked by wyverns at the waterfall."

Miranda shivered involuntarily.

Justin held up his hand. "Wait a minute. You mean Em was attacked in the same place, as Miranda was ... by the same dragon-wannabes?"

"The coincidence didn't escape me—or your granddad. But yes, exactly like that—with one big difference: Em was ... killed"—the word caught in his throat—"or, well, at least that's what we thought." He pulled another picture off the map that was pinned somewhere in the Middle East and handed it to Justin. "The night you two arrived, I was given this."

Justin looked at it for a moment, then snatched the first photo from Miranda's hand. He held them side by side, studying them intently. "They sure look similar. Are you sure it's really her?"

"Very." Mr. O'Faron indicated that Miranda should take a look.

Miranda took both photographs from her brother. When she saw the woman in the picture, she almost screamed. Sitting in a dark corner of a stone room, her knees pulled tight to her chest, was the woman from Miranda's dream back in New York. The image of the woman chained to a stone pillar deep underground, exhausted and beaten, flashed back into her mind. Miranda could hear her aunt's voice whispering to her, *Heal Storm!* over and over again.

"Are you okay?" Mr. O'Faron asked.

Miranda realized she was shaking all over. "I'm fine. Where did you get this?"

"At the last council meeting, a drac told me Em was alive, and the same one gave me that picture the night I picked you two up from the airport. You remember the warehouse I stopped at, right?"

Miranda nodded. There was no way she could have forgotten that creepy warehouse and the dracs trying to lure them in even if she tried.

"Well, the drac said he had information on exactly where she was, but that her captors wanted something in exchange." He seemed to be staring right through them, lost in thought. "But the price—" Mr. O'Faron paused, focusing his eyes now unnervingly first on Justin, then Miranda. "The price was just too high. I'll find another way."

"So that's why you've been stealing from our family, to get information on where she is?" Justin said.

Mr. O'Faron frowned. "I'm not stealing from your family. But not telling your granddad what I've found out does feel wrong."

"Then why don't you tell him?" Miranda looked around the room for anything resembling gold or dragon eggs, realizing in the same moment that she had no idea what dragon eggs might look like, or even how big they were.

"I tried talking to Mac. Many times in fact. But this topic is so painful, he just shuts me down before I can even get a word out. So before I tear open old wounds, I need to be absolutely sure it's true. I'm not going to risk breaking the old man's heart all over again." Mr. O'Faron gestured toward the boxes stacked against the wall. "I saved everything I could of Em's. It was just too much for Mac to have reminders of his daughter around, so he asked Mrs. Lóng to remove anything that was hers from the ranch house. But before she could, I hid it all here."

"Go back a second. We saw you give the dracs something at the warehouse. If you didn't steal it, what did you give them?" Miranda crossed her arms over her chest, trying to look as menacing as possible, but really to stop her hands from shaking.

"Believe it or not, not everything on the ranch belongs to your family." Mr. O'Faron sighed. "Look, it's a long story, but I gave the dracs some stuff that was here from the time before the McAdelinds kicked them out." He turned around. "I'll explain it all later. Right now, we need to get back to the ranch before we're missed. I can't afford to have what I'm doing jeopardized, not when I'm so close to finding her."

"Hold on a moment there, cowboy." Justin furrowed his brows. "What kind of *stuff*?"

Mr. O'Faron shifted uncomfortably. "Nothing big, just some really old scrolls and a rusty old knife. But trust me when I tell you that I am not the person stealing from your family." He looked at his watch again. "Really, we need to get moving before—"

"I trust I am not interrupting anything important." Everyone jumped, including Mr. O'Faron. Mrs. Lóng was standing right behind Justin and Miranda. Her normally glowing face seemed darker somehow.

Mr. O'Faron walked forward, pushing his way past the kids. "What are you doing here?"

"William, you are needed at the house immediately," Mrs. Lóng said.

He paled. "What's wrong?"

She let out a long sigh. "Lord Drake is here."

* * *

Miranda and Justin struggled to keep up with the two adults as they speed-walked back to the main entrance to the Warren. Mrs. Lóng had one of the ranch's trucks waiting for them. However, unlike the one Mr. O'Faron had picked them up in at the airport, this one only had one row of seats, so Miranda and Justin were relegated to the truck bed. The view through the small back window showed a very heated, if inaudible, conversation between the mysterious cook and the enigmatic ranch hand.

"What do you think they're talking about?" Justin said in a loud whisper.

Miranda shrugged. "Maybe what this Drake guy is doing here, or maybe what they are going to tell Grandpa about us sneaking around, or maybe about how messed up it is that Mr. O'Faron has been keeping the fact that our aunt is alive a secret and making deals with those creepy draconians."

"I'm going to bet on the last one." Justin flew into the air as they hit a large bump. "So, do you think he's lying about not stealing the other stuff?"

Miranda shrugged again. "Not sure." She paused. "He's sneaking around, and he has a motive. Seems like a pretty big arrow pointing right to Mr. O'Faron if you ask me. But … he does sound sincere."

Justin nodded. "Do you think this Drake guy is the old dude Miss D told us about?"

Miranda scrunched up her face. "Of course not, that was, like, a hundred years ago."

Justin scrunched up his face to match hers. "Duh, I know that. I meant, is he from the same family?"

Miranda gave him her best *Of course he is, don't keep asking stupid questions* look. Justin stopped talking and turned his attention to the road ahead, twisting around to peer through the truck cab's rear window.

The truck skidded to a halt in the circular driveway of the

ranch house, joining several large black SUVs with tinted glass. Mr. O'Faron hopped out of the truck and helped both Miranda and Justin out.

"Looks like the president's here," Justin mused.

"Something like that," Mr. O'Faron muttered under his breath.

Two very large guards in dark suits were flanking either side of the front door. Mr. O'Faron pushed past them, with Miranda, Mrs. Lóng, and Justin not far behind. They followed Mr. O'Faron as he tried to force his way past two more guards and into the study but were blocked.

Miranda could barely see around the guards to the room beyond. She thought the whole scene could be right out of a bad conspiracy-theory movie. Six men in dark suits stood by the windows and in every corner, their eyes darting back and forth. Her grandfather paced in front of the large fireplace, occasionally giving one of the men a dirty look. Rounding out the bizarre scene was a very pale man with slicked-back brown hair and golden eyes sitting calmly in one of the overstuffed leather chairs. Standing behind him was an equally pale boy, in almost every way the older man's younger twin.

The golden-eyed man turned to his guards at the door. "That one"—he gestured with a flick of his wrist toward Mr. O'Faron—"needs to remain outside. This business does not involve the O'Farons. Honestly, William, I am surprised you are still here." He spoke with an English accent, and a very snooty one too, Miranda thought.

Mr. O'Faron's face flushed. "I have as—"

Grandpa held up his hand, cutting him off, and addressed the man in the chair. "William has as much right to be here as I do. You know that as well as anyone, so cut the pretense and get on with telling us why you're here."

The man nodded lazily to his guards, and Mr. O'Faron

elbowed his way into the study. Miranda and Justin followed him in silently.

"And what lovelies do we have here?" the man in the chair asked.

Miranda noticed her grandfather stiffen slightly and stop pacing. Lines of worry formed on his rough face. "These are my grandchildren, Archibald."

"What a ... pleasant ... surprise. I was unaware that you had grandchildren." The slightest smile curled at the edge of his thin, wet lips. "Children, allow me to introduce myself. I am Lord Archibald Drake, high dragon lord and leader of the Council of Twenty." He turned in his chair slightly toward the boy standing behind him. "And this is my son, Winston."

The pale boy glared at his father, but when he realized that everyone was staring at him, he inclined his head slightly toward Miranda and Justin, saying nothing.

Lord Drake turned to their grandfather. "Well, Mac, you do like holding your cards close to your chest, don't you? I'm assuming these two are the offspring of Robert and that *savage* girl ...What was her name again ... Kale or something?"

Miranda felt her face flush. Who was this pompous man and how dare he talk about her mother like that? She clenched her fists and stepped forward. "I don't know who you think you are—"

Someone put a hand on her shoulder, and she turned around to see Mr. O'Faron looking down at her. Something in his expression—both angry and sympathetic at the same time—told her to drop it.

"Let's cut the crap, Drake," her grandfather said. "Trying to rile everyone up isn't going to get you anything except your butt kicked. I don't care how many of these goons you've brought with you. So, for all our sakes, why not just say what you want?"

The high dragon lord frowned. "And here I thought you Americans enjoyed breaking the ice with a little small talk first. Really, the art of civil conversation is completely lost in the New World." He crossed his gloved hands across his lap. "I think you know why we are here. But very well, I'll play along. I am here to put you on official notice. A major breach in our most sacred laws needs to be rectified. Immediately."

"I imagine you're referring to our security issues," Grandpa said through clenched teeth.

Lord Drake emitted a tiny, humorless laugh. "If that is what you call multiple thefts and possible exposure of our world, then yes, we—that is, *you*—are having some 'security issues.'" He looked down at his gloved fingertips. "I am here, my dear sir, to ensure that one way or another this problem is solved. You can either resolve it yourself by week's end, or I will find someone who can."

"We're handling it," Mr. O'Faron said.

"Oh, indeed, I can see how effective *you* are. Especially since two young children were able to bypass your ... *security* measures and break into the sanctuary unchallenged."

Grandpa paused in his pacing and looked at Lord Drake seriously. "Wait a minute, how did you learn about that?"

"Oh, McAdelind. Do you really think for one moment that I leave my responsibilities to chance? It is my business to know what the other lords are doing—or in your case, *not* doing." He met Grandpa's stare with equal intensity. "I am not in a very generous mood, however. One more violation and I am taking control." He stood and began walking toward the front door, his son and security detail falling in step behind him, as if the move had been choreographed and well rehearsed. Lord Drake paused at the door and turned to face them. "It would be a shame for there to be any more ... incidents." His gaze falling on Mr. O'Faron, he added, "I am placing some of my men near the entrance of the sanctuary in case they are needed. Come, Winston," he said and exited the house.

Miranda watched as the Drakes and half the procession of oversize security officers got in their cars and sped down the dirt road and off the ranch. The other half drove off up the dirt road leading to the Warren. After they were well out of sight, Grandpa walked over to one of the high-backed chairs and plopped down with a grunt.

Mr. O'Faron's eyes narrowed and he punched a fist into the palm of the other hand with a loud smack. "How in the world did they find out about the thefts?"

"What really matters is, we not only have a thief who knows our security systems inside and out, but an informant to the Council in our midst," their grandpa added, rubbing his temples.

"What's going on? Who does that bigot think he is anyhow?" Miranda said, still seething about the rude way Lord Drake had referred to her mother. Whenever anyone found out their mom was Native American, they would always ask at least one idiotic stereotype-motivated question: *Did she grow up on a reservation? Does she wear feathers in her hair? Did she speak English as a child?* But never had anyone referred to their mother as a "savage." Lord Drake sounded as if he had walked right out the Middle Ages or something.

Grandpa let out a long sigh. "That self-important piece of work, and 'bigot' as you so correctly put it, is High Dragon Lord Archibald Thomas Henry Arthur Charles Drake the Twelfth. Master of gold dragons, head of the Nineteen Families, leader of the Council of Twenty—and a world-class pain in the you-know-what."

"But why is he threatening us?" Justin asked. "I thought the Drakes gave our family this land in the first place."

"Mostly, because he can. Under certain circumstances, this

land, my title, and even our family's name could be seized by the council and given to one of the other families. Drake and I go way back, and there is no love between us, as you saw. He's probably been watching me for years, waiting for just this moment to make his move."

"Why does he hate you so much? Did you beat him up or something?" Justin laughed slightly at the thought of his larger-than-life cowboy grandfather punching the scrawny Drake.

"Indeed I did, son," Grandpa said with a weak smile. "But that isn't what this is about. It's about power and control, not revenge." He looked at Mr. O'Faron. "William, gather the staff."

"Why, Mac?" Mr. O'Faron's face was suddenly creased with concern.

Their grandfather stroked his chin thoughtfully. "We're out of time and I can't afford to have the Drakes take this all away from us. So, effective immediately, I'm closing all access to the Warren to everyone except you, me, and Cisco."

CHAPTER 34

MIRANDA
The Secret Passage

"WHAT? YOU CAN'T DO THAT," Miranda said, jumping to her feet.

Grandpa arched an eyebrow and crossed his arms over his broad chest. "I can, and I will. I don't think you fully grasp what's going on. We're one mistake away from losing everything."

Justin stepped forward. "But what about Red and the other dragons? Who is going to take care of them?"

The old man's hard expression softened slightly. "This matter will be resolved one way or another soon enough. Mr. DeSoto, and Mr. O'Faron, and I can manage everything until then."

Panic began to build in Miranda. She needed to tell Storm that Em was alive. She needed to give the dragon hope again. "But I need to see Storm. Please, Grandpa, just let me talk to her one more time."

His face hardened again. "Why in the world do you need to see that worthless lizard?"

Miranda clenched her fists. "She's not worthless. She's

brave, and strong, and she needs my help."

Her grandfather's face began to redden. "I know she showed up the other night in the valley, but trust me, I know her far better than you, and she's not worthy of the concern you're giving her." He touched the scars on his face. "My decision is final."

Miranda stomped her foot down hard. "But I need—"

"End of discussion, Miranda!" he yelled.

Miranda turned on her heels and exited the room, shooting Mr. O'Faron a dirty look before stomping up the stairs. When she got to her room, she made sure her door slammed shut with enough force to rattle the windows before throwing herself on her bed and hammering her fists into the pillows.

As Miranda rolled onto her back, she heard something make a crinkling noise in her pocket. She thrust her hand in and pulled out the two photographs from Mr. O'Faron's secret room. She had forgotten that she had stuffed them there when Mrs. Lóng showed up unexpectedly.

The photo of her aunt in the cell chilled her. In it, her aunt was looking directly at the camera. Her eyes were the same stunning blue as her father's, brother's, grandfather's—and her own. Em didn't look scared, or even broken, but defiant. Did that mean she had been a prisoner for twenty years? Miranda couldn't even fathom what that would be like. She looked around her spartan blue room and couldn't imagine spending a single day there, let alone more time than she had been alive.

Miranda shuffled the two pictures to look at the older one. Faded with age, it had taken on a reddish tint. She had seen very few pictures of her father when he was younger. He looked a lot like Justin: thin yet sturdy, but with blond hair and light skin. He had on a tan cowboy hat, and was dressed up a bit, in a nice pair of Wranglers, a white button-down shirt, and a clean tan jacket. Opposite him, wearing all black, including his signature black hat, was Mr. O'Faron. It was scary how much Billy resembled his father in almost every way—except for the smile. In the photo, Mr. O'Faron's smile was genuine, the smile of someone truly happy, totally in love. Billy's smile never seemed sincere.

Miranda set the photo of her aunt in the cell down gently on the bed next to her, and held the other one up high. As the light hit the back of the photo, Miranda saw faint lines crisscrossing the back of the image. She turned it around to see what was on the other side. To her surprise, there was a hand-drawn image of—something, a picture of a house, with a solid line leading to a waterfall, then a dotted line going from behind the waterfall to a picture of a dragon.

She sat up quickly. "No way." It was a map. But not just any map: a secret way into the Warren.

"Thank you, Aunt Em." Miranda kissed the map excitedly. "Thank you."

* * *

"The whole place is locked down tighter than Fort Knox," Justin said. "For something with only one entrance, you'd think they could've secured it before now. And frankly, I don't get the whole 'No one enters' deal. Can't they just search all of us as we go in and out?"

Mrs. Lóng pirouetted into the dining room carrying a full plate in each hand. "It is only for a couple of days, dear. Drake can't stick around forever. He has many responsibilities of his own that need attending too. Trust me, he will be gone soon enough."

Justin frowned, "I suppose so, but who knows for sure how long that will actually take? We might be gone by then. Seems totally unfair to lock Miranda and me out. We didn't take anything."

After depositing the plates on the table, Mrs. Lóng settled down next to them. "That is true, but your grandfather needs to be sure he has the situation totally under control before he can start getting to the bottom of the thefts." She turned to Miranda. "You have hardly eaten anything in days. Are you feeling well?"

"Sure. I'm good. Just not hungry." But in truth, Miranda was preoccupied, mentally walking through the plan of skipping her morning chores and finding the secret entrance to the Warren while everyone else was busy. She had been gathering supplies over the previous two days, trying to prepare for every conceivable obstacle save one—another wyvern attack—and she was counting on the light of day to help her with that.

"Earth to Miranda," Justin mumbled through a mouthful of biscuit.

"What? Sorry, did you say something?" Miranda looked from her smirking little brother to the frowning cook.

"I just asked you what you were thinking about that made you mutilate your food like that," Mrs. Lóng said. Miranda followed Mrs. Lóng's gaze to the dissected meal on her plate.

"I was just wondering why you never said anything to Grandpa about Mr. O'Faron's secret room," Miranda said, trying to turn the conversation away from herself.

The old cook sighed. "Of course he knows about the shrine to your aunt. He knows how much William loved her. But your grandfather would never go in there, or even acknowledge the place's existence. Doing so would bring up too many bad memories."

"That's just crazy. She's his daughter." Miranda pushed the remains of her meal away.

"It is a terrible thing to outlive your own child." Mrs. Lóng seemed to gaze inward and caressed her pearl necklace absentmindedly. "There is no right or wrong way to grieve over that kind of loss." She stood up suddenly, swept up the dishes, and disappeared into the kitchen.

Justin pushed back from the table and stood up. "That's my cue. Time to go and see if I can figure out how to turn that hidden TV on before I start self-defense practice."

"I thought you did that at night?"

"I know, right? For some reason, Mrs. Lóng switched my schedule around today." He smiled at Miranda and walked into the study.

Miranda took a deep breath. Well, no time like the present. If she didn't leave now, she might be spotted by her brother or the sneaky cook. Miranda stood and quietly walked to the front door, grasped the knob, then hesitated. She closed her eyes, and in her mind she saw the glowing eyes of the wyverns looking back at her. Ever since that night in the valley, so close to death, she had found the thought of going back there insane. Then Miranda pictured her aunt sitting in a frigid stone cell for years, bravely facing her fate. She had somehow reached out to Miranda and pleaded with her to help Storm. The dragon was the reason Miranda needed to do this, and somehow the key to finding her aunt.

Miranda pushed the door silently open and eased it shut behind her. Once off the porch, she sprinted around the house, over the bridge, and up the hill to the fire pit. When the ranch was completely out of view, she slowed to catch her breath. The sun was rising, blanketing the land in orange light. Redoubling her pace, she soon came to the hidden backpack she had stowed under a bush by the steep path down into the valley. She shouldered it and half ran, half slid to the riverbed below.

At the table rock, she stopped and looked around nervously. The feeling of being watched was overpowering. Her heart was racing with equal parts exertion and fear. She scanned the high cliff walls but saw no signs of any creature, great or small. The possibility of wyverns being so bold as to fly onto the dragon ranch in the light of day was remote, but after being attacked by the beasts, she couldn't rule out anything.

Pulling out a flashlight from her pack, Miranda quickly walked over to the base of the waterfall. It wasn't very big, maybe as tall as the ranch house, and ten feet wide, but even so, there was an impressive amount of thundering water spilling over it.

Miranda flipped on the light and shone it around the edge of the falls, looking for anything that resembled an entrance. When she came to the cliff wall, she noticed fresh sets of footprints in the grayish mud. "So, Mr. O'Faron," she said. "This is how you've been sneaking in and out right under Mr. DeSoto's nose."

She used the footprints as her guide, and they soon led her to a narrow ledge that disappeared behind the waterfall. It was wide enough to walk on, and except for getting a little wet from the spray, Miranda easily navigated her way behind the rushing water. She turned her light toward the cliff, where she saw an opening in the rock face, just big enough for an adult to squeeze through.

Miranda took a deep breath and stepped into the darkness beyond.

CHAPTER 35

MIRANDA
The Heart of Storm

IRANDA FOUGHT BACK A SURGE of panic as the narrow walls seemed to press in from both sides. She took deep breaths, trying to push back the feeling of being crushed under the table rock all over again. She started to move faster, slipping occasionally on the slick stone floor, scraping her elbows and knees on the walls. The tunnel was completely dark and pin-straight. If it hadn't been for the sound of the waterfall gradually fading to a faint whisper behind her, she would have believed some force was holding her back from moving forward.

Miranda was beginning to think she was walking to the center of the earth itself, when the walls ended and she found herself in a huge open cavern. Unlike the Grand Corral, with its elaborately carved pillars and arches, this was clearly a natural cave. Thousands of stalactites shed droplets of water down from the ceiling, like dirty icicles melting into their twins on the floor. She followed a worn path among the largest stalagmites to the center of the cave, where the path turned abruptly to the left and disappeared into another tunnel, this one obviously human-made. Thankfully this passage wasn't nearly so long as the first, and only after a couple of minutes, it ended in a wall of dressed stone with a square panel of images carved on it at eye level. Miranda ran her flashlight over the surface and inspected it closely. There were nine different symbols in all, each cut into the surface of a small individual block of stone, tightly aligned but with no mortar around them, and arranged in a tic-tac-toe–like grid. The top row had a lightning bolt, a spear, and a temple. The next row down had several wavy lines that appeared to be water, followed by a net, then a dragon. The final row had a bow, a club, and a symbol that looked like fire. Miranda pushed against one of the symbols, the bow sign, and the block sank slightly into the wall. This must be some kind of code, she thought. But what order do you press them in?

Miranda tried pushing on more of the glyphs at random: net, club—when she pressed on a fourth symbol, fire, all the pushed-in blocks popped back up flush with the surface again with a faint clinking sound. She shrugged and pushed on the wall with one shoulder. Nothing happened. She tried another sequence of symbols, this time just three, then pushed on the wall once more. Still nothing. When she touched a fourth, again all the depressed blocks reset.

So she needed to pick three of them, but which three, and in what order? This could take days, and she didn't have days. She needed to get to Storm before anyone discovered she was missing. How in the heck did Mr. O'Faron and Em know how to get in here? On a hunch, she pulled out the picture with the map drawn on the back. A house, with a line to a waterfall, then a dotted line to a dragon.

She reached up and pushed the symbol of the temple, which kind of looked like a house, followed by the water, and finally the dragon. There was a soft click, and Miranda couldn't help but giggle. "Thanks again, Aunt Em."

Miranda pushed against the wall lightly, and this time a door-size panel of stone began to pivot inward. She turned her light off, just in case it would be spotted on the other side of the secret door, placed her hand against the spot, and pushed hard. The secret door felt deceptively light, and it swung open quickly. Miranda lost her balance and tumbled into a dark room, dropping her flashlight in the process. The sound of metal striking rock echoed around the room. Miranda lay perfectly still, hoping no one, and nothing, was nearby.

After several long seconds of straining to hear anything over the sound of her own thundering heart, she decided it was safe to proceed. Groping around in the dark for the flashlight, Miranda jammed her finger into something hard. She stifled a scream, massaged her hand, then moved more slowly. Soon her fingers closed around the light, and she flipped it back on.

The room was filled with wooden boxes of every kind, some larger than her body, some the size of a picnic basket, and every size in between. The entrance she had just come through was behind several large boxes set about six feet away from the wall. Miranda walked back over to the stone door and gave it a small push to close it. It swung slightly past flush before coming to rest, invisible again. "Just like a saloon door," she mused. It appeared that from this direction, the secret door didn't need a code to unlock it; it was obviously designed to keep people out of the subterranean complex, not trapped inside it.

She turned and navigated through the crates to the opposite wall, where there was a large wooden door with an iron handle. Miranda flicked off the flashlight and pulled the door open slightly. In the corridor beyond, she could see a very faint light in the distance. She decided it would be better to use the flashlight as sparingly as possible until she figured out exactly where she was in the Warren.

At the end of the corridor, she came to a large circular chamber with several pitch-black passageways branching off of it, and on the far side, a broad stone staircase leading up. Creeping over to the stairs, she began to ascend silently, keeping her back against the wall.

As she neared the top, Miranda realized she was about to enter the trophy room from below, and the light she had seen was coming from here.

Just as Miranda's eyes came level with the trophy room floor, she heard a noise and looked over to see Mr. DeSoto, his back to her, looking intently at one of the statues between the shelves. Miranda's heart all but stopped and she silently slipped back down out of sight. Did he somehow know she was here? She looked back down the stairs. If she left now, she could be at the ranch in less than an hour, and no one would be the wiser.

She shook her head. I can't back out now, she thought. This might be the only chance I get to talk to Storm. Miranda counted to one hundred, then slowly peeked over the threshold. The room was empty. Had she just imagined Mr. DeSoto? Where could he have gone so quickly and so silently? Could he be hiding, waiting for her to emerge? She gave the room one last scan. It was too well illuminated for him to be hiding in a shadow. She crept up the stairs, quickly crossed the room, then broke into a run toward Storm's lair.

When Miranda got to the Grand Corral, she stopped at the entrance, looking for Mr. DeSoto and for any dragons who might be roaming about. Despite the dimness and quiet, she felt a presence nearby. It was looking for something and getting closer. Miranda turned and started running back to the trophy room, but came to a skidding halt when she realized the feeling was coming from somewhere ahead of her. Pressing herself back against the wall, she held her breath and waited. A distant sound of scales scraping on stone grew gradually louder.

"I can smell your trail, thief. You are close, I'll find you soon, then you will pay."

Miranda recognized the voice immediately: Azuria, the wild blue dragon who had attacked her a couple of weeks before. She had been terrifying then, but at least there were other people with Miranda. This time, Miranda was completely alone. Where was the dragon? How close? Miranda began to back down the passageway on tiptoe, never taking her eyes from the corridor leading to the trophy room far ahead.

Risking a backward glance, Miranda saw that she had about ten feet to go before reaching the large arena. When she turned around, she screamed. Azuria had somehow come silently into the tunnel and was heading quickly toward her.

"I've got you now. Vengeance will be mine," she growled and threw herself forward.

Miranda turned and sprinted into the open space of the corral, heading toward the archway leading to Storm's lair. If she could only get there, she knew she would be safe.

She heard the sound of wings flapping as Azuria took flight. Miranda's heart sank. She wasn't going to make it. Azuria was descending upon her. Anger radiated from the dragon, and Miranda sensed electricity building within the beast as her scales began to vibrate and shimmer. There was no hope. Miranda was alone and this dragon was going to kill her.

Something suddenly snapped in Miranda's mind, and she stopped. Her scared, helpless little brother had revealed more courage than she was showing, and here she was, running for her life and about to be attacked from behind—

again. "Not again," she whispered. "If I'm going to die, then I will die fighting." She turned and yelled, "How dare you threaten me!" A warmth began to spread throughout her body, and her fingers tingled.

Azuria paused, hovering above her in midflight. Miranda's boldness seemed to confuse the dragon's predatory instincts, but only for an instant. She inhaled deeply, electricity now dancing in undulating arcs all over her body.

Miranda did not try to dodge out of the way. She stood rooted in place, her fists clenched at her sides, her eyes narrowed in defiance.

A lightning bolt shot from the dragon's mouth with a thunderous crack. Miranda flung out her arms, palms open before her. The lightning bounced off her hands and exploded against the ceiling high above. Stone fragments rained down between the still-hovering dragon and Miranda, but neither moved an inch.

Azuria roared in frustration, *"Give me back my child, human!"*

"I don't have your child, *dragon!*" Miranda spat back.

The sound of something large moving rapidly behind her caught Miranda's attention, but she dared not take her eyes off the murderous blue. Red came bounding into view and planted himself solidly, rearing high on his haunches between Miranda and Azuria. *"Are you okay?"*

"I'm fine," Miranda said through clenched teeth.

Red turned to look at her. *"But I thought I heard a lightning strike?"*

Miranda looked down at her hands. They were tingling, but there wasn't even a mark on them. "I'm fine, Red." She glanced up at the dragon. "Can you keep an eye on her and make sure she doesn't shoot me in the back. I need to show Storm something."

"Sure, no problem. You go on ahead and have a nice chat,

I'll just hang out here and babysit the psychotic blue dragon ... All by myself."

Miranda ignored the comment and turned to leave, but an intense feeling of being watched made her look back at the entrance to the trophy room. She thought she saw something move in the shadows. She couldn't afford to be caught now. She turned and sprinted as quickly as she could down the hall to Storm's lair. Even if she had only imagined the movement out of fear, surely someone would have heard the lightning besides Red and be coming to investigate? If she got caught now, her grandfather would never allow her back in here.

When she arrived at Storm's lair, she quickly pulled open the door, slid inside and silently shut it behind her.

The room was pitch black, but she could sense the dragon nearby. Miranda flipped on the flashlight and saw Storm curled into a ball near the corner, watching her. *"How are you here, young one? I overheard Lord McAdelind say the ranch was locked against all but him and two others."* Storm lowered her gaze. *"I was worried I would never see you again."*

Miranda walked over and stroked the dragon's cheek. "I have something to show you." She fumbled in her pocket, pulled out the recent photo of Em in the stone prison, and held it up for Storm to inspect.

The dragon withdrew from it as if it were poison. *"What trickery is this?"* she demanded, backing away even further.

"It's no trick," Miranda assured her, although it had never crossed her mind that the photo might be fake. "At least Mr. O'Faron believes it's real, and it sure looks like Aunt Em."

"It can't be her. She's ... dead. ... I was there when it happened."

Miranda sat down in front of the dragon. "Are you positive? You were young and scared, maybe she actually survived."

Storm shook her massive head emphatically. *"Em was ... ripped ... apart,"* she stammered.

Miranda reached forward, laying her hand on one of Storm's front paws. To her surprise, Storm didn't withdraw it. "Mr. O'Faron's convinced this is Em, and so am I." She looked down. "Listen. This is going to sound crazy, but I *saw* her." Miranda shook her head. "Well, not with my eyes, but in my mind. Like when I see your memories, or see what the other dragons intend to do. Does that make sense?"

"No, young one. None of this makes sense."

"The night before Justin and I came to the ranch, we had a dream. Both of us. The same dream. Only it wasn't a dream, it was more like"—she sucked in a breath sharply—"like a desire, or … a plan. Oh no!" She stood suddenly and started to pace back and forth, lost in thought.

"What are you talking about?"

Miranda looked up at the dragon. "I didn't know at the time what was happening that night. It was the first time I'd felt anything like it—I thought it was a dream. But it wasn't. I just realized, I was reading the thoughts of the draconian who came to our apartment. He was thinking about what he was going to do to my Dad and my … aunt. He was thinking about hurting them." Miranda fought back her tears. "Then I saw him knock on the door to our apartment, like I was doing it myself." She placed a hand on the dragon's snout. "No, Storm, she's alive, but she's in danger. We need to find them before it's too late."

Storm closed her eyes tight and lowered her head. *"I am sorry, but she is not, and it is my fault. I killed her."* Her body was suddenly racked by a shuddering spasm.

Miranda stroked her cheek gently. "I know this is painful, Storm, but I need to see for myself." She cupped the dragon's chin with both hands, and lifted it so that they were eye to eye. "I know I am asking a lot, but it's a place we need to go together."

Storm nodded slowly. *"It is a place I know well."* She opened her eyes and looked right through Miranda. *"A place I can never leave. It is my punishment. It is my prison."*

CHAPTER 36

MIRANDA
Scars

MIRANDA WAS INSTANTLY TRANSPORTED back to the canyon. The experience of sharing a memory, especially a vivid one, was disorienting. Even though she knew she was actually standing in Storm's lair, under a mountain of rock in the Warren, she felt that she was a part of this other world of memory, not just an observer.

Something nudged her in the side, causing her to look over her shoulder. If Miranda thought jumping into a memory was confusing, seeing herself as a dragon was even more so.

Sitting on her back, in front of her wings, was a slender girl with brilliant blue eyes and light-golden hair. A rush of love, longing, and sorrow overwhelmed Miranda. She needed to concentrate, to notice any details the dragon had missed. Miranda focused on the girl, how her hair was pulled back into a tight braid that fell over one shoulder, how she sat with impeccable posture in the saddle, and how her eyes shone with the same strength Miranda had seen in the photo taken when Em was older.

The girl suddenly pointed to the sky, and Miranda's field of vision rose, following her gesture. Just over the horizon several dark shapes, their batlike wings beating in unison, were rapidly approaching. Miranda recognized the wyverns long before she could see any of their other telltale features.

This didn't make any sense. Why was her aunt waiting for a bunch of those vile creatures? Miranda felt Storm's muscles tense, felt her stomach twist nervously, and her overwhelming desire to flee.

Em's hand caressed the dragon's shoulder lovingly. "It's all right, girl, this was my idea, remember. They're the only ones that can help us. If things go bad, just wait for my signal."

Miranda tried to change the point of view, to look at her aunt's face and figure out why in the world she would have invited these savage killers to the ranch, but of course her view was locked into Storm's memories of what the dragon had seen. It didn't make any sense. Em was only sixteen or seventeen years old at most. What could she have been doing?

Within moments, five huge wyverns were coming in for a landing. Three touched down around the canyon ridge, continuing to beat their wings slowly, their long snakelike necks swaying back and forth, scanning the canyon with hungry eyes. The other two landed between her aunt and the river.

To Miranda's sudden horror, she realized that all escape routes were effectively closed off. They were trapped.

She felt Em slide off Storm's back before coming into her field of vision, walking slowly but with purpose toward the wyverns on the ground. "We agreed you'd come alone," she shouted up toward the larger of the two beasts. At first, Miranda thought she was talking to the wyvern itself, until she noticed that both had thick leather straps crisscrossing their chests. Two dark figures in black robes slid to the ground from the wyverns' backs, landing silently next to their mounts. Deep hoods concealed their features.

One of the robed figures started walking forward, while the other remained near his mount. "Unfortunately my dear, the situation has changed," a raspy voice hissed.

"What do you mean, changed?" Em said, her hands now balled into fists. "You promised if I gave you the gold and allowed you to see the stone shard, you would restore Billy's good name."

"As I said, the situation has changed. Someone a little more … *influential* was willing to pay a great deal more to ensure that the O'Faron family is never reinstated."

What were they talking about? Why was her aunt trying to get Billy back his name? Was Billy even born yet? *"Storm,"* Miranda asked. *"What does she mean about reinstating the O'Faron name?"*

But the dragon did not respond.

"Why, you double-crossing snake! You swore to me this was a done deal," Em growled. "I want those gold bars back, and you can kiss this"—,she held up a triangular stone shard— "goodbye. Forget about ever seeing it again!" Miranda sucked in a quick breath. She was looking at another piece of the stone tablet from her dream, similar to the one their mom had hidden in Justin's luggage.

"As a matter of fact, this very lucrative deal came with another condition that we consider … a win-win." Miranda could just barely make out the draconian's sinister smile hidden in the deep shadows of the cloak.

Even though Storm's attention was squarely focused on the exchange between Em and the lizard-man, Miranda caught a subtle motion of the lead draconian's hand directed toward his companion. She concentrated on the dragon's peripheral vision and saw the second draconian move closer to his wyvern mount and start to pull something off its back.

"*Storm. What did he just pull off the wyvern's back?*" Miranda asked, but her voice sounded far off and warped, distorted.

Storm did not respond, keeping her focus intently on the exchange between Em and the draconian. Miranda tried again to get her attention. "*Storm! I need you to focus on what I'm asking. What was on the wyvern's back?*"

She felt the dragon begin to shake violently. "*I can't ... this is where it all changes ... where it all goes wrong ... this is where it all ... ends ... .*"

Miranda was drawn back to the memory, back to her aunt. Miranda watched Em take a step backward, place the stone in her pocket, and raise her hands high above her head as if the draconian were holding a gun aimed at her chest. "What are you talking about?" Em stammered, then out of the corner of her mouth whispered, "*Now, Storm.*"

"I'm talking about the destruction of the McAdelinds, child. We can't go after a dragon lord directly, but we can go after his children." The draconian took a step closer to Em. "And in doing so, we can break him from the inside."

Em stretched her arms up even higher. "Storm! Now!" she shouted, but Miranda could feel the young dragon frozen with fear. Miranda had no idea what her aunt expected the terrified blue to do. She was hopelessly outnumbered.

At a command from the draconian, the large wyvern struck, leaping at Em with its jaws open wide, ready to devour her in a single bite. Em barely had time to dodge out of the way. The wyvern shot past her, but its tail hit her in the head like a giant club, and she crumpled to the ground, unconscious.

It was only seeing her friend in mortal danger that allowed Storm to overcome her terror enough to move. She sprang toward Em, but just before she could reach her, a crushing weight pinned her to the ground. Sharp, burning pain shot across her back. Storm tried to roll free, but was held down firmly in place. She looked behind her, and Miranda could see that two of the wyverns from the cliff had descended and were both pinning Storm down with one foot while raking her back with the claws of the other. As blood streamed from the young dragon's wounds, her mind began to cloud.

Summoning all her strength, Storm surged forward, knocking the beasts off balance. She beat her wings, trying to get into the air, where she might have a fighting chance, but was hit hard from the side and sent into the canyon wall. Darkness began to close in around her as she searched hopelessly for Em.

Before Storm passed out, Miranda noticed two minor—but as she would soon realize, very important—details. First, the lead draconian was busy pulling her aunt's boots off; and second, his lieutenant was desperately unrolling the large bundle he had removed from the wyvern's back earlier.

Then everything went black.

* * *

"Storm. What happened next?" Miranda pressed, knowing how painful this was for the dragon, but needing to see it all for herself. "I need to know everything."

The dragon said nothing, but Miranda felt her shaking violently as the darkness gave way to a slightly different scene. The sun had apparently set some time before, but the valley was all aglow from the light of a full moon.

Only two of the smaller wyverns were left. One was feeding ferociously near where the second draconian had been frantically unrolling something. Blood dripped from its fangs as it dove in for one ravenous bite after the other.

The second wyvern was walking slowly toward Storm, its mouth gaping, its spiked tail poised above its head, ready to strike. Miranda felt the dragon let out a long sigh, then close her eyes, waiting for the end.

A primal yell in the distance made Storm open her eyes. Sprinting down the steep hill on foot was Grandpa. He was shouting and running directly at the feasting wyvern. Storm tried to get to her feet, but her left foreleg buckled and sent her to the ground again. It was broken. She pulled herself back up, careful not to put weight on the injured limb, and began to limp toward the second wyvern. It had turned its attention to her grandfather, advancing toward him with short two-footed jumps.

Miranda was amazed that her grandfather, who looked basically the same, except with a lot less gray hair and no scars, continued charging toward the creatures completely unarmed and with no support.

The first wyvern, blood still dripping from its fangs, stepped over its meal and raised its wings and tail defensively. It let out a terrible screech. Her grandpa, not slowing, drew something long and metallic from a sheath strapped to his back and leaped at the wyvern's head. The creature moved forward to snap its vicious jaws at him but recoiled in pain as a silver blade cut deeply into its snout. A spray of blood was followed by another and another as her grandfather swung his blade in blurring arcs. The creature tried desperately to back away, but he kept advancing, slicing deeper with each stroke into the creature's scaly body.

The second wyvern was now approaching Grandpa from behind. Miranda wanted to scream out a warning, but she knew it would do no good. The wyvern swung its tail, knocking him off his feet. He tried to roll up into a fighting stance again, but the creature slammed its tail down, forcing him to roll out of the way.

Storm was trying her best to move forward, but the pain came in waves from all over her body, and she found it hard to breathe. Miranda realized she must have several broken ribs. The wyvern's tail came back near her as it prepared for another strike. Storm leaped forward with all her strength and bit down hard. The wyvern screeched, trying desperately to dislodge her, but even through her pain, Storm refused to let go. The beast turned away from Miranda's grandfather to focus on the injured dragon.

Miranda could see her grandfather get to his feet and charge the distracted wyvern. He vaulted into the air, using a big rock as a ramp, and slashed with his sword in a diagonal stroke. Blood poured from the open wound in the wyvern's neck. Its head was attached only by a small sliver of flesh. Storm maintained her grip on the creature's tail until its last ounce of life drained away.

But now the first wyvern, eyeing its chance, crept forward and swung its tail hard at Grandpa. His quick reflexes saved him as he raised his sword just in time to block the barb from piercing clear through his body. Unfortunately the force of the blow knocked him hard to the ground.

The wyvern pivoted and pinned his sword arm to the ground with one of its taloned feet and raised the other over his head. It slowly dug its claws into his scalp and dragged them down the length of his face, his neck, his chest. His blood flowed freely, and he screamed.

Storm dropped the tail of the dead beast, beat her wings several times to gain speed, and crashed into the flank of the wyvern pinning Grandpa down, knocking it away from the bleeding man and onto its back. Storm's vision began to fade again as pain overwhelmed her.

Miranda watched as Grandpa staggered to a standing position, one side of his face mangled and gory, then slowly walked over to the prone wyvern. He brought the silver sword down again and again, hacking fiercely at its head and neck, even long after the beast had stopped moving.

All of the man's strength seemed to give out all at once.

He dropped his sword and staggered to the spot where the wyvern had been feeding. His knees buckled and he fell to the ground, staring down at a bloody pair of blue cowboy boots. He threw his head back and let out a scream that seized Miranda's heart. He lowered his head and began to cry, deep, sorrowful sobs. "No. No! Not my beautiful little girl. Not my Miranda ... ."

Storm crawled over to where her grandfather was kneeling, and Miranda could see there wasn't much left of her aunt. Besides the cowboy boots there was nothing but a clump of dark-blond hair and torn bits of clothing. Miranda's stomach was turning but she fought the feeling back and concentrated on the hair. It was slightly ... off—not the right color, too dark, and loose, with no trace of a braid.

Her grandfather turned on Storm, half his face now caked in drying blood, his left eye swollen shut, the other red and swimming with tears. "Why didn't you save her? It was your duty to protect my little girl with your life. Your life! That is your bond. You failed to save her!" He looked away from the dragon in disgust. "You are as dead to me as she is." Then he began sobbing again, repeating "No!" over and over until the vision faded.

* * *

Miranda found herself back in Storm's lair. She was still holding the dragon's chin in her hands. "It wasn't your fault, Storm."

"Of course it was. I failed. I was too afraid to act, and I got my mistress killed."

Miranda shook her head. "What were you supposed to do? You were a young dragon against five wyverns."

"We had a plan. I panicked."

"What plan?"

Storm hesitated for a moment before replying. *"When Em raised her hands, I was supposed to fly as fast as I could, grab them in my front paws, and vault her onto my back, so we would make our escape."*

"What? That's crazy, you would have killed her."

Storm shook her head. *"We had done it many times. That is how we would begin the ring-racing competition, and why Em received such high scores. It would have worked if I had been brave. The wyverns would not have been able to react in time and we would have been long gone before they could attack. She is dead because of my cowardice."* Storm lowered her head.

Miranda sat back down on the floor. "Actually, I am more convinced than ever that she's alive."

"You saw with your own eyes. How could you think such a thing?"

"Because I was looking at everything, not just at what the draconians *wanted* you and Grandpa to see." Miranda took a deep breath to collect her thoughts. "First, what was in the large sack? Why were there only two of the smaller, younger, wyverns around after you woke up? Why was the drac pulling off Em's boots when she was knocked out—and why was the hair of the dead girl not Em's hair?"

Storm closed her eyes for a long moment, then they sprang open. *"How did I miss that? You are correct, the hair is not hers."* She stood up. *"What do you think happened?"*

"I think they did a switch. There was a body, or something—an animal or meat maybe—in the sack they pulled down, and it looked enough like a person to pass for Em's body—especially if a wyvern had enough time to make a meal of it. They left Em's boots there to make it look more convincing. I think the whole reason for them coming here was to take her alive but make it look like she had died, so Grandpa wouldn't look for her. To him it just looked like two wild young wyverns had killed and eaten his daughter."

"But why would they want Em alive?"

Miranda shook her head. "I have no idea. In the dream … or vision … or whatever, that Justin and I had, she and our Dad were chained to pillars in a cave. I think they were there to be sacrificed." Miranda paused in thought for a moment. "Actually, she wasn't in Justin's dream—*I was.*"

"There is a connection between you and your aunt. I could feel it right away. The wyverns must have been after you as well."

"Maybe, but they weren't trying to capture me. They were trying to kill me." Miranda reached into her pocket and pulled out the old note she had found under her bed. "I found this letter to Em, thanking her for something, but the name is torn off. Do you know who wrote this?"

The dragon looked at it and nodded. *"It is from Billy. He must have written this after she gave him the black hat."*

"Wait a minute. You're talking about Mr. O'Faron?"

"Of course. The one who you call Mr. O'Faron, or William, I know as Billy. I always have. It is what my lady called him."

Miranda's mind was spinning. "So the other night, when the O'Farons were arguing, and you said, 'I feel sorry for Billy, he deserves better than that,' you were actually talking about Mr. O'Faron?"

"Indeed. He has had a hard life. So much loss. Nothing to his name. That whelp of his should show more respect to him and to Em. She was trying to get the O'Faron name reinstated when she was betrayed by those treacherous snakes."

"What do you mean by 'reinstated'?"

A siren began to blare in the corridor. Miranda covered her ears, trying in vain to block out the noise. She peeked out through the open door to see what was happening. Rough hands grabbed her, pulling her into the corridor.

"Miranda. What in the Sam Hill are you doing here?"

Grandpa was red-faced and breathing heavily. "You know you're not supposed to be here … wait a minute … how did you get in here?" He looked behind her into the lair beyond. "And what are you still doing around that worthless lizard? I told you to stay away from her."

Miranda's face flushed. She knew now why her grandfather felt the way he did, but she also knew it wasn't Storm's fault. Miranda started to protest, but yelling and footsteps made her pause.

Her grandfather pushed her in the opposite direction of the people coming, pointing a finger at her harshly. "Go straight back to the ranch and wait for me there. Don't even think about wondering off somewhere. You and I are going to have a very serious conversation about this, young lady. Now go, before Drake's goons see you. I'll distract them long enough for you to exit."

Miranda didn't hesitate. She turned and ran as fast as she could toward the secret door.

CHAPTER 37

JUSTIN
Mud

JUSTIN MOVED QUICKLY TO THE RIGHT as Mrs. Lóng brought a wooden knife down toward his neck. In one fluid motion he grabbed her wrist, stepped toward her and under her arm, and sent the old cook flipping onto her back. At the same time, Justin twisted her wrist, making the knife fall to the ground.

"That was great, dear. Your best yet." Mrs. Lóng clapped her hands together excitedly in a quick, tiny motion above her chest.

Justin blushed slightly. He offered his hand and pulled her to her feet. For someone who had to be at least seventy years old, she was astonishingly durable. They had spent every day working on breaking out of holds, dodging and countering punches, disarming and disabling opponents. Compliments had been rare. "Thank you, Mrs. Lóng." He bowed. "But why are we practicing how to disarm a knife attack? I've never even seen Billy with one before."

She looked away for a moment before saying in a quiet voice, "You would be surprised. You never know when you may need such knowledge. It is always better to practice and not need a skill than to die out of ignorance."

Justin raised an eyebrow. "Okay—I'll have to take your word on that one. So, what do I do once I have my opponent on the ground?"

Mrs. Lóng looked him up and down critically. "If I were you? I'd run."

"Nice."

She pursed her lips and placed her hands on her hips. "I'm being completely serious. You aren't strong enough to cause any real harm to a bigger opponent, and we haven't worked on any offensive moves for someone your size."

Justin scowled. Of course he agreed with her, but he didn't like hearing that said out loud. "So, when do I learn some of the—"He kicked his leg as high as he could, threw a couple of punches into the air, and yelled, "Kee-yah!"

Mrs. Lóng shook her head. "Never, if you make that noise. Once again, that's Japanese, not Chinese." Then she smiled and laughed loudly. "Okay, okay, I think you've got some of the defense fundamentals down. Let's see what we can teach you about offense."

Over the next hour they worked on several strikes, specifically to the "soft" areas, as Mrs. Lóng described them. Mainly she was talking about the groin, the knees, and the elbows. By the end of the exercise, Justin was sweating and breathing hard.

"That last part was adequate, but you have a lot of work to do. Practice some of the strikes, and for goodness' sake, do a pushup or two—or a hundred. I was stronger at five than you are now." Mrs. Lóng shook her head and headed back toward the ranch. "Lunch is in one hour."

Justin watched her until she disappeared through the door leading to the kitchen, then kicked off his shoes and socks and stepped into the river. Given how hot the day was already, the water was shockingly cold. He sat down on the rocky bank and closed his eyes, intending to relax for a moment before continuing his exercises.

"Hey, dork," Billy called from behind him.

Justin jumped quickly to his feet and stumbled backward a couple of steps into the river, almost losing his balance. "What do *you* want?"

The older boy smiled. "Why so hostile? Are you worried I'm going to knock you on your butt again? Don't worry, McAdelind, I've got bigger problems. Have you seen Mr. DeSoto this morning?"

Justin balled his fists. "Why? Planning on blaming me for something else? Maybe a flood this time?"

Billy scowled. "I don't have time for witless banter. Did you see him or not?"

Justin glared up at the older boy standing on the riverbank above him, a position that made him seem even larger and more intimidating than usual. Billy was also filthy, his clothes streaked with dirt and his boots covered in grayish mud. "He was driving up toward the Warren about an hour ago. Why?"

Billy's body stiffened. He glanced at the road leading to the dragon sanctuary, then ran off in the other direction, toward the bridge that led to the valley.

Justin waited until Billy was out of sight before trudging up the riverbank. "What a freak." he said. He looked down at the reddish muck on the riverbanks, choosing his steps carefully, trying not to slip. Something odd about Billy's ragged appearance nagged at him. Why was Billy so dirty, and where in the world was there gray mud on the ranch?

* * *

Justin was almost finished with his lunch when Miranda came skidding into the dining room. She was holding her left side, bent over and breathing heavily.

"Uh—are you okay?" Justin asked, looking behind her to see if she had been chased into the room.

She held up a finger. Justin just shrugged and took the moment of silence as his window to quickly shovel all the rest of the food off his plate and into his mouth. When he was done, he looked up to his sister, who was staring at him with a look of disgust. "What?" he mumbled through a mouthful.

"That's ... repulsive. Seriously ... where did ... you get ... your manners?" Miranda panted.

Justin just shrugged and swallowed with a gulp. "At least I don't look like I was rolling around in the dirt." Then he paused. Her hair was disheveled, her clothes were dirty, and her boots were covered in gray mud. "Hey. Wait a minute." He stood up and crossed his arms. "You weren't with Billy, were you?"

"What? No," Miranda said, making a face. "Why?"

Justin looked her up and down one more time. "Come on. Tell me the truth."

"Don't be such a dork. I *am* telling you the truth."

"Then why do you look like you've been rolling around in the dirt and have the same gray mud on your boots that he does?"

She looked at him, bewildered. "What do you mean, the same gray mud?"

Justin pointed down at her boots. "That mud. I don't know where you both got into it. All the mud around here is *red.*"

He watched as his sister looked down at her feet. Then her eyes widened. "Oh, no," she whispered. "It's been Billy this whole time."

Justin waited for a moment, thinking she would continue, but when she didn't, he asked, "It's Billy *what* the whole time?"

"Billy's been stealing from our family, Justin. He's the thief."

CHAPTER 38

JUSTIN
To Catch a Thief

"I HATE TO SAY I TOLD YOU SO, but I totally did." Justin grinned broadly. "Billy is a complete jerk." Miranda was silent. Justin realized that he had been so caught up in his own glee at being right about Billy, he had not paused to consider her feelings. "Uh … I mean … are you sure? It's possible Mr. O'Faron could still be behind the thefts. It's just some gray mud. Billy might have gotten into it somewhere else."

Miranda shook her head. "It's more than that. What was stolen, when it was taken, and the attacks, it all adds up," she said, indicating her boots. "I didn't realize it until you pointed out the mud though." Miranda began to pace around the room. "The only place I've seen that gray stuff is behind the waterfall, at the secret entrance to the Warren."

"Wait. What are you talking about? What secret entrance? And you went there without me?"

Miranda was too distracted to listen. "But why me? Why does he want to kill me?"

"What do you mean *kill* you?" Justin clenched his fists.

"Did he attack you?"

Miranda shook her head. "Not directly, but he *had* to be involved in the wyverns' attack and both times Azuria attacked me. He must have been watching me and let her out of the wild area when I was there."

"*Both* times?"

Miranda nodded. "She shot another lightning bolt at me this morning when I went to go talk to Storm." She paused. "But ... I blocked it with my hands."

"You what?" Justin went to his sister and took her hands in his own to examine them closely. "There isn't even a mark."

Miranda gave him a weak smile. "Something bigger is happening here, and I think Billy is trying to stop us before we figure out exactly what."

"Not us, *you*. And do you really think a sixteen-year-old could be the mastermind behind something like this? Come on, the guy is a complete dolt. I bet someone else is working with him. Someone like his father."

Miranda shook her head. "Mr. O'Faron loved, I mean, he loves Aunt Em too much. I don't think he would sacrifice her family to get her back."

Justin shrugged. "Maybe. There is still something fishy going on with him beyond what everyone is telling us. If he isn't helping Billy, who is? We need to tell someone what's going on. We can't do this alone. My vote is Mrs. Lóng."

Miranda shook her head emphatically. "No way. She's too weird. Plus she has been appearing and disappearing all over the place at suspect times. She may be involved as well."

"Mr. DeSoto then?"

"I'm not sure. I don't really trust him.

Justin scratched his head. "I'm not sure I trust him much either. He seems kind of shady to me."

Miranda crossed her arms over her chest. "We really can't trust anyone, can we?"

"Well, there is someone. The person who has the most to lose: Grandpa."

Miranda nodded and let out a long sigh. "How do we make him listen to us though? Every time anyone brings up Em, he cuts them off."

Justin frowned. "We have to try. We can't do this by ourselves." He snapped his fingers. "I've got it. If he won't listen to us, then we need to show him."

Miranda tilted her head. "What do you mean?"

"I mean, we take him to the secret passage. That should get his attention, right? As a matter of fact, I saw Billy heading that way over an hour ago. You two must have just missed each other. If we are there to catch him red-handed, even better."

His sister nodded. "Actually, brother, that's an excellent idea." She turned and sprinted from the room.

Justin followed her as she ran out the front door to the ranch. "Wait! Where are you going? I thought we were going to wait here for Grandpa to get back."

Miranda shook her head. "No time. We have to catch Billy red-handed. And don't worry about Grandpa, he'll find us. He told me to come back here and wait for him. When he finds I'm not here, he'll come looking for me."

"How will he know where to find us?"

"He caught me in the Warren with Storm. When he can't find me here, he'll come looking for me, and he will most likely start in the valley. Every time he asks us not to do something, we end up doing it anyhow, and he specifically told us *not* to go to the valley." She grabbed Justin's hand. "Come on, let's go and wait for Grandpa to find us, and if Billy happens to show before he does, then we can nab that creep ourselves."

Justin looked at her skeptically. "I'm not so sure about that."

She gave him a wicked smile. "I am. Billy told me where they keep all the bear mace."

* * *

Justin was having a hard time keeping up with his sister as she leaped like a gazelle over deep erosion ditches, rocks and low bushes. A sharp pain flared in his left ribs, and he slowed, grabbing the spot where the stitch had formed.

Miranda must have sensed him slowing and adjusted her pace. "You okay?"

He nodded. "Just ... a stitch."

"We're almost there, just around those big boulders." She pointed at two big rocks that framed the winding path. Justin had only been this way once while riding on the back of a dragon, so none of this looked familiar to him. Miranda slowed even more as she peered around the edge of the trail before moving forward. She turned and whispered back, "Looks clear. The ground is a little loose up ahead by the cliff, so let's walk the rest of the way. You coming?"

Justin sighed and jogged to catch up. Miranda was crouched low behind some scraggy-looking shrubs. She motioned for him to drop lower as he moved toward her. On the other side of the brush, the valley dropped off in a steep cliff. From this vantage point, Justin could easily see the waterfall ahead and the creek flowing down to the ranch house.

"We should be able to see Billy come out of the tunnel from here," Miranda said, pointing toward the waterfall. Then she turned back and gestured toward the rocks they had just walked between. "When he comes this way, we can drop back and ambush him there."

Justin nodded, but felt very skeptical about the idea that

the two of them could stop Billy from doing anything. "Okay, hand over that bear mace you were talking about."

Miranda tossed him one of the cans, which she had snatched from a storage cabinet in the stable before heading to the valley. "You pull that tab thingy first, then point the nozzle and pull the trigger. Make sure it's directed the right way, and make sure the wind won't blow it back in your face. Other than that it's pretty simple."

Justin frowned at the can. "Are you sure this will work?"

"It worked on a wyvern, it will definitely take down a stupid boy."

Motion below caught Justin's attention and he raised a finger to his lips. Someone was walking slowly out from behind the waterfall: Billy O'Faron. They watched as he walked slowly over to the pool at the base of the waterfall and stared into it for a long moment, then in one motion picked up a rock from the ground and threw it as hard as he could at the rock wall.

"What do you think that was about?" Justin whispered.

Miranda shook her head. "I'm not sure. He's frustrated about something though."

"He's not carrying anything out, so maybe he got stopped from taking whatever he was trying to get."

"Maybe," Miranda said, and frowned down at Billy as he walked slowly toward them, his hands thrust deep in his pockets and his eyes on the ground. She rose into a low crouch and scuttled silently back toward the large rocks. "Let's get into position. He'll be here in a couple of minutes."

Once they were behind the protection of the boulders, Miranda stood and gripped the mace tightly in both hands. "You ready?" she said, her voice shaking slightly.

Justin nodded, and squeezed into a space between two of the rocks so he would be unnoticeable from the direction Billy was approaching. His sister gave him a thumbs-up and disappeared back behind the bend. Justin strained to listen for any sound of Billy approaching, but all he could hear was the sound of his own heart beating rapidly.

What seemed like several minutes went by before Justin heard the crunch of gravel. He tightened his grip on the can of mace and held his breath. The older boy came slowly into view. His head was still lowered and he shuffled his feet as he walked.

Justin's muscles tightened, ready to spring out as soon as he passed by. But before he could even react, Billy's hand shot out toward Justin and grabbed him by the hair. He let out a yelp of pain and surprise as the bigger boy yanked him hard and fast out from between the rocks.

But Justin's recent martial arts training took over, and he grabbed Billy's hand on his hair and held it tight to his head. At the same time he swung the can of mace at the outside of Billy's elbow. Justin saw the older boy's joint hyperextend and felt Billy's grip on his hair loosen. Before Billy could even cry out, Justin moved in closer and sent his fist into Billy's diaphragm, knocking the wind out of him and dropping him to the ground.

Justin aimed the can of mace at Billy's face, and yelled, "Freeze, scumbag! Your days of stealing and trying to kill my sister are over!"

Billy was curled into a fetal position, gasping for breath. "What are … you talking … about? You're … completely crazy," he wheezed, looking up at Justin. "How many … times do I have to tell you, … I'm not trying to hurt anyone." He let go of his injured elbow and winced as he pushed himself into a sitting position.

"Yeah, right. You're not trying to hurt anyone—except me!" Justin spat. "But forget that. You've been sneaking into the Warren and stealing from the ranch. And you set up situations where a wild dragon and a group of wyverns attacked my sister. Those seem like the actions of someone trying to hurt my family."

Billy laughed humorlessly. "You really are as dumb as you look. I'm not the one stealing from your stupid family ..." Then his eyes went wide and shifted their focus to look to something behind Justin. "He is."

Justin took a step to one side, not wanting to turn his back on Billy, desperate to see the path behind him. It took him a moment to understand what was happening. Miranda, her face hard with anger, was walking in front of Mr. DeSoto, with her hands held up in front of her. Mr. DeSoto was following closely behind, his lips curled into a smile. He winked at Justin and shoved Miranda roughly to the ground.

Justin moved quickly to his sister. "What the heck is wrong with—" Justin stopped in midyell as he noticed the pistol leveled at them. He slowly helped Miranda to her feet, and they stood side by side facing the grinning man with the gun.

Billy forced himself to his feet and stood with Miranda and Justin. "You two wanted to catch the thief?" He inclined his head toward Mr. DeSoto. "Well, there he is. Let me introduce you to Francisco DeSoto, wannabe dragon lord of North America, and world-class slimeball."

CHAPTER 39

JUSTIN
Flight

MR. DESOTO'S LIP TWISTED into a snarl. "Not *wannabe, chico.* I think the word you are looking for is *rightful.* After today, the McAdelinds will fall, just like the O'Farons, and I will reclaim what was taken from me. I will be the dragon lord of North America." He glanced at his watch, "Soon Lord Drake's men will discover that another break-in has occurred, and your families' fates will be sealed."

"But you're the head of security. It makes you look like a complete idiot. Why in the world would anyone hand this all over to you? That doesn't even make sense." Justin said.

"Oh, I have some powerful allies making sure it will." Mr. DeSoto's face hardened, and he waved the gun, pointing back toward the valley. "Now move. We have a rendezvous to make. My time has come, and I'm not going to be late."

Miranda stood her ground. "You won't get away with this. My grandfather knows where we are. He'll be coming any minute now."

Mr. DeSoto made a *tsk-tsk* sound and shook his head.

"Actually, I imagine he'll be held up for quite a while with Drake's men." Mr. DeSoto smiled. "After years of working for the dogs who stole this land from my family, I am finally about to take it all back. And the best part is, you and your brother provided the perfect opportunity to make this all possible."

"What opportunity?" Justin asked.

"Why, trading your lives for this ranch," he laughed. "After all of these years, feeding Drake information on this place for a shot at getting back my birthright, this was just too good to pass up."

Justin clenched his fists and glared at Mr. DeSoto. "So, it was you trying to kill my sister?"

"And *you*," he said and winked at Justin, then turned to Billy. "But little O'Faron here has had that figured out for a while now, haven't you?" Billy just glared at Mr. DeSoto, who shrugged. "Always a moment too late to save the girl, but there when the boy needed you most. Doesn't really matter in the end." He pointed the gun at Miranda. "You will be pleased to know, your death is no longer part of the arrangement. My associates originally said they wanted you 'dead or alive.' Dead is always easier in my opinion, but when I told them I had seen you with my own eyes block a lightning bolt from the wild blue, they said they were coming immediately to collect you themselves. So alive it is. But you two," he said, indicating Billy and Justin, "are not really part of the deal. Your deaths will serve to finally break the old man and bring both the McAdelind and O'Faron lines to a well-deserved end."

Justin shot a look over at Billy. "What does he mean, *you* saved me?"

The older boy never took his eyes off Mr. DeSoto. "The night we caught the escaped dragon in Denver. There was a wyvern after you. Nightshade and I took care of it."

Justin's mouth dropped open. He remembered sensing a dragon's intent to kill; he had assumed that it was after the wyrmling, but even that intention had been unclear. Now it all made sense. Justin had been picking up on the black dragon's intent to rip into the wyvern that was after Justin, not the baby dragon. Justin couldn't believe it. The boy he had disliked for the past couple of weeks had actually saved his life.

"Why steal my shirt?" Miranda asked.

Mr. DeSoto laughed. "I was looking for something else actually. Something my associates thought might be with you, but alas, it was not."

Justin had to restrain his hand from reflexively touching the rough carved stone fragment in his pocket.

"But while I was there," Mr. DeSoto continued, "I figured I'd grab something of yours. By now you know dragons have a very acute sense of smell." He shrugged. "Making that stupid blue think you stole her egg was surprisingly easy. Now—"

"You started the fire on the hill too, didn't you? Why risk destroying the ranch if you want it so badly?" Justin said.

"I needed time to move some of the bigger items," Mr. DeSoto replied. "Your pyromaniac tendencies gave me the perfect excuse. Everyone would have to respond to a fire." He looked over at Billy. "Well, almost everyone. Little O'Faron here has been on to me for a while, but he could never get there fast enough to catch me in the act. And I don't really give two beans about this land. What I care about is located below it."

Miranda turned to Billy. "So you were sneaking into the Warren to catch him?"

"I figured there had to be some evidence," Billy said. "Someplace he was stashing the stolen stuff. He never leaves the ranch. It has to be here somewhere."

"Why didn't you tell my grandpa or your dad? They could have taken care of this ages ago."

Billy shook his head. "I couldn't accuse one of the Nineteen Families of stealing without proof. I would have been kicked out of this place for good. And lately my dad has been putting his own family second to a dead ex-girlfriend."

Mr. DeSoto threw his head back and let out a loud laugh. "You want to compare fathers for a moment. Let's see, mine forced me into a pen with a wild dragon—when I was ten years old mind you—to make me "more of a man". Oh, and it ended up biting off my leg. Then he stripped me of my birthright—I am the oldest after all—and instead gave everything to my sniveling, idiot brother. The last thing he did before kicking the bucket was to exile me from my own family. I'm not sure your old man can beat that." He shrugged. "But none of that really matters anyhow. My treacherous brother can have that worthless piece of land and those evil lizards that come with it. I'll be living here as one of the richest dragon lords"—he waved his gun at his three captives again—"and you'll be dead. Now get moving, before I shoot you all here and now."

"But, why kill us?" Justin pressed, hoping beyond hope that help was on the way. "I mean we could—"

Mr. DeSoto pointed his pistol at the ground and shot. Justin jumped back away from the spray of stone fragments. The sound of gunfire echoed off the canyon walls. "I said, move," Mr. DeSoto growled.

Justin, Miranda, and Billy turned slowly and started walking toward the valley. Justin leaned slightly toward the older boy and said, "I guess I should ... thank you ... for saving my life, and all ... not that it matters much now."

Billy continued to look straight ahead. "I didn't do it for you, McAdelind. I did it for me."

Justin raised an eyebrow. "How does saving me possibly

help you?"

Mr. DeSoto laughed. "Because if anything happens to the McAdelinds, the O'Farons lose any chance of ever being a recognized family again. Didn't you ever wonder why the Council of Twenty only has *nineteen* families? It's because the O'Farons were kicked out in disgrace." Billy clenched his fist and stopped walking. Mr. DeSoto limped to a halt, raising his gun. "Keep moving, boy."

Billy turned slowly and glared over his shoulder. "This isn't over yet, traitor. You'll get what's coming to you." He spat on the ground behind him before turning and heading along the path.

They continued on in silence past the place where they had spotted Billy emerging from behind the waterfall and then beyond the path leading down to the canyon floor. Soon they were standing in an open area where the path ended at a top of a steep cliff. The space was clear of trees, shrubs, and rocks. There was no place to run or hide. They were trapped.

"We're here. Keep your backs to the cliff and I want to see those pretty little eyes on me," Mr. DeSoto said, holding the pistol leveled at their chests. He shot a quick glance over his shoulder. "Ah. Excellent. They got here quickly."

Justin looked to the sky. On the horizon, six dark shapes moving low and fast were closing in on them. Their wings, barely visible from this distance, were mere tiny wisps beating in unison at their sides. Justin closed his eyes and reached out with his mind, trying to sense the approaching creatures' thoughts and intentions. There was something there, not a dragon's mind, but something … very familiar. Something he hadn't sensed since … His eyes opened wide. "You're working with the draconians!"

Mr. DeSoto glanced over his shoulder and squinted, then turned back, a smile on his face. "I'm impressed, *chico*, you have some seriously good vision. And I'm not working with them, I'm working *through* them. But don't be so surprised, I would have worked with *el diablo* himself if it would get me back what I deserve."

Miranda shook her head. "Don't be a fool, Mr. DeSoto. My aunt tried working with them, and look what happened to her. Be smart, let us go, or this won't end well."

Mr. DeSoto just smiled. "I know you are new to how things work in this world, but the draconians serve the Nineteen Families. They'll honor our agreement because they have to." He shifted his position, putting more weight on his real leg. "It's a win-win. They serve their masters, and I get the ranch."

Justin kept his eye on the horizon as the draconians drew ever closer. He was now able to make out the distinct forms of six big wyverns, each bearing a humanoid figure on its spiky back. Time was running out. Once the dracs got there, not even his grandfather could save them. If they were going to try something, now would be their last chance.

Justin looked over at Billy. He was still cradling his injured arm against his chest. Smooth move, kung fu master, Justin thought. Take out the one person who actually had a shot at saving them. He looked past Billy to his sister, standing motionless. She had been quiet for a while. Her eyes were squeezed tightly shut and her brow was furrowed in concentration. She must be trying to reach out to the dracs, Justin thought, maybe trying to see why they want her alive. Suddenly her eyes opened, and a small smile spread across her lips. She glanced over her shoulder. Justin followed her gaze to the sheer drop to the valley floor, some fifty feet below. She wasn't crazy enough to jump, was she? Maybe she thought death at her own hands would be better than anything the creepy lizard men had planned for her. He looked at her again, she met his eyes and … winked.

Miranda slowly began to raise her hands above her head. Mr. DeSoto raised his gun level with her chest, and his lip curled into a smile. "I'm not robbing you, *chica*. You can put your hands down." She continued to raise her arms farther until they were straight in the air, never taking her eyes off the man with the gun. Mr. DeSoto's expression turned from amused to annoyed. "Seriously, put them down. Now." Miranda just stared at him, reaching high. He raised the gun, pointing it at her head. "I'm not playing games here, girl," he spat. "Put your hands down now, or I will shoot them off." Miranda stood on her tiptoes, stretching as far as she could.

Billy turned to her. "Miranda. He's serious. Put your arms down."

She glanced at him out of the corner of her eyes. "I'd move away if I were you," she said. Then she looked at Mr. DeSoto. "You might want to consider running, thief."

Justin was about to step in front of his sister when he sensed something that made his heart stop: a dragon, full of rage and purpose, flying at top speed directly toward them. He quickly scanned the sky. Nothing. He looked back at his sister, who gave him a slight nod, then looked straight ahead and closed her eyes.

There was almost no sound as Storm came soaring up from the valley behind them. In one fluid motion, she grabbed Miranda's outstretched arms, and tossed her into the air.

Billy and Mr. DeSoto dropped to the ground, but Justin could only watch in amazement as his older sister did a flip in the air and landed soundly on the blue dragon's back. It was only then that she opened her eyes. She looked back at him and shouted, "Run, Justin!" before Storm banked hard to the left and sped toward the mountains. The wyverns let out a collective cry of rage, and five of the six turned to pursue Miranda and Storm.

Justin realized that if he was going to make a move, it was now or never. Mr. DeSoto was still lying flat on the ground, watching Storm and Miranda disappear from sight. Justin ran at the crippled man. But Mr. DeSoto moved faster than Justin would have thought possible, and sprang to his feet with his gun once again leveled at Justin's chest.

Justin skidded to a stop. "What are they planning to do to my sister?"

Mr. DeSoto scowled at him murderously. "I never got around to asking." He glanced quickly over his shoulder as the one remaining wyvern landed behind him. "About time. Now, finish these two and join the others before the girl warns her grandfather."

The drac on the wyvern's back let out a long, weird hiss. "All in good time, Francisco DeSoto. All in good time." His hood fell back slightly, revealing his wide reptilian mouth. "But first, I need to take care of some other business."

Mr. DeSoto's face looked perplexed. "What other—?"

The wyvern's tail whipped out behind Mr. DeSoto and pierced his back, cutting him off in midsentence. A look of shock crossed his face as he stared down at the blade-like barb, which extended a foot beyond his chest. The beast shrieked and yanked the barb free. Mr. DeSoto toppled to his knees, blood flowing from the gaping hole near his heart. He dropped the gun, looking at Justin for an instant with wide-eyed terror and said, "The tablet—." Then fell face down into the dirt.

The wyvern took a step forward, blood dripping from the tip of its raised tail. The draconian spit on the back of the fallen man and hissed, "We are done taking orders from humans." He made that strange hissing noise again, and Justin shivered as he realized that the bizarre and creepy sound was the draconian laughing. "Now. Who's next?"

CHAPTER 40

MIRANDA AND JUSTIN
The Wall

IRANDA FELT LIKE SHE WAS going to pass out, until she remembered to start breathing again. She had been holding her breath ever since she felt Storm about to grab her arms. She looked down at her wrists and could already see large bruises blossoming where the dragon had grabbed her. Her knuckles were white from grasping the saddle tightly as Storm flew close to the treetops through the winding valley. How in the world had her aunt done this all the time and not lost her arms completely?

"*She wore leather guards,*" the blue dragon said offhandedly, reading Miranda's thoughts. "*I was also never moving quite so quickly and never approached from that angle before. You did well, Miranda. Your aunt would be impressed.*"

"*Thanks, I think.*" Miranda thought back, realizing this was the best way to communicate over the deafening roar of the wind. She looked back over her shoulder at the five wyverns in close pursuit. Crap! She had planned on all of them following her, and giving her brother and Billy a chance to take down Mr. DeSoto. *"It will be even more impressive if we can all escape."*

Storm was silent for a moment as she made several complicated banking maneuvers around sharp turns in the valley, then said, *"Escape is not an option. We will need to fight."*

"What? We've tried that once before. One against five was a bit of an issue."

"This time there are six. Do not forget the one that landed near your brother."

Miranda's heart sank. *"Trust me. I haven't."* She couldn't help but think she had left her brother to die.

"Do not let your thoughts about your brother distract you from the task at hand. He is very resourceful. Even now he calls to the Welsh Red. You need to focus on the here and now. We are good to no one dead."

"You're very inspiring, has anyone ever told you that before?" Miranda said.

Storm ignored her sarcasm and continued. *"I've been thinking about this much. I believe there is a small chance we can emerge victorious, but you and I are going to have to try something that has never been done before, and will most likely kill us both in the process."*

Miranda frowned down at the dragon. *"I'm not sure I like the sound of that."*

Storm turned her head slightly so she could look back at her rider. *"Wyverns are pack hunters, and deadly in their own right. With the help of their draconian riders, they will strike us with a coordinated attack that we will not survive. Our only hope is to hit them even harder first and try for a quick victory. We don't have time to hope for help. They are already starting to implement their hunting strategy."*

Miranda looked back and saw what Storm meant. The largest of the wyverns, obviously their leader, was behind them in pursuit, while the two on either side began to break off. *"They're trying to surround us,"* Miranda said with horror.

Storm focused once more on the way ahead, concentrating on the twists and turns of the valley. *"Yes, they will fly up and around and come at us from three directions at once. Our best hope is to engage two of the flankers first, then work on the other flankers, before attempting to engage the leader."*

"Wouldn't it be better to just attack the big one first, and break their spirit? One-on-one seems better odds to me."

"Not this wyvern, and not that draconian." The dragon shuddered.

Miranda looked back again and realized something unsettling. *"Those are the same two that attacked you and Aunt Em."* Storm said nothing; she didn't need to. *"Okay. What did you have in mind?"*

The dragon was silent for a moment, but Miranda could sense her conflicting emotions before she spoke. *"We are going to hit them with lightning."*

"What? Uh, if you remember correctly, that almost caused you to explode," Miranda shook her head. *"I think that is a quick way for both of us to die."*

"Perhaps. But ... I can't explain it. We were close. Very close. But neither of us knew what was happening, and we were both holding back."

"And now?"

"Now we have nothing to lose, and neither you nor I will hold anything back this time. It is either fight with everything we have, or die."

Miranda couldn't help but smile. Her aunt's words to her in the dream had been the command, *Heal Storm!*, but she hadn't been sure what that meant until now. She reached down and traced her finger along one of the jagged scars that crisscrossed the dragon's back. It meant more than just helping Storm get over what had happened to Em. It was also to help her fight her fears. *"I think it's about time someone taught these lizards to never mess with a McAdelind,"* she shouted, *"or their dragons!"*

* * *

Justin couldn't stop shaking as he backed toward the cliff. He had never seen a dead person before. But there was Mr. DeSoto, lying flat on his face, not ten feet away, his blood still draining from his lifeless body.

The wyvern that had just stabbed him through the heart let out another screech. It was hopping awkwardly toward them on its two hind legs, using its fanned-out wings for balance.

It would be on them in moments. They had to do something fast. Justin shot a quick look over at Billy. He was pale as a ghost. Apparently this was the first dead person he had seen too. *"Red! Where are you?"* Justin shouted in his mind. He had figured Miranda must have been communicating to Storm this way, so he should be able to reach Red. *"If you don't hurry, I'm going to be a kebab in about ten seconds,"* Justin said. The wyvern stepped on Mr. DeSoto's body, and the sound of snapping bones almost made Justin throw up.

"On my way. Try not to die. I'll be there in a jiffy."

"Okay, I'll be standing at the edge of the canyon with my arms up," Justin said, and started to slowly raise them above his head. He could feel Red in the open air now.

"Why in the world would you do that?"

"That's how Storm grabbed Miranda," Justin said.

"Ah—no. I'd rip your arms clean off your body. Don't get me wrong, that gets a lot of applause and all at the rodeo, but it's completely impractical for a real-life situation."

Justin frowned, lowering his arms back down again. *"Plus, you have no idea how to do it."* The wyvern cocked his head at Justin's sudden arm movements but kept advancing.

There was a long pause before Red answered. *"And … I have no idea how to do it. When I get there, drop low."*

Justin felt air beneath his heels, he had reached the edge of the cliff, and franticly circled his arms, trying to keep his balance and not do a back flip off the ledge.

"Any last words, human?" the draconian rider hissed.

Justin grinned up at the lizard-faced creature. "Sure. Duck!" He hit the ground. Billy didn't even hesitate and instantly dropped too.

Red came over the canyon wall and slammed hard into the off-balanced wyvern, sending it sprawling onto its back. The draconian let out a cry as the wyvern rolled onto him, instantly crushing the life from his body.

In two quick bites, Red ripped the wyvern's throat out. When he was satisfied that the creature was dead, he leapt back over to Justin. *"Hop on."*

Justin reached up, grasped the saddle's horn with both hands, and pulled himself up. Even with the wyvern Red had just dispatched, it was still five against two, and the leading wyvern had looked bigger and nastier than all the others. They were going to need help. "Billy, can you make it back to the ranch and let my grandpa know what's happening?"

Billy nodded. "Go save your sister." He turned to leave, then looked back over his shoulder. "Good luck, Justin," he said, then took off at a sprint down the trail back to the ranch.

Red scanned the sky. *"Where are they now? I don't see anything."*

Justin closed his eyes and reached out with his mind for Storm. Then he pointed toward a mountain slightly to the left. *"They're flying low and headed toward that peak over there."*

"Okay. I know a shortcut. Hold on to something." Red dove

off the side of the cliff into the valley below.

Justin's stomach shot into his throat. The sensation of freefall intensified as they plunged toward the ground. Just before they would have hit the bottom of the valley, Red pulled into a rapid climb, causing Justin's stomach to lurch even more. If he hadn't practiced riding so much lately, he thought, this little maneuver would have caused him to barf all over the dragon's back.

Red was flying faster than Justin would have believed possible, as each powerful beat of the dragon's massive wings launched them forward through the air. It wasn't long before they caught sight of the wyverns. Justin let out a sigh of relief: the beasts hadn't caught up to his sister and Storm yet. He watched them as they began to split up into some kind of maneuver to surround Miranda and Storm from three sides. *"So? What's the plan?"*

Red let out a harsh laugh. *"We catch them. We kill them. That simple."*

"You make it sound so easy," Justin said sarcastically.

"If it were easy, it wouldn't be very much fun, now would it?"

Justin shook his head. *"I'm glad you're enjoying this."*

"I'm a dragon. This is what I do." Red tilted his head slightly so Justin could see one of his large eyes, reptilian but with the round pupils characteristic of domestics. *"Which one do you want to kill first?"*

Justin looked at the spreading formation ahead of him. *"Let's get the big one in the middle. I think he's the leader."*

"Sounds like a plan to me."

Justin's eyes narrowed on the nearest wyvern. *"We're coming, Miranda."*

* * *

Storm banked hard to the left, almost throwing Miranda off in the process. She lost her grip with her right hand and dangled from the saddle with her left. Storm shrugged a shoulder hard and gently tossed Miranda back into place. *"Clip the safety harnesses on before you fall to your death."*

"You might remember that this is my first time riding a dragon." Miranda looked around and noticed a belt attached to two leather straps coiled behind her. She quickly secured it around her waist and gave it a hard tug just to be safe. *"How did you get this saddle on anyhow?"*

There was a long pause. *"That is a discussion for later. Right now we have work to do."* Storm beat her wings rapidly, gaining altitude and placing them a little higher than the two wyverns they were heading toward. *"Are you ready?"*

Miranda could feel the bile rising in her throat. What they were about to attempt was either going to save them or kill them, and their fate rested firmly on her shoulders. *"As ready as I'll ever be."*

"I was hoping for a show of greater confidence, but that will have to do." Storm began to slow slightly. Miranda could sense the fear in Storm suddenly overwhelmed by resolve. *"This is for you, Em. Let us begin."*

Miranda placed both hands on Storm's neck and focused on the creatures in front of them, taking the measure of not only the mindless wyverns but also the robed lizard-men on their backs. They had come to capture her. They had come to kill her little brother. She was going to make them pay for that.

Miranda closed her eyes, embracing the primal desire to fight, to kill, to protect. Energy began to build deep within her. She wasn't scared this time. This time she was going to win. She pushed the energy forward into the dark place where Storm said domestics can't go. She was met with the same resistance, but this time, she felt the dragon's presence beside her pushing as well. The wall was strong, but they were stronger, and she could feel the barrier begin to crack and groan under their combined effort. Miranda gathered all the energy around her, making it surround her, permeate her. And just when she thought she was going to burst into flame, she threw it at the wall.

And the wall fell.

Miranda's eyes sprang open. Electricity was arcing all around her and Storm in dancing blue-white loops. The scales along the dragon's back were vibrating so quickly, her hide was shimmering like a mirage. It was only then that Miranda realized this was how blue dragons must generate electricity. They were able to create a massive static electric charge by making their scales rub together fast. She could feel Storm's chest expand almost painfully, then in one rapid release of pure energy, lightning erupted from Storm's mouth in a continuous blinding stream followed by a deafening crack of thunder.

Miranda watched in grim satisfaction as a great zigzagging bolt of lightning struck first one, then the other wyvern. Their charred flesh blistered at the point of impact killing both wyverns instantly. Their draconian riders screamed as they plummeted helplessly to their deaths.

Storm suddenly lost altitude and began to drift slowly to earth. Reaching out with her mind, Miranda felt the dragon's exhaustion. *"Storm, you need to keep moving. The others will be here soon."*

The dragon moved her head to the side so she could see Miranda. *"That ... took ... too much ... out ... of me."* She tried to beat her wings harder to regain some altitude, but they refused to respond, and she continued to sink toward the ground. *"I'm afraid ... we ... are done ... young one. I have ... failed you."*

Just as they were about to crash into the trees, Storm fanned her wings out like a parachute and slowed them enough to land hard in a small clearing. The impact forced the air from the dragon's lungs as her legs collapsed underneath her.

Miranda quickly unfastened her safety harness and jumped clear of the dragon as Storm rolled onto her side and lay still. Miranda ran over and gently stroked her face. Storm was panting, taking short, shallow breaths. Miranda feared she would soon cease breathing altogether.

They had pushed too hard, and it had almost cost them their lives. Worse still, even though they had taken down two of the wyverns, there were still three more on the way. Miranda's heart sank. It hadn't worked. They had fought for nothing.

Miranda leaned back against the dragon and slumped to the hard, rocky ground. She heard the flapping of large leathery wings and looked to the sky. Two wyverns were circling above them like vultures over carrion with their draconian riders leaning over to get a better look at their prey. They would capture her soon, and with Storm out of the picture, there was no one who could rescue her now.

CHAPTER 41

JUSTIN AND MIRANDA
Sitting Ducks

J USTIN KEPT HIS EYES ON THE WYVERN ahead of them. Both mount and rider were so intently focused on his sister, they failed to notice the great red dragon bearing down on them from above. When Justin and Red were less than five hundred feet away, the hairs on Justin's arms began to stand on end. For a second, he thought it was because he was terrified of what they were about to do, but then he felt the air crackle with electricity. He became aware of his sister's will uniting with Storm's against some unseen force. He could feel their rage focused on fighting and protecting. Miranda was wrapping herself in that rage, turning it into a massive amount of energy, until—

A brilliant flash of light, off to Justin's left, was followed by a tremendous thunderclap. He cupped his hands over his ears, but too late to save them from ringing painfully. Red slowed to a hover, and Justin asked, *"What was that?"*

Red looked to the left, and in a tone Justin had not heard before, maybe awe, maybe fear, said, *"That was ... Storm. She actually breathed lightning. A domestic dragon used a breath weapon. No freaking way. That ... rocks!"*

"I thought you guys couldn't do that?"

Red looked down at the big wyvern hovering a safe distance away from where the attack had taken place. *"I didn't think we could. But you know what? Neither did they."* He turned his long neck so that he looked Justin right in the eyes. *"Now's our chance. You ready?"*

Justin forced a smile to his lips even though the butterflies in his stomach felt like they wanted to escape through that same smile. But the dragon was right, the dracs and their mounts were completely distracted: now was the time to act. Justin kicked Red in the ribs with the heels of his boots and gave a loud mental *"Kee-ya-a-ah!"*

Red tucked his huge leathery wings tight to his body and dove with such speed, the wind made Justin's cheeks ripple with tiny waves as tears streamed freely from his eyes. They were heading directly toward the wyvern's back.

Justin could feel the dragon's body tense under him, and he braced himself for impact. Red extended all his claws before him, ready to shred the huge wyvern's wings and send it plummeting to the ground like a stone.

The draconian, as if sensing the impending attack, pulled hard on the dorsal spines of his mount, sending it into a banking dive and just out of reach.

"Crap!" Red shouted, leveling out. *"Almost had him."*

Justin continued to watch the pinwheeling wyvern, thinking it might crash into the trees below, but at the last second it righted itself and shot toward them. *"Red! Look out! The big one's coming up from below!"*

Instead of turning to the sky and trying to outrace his attacker, Red tucked his wings back against his sides once more and dove directly at the wyvern and rider. The creature screeched in surprise and tried in vain to avoid colliding with the dragon, but it was too late.

The two beasts rammed into each other with a deafening metallic crash. Every one of Justin's bones rattled in his body, and he shook his head, trying to clear the fogginess away. The whole world was spinning around him as Red and the wyvern, locked in combat, fell out of control to the earth below, each raking his claws on the other's legs and underbelly, jaws snapping, trying to find the soft underside of each other's throat.

Ribbons of drool streamed from the beasts' open maws, showering Justin in a slimy spray. "*Gross! I just got lizard spit in my mouth!*"

"*Instead of complaining ... how about ... helping me out?*" Red said between pained grunts. They were spinning and turning through the air, and the ground was rushing up to meet them.

"*Well, we're about to make a huge crater. Does that help?*"

Red looked around at Justin for an instant. "*Actually kid, it does,*" he said, and with a loud grunt kicked himself clear of the wyvern. Once he was out of reach, Red extended his wings, caught the wind, and slowed enough to pull into a glide over the tall pine trees. The wyvern tried to execute a similar maneuver, its rider pulling back hard on its dorsal spikes in a vain attempt to send it back into the sky, but they couldn't pull up in time and crashed into the forest. The sound of snapping tree branches was immediately followed by the creature's hair-raising scream.

Red continued flying away from their opponents, beating his wings hard to gain speed and altitude. Justin realized with a sinking feeling that the red dragon wasn't circling for another attack but was really heading in the opposite direction.

"*Red. Where are you going? What if it's not dead? We need to go back and finish him.*"

"*I saw Storm go down after she used her lightning. She is on the ground now. If we are going to do something crazy and heroic, we need to even the odds up a bit."*

Justin sensed that Red was leaving something important unsaid. That big wyvern wasn't like any of the others he had seen, and Justin could tell that Red was a little unsure of his ability to take it on alone. But he decided that now was probably not the time to bring that up and asked, *"So ... we're going after the other two?"*

Red nodded. *"Do you think we can do what your sister and Storm did? Do you think we can unlock my breath weapon? If I were a wild dragon, it would be fire ... ."*

Justin hesitated before responding. He had been able to feel what Miranda and Storm were doing right before the lightning strike, something like a wall falling, but he wasn't even sure how they had gotten to that point. *"I don't think so."*

"We're running out of options here, kid. That big guy back there is almost a match for me. And we still have two others to contend with. We need to try something—unexpected." Red looked back over his shoulder at Justin. *"You can do it. We can do it. I know we can."*

Justin swallowed hard, and nodded. *"What do we have to lose, right?"*

* * *

Miranda was trying to shake Storm awake as she watched the two wyverns above them. What were they waiting for? If they landed now, they could put an end to Miranda and Storm in seconds, but they just continued to glide in a great circle overhead. It occurred to Miranda that the draconians actually might think that she and Storm were bait in a trap. After the surprise lightning attack, the dracs might be wondering if Storm was playing dead to lure them to their deaths.

Miranda could only wish that were the case. She placed both hands gently on either side of Storm's face and closed her eyes. *"Storm. Storm. You have to get up. We're in danger. You have to get up."* But there was no response.

Miranda knelt down in front of the blue dragon's head and gently held her muzzle. She closed her eyes again. *"Storm. I know you're there. I need you. It isn't just our lives that are at stake."* Miranda felt a little underhanded saying this, but there was no other choice. *"Em needs you too."*

Miranda felt a quiver of recognition, and knew she had to keep pushing, but she hated herself for what she had to say. *"Are you really so afraid ... are you really such a coward ... that you will give up and let Em die ... again?"*

There was a flash of light in Miranda's mind that yielded to the shimmering image of a mighty blue dragon before her. *"I fear no one, I am no coward, and I will not let another soul do my mistress harm."*

Miranda nodded. *"Then what are you doing lying around waiting for death to take you?"*

Storm's body shifted slightly under Miranda's hands and the dragon opened her eyes. *"You are full of surprises, young one."* Storm strained to pull herself into a crouch, but gravity itself seemed too much for her. *"I am here now. And I will not fail you—or Em."*

Miranda reached up and stroked the dragon's neck. "I know you won't. I'm sorry. I just thought—"

Storm shook her head. *"You said what you needed to, nothing more, nothing less."* She looked skyward, to the two circling wyverns. *"What are they waiting for?"*

"I think they were waiting to see if this is a trap. But now they must know it isn't." No sooner had Miranda uttered the words than the wyverns dove directly at them.

CHAPTER 42

JUSTIN

Fire

J USTIN CLOSED HIS EYES and tried to feel for the spot Miranda and Storm were pushing against, but he couldn't find anything like that. Red had no spot. No barrier. No dark area in his mind. No protective rage. No sadness. Nothing.

"Anything?" The dragon asked. They were coming up on the circling wyverns, and they were running out of time.

"I can see you're hungry."

"Always."

"You like to sleep."

"That's a given."

"Oh, and you like to fight."

"Obviously."

"But there is nothing in there that even closely resembles rage."

"What can I say? I'm balanced."

Justin sighed. *"Balanced or not, if we're going to release the inner pyro in you, we need to figure out how to break down the barrier you domestics have. Is there anything that makes you really mad?"*

Red thought for a moment. *"Let me see ... Being hungry, not getting enough sleep, and not fighting on a regular basis."*

Justin opened his eyes and punched the back of the dragon's neck. "Not helping." Then silently added, *"Okay, this isn't going to work, let's just do what you were going to do to the leader."*

"Won't work. They're too far apart and as soon as we engage with these two, the big one might loop around and hit us from behind."

"Are you sure there isn't something that makes you mad?"

There was a pause, and Justin caught a glimpse of intense emotion, but then it was gone, replaced by the very basic thoughts of food, sleep, and combat. *"There was something there, just for a second. What was it?"*

"Nothing." Red sounded annoyed.

Justin pushed. *"It didn't feel like nothing."*

The same emotion flashed again. *"You know what, kid? I think your plan will work. We should just—"*

"Red, you were the one who wanted to do this." Justin closed his eyes and pushed his mind toward the feeling. It was like chasing a shadow through a dark room. It kept hiding behind some of the most mundane thoughts, trying to evade him. But now that he saw it, now that he knew its tactics, Justin could catch it. He reached out and touched the shadow, and the world suddenly shifted, as the emotional shield Red had been hiding behind came crashing down. Curled up in the corner of a dark, quiet, cavelike lair was a juvenile red dragon. It was looking around nervously and shaking. Justin realized he was actually seeing an image of how Red saw himself.

The dragon's voice boomed out of the darkness, angry and urgent. *"You need to leave here, now!"*

Justin ignored him and walked over to the young dragon.

He knelt down so he was eye to eye with it. He reached out and stroked the side of its face, and this version of Red leaned into his touch as if hungry for comfort. *"It's okay. I'm here now."*

The young dragon looked up at him with sad eyes. *"Why did he leave me?"*

"Who left you?"

"Your father. He was my friend and he left me." The face of a young man, Justin's dad, suddenly appeared and said, *"I'm not sure when I'll be back, Red, but I promise you I'll return. I need to find my sister. I know she's still alive, and I need to save her. Do you understand?"* Then he smiled and disappeared.

Red's voice came quietly from the darkness, *"A part of me has been here ever since. Waiting for him to come back. Waiting for my friend and my ... Father ... to return."*

There was a part of Justin that felt the same way. He was waiting for his dad to come sweeping in at any moment and save him and Miranda, but somehow he knew that wasn't going to happen. *"Red, he isn't coming back—at least not right now."* And as Justin said the words, he knew they were true. *"He's lost somewhere and we are on our own."* Justin shook his head. *"It's time for both of us to grow up. We can't be the scared kids in the corner any longer. We need to be more than that."*

Instinctively, Justin reached out to this strange embodiment of Red's insecurity and placed his hands on its neck. *"My dad may not be here, but I am. And I am your friend. I am your ... brother."* He leaned over and gave Red's inner wyrmling a tight hug.

Suddenly it felt hot. Really, really, hot. Like fire. Justin looked down and saw that he was surrounded by flames. He felt the warmth, but it didn't burn him. *"Red. Are you feeling this?"* There was no answer, but he felt the dragon's presence. Justin gathered the fire around him, feeling it dance all around his body. But the more he gathered, the more he felt a pressure trying to push it away. That must be the force Miranda had encountered, something that blocked the domestic dragons from being able to use this ability. Justin started to push against it, felt it push back, and pushed even harder. *"We need to do this together."* Justin groaned from the strain of the unmovable force. If his sister could figure this out, so could he.

Red's will joined Justin's, and they pushed in unison. Nothing happened at first, but then the wall of force started to move. He felt it begin to crack under the pressure, and in his enthusiasm he tried to throw everything he had at it, but Red held back. *"Why are you stopping? We're almost there."*

"Call it a feeling, but your sister and Storm fell from the sky after they did this. Let's try a more conservative approach."

Justin laughed; he couldn't believe Red was actually telling him to be cautious. But the wily dragon was probably right. Justin pulled back a little and kept the pressure on one spot. More cracks began to appear as a spiderweb of light and fire. Justin concentrated on one of the bigger fissures and forced it to widen. There was a sound like a massive bonfire roaring, and the wall came down.

Justin opened his eyes, and saw the wyverns diving directly at Storm and Miranda. He saw grim determination in his sister's face. She was going to fight to the death, even when she knew the odds were against her.

Red took a deep breath, and … belched. The largest smoke ring Justin had ever seen came out of the dragon's mouth, quickly dissipating in the air around them. *"Not exactly what I had in mind."* Justin said.

"It's harder then it looks." Red inhaled again. This time Justin could feel the heat swirling inside them both, and they drew it all to one spot, containing it, making it even more intense. When it felt as if they were going to burst into flames, Red

let the fire free.

A white-hot cone of flame shot forward into the backs of the diving wyverns. Their riders didn't even have time to scream before their charred forms plummeted to the earth below. Wails of agony erupted from the dying wyverns as their scales blistered and their wings began to burn like dry leaves. Their screams were suddenly silenced when they crashed full speed into the trees near the clearing in the woods.

Red spread his wings and slowed their descent. He shook his head to clear it. *"I don't feel so great."*

"Just get us down to the ground near Storm and Miranda," Justin said, pointing to the open area.

The dragon made a series of tight descending circles on his approach. From experience, Justin could tell they were moving way too fast and braced himself for a rough landing. Red hit the ground hard, his legs buckling underneath him. Justin lost hold of the horn and found himself dangling from the saddle upside down, hanging by the safety straps. Rock, sand, and dust were thrown up into his eyes and mouth as the dragon's body, like a meteor skidding to a halt, plowed a wide trench in the earth.

When they finally came to a stop, Red groaned, *"Ow. That really, really, hurt."* He laid his head on the ground.

Justin struggled in his inverted position to unhook the safety straps, and when he couldn't figure out how, simply unfastened the belt and plopped unceremoniously into a clumsy handstand. He stood up and shook the dust and dirt from his hair.

He ran over to the dragon's head and knelt down. Red opened one eye. *"Am I dead?"*

Justin laughed. "Oh, come on, you look fine. You know what they say, any landing you can walk away from is a good one."

"Whatever idiot said that never fell out of the sky into a pile of rocks." Red struggled to his feet. *"Ow, ow, owie."*

When the dragon had succeeded in hauling himself up into a semistanding wobble, Justin cringed. Red's chest and belly were cut all over, and he was bleeding freely from several of the larger gashes.

Red followed his gaze down. *"So that's what hurts. It looks worse than it is. I'll be fine. I need to lick it a bit. But—ow, that smarts."*

Justin nodded, not really believing Red was being completely honest. "Well, in that case, we should grab Miranda and Storm and get the heck out of here. That big wyvern and the draconian might be here any second."

Red laughed. *"Now that all his friends are dead, he'll probably hightail it back to whatever hole he crawled out from."*

Justin turned around and saw his sister walking toward them. She was holding a rock in each hand, obviously the only weapons she could find. Her hair looked as if she had lost a fight with an electric eel, and she had a huge smile on her face.

Then she stopped, her eyes widened, and she started to back quickly toward Storm.

Trees creaked behind Justin, and he turned to see the huge wyvern knocking pines aside as if parting a curtain, its scorpion tail poised menacingly above his head, ready to strike, its mouth open wide, exposing rows of dagger-like teeth dripping with thick saliva.

When the creature had emerged completely into the clearing, it stopped, and its draconian rider slid off its back and down onto the ground. His black robe, Justin noticed for the first time, was different from the other riders', decorated with strange gold symbols, like the robe Justin had glimpsed worn by one of the dracs at the warehouse in Denver. Could this be the same one?

In one of his clawed hands the drac clutched a staff, in the other, a long curved knife. He stopped in front of the wyvern and shook his hood free. Up until this moment, Justin had had only a vague idea of what a draconian might really look like close up. What he found himself staring at now was a thing out of a nightmare. The creature had a short snout with slit-like nostrils and two parallel rows of small protruding horns that ran from his nostrils all the way to the crown of his head. He sniffed the air around him, and his enormous yellow-and-red eyes came to rest on Miranda. He spread his feet slightly and twisted the knife in his hand. He opened a mouth full of long, sharp teeth, licked his lipless mouth with a forked tongue. "That is where you are wrong, *dragon,*" he hissed at Red. "I will crawl back under my *rock* when I have gotten what I came for."

CHAPTER 43

MIRANDA AND JUSTIN
The Draconian

MIRANDA FELT A SCREAM STARTING to build somewhere deep inside her, but it caught in her throat, escaping only as a gasp.

She hated wyverns. Almost getting eaten by a group of them more than warranted that feeling, but she had also experienced Storm's memory of the wyverns' attack against her aunt and Storm so vividly, it felt as if she had really been there herself. Wyverns had become her least favorite things on the planet—until she saw this draconian close up. The vile creature made her feel like she might faint *and* throw up at the same time.

The drac's eyes were locked on her, and Miranda knew there was no running from him. She backed away until she collided with Storm. Miranda knew too that the two dragons couldn't overpower the enormous wyvern, let alone the draconian, in their weakened state. Without their help, her brother would die at the lizard-man's hand, and she would be his prisoner.

The drac's tongue flicked out, tasting the air. "You are wise to be afraid, human."

"W-who says I'm a-afraid," Miranda sputtered.

A series of short hisses escaped the draconian's mouth and his tongue flicked toward her again. "I do, because I can taste your fear." He took a couple of steps forward, followed closely behind by the wyvern. "This will be so much easier if you don't resist."

Justin stepped between the draconian and Miranda. "That's what all you bad guys always say. Is there a class somewhere where you learn that kind of crap?"

Miranda watched in disbelief as her brother, the little brother she was always rescuing, and who had been afraid of, well, basically everything, stood up to the scariest thing she had ever seen.

Justin bent his knees slightly, slid one of his feet back so that his torso was turned at a right angle to his adversary. "If you want my sister, you're going to have to get past me first."

The draconian stopped walking forward and tilted his head, his tongue darting out toward Justin. "That was indeed my intention."

"So, how do I taste, lizard?" her brother asked.

The draconian wasn't laughing now. "Your confidence will not change the outcome. You will be dead in moments."

"Bold words for someone outnumbered two to one," Justin said.

Miranda saw Justin's eyes dart to meet Red's.

"This is your last warning," Justin said. "Leave now, and we promise not to kill you."

"Kill me? With what? Two lame half-breeds, and two children, with only their clawless fists and fangless mouths. You are only stalling for time. No one will come to save you before I gut you alive."

Miranda felt a focused thought directed her way by Storm, a whisper. "*Your brother is buying you time to escape, but there is no running from this creature. We must stand and fight."*

"Okay, but how?" Miranda replied, looking at the two stones she was still gripping, realizing how useless they were. *"The drac's right. We have nothing to fight them with."*

"Behind the saddle there is a long leather saddlebag," Storm whispered urgently. *"What is in it will help. But you must move quickly."*

Miranda moved without hesitation. As Storm raised one wing, shielding Miranda from the draconian's view, she glided back and around Storm's flank to reach the rear of the saddle.

To Miranda's surprise, there was indeed a long flattened leather tube behind the saddle. Why hadn't she noticed it before? Well, probably because she had been fleeing for her life. Miranda pulled open a tie at one end and pushed back the leather flap protecting what was inside. She could see an old sword grip, its once-black leather worn gray and crisscrossed with white scars. She wrapped her fingers around the grip and pulled. She sucked in a quick breath of surprise as she recognized the strange silvery metal of her grandfather's sword, the one she had seen in Storm's memory of the night Em disappeared. "Wait, how did you get this?"

"Sssh!" Storm whispered harshly. *"There is no time for talk."*

The sword made a tiny, thrilling *shing!* sound as Miranda pulled it free of its scabbard. Even though it was almost as long as she was tall, the weapon was surprisingly light and perfectly balanced. She gave it a couple of quick swings, testing its weight. No wonder her grandfather could wield such a long blade effortlessly. *"I don't really know how to use one of these."*

"What is there to know? Swing it at your enemy."

"You make it sound so easy."

Miranda heard Justin say, "Are we going to do this, or are you just going to stand there looking stupid all day?"

The draconian roared. Storm raised her wing in time for Miranda to see the lizard-man charge her little brother, his wicked curved knife raised high above his head, a murderous look in his red reptilian eyes. Justin didn't even move. He just bounced lightly on the balls of his feet in the stance he had adopted before, waiting for the draconian to come.

* * *

"I'm dead! I'm totally dead! What the heck was I thinking? This creep is literally going to tear me apart!" Justin said, sending his thoughts to Red. It seemed that as long as he stayed focused on the dragon, the draconian couldn't overhear their mental conversation. Despite everything telling him to turn and run, his sister's life depended on Justin's holding his ground. While he had been taunting Mr. Ugly, who consequently was running at Justin full speed, he and Red had been working out a strategy to try to buy Miranda time to escape.

"I actually think it might work. Don't lose your nerve." Red shifted to his right to give himself a clear line of attack at the wyvern. *"Let me know when."*

For Justin, time seemed to slow and his vision to become unnaturally clear. The draconian was now less than five feet away. Justin stopped bouncing and yelled, "Now!"

Red gathered a pawful of dirt and pelted the running drac in the face, then launched himself at the wyvern.

By the time the dirt hit the draconian, he was already bringing the long knife down at Justin's neck. The drac let out a piercing cry as the sand and gravel hit his eyes. Justin shifted quickly to the right and in one practiced, fluid motion grabbed the drac's thick wrist. He pivoted, using his opponent's own momentum to toss him into a flip. Throughout the arc of the throw, Justin maintained his grip on the drac's wrist. As the draconian hit the ground hard, gasping, Justin twisted his clawed hand sharply, and the knife fell free.

Justin stood in shock for a moment. It had worked! He had totally beaten the scary lizard-man in one move. Thank you, Mrs. Lóng!

Before he could finish congratulating himself, something hit Justin in the chest, sending him flying through the air. He smashed backward into the ground and tried desperately to take a breath. Sensing something coming at him, he rolled to one side. A heavy wooden stick slammed down on the ground where his head had been a second before. Of course. That must have been what had hit him. Stupid, stupid, stupid, he said to himself. You were so concerned about the knife, you forgot the staff.

Justin scrambled to his feet. He raised his fists, bouncing lightly in place, keeping in constant motion. The drac swung his staff like a baseball bat, but Justin could perceive his intention to move a fraction of a second before he acted. The drac let out a yell of frustration, and attacked again with such inhuman speed, the staff was little more than a blur. But Justin was moving even faster, having foreseen the attack before it began, and he easily dodged everything the drac threw at him. Justin could tell the creature was starting to tire, and he was thinking of pressing an offensive move, when his foot caught on a rock and he lost his balance.

The draconian hissed excitedly and sprang forward. Justin was on his back again, looking up at the murderous lizard, who gripped his staff in both hands above his head. He was straddling Justin, ensuring that the boy wouldn't roll out of the way. A wicked smile spread across his wide reptilian mouth. "I'm going to enjoy feasting on you, human."

* * *

When the draconian began running toward her brother, Miranda and Storm sprinted at the wyvern. There was no way Red, in his current condition, could hold off the huge beast for more than a couple of seconds.

Miranda saw Red throw something at the drac, then spring at the drac's mount. The dragon slammed into the wyvern's side hard, but not hard enough to knock it over.

The wyvern responded by striking the red dragon across the back with its tail. Luckily for Red, the angle did not allow the poisonous barb to find its target, and the blow glanced off his thick scales. But the force of the strike was still enough to send Red flat to the ground.

Miranda could feel Red's exhaustion and his determination to save them, even if the effort cost him his life. She tried to move her legs faster, but there was still too much ground to cover, and even though the long sword she held was astonishingly light, it was still awkwardly long.

The wyvern growled and thrust its ugly head at Red's neck. The dragon let out a low cry of pain as the beast sank its teeth into his neck. It raised its tail high, ready to strike a killing blow.

Storm shot past Miranda and clamped her jaws down on the wyvern's long neck. It reacted instantly, releasing Red, and tried to shake free of the blue dragon. But Storm wouldn't let go. She hung there, shaking her head viciously back and forth. The thrashing creature in her jaws managed to hit her in the ribcage with one wing, forcing her to release her grip. Yet in the process, she was able to tear a mouthful of thick scales away from the wyvern's throat, causing dark-red blood to flow freely from the wound. The wyvern screamed and stomped down on the blue dragon's head with one foot, pinning her to the ground.

Miranda realized it wasn't by accident that Storm had ripped open that particular spot on the creature's neck. The dragon was showing her where to hit the beast in order to kill it.

The wyvern drew up its tail, and the barb came speeding at the prone dragon. Miranda used Storm's back as a ramp to leap into the air. She swung her sword like a bat in an upward motion, hitting the poisonous tail with all her strength. It felt like cutting through a watermelon with a meat cleaver. The severed part of the tail dropped to the ground.

The wyvern threw back its head and howled in pain, exposing the now scaleless spot on its long neck. Miranda jumped off the dragon, and with both hands gripping her grandfather's sword, swung it down at the creature's throat.

It let out a short gurgling cry before its severed head dropped to the earth.

* * *

The draconian pulled back his heavy staff, preparing to bring it down with all his strength.

Justin raised his arms in a feeble attempt to block the deathblow.

There was a gurgling screech, and something impossibly heavy fell to the ground, causing the trees and rocks to shake. Justin looked up and noticed the draconian's attention swing to something behind him. Without hesitation, Justin brought his foot up as hard as he could into his assailant's groin. For a second, he was worried that the lizard-man's anatomy wasn't like a human's, because he didn't react. But then, the staff fell to the ground, followed by the drac.

Justin rolled out of the way just in time to avoid the collapsing draconian, who was clutching his groin and moaning weirdly. Justin scrambled to his feet and looked around. Red and Storm were slowly getting up. The wyvern was dead, its head neatly severed from its neck. And his sister was walking toward him, a shining silver sword in her hand.

"Seriously? You had a *sword* the whole time? You could have let me know. It would have made kicking his butt a lot easier."

Miranda smiled. "Here you go," she said, and tossed the weapon to him.

Justin expected the sword to crash to the ground as soon as he grabbed it, but it was surprisingly light. He swung it back and forth a couple of times. "Nice. Where did this come from?"

"Good question. Not sure." Miranda shrugged. "We'll figure that one out later."

Justin nodded and swung the sword down, pressing its tip at the draconian's throat, pinning him. "If you remember, I *did* warn you to leave. But since you decided to stay, how about you answer a couple of questions. Let's start with why you want my sister."

The draconian's reptilian face remained expressionless and he said nothing. But in his mind Justin saw clearly the image of his sister tied to the stone pillar in the underground cavern.

"Okay, I've seen that before. What's up with the stone pillar and why do you want to chain my sister to it?"

The draconian's eyes opened wide, and Justin now saw the wall of fire with a dark dragon-like thing within it. Whatever was behind the flames started chanting something.

"Who is that?" Justin's thigh had started to get hot, and he looked down to see the stone shard glowing in his pocket. "What the—"

The draconian closed his eyes and arched his back, then

screamed as his eyelids sprang open and flames erupted from the now empty sockets.

"Get back!" Justin yelled, and pulled Miranda away from the writhing creature. Fissures crisscrossed the draconian's body as dancing flames spread rapidly all over it, consuming him alive.

Somewhere deep in the flames Justin heard harsh laughter. He recognized it instantly. Weeks before, when he and Miranda had opened the package from his mother, and his sister had passed out, this was the voice they had heard. *"Every day I grow stronger. Every day my return becomes more imminent. Soon, soon I will rise, and when I do, the world will be made anew."*

Justin gulped. He didn't like the sound of that at all. "Who are you? What do you want from us?"

"I want it ... All!" the voice hissed. Then, as the fire died, the voice began to fade. *"Soon ... Soon ... Soon ..."* And then it was gone completely.

Justin was left staring at the spot where the draconian had been only moments before. All that remained was a blackened shape, like a permanent shadow, etched into the rocky ground.

Justin felt his sister put her arm across his shoulders and he leaned into her. He suddenly felt very tired. "What do we do now?"

She gave him a reassuring squeeze. "I don't know. But whatever it is, we'll do it together."

CHAPTER 44

MIRANDA
Revelations

MIRANDA SHIELDED HER EYES with her hand and scanned the sky. Justin had felt something frantically searching for them close by. He hoped it was a dragon with Grandpa on its back, but he didn't want to take any chances. "See anything?"

He shook his head. "It's still too far away, but I can definitely sense it."

"Any idea if it's a friendly?"

Justin shrugged. "No. It's definitely looking for *us*, and it seems kind of mad, but ..." He closed his eyes. Then he laughed. "Never mind, it's Argo, with Grandpa riding him. I'm calling for him now." Then he opened his eyes and plopped down under the shade of a big pine. "They'll be here shortly. We might as well have a seat and wait."

Miranda nodded and sat down on a rock near the river's edge. She was impressed by how well her brother could sense the dragons clearly and at great distances. When he had been questioning the draconian, she could barely see any of the lizard-man's thoughts. They were all just jumbled images to her, but to her brother it was just like watching a movie.

Miranda set Grandpa's sword next to her on a rock, feeling much safer with it close by, then took off her boots and socks. It had been a really long walk down the valley on their way back to the ranch, and her feet were killing her. She put them into the icy river water, hoping to numb the soreness away.

Storm came over next to Miranda and submerged her entire head in the water. She pulled it out and shook vigorously side to side, spraying Miranda with a frigid shower. *"That feels much better."*

"Speak for yourself. Now I'm soaked." Miranda used the bottom edge of her shirt to dry the water from her face. "So, are we going to talk about how you got that saddle on, and how you just happened to have my grandfather's sword with you?"

Storm swung her head around until her eyes were level with Miranda's. *"When you called for me, I ran to the only exit I knew, the main one. But when I got there it was locked tight. I turned to see if I could find a way to open it, and the cook was standing behind me."*

"What? Wait a minute. Cook? You mean Mrs. Lóng?"

"The same."

"How did she—why was she even—" Miranda stammered.

"I do not know the answer to any question other than the one you asked me before. The cook had the saddle in her arms. She put it on me, told me that the sword was there, then unlocked the door." She looked up to the sky, and Miranda followed her gaze. A dragon was sweeping toward them. *"Take care with that one. She is not what she appears to be."*

Miranda nodded then slipped her socks and boots back on and hopped off the rock. Justin stood up from his resting spot in the shade and came over to stand beside her as they waited for Grandpa to land.

As soon as Argo touched the ground, Grandpa jumped off and came running to them, his face twisted with apprehension. Then his large gray mustache curved into a smile and he scooped Miranda and her brother into a big bear hug. "I saw the wyvern and began to fear the worst … ." Miranda followed his eyes to the sword lying on the rock at her feet. "Well, that answers a couple of questions." He shook his head and laughed. "I'm not even going to ask how you got that out of my safe."

He looked over at Red and Storm. "The dragons look the worse for wear. We should get them back to the ranch and have Miss Ddraig patch them up."

Miranda shook her head. "Not yet. We need to tell you what happened." Then she looked over at Justin, who nodded. "And it's time you knew everything."

Grandpa looked skeptical, so Justin added, "It's important we talk before we get back to the ranch. We know we can trust you. But, we're not totally sure about anyone else."

Grandpa studied them for a long moment, then nodded. "Well, let's have a seat then. Where do you want to start?"

Miranda sat back down on the rock and placed her hand on the sword's cool, silvery blade and pulled the photograph of Aunt Em from her pocket. She paused, then pressed the picture to her heart. "I think we need to start at the beginning. The night before we came to Colorado, the night Dad called you, we were visited by a draconian … ."

* * *

By the time Miranda and Justin had finished recounting everything that had happened since the draconian's arrival at their apartment in Manhattan, the sun was low in the sky. For the most part Grandpa remained quiet, only asking an occasional question. Now he sat on the ground staring at the picture of his daughter, lost in thought.

"Grandpa?" Justin asked, "Are you okay?"

He shook his head, "No, son. Not really." Then he stood up and walked over to Storm. She lowered her head, refusing to look at the dragon lord. He slowly lifted her chin until their eyes met. They stayed like that for a long moment before he said in a hoarse voice, "I'm sorry, Storm. I—owe you an apology." The dragon shuffled forward and rested her chin on his broad shoulder. They stayed that way for a long time too, quite still. Then Grandpa pulled back. "I'm not going to rest until I get my little girl back. Nothing is going to stand in my way. Too much time has been wasted already. I will not have my daughter rotting away in some godforsaken cell. You have my word on that." He shook his head. "This whole time, William was right. What an old fool I am."

"Miranda, please tell Lord McAdelind he was not alone in his mistaken belief. I have loved no one so much as I love Em, and I too thought her lost. I will follow him to the ends of the Earth and beyond to get her back."

Miranda relayed Storm's words and Grandpa smiled. "Do you have any idea what I would give to be able to have the dragons speak to me like that?"

"I'm not going to lie, it's pretty cool," Justin said. "Well … for the most part. Listening to Red's endless complaints about how hungry he is gets kind of old after a while."

Red gave Justin a dirty look that made all the humans laugh.

"What are you going to do about Lord Drake?" Miranda asked.

Grandpa stroked his jaw. "You said Cisco was working through the dracs. That means someone is behind all of this, pulling the strings. But we don't know who or why. It could very well be Drake himself, or some threat we haven't uncovered yet. We must be careful. Mr. DeSoto's confession to you three and his dead body should be enough. It's a shame we weren't able to get back what he took. If only we knew where he stashed everything, Drake would have no choice but to drop this once and for all."

Miranda nodded. "Billy said he suspected Mr. DeSoto the whole time, but he never saw him leave the ranch. Billy also knew about the secret way in through the waterfall. The front entrance was usually heavily guarded, so he was watching the back. I think everything Mr. DeSoto stole is still here somewhere."

Grandpa stroked his chin again. "I've been over every inch of the complex. Where could he have stashed it?"

Miranda snapped her fingers. "We already know there is one secret passage in the Warren, I'm willing to bet there are more."

Grandpa nodded. "Yes, but where? I've lived here my entire life and didn't even know about the one behind the waterfall. I don't even know where to start."

Justin raised his hand. "Oh, oh—I know. There must be a hidden stairway or something behind that creepy statue in the trophy room."

"What creepy statue?" Grandpa asked.

"You're joking, right? The one whose eyes follow you everywhere," Justin said, shuddering. "The one that looks like an evil dragon lady."

Their grandpa let out a bark of laughter. "I know the one. I've always hated that thing too. But why there?"

"I saw Mr. DeSoto standing by it several times, and the last thing he said before ... dying ... was 'the tablet,' and that statue is holding a stone tablet."

Miranda frowned. "But why would he tell you where he stashed everything?"

Justin shrugged. "Maybe trying to make things right in

the end. Who knows?"

Grandpa stroked his mustache. "Seems as good a place as any to start looking. We're still several miles away from the ranch. I think the three of us should ride Argo back and take a look at the trophy room. He inclined his head to Red and Storm. "Are they okay to walk back?"

Red nodded. *"I'll be fine."*

Storm inclined her head. *"I am feeling better than I have in years."*

"They'll be okay," Miranda said.

Grandpa nodded. "Then let's ride, and get back what that dirty dragon rustler took from us."

"What's a *rustler*?" Miranda asked, as Grandpa helped her onto Argo's back.

"Another name for a thief. You know, if someone steals cattle, they're called cattle rustlers." He hoisted Justin into place behind Miranda.

"Why don't you just call them cattle thieves then?" Justin asked.

Grandpa climbed onto the dragon's back and patted it on the neck. "I tell you, Argo, we got ourselves a couple of real greenhorn city folk for grandchildren." He gave the dragon a gentle kick in the sides and Argo launched himself into the air. "Because, son, you're in the West now. And here we call them *rustlers*."

CHAPTER 45

MIRANDA
Tiamat

MIRANDA BIT HER LIP as she watched Justin inspect the tablet in the dragon lady statue's hand for a way to open a secret door. This seemed like a long shot to her. Even if Mr. DeSoto had been trying to make it up to them in the end, he could have meant a hundred different things by his final words. And for all they knew, this could be a trap. One last way for him to get revenge on the McAdelind family.

Justin snapped his fingers, causing her to jump. "Got ya." He grabbed the tablet, pulling it toward him as if he were trying to snatch it away from the evil-looking woman. A section of wall behind the statue rotated to reveal a spiral staircase leading up. "I was totally right. Take that, Sherlock."

Grandpa pulled out three flashlights from Argo's saddlebag, handed one to Justin and one to Miranda, then flicked his on and shone it around the opening. The dragon watched the proceedings intently. "Don't go patting yourself on the back too much. This still might be a trap," Grandpa said. "Okay, stay behind me." Then he slowly walked past the statue and up the dark stairs.

As soon as they were all past the door, it closed behind them. Miranda shuddered and moved closer to Grandpa. They climbed for what felt like miles before reaching an archway carved with strange symbols. Faint light was coming from the room beyond.

"Looks like we're here. Let's see if we can find any of the stolen items," her grandfather said, walking through the portal.

Once inside, they fanned out. Shining their lights around, Miranda saw they were in a vast cathedral-like hall. It was similar in design to the Grand Corral, with massive pillars rising high into the air to support a vaulted stone ceiling. Benches in neat rows flanked a wide central aisle. From the direction the seats faced, Miranda assumed they must have entered through the back of the room.

"I think I found a balcony," Justin said, standing by an archway to the right, which provided the room's only source of dim light. He poked his head through the opening. "Whoa. I can see the trophy room. It's a long way down. Hey, Argo! We made it!" he yelled, waving to the dragon below.

Miranda shook her head at her dorky brother and continued to walk slowly down the center aisle. A strong odor washed over her, and she pulled her shirt up over her nose and mouth. "Yuck." It smelled like old leather and sulfur.

Both her brother and grandfather came running over to her. "Ugh! Gross," Justin said and pinched his nose close. "Stinks like ... Miranda's feet."

Grandpa shone his light farther down the room, illuminating a bunch of large oval objects in a pile. "That's the smell of dragon eggs. Specifically, ones that have expired." He shook his head, and walked quickly over to the mound.

Miranda watched as he held up one egg the size of a

basketball, and shone a light behind it, looking for any sign of movement from the embryo within. After setting several of the eggs aside, he held up a bright-blue one with something wiggling inside. He let out a laugh. "Well, this little fighter is still alive." He handed it to Justin. "Hold this for a moment, son, while I look through the rest.

Justin grunted and dropped his flashlight in an effort to hold the heavy egg. "Don't worry about me, I'm good," he said in a strained voice. Miranda laughed and ran over to help him keep it from falling.

Grandpa inspected the remaining half dozen or so, but they all turned out to be dead. He shook his head. "This is a terrible tragedy. Dragons don't breed often." He gestured toward the stinking pile. "These are from some of our healthiest lines." He reached over and took back the one Justin was holding. "Well, at least this little one was strong enough, and he's a wild blue to boot. Their young can be less hardy than a domestics.'"

"If you have all these eggs, why aren't there more baby dragons around?" Justin asked.

"Over the centuries, we've developed methods for controlling the dragons' fertility. We can't afford to have a massive increase in the dragon population. Still, every egg we do choose to keep is precious." He shook his head again. "What DeSoto did here is a high crime in our world. The use of dragon eggs for personal gain is akin to murder." He cradled the egg in one arm and picked up his flashlight. "Come on. Let's see what else we can find in here."

A short distance away on one of the benches lay a dozen gold bars. "Whoa!" Justin exclaimed in awe. "Holy cow. We're rich. Uh ... I mean ... *you're* rich. I've never seen anything like that before."

Grandpa winked at Justin. "That's nothing. Wait until I show you guys the vault. And you were right when you said *we're* rich. Everything I have is yours too." Then he tilted his head. "Well, eventually it will be. You two have a lot to learn first."

Justin rubbed his hands together. "So, does this mean I can have a TV in my room?"

Grandpa shone the light around. "We'll see … Wait a minute. What's this?"

Miranda looked up to see two stone pillars rising up to the ceiling, both with rusty chains dangling from them. Her breath caught in her throat. Beyond them was a wide altar flanked by bronze bowls. She quickly backed away from them, her rising panic making it hard to breathe. This was from her dream.

Miranda shook her head. This couldn't be right. As her gaze swept rapidly around the room she started to calm down. Well … not exactly like the place in her dream. This wasn't an inconceivably vast cave. But it was so similar. Cold sweat ran down her spine, and she felt a strong desire to flee. As she continued to back away from the altar, her heel hit something and she tripped, falling hard onto the floor.

Justin and her grandfather ran over. "Are you all right?" Justin asked.

She shook her head, and her words came out in gasps. "This place—the dream—it's not quite right … ."

Justin looked around. "I know, it's too small. Not a big cave. But the rest is the same, like a miniature version of the place we saw. What the heck do you think this is?" He looked down at something on the ground and picked it up.

Miranda realized it was the object she had tripped over, which turned out to be a package wrapped in brown paper. Her brother's face turned pale. "What is it, Justin?"

"It's from Mom and Dad." He shook his head. "They *did* try to contact us. That loser Mr. DeSoto took this so we wouldn't know." His face fell into a frown. "The postmark is from right after we got here."

Justin passed the package to Miranda. It was covered in several big stamps and labels in Spanish. She walked over to the nearest bench, ripped the package open, and dumped out its contents.

There was a letter in her mom's loopy handwriting on top of a pile of pages of handwritten notes, including what looked at a quick glance like an account of a Native American creation myth, followed by several maps, some photos, and finally a key with *312* written on it in black marker. Miranda grabbed the letter and read it quickly.

"What does it say?" Justin asked eagerly.

Miranda took a deep breath. "'My dearest Miranda and Justin,'" she read. "'I'm so sorry we had to leave you and in such an abrupt manner, but I trust your grandfather is taking good care of you. He is an honorable man and can be trusted. You can't believe how hard that was for me to write, but despite our history, I can't deny the truth of those words.'"

Miranda and Justin looked at their grandfather, and his face flushed. "I was sort of … Well … I was quite vocal in my objections to your mother and father … dating."

Miranda shook her head disapprovingly and continued reading: "'I can only imagine how frustrating this must be for you both. Hopefully you are getting along well and learning more about your heritage. Take my word for it when I tell you, family is not always what it appears on the surface.'"

Justin laughed dryly. "No joke, Mom. That's the understatement of the century."

Miranda continued. "'Our intention was to take care of this business quickly and come to get you. Unfortunately, something has happened, and your father and I aren't able to make it at this time. I can't put too many details here. We can't afford to have our current whereabouts exposed. Too much has been compromised already. Some we thought to be our allies have turned out to be working against us, and now everything is in jeopardy.'"

"'If you don't hear from us by the end of the summer, we will have failed. But for everyone's sake, we cannot. I know this is hard to understand, but what your father and I are doing is bigger than all of us. I'm asking you both to be brave, sit tight, and wait for us to contact you.'"

"'I'll write again in a week. However, in the event that you don't hear from me, give the information included in this package to your grandfathers. They will figure out what to do.'"

"'We love you both so much. Take care of one another, trust each other, and trust your family.'"

"'Love, Mom and Dad.'"

Miranda paused. "'P.S. Do not give that same trust so easily to others, and do not try to go back <u>home</u>, there is nothing for you there any longer.'"

Justin grabbed the letter out of Miranda's hand and read it again. "What does she mean, 'do not try to go back home, there is nothing for you there any longer'? And why is *home* underlined? Does that mean we're never going back to New York? Wait a minute. You don't think they're really spies or are in the witness protection program or something. What's going on? And what does she mean by 'grandfathers'?"

Grandpa's face flushed. "She means *her* father," he said as he continued to look through the photos, notes, and maps from the package. His eyes went wide when he came to one image in particular, which seemed to prompt him to shine his flashlight at the wall behind the altar. The light revealed a mosaic that stretched across the entire wall. He shook his head, not taking his eyes off the image. "I'm not completely sure, son. But I'm willing to bet it has to do with … *her*."

The mosaic represented a dragon lady similar to the statue in the trophy room below. Her skin was the color of night, and she was rising up out of green flames. A shiver went down Miranda's spine. The woman's face was almost beautiful—*almost*: perfect features, almond-shaped eyes, high cheekbones, dark flowing hair. But long horns sprouted from the corners of her eyebrows, her eyes had snakelike pupils, and her open mouth revealed rows of sharp teeth. Hers was a nightmarish beauty. "Who do you think that is?" Miranda asked.

"On this photo," Grandpa said, holding it up, "your father circled the face and wrote *Tiamat* in the margin."

"So that's what you call a half-woman, half-dragon thing? A tiamat?" Justin asked.

"Tiamat is not a type of monster, she's the queen of monsters." Grandpa nodded toward the mosaic. "The legend is that she created dragons, and other creatures, to do battle against the gods."

"I take it she didn't win," Miranda said.

"No. She was defeated by a younger god named Marduk. As a matter of fact—or legend—the twenty families are supposedly descendants of Marduk's most trusted warriors. He gave them the task of ridding the world of the monsters Tiamat had unleashed."

"But we raise dragons. Isn't that a bit of a contradiction?" Miranda pointed out.

Grandpa shrugged. "I suppose. But most of these stories exist to provide an explanation for why things are the way they are—why the sky doesn't fall into the sea, why the ground shakes from time to time, why rivers flood. I seriously doubt there were any *real* gods doing battle—probably just some kings fighting each other. And the stories were exaggerated over time."

"Um, may I point out the obvious? Dragons actually exist."

Justin indicated the picture on the wall. "I think we should assume some of the other stories might be true as well."

"Point taken," Grandpa said, then glanced up at the scary-looking woman again. "We got what we came here for. Let's get out of here. This place gives me the creeps."

CHAPTER 46

MIRANDA

The Next Move

THE SECRET DOOR CLOSED SILENTLY behind them as they walked back into the trophy room. Miranda glanced back at the statue of the dragon lady and shivered. Miranda now knew her name, Tiamat, and somehow that made her even creepier.

"There was only one egg taken from a wild. We should get this to her at once before it dies," Grandpa said, walking over to one of the doors they were not allowed to enter. Like the other archways, this one was large enough for a dragon to easily fit through. He placed his hand flat on a black panel, and a red light scanned up and down his palm several times. There was a loud click and the huge door swung open.

Miranda walked close behind him as they entered the great space, where two wild dragons were flying around. When they spotted the three McAdelinds entering, they paused, hovering in the air for a moment with beating wings to regard the humans.

Grandpa stepped forward. "I bring this egg back to the one who bore it."

"Oh, look. Our jailor speaks to us as if we suddenly matter," one wild blue dragon said, his voice in Miranda's mind deep and slow.

The blue to the right sniffed the air. *"It is Azuria's missing offspring. Maybe we should tell her the humans have returned it—dead."*

The first one laughed. *"And see what chaos ensues."*

Miranda stepped around Grandpa and said aloud, "That would be stupid on your part. I'm sure she would turn on both of you once your lie was exposed."

Suddenly both angular reptilian heads swiveled to face her.

"This must be the one Azaria has spoken of. The heiress who is immune to our lightning," said the first.

The second dragon nodded. *"Since her offspring is not actually missing, I'm willing to bet Azuria's tale about this human is equally untrue."* Then it looked at the first dragon and added, *"Shall we find out?"*

The first dragon licked its sharp teeth. *"Why not?"*

"Get back!" Miranda cried.

"Why? Why? What are they saying?" Grandpa asked.

"You don't want to know," Justin said, grabbing his grandfather's shirttail and pulling him hard back toward the door.

Both dragons sucked in deep breaths. Their scales seemed to ripple as electricity started to arc across their lean serpentine bodies.

Miranda spread her feet wide and clenched her fists, feeling the static electric charge building in each of the dragons. She concentrated on that feeling as it touched the primal part of their minds.

"Stop!" Grandpa's cry was cut short by the deafening clap of thunder as two bolts shot toward Miranda.

She threw up her hands, absorbing the energy, feeling it move through every cell of her body. She looked down at her fists and saw electricity dancing up and down her arms. She closed her eyes, and mentally pushed all the energy into her hands. It felt as if she was going to explode if she didn't do something with it, and soon. Her eyes snapped open, and she threw her arms up toward the two hovering, wide-eyed dragons. Lightning exploded from her hands, hitting both beasts squarely in the chest. The impact sent both of them flying backward and crashing to the ground.

Miranda ran toward the closer one and grabbed it roughly by the snout. Its eyes were wild with fear. "How dare you defy a dragon lord, you worthless worm! Your stupidity could have well caused the death of Azuria's baby." Miranda let go of the beast's snout and shouted. "Azuria! I have returned with your child!"

There was a roar from one of the passageways to the left, and the blue dragon came bounding out. Her eyes darted to the two dragons on the ground, then to Miranda. She sniffed the air, then stalked slowly over to where Grandpa stood.

He held out the egg with both hands toward the dragon. She bent lower, sniffing at it, then, ever so gently, took it out of his hands to hold it in her mouth.

Miranda approached her. "As I told you, I am not the one who took your child. We just recovered it from the traitor Francisco DeSoto. He died by a wyvern's sting."

The blue regarded Miranda for a long moment, then turned and walked slowly back to the archway through which she had entered. Before disappearing out of sight, she met Miranda's eyes again. There they stood, motionless. Then Azuria lowered her eyes and inclined her head in a deep bow before exiting.

Grandpa let out a low whistle.

"What?" Miranda asked.

"I thought blocking lightning with your hands was

impressive, but that was something else."

"What was?" Miranda said. "She didn't even thank us."

"No, but she did something even greater. Something I've never seen a wild dragon do before. She *submitted* to you."

Miranda shrugged. "Okay. So? I'm not sure I know what that means."

"Among dragons there is always a hierarchy. For a domestic, the *human* it pairs with is its—for lack of a better term— leader. For wilds, the leader is always the strongest dragon in the pack." He smiled. "Azuria just recognized *you* as the strongest—the strongest dragon."

* * *

Miranda jumped out of the truck before it came to a complete stop, and took the steps into the house two at a time. It had been almost an entire day since she had eaten anything. If she didn't have something soon, she thought she would die. Her grandfather had radioed ahead to let Mrs. Lóng know that they were on their way and to have dinner ready. At this point, anything less than a seven-course meal wouldn't be enough to satisfy her, Miranda thought, and she might attack someone, probably the quirky cook herself.

Miranda sprinted inside and came to a sudden halt. In the weeks they had been here at Thunderbird Ranch, she and Justin had eaten all their meals alone together. Not even Mrs. Lóng had ever joined them. But this time the table was set for seven.

Justin ran into Miranda from behind, almost knocking her down. "Cool. Looks like we have company tonight," he said.

Mrs. Lóng came spinning through the swinging door from the kitchen, dozens of steaming platters balanced up and down both arms. "Have a seat, dears."

Miranda and Justin sat down and watched in wonder

as the eccentric cook pivoted this way and that, expertly placing each platter down on the table.

Justin had a huge smile on his face. "You're going to have to teach me how to do that someday, Mrs. Lóng."

The cook stopped and frowned. "Oh, child, if only I could. Such moves take years to master. Centuries, even."

Justin just shook his head and smiled. "We'll see. I'm a pretty quick learner. I took out a draconian today. Soon I'll be taking you down too."

This time Mrs. Lóng threw her head back and laughed loud and merrily. "Not if you live ten lifetimes." Then she suddenly got very serious. "Before the others get here, I do want to tell you both how profoundly proud I am of you. You have exceeded every expectation I had." She placed the last platter down and sat next to Justin. She leaned in, motioning for them to do the same, and whispered, "But this is only the beginning, and there is such a long difficult road ahead. Trust and believe in one another." She grabbed their hands and pulled them together. "Your survival depends on this."

Miranda looked at her little brother. He seemed so much older than the scared, annoying boy he had been back in New York, full of new power and confidence. She realized that for the first time in their life she actually felt ... proud ... of him. "We will."

Justin nodded. "No matter what happens."

Miranda looked over and saw tears in the old cook's eyes. "How did you know we would need Storm and Red? And Grandfather's sword?" she asked.

Justin nodded. "Not to mention teaching me the one move I would need to know in order to beat the draconian."

Mrs. Lóng let go of their hands and stood. She brushed at her apron, smoothing it out. "I'm sure I have no idea what you are talking about. I am just a simple old cook." She winked at them before quickly disappearing through the kitchen door.

At the same moment several people entered the room from the front hall. Grandpa took the seat at the head of the table. Mr. O'Faron and Miss Ddraig followed and sat on either side of Justin. Next Billy came in, his arm in a sling. He paused at the archway for a moment, looked back at the door, then turned as if reconsidering something and sat down next to Miranda. Mrs. Lóng entered with even more platters and after depositing them sat at the opposite end of the table from Grandpa.

Grandpa cleared his throat, drawing everyone's attention. "Miranda and Justin, I don't even know how to begin to thank you. You have saved this ranch, and our family. We owe you both everything." He winked at them, then continued. "But before we get started on a well-deserved meal, I need to say a few words." He spread his arms, encompassing everyone seated at the table. "A month ago, I felt as if I had no family left. My daughter was dead, my son was estranged, and my wife … well … let me just say, I felt pretty darn alone. Today, I look around this table and realize what an old fool I have been. I was so caught up in my own grief, I drove the people who mattered most away. I shut everyone out, and I failed to see what was going on right under my nose." His face became very serious. "One of our own was trying to destroy us from the inside and take everything our family"—he paused to look at Mr. O'Faron—"everything our *families* have been building for centuries. But it's high time I got my head out of the sand and took action. My daughter is alive and rotting in a cell somewhere. My son and daughter-in-law are most likely in danger. Someone is behind all of it. The fact that the high dragon lord appears to be involved leads me to believe we can't give our trust blindly in any of the other families. And based on what Miranda and Justin have told me, the dracs may even have their scaly hands in a lot more than just what has happened here. They may be working independently, with some evil designs of their own." He balled his hands into fists. "But I'll tell you one thing for certain, I'm not going to sit for one more moment with my eyes shut. I am going to get my kids back." His expression softened, and he looked at each face around the table in turn. "But I know I can't do this alone. I need each of you to help me. I need my family."

Mr. O'Faron stood up. "I'm with you, Mac. I always have been."

"Aye, me too, sir," Miss D piped enthusiastically, springing to her feet.

"I've been with you all along, Mac, you know that," Mrs. Lóng, said, inclining her head toward Miranda and Justin.

Miranda glanced over at Billy, who was just staring silently at the plate in front of him, his face flickering with conflicting emotions.

"Kids," Grandpa said, drawing her attention back to him. "I don't think it would be safe for either of you to go with us. I don't know what I would do if anything happened to you while under my watch."

Miranda exchanged a look with her brother. "With all due respect, Grandpa, this is already as much our fight as it is yours. Maybe even more so. And if the last couple of weeks are any indication, no place is very safe for us. We are going with you. And when it comes time to stand and fight … we fight."

Grandpa slammed his fist onto the table. "Then it's settled! We do this together, we get all our loved ones back, and we punish whoever's responsible for their suffering." He met everyone's eyes once more, then said, "Well, what are you waiting for, people? Eat up. We need our strength, because we start tonight."

The adventure continues in …

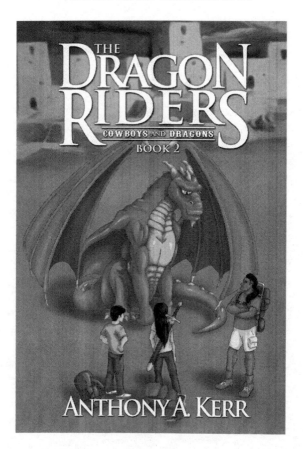

CHAPTER 1

MIRANDA
The Warehouse

MIRANDA JERKED AWAKE as static burst over her helmet speaker. She frantically grasped the saddle's horn, sucking in several quick breaths in an attempt to calm her racing heart. *Thank you, safety harness!* she thought.

"Are you okay, Lady McAdelind?" asked Indigo, the juvenile blue dragon she was riding, her smoky voice resonating in Miranda's mind.

"Yeah, fine. I'm just tired," Miranda replied telepathically. *"And please, call me Miranda."*

"Keep sharp everyone," Mr. O'Faron's voice crackled over Miranda's helmet speaker. "We're almost there."

Miranda gazed ahead to where an eerie orange light illuminated the clouds they were soaring above. She reached up and turned a knob on her helmet radio control panel until she was on a private channel with her brother. "Is that Denver, already?"

"Yes. Did you doze off too?" Justin said through a yawn. "This has been the longest day of my life. I could have really used a good night's sleep."

"I agree, but we needed to do this tonight," Miranda said. This had easily been the longest day of her life too. It had begun with her sneaking off to the Warren to let Storm know that the old dragon's former mistress, and Miranda and Justin's aunt, Em, was alive, then quickly turned into a fight for her life against a half-dozen wyverns and draconians. A chill shot down her spine at the thought of the vile lizard-men and their scorpion-tailed mounts. Yet here she was, heading directly into another encounter, and maybe another battle, with the same terrifying enemies.

"Remind me again why this couldn't have waited until tomorrow night?" Justin asked.

"Because there's a good chance the dracs would have disappeared by then. We need to strike while we know where they are." During dinner Grandpa McAdelind—or Grandpa Mac, as Miranda and Justin had started calling him—had decided to raid the only known draconian hideout for information: the warehouse where Mr. O'Faron had met with the draconians after picking up Miranda and Justin from the Denver airport only a few weeks before. So much had happened in such a short time. Their home and their life back in Manhattan seemed like a dream now. And yet here they were, riding dragons through the night sky. "Should be pretty simple," Miranda added.

"Nothing is going to be simple on this idiot of a beast," Justin grunted, and shook his head at the very young grayish-blue dragon he was riding, Steel. "I really miss Red."

Miranda glanced down at the inexperienced blue dragon she was riding and wished Storm was with her as well. In just a short time, they had been through so much together, and Miranda knew, without a doubt, that the fierce dragon would always do everything in her power to protect her.

But Red and Storm were both recovering from their battle with the wyverns, and despite their unrelenting protests, Grandpa Mac had decided the best thing for them to do was to recuperate. Breathing fire and lightning to fight against an overwhelming force—something no domestic dragon had ever done before—had taken a lot out of them both, and until Grandpa declared both dragons healthy again, they were grounded.

Plus, according to Mr. O'Faron's information, there would only be a handful of draconians at the warehouse anyway, so five dragons should be more than enough to overpower them.

Even so, Miranda still couldn't help but wish that Red and Storm, and … O'Faron's son, Billy were with them now too.

She felt her face flush slightly at the thought of the handsome older boy. He was still a little mad at her and Justin for thinking he had been the person stealing from their family. Despite his feelings, he had insisted on coming along. But his arm was still healing from a fight with Justin, during which her brother had managed to smash Billy's elbow with a can of bear mace, and Mrs. Lóng, Grandpa Mac's mysterious cook and confidante, had said it would be another day or two before he could ride again.

"We're almost there, Indigo! Ready to bust some heads?" Miranda said.

The blue dragon shuddered. *"I'm hoping that if we ask politely the draconians will just cooperate with us."*

Justin laughed. "A diplomatic dragon. Nice."

"Well, I'm ready to bust their heads, boss," Steel chimed in enthusiastically. *"You give the word, and I'll tear those filthy lizards into smithereens."*

"Looks like we got the wrong dragons, Justin. Want to

switch?" Miranda teased.

"I wish. Next time, I get to pick my dragon first."

Mr. O'Faron held up one arm to signal that he was about to make his descent, and Miranda hurriedly switched back to the main radio channel. "Okay, here we go!" he called, lowering his arm. Thunder, his blue dragon, banked into a steep dive and vanished into the clouds.

"All right, kids. Once we get to the warehouse, wait for my signal that it's all clear before entering. Understand?" Grandpa Mac said. Seeing that Justin and Miranda had both nodded, he guided Argo, his massive gold dragon, after Thunder.

Then less than a heartbeat later they were followed by the young dragon trainer, Miss Ddraig, on her red dragon, Flare.

"Okay, Steel," Justin said sternly. "Let's keep it simple. Follow the other dragons down to the warehouse. Nice and easy."

"Sure thing, boss-man!" the young blue replied, sounding excited.

Justin let out a high-pitched yell as Steel tucked into a tight barrel roll and dove into the thick clouds below.

"All right. Our turn," Miranda said, leaning forward to direct Indigo to dive, but the dragon's only response was to shake uncontrollably.

Miranda sighed. "Come on, Indigo. This will be a breeze. You have nothing to worry about."

She could feel the young dragon's hesitation. "But what if it's worse than we expect? What if there are twice as many draconians as we think?"

"Then we'll deal with all of them," Miranda said, with more confidence than she felt, and patted Indigo's rough, scaly neck reassuringly. "Don't worry. I won't let anything happen to you. I promise."

The dragon nodded once before drifting slowly downward into the clouds.

Miranda had always imagined clouds to be warm and soft like pillows, but passing through them felt more like being in a cold carwash with all the windows down. Before she knew it, she was soaked to the bone and shivering uncontrollably.

After what seemed like an hour, Indigo spread her wings out like a pair of giant sails and landed softly on the gravel-covered roof near the four other dragons.

Something was wrong. Everyone had their helmets off, worried looks darkening their faces.

"I said slowly, you oaf!" Justin whispered harshly to the slinking Steel. "Your clumsy landing alerted everyone inside that we're here."

"Are you positive?" Grandpa Mac asked.

Justin closed his eyes, as if reading signals only he could detect, then nodded. "Yep. They're running around, thinking about … fire. That's weird."

"They must be burning any evidence we might be able to use to find Robin, Kaya, and Em. We have to go in now before they destroy everything. Remember, our goal is to grab anything that will lead us to the imprisoned members of our family. William, on the count of three," Grandpa Mac whispered, and held up one finger, then two. As soon as his third finger went up, both he and Mr. O'Faron gave their mounts a slight kick.

As if they had rehearsed this many times before, the two dragons each slammed one massive clawed forepaw into the roof and started peeling the corrugated metal back as if they were unwrapping a huge Christmas present. When the hole was big enough for a dragon to squeeze through, Argo launched himself in, followed immediately by Thunder.

A weird droning sound erupted from inside the warehouse—the creepy chanting the draconians seemed to love. The plan was to wait for a signal indicating it was safe to enter, but there was so much noise, Miranda couldn't make out a single word.

Justin had his eyes closed again, and his head cocked to the side. When he frowned, Miranda asked, "What's wrong?"

"I'm not totally sure. The dracs aren't surprised or scared. And their thoughts are ... hard to read. I can't even get anything from Argo or Thunder to see what's happening."

Miranda closed her eyes and tried to connect with the dragons' minds. If Justin were having difficulties sensing the dracs, it would be even harder for her. Her brother had a knack for reading the thoughts and intentions of both dragons and draconians. But Miranda couldn't see or feel anything but a big black spot, as if they were intentionally being blocked. Her eyes shot open. "Something's wrong, Justin. We're being *jammed!*"

"How is that even possible?" Justin asked.

Miranda shrugged. "How is *any* of this possible?"

Steel was dancing impatiently back and forth, and then as if the waiting had just become too much for him to handle, he crouched at the edge of the hole. *"We're missing out on all the fun. I'm going in."*

"Oh, no you don't! We're supposed to wait for the signal, you stupid dragon!" Justin screeched, as Steel leaped into the warehouse, disappearing into the darkness below.

Miranda turned to Miss D. "What do we do now?"

The dragon trainer smiled wickedly and shrugged. "If you think I am missin' any of this, you're mental, you are." She urged the hesitant Flare into the opening.

Indigo started to rapidly back away from the hole. *"I don't think this is a good idea. Not a good idea at all. We need to wait for the signal. I have a bad feeling about this."*

Miranda agreed with the trembling dragon, but if they didn't move now, any evidence leading them to her parents and aunt would be destroyed. "I need to find out what those dirty lizards know. So I'm going in, with or without you."

"Oh, no, no, no! Lady McAdelind, it is my duty to protect you, and this is far too dangerous. We should just wait here a little while longer."

A wave of heat shot up through the hole in the roof, followed by screaming and shouting.

"We need to go. Now!" Miranda yelled and kicked Indigo with both heels to spur the beast into action. The dragon hesitantly jumped forward and plunged down into the warehouse.

Intense heat hit Miranda and took her breath away. Indigo swerved hard to the left and away from the source of the blistering air. The dragon landed on a tower of metal scaffolding at the far end of the warehouse. She turned to give Miranda a better look at the chaotic scene unfolding below.

The structure was much larger than Miranda had expected. Not nearly as big as the Grand Corral in the Warren on Grandpa's ranch, but close to the size of a football stadium and several stories tall. Crates and metal enclosures of all sizes had been pushed and stacked haphazardly around the edges of the warehouse. Miranda had expected to see the draconians burning any evidence they may have had, but instead she saw Grandpa Mac, Mr. O'Faron, Miss Ddraig, and Justin all trapped in a cage constructed completely out of green fire. The entire center of the warehouse had obviously been cleared for just this purpose. The dracs must somehow have anticipated their arrival. It was a trap.

Miranda coughed and tried to take in a deep breath, but the fire was quickly consuming the oxygen within the warehouse. Not only that, but there was a strong odor, like rotten eggs, that almost knocked her out of her saddle.

Miranda grabbed her nose. "Pee-yew! Do you smell that?"

Indigo looked around nervously. *"Yes. It smells like gas. I told you this was a bad idea. We need to get out of here immediately. I need to get you to safety.*"

"No! We need to save everyone!" Miranda shouted back. But she wasn't sure how she was going to do that just yet. Surrounding the cage of fire were hundreds of robed draconians chanting, their arms held out, palms facing the flames. Not just five or ten, as they had thought. And there were still more dracs, about a dozen, not taking part in the chanting but busy doing something around a large brass urn that stood next to a heavy wooden table stacked with items of various sizes that Miranda could not identify. Destroying papers and other evidence maybe? A few steps away from the urn she also saw several large wooden crates, placed too near to be there by accident. And what could be in those? she wondered.

Miranda's eyes narrowed on this group of lizard-men. She had to stop them first.

"I think if we knock a section of the roof down, we might be able to crush some of the draconians and create a breach in the fire trap," Indigo stammered.

"Good idea," Miranda said, not taking her eyes of the dracs in the corner. "But we need to stop those creeps over there first."

"But what about the others? They need our help. I thought you said we needed to save them."

"And we will. But we need to stop those filthy lizards from destroying any clues about where my family might be located. That is our primary mission and what we came here for."

Indigo swung her head toward the spot Miranda was indicating. *"There are more than ten draconians. I can't fight all of them by myself."*

"Sure you can," Miranda said, cracking her knuckles. "I have an idea. How do you feel about … lightning?"

THE ADVENTURE IS ONLY BEGINNING

Don't miss a moment of Miranda, Justin, Red and Storm's adventures as they try to save their family and stop the dark queen Tiamat from rising, by visiting www.aakerr.com and staying informed of upcoming book releases.

If you've enjoyed the *The Dragon Rustler*, please help spread the word by telling your friends and leaving a review.

Thank you so much for reading!

ACKNOWLEDGEMENTS

This book wouldn't have been possible without the help and support of several very important people.

First, my wife Jenifer, who not only encouraged me to start writing in the first place, but has carried the burden of our family on her back. Every day I realize how blessed I am to have found someone like her.

My alpha-readers: Lilia, Alisia, Ryan, and Sarah. Your support and encouragement helped me make it through many rounds of revisions.

My beta-readers: Greg, Morgan, and Chau. Your excitement kept me moving forward when things started to slow down.

My family and friends: Andre, Lilia, and Alex, Mom and Dad, Ryan and Sarah, Becky and Will, Alisia and Sergio, Bonnie and Jim, Carrie H., Paul, the Hustwits, the DeRodeses, Kevin, Heidi, Maureen, Andrew, and many others who were, and still are, supportive of me throughout the entire process.

The instructors at Lighthouse Writers Workshop, William Haywood Henderson and Sarah Ockler for being the perfect mix of teacher and counselor when I needed both.

The Indie book community, especially the guys at Sterling & Stone; Johnny, Sean and Dave, for not only making me laugh every week, but also teaching me how to be an Indie. Joanna Penn, for her detailed books on how to make a living as a writer. And David Gaughran for writing excellent books on marketing.

Christopher Farnsworth, who took the time out of his busy schedule to give me advice and encouragement.

Robin Marley, for giving me the idea that a story about cowboys and dragons would sell a ton of copies. I hope he's correct.

Carrie Dillon, for not hesitating to support an old friend in a new venture and leading me to the perfect editor.

And last but not least, my editor Christopher Caines. Without his help, guidance and support, *The Dragon Rustler* would still be a story and not a finished novel.

ABOUT THE AUTHOR

Anthony A. Kerr has always been a storyteller. Whether it was acting out elaborate plots with Star Wars figures when he was little, writing really, really, bad movies in high school, or creating weekly comic strips at work. Stories are always swirling around in his head, yelling at him to put them down on paper.

The Dragon Rustler is the first of many books yet to be released. To stay informed on upcoming books in the Cowboys and Dragons series, as well as other book series and stand alone novels, please visit www.aakerr.com and sign up to be alerted to upcoming publication dates and events.

Anthony lives in Denver Colorado with his wife and three children.

Made in the USA
Charleston, SC
29 October 2016